THE MIDNIGHT CHILL

Also by Marten Claridge

Nobody's Fool

THE MIDNIGHT CHILL

Marten Claridge

HEADLINE

First published in 1992
by HEADLINE BOOK PUBLISHING PLC

10 9 8 7 6 5 4 3 2 1

British Library Cataloguing in Publication Data

Claridge, Marten
The Midnight Chill.
I. Title
813.54[F]

ISBN 0-7472-0527-2

Typeset in 11/13pt Times by
Falcon Typographic Art Ltd,
Edinburgh

Printed and bound in Great Britain by
Richard Clay Ltd, Bungay, Suffolk

HEADLINE BOOK PUBLISHING PLC
Headline House
79 Great Titchfield Street
London W1P 7FN

In memory of
Joan Ker
Kenneth Marten Ker
&
Eileen Ker

ACKNOWLEDGEMENTS

To these fine people I owe my gratitude:
Kirsty Anderson; John Capstick; John Edwards; Robert Firth; Nigel Gatherer; Alastair Greigson; Janet Hay; Heart of Midlothian FC; Tam Hendry; Tom Hunter; Terry Kivlin; Gérald and Marie-Hélène LeDucq; Lothian & Borders Fire Brigade (Bob Virtue & Dick Church-Michael); Marc Marnie; Joe McEwan; Iain McKinna; Mark Miele; Davy Pringle; Pat Robertson; the Scottish Arts Council; David Sharp; Paul Tebble; Vinyl Villains; Iain White; Liz Williams.

CHAPTER 1

Picture this:

The villa sits high and secluded on the southernmost slope of Calella de Palafrugell on the Spanish Costa Brava. Its white stucco walls and sun-bleached tiles are set hard against a backdrop of cypress and pine, and from the poolside patio you can look down across the confusion of rooftops and narrow winding streets of the hibernating resort to the shimmering turquoise of the bay beyond: there the three sparsely populated beaches, the bobbing boats and the gently lapping waves; there the knot of weathered fishermen repairing their nets in the shade of the beachfront arches.

And this:

Edinburgh, the Big Chill. Mid-December Gorgie. Gloomy wind-whipped streets cowering beneath turbulent skies and lashing rain. Tenements huddled together, close on sooted wynds, broken cobbles glistening a bloodless orange in the streetlight wash. Not just the polished gloss of the city the tourist saw, but the real city where punters battled along dark, littered streets, crunching broken glass as they scrunched against the elements, past boarded shop-windows and lean, scavenging dogs. Where cold, hollow eyes reflect cold, hollow lives, and anger offers the only semblance of any emotional warmth. Where winter is a long and soulless night of far too many days.

Where would *you* live, say you had the choice?

Say someone called you up and said, 'Hey, Billy, how would you

1

like a holiday? A long-term stay in an exclusive villa on the Costa Brava, all expenses paid?'

And all you had to do was kill someone. What you liked doing best anyway.

What would you do?

What would any poor man do?

It wasn't as though it was easy out here. Fuck no. Life was hard. Decisions had to be made. Like should he go to the toilet or just piss in the pool? Hard indeed. The only advantage was Sunday mornings you could sit out here in the shade on the patio with a San Miguel in one hand and a coming-down head in the other. Watch the girl turn lazily in the pool and try to remember exactly how she got there.

Foxy-looking chick, too. Wearing one of those black string bikinis that reveal more than they suggest. Her skin was pale, her face and shoulders freckled and her hair a tangle of long blonde curls. But spread like seaweed now, as she lay face down in the swimming-pool with the axe still lodged deep between her shoulder-blades. A sight for sore eyes.

And Billy's eyes *were* sore. Studying them in the mirror this morning they had looked like raw, suppurating wounds; as though someone had poked through the sockets and given his brain a stir. Which was exactly how it felt now. Addled. And not just a little confused as he tried to piece together the events of the night before.

She was an art student. Sandra something. English. She'd hitched her way down through France and had arrived in Spain at the same time as the heat-wave. Had decided to take a little sun before heading on down to Barcelona. Which was how she ended up dead in Billy's private swimming-pool.

Well, not quite. There were still a few blanks to fill in, foggy places in his mind where memory feared to tread. Perhaps another San Miguel would help.

William P. McCulloch dragged his weary bones off the recliner, padded naked across the patio to the cool marbled floor of the kitchen; the effort almost draining him. He took two bottles from the refrigerator, opened one and gulped. Then almost bit off its neck as the portable phone shrilled on its wall-attachment.

He glared at it, willing it to explode. For eighteen months now it had only ever rung on the first Sunday of every month.

Until now.

And still it rang. On and on. Shredding his nerves as he stood with his dick in the ice-box trying to decide – answer it or smash it to a million tiny pieces?

Decisions, decisions.

And today of all days, all strung out the way he was and trying hard to understand how there were bloodstains all across the wall in the hall. Look at him, all wound up, taut as a fucking bowstring. And all because the phone was ringing when it shouldn't – the *second* Sunday in December.

As he reached for it the ringing stopped.

Typical.

He took it from the wall and carried it outside with his beer.

Pure dynamite. The benefits of a common market. Even the lowest European common denominator was proving better than anything ever Made In Britain. For instance. The acid here, they brought down straight from Amsterdam on the overnight express, Paris to Barcelona. Leave your passport with the guard, sleep right through, step off bleary-eyed in Gerona saying, 'Customs? What customs?'

And strong stuff, too. What had Alfonso called it? *Estrella Roja*, red star. Billy had his own name for it. Life Saving Drug. And a thousand tabs was going to cost you maybe only a fiftieth of the profit you made. You had the same outlook on life as Alfonso, a hundredth.

But worth it.

Look at Billy.

One tab and twelve hours later he was still jumpy as a cat in a threshing machine. Or maybe it was the heat, he thought. Affecting his head. Christmas just around the corner and here he was cooking like a haggis in the middle of a heat-wave. He opened the second San Miguel on his teeth and carried it across to the low balustrade overlooking the bay.

One thing about Sandra, she knew how to float. She'd been doing it now for hours. Turning softly like a starfish in the centre of the pool, the shaft of the axe like a listing mast in the centre of her back. Around the lips of the wound the blood had dried, crusty and dark, accentuating the paleness of her skin. She looked unreal, Billy thought, almost waxlike against the pink-stained water.

A breath of warm sluggish wind pushed at his hair, the smell of olive-oil and garlic wafting up from one of the villas further down the headland. Soon it would be time for chill-out, what the Spanish liked to call *siesta*. He removed his shades and mopped his face, thinking suddenly of the claustrophobic, hop-laden air of his native Gorgie. So far away, yet somehow brought close by the sound of the telephone. Not just garlic, but a sense of change in the ether.

He noticed for the first time the wound just above the elbow of her right arm. Four inches long, it had the gape of a screaming mouth, the bone within winking like a pearl in the sun.

So at least she had struggled, he thought. In the hall outside the kitchen, where the bloodstains climbed the wall . . . A forehand, then. With her running towards the patio in her near-nothing bikini. Screaming?

Yeah, they always screamed in the films.

The telephone shrilled again. This time he didn't jump a foot in the air, he merely let it ring.

There were more bloodstains, he noticed, on the patio near the lip of the pool. Had he caught up with her there? Or here on the far side, by the low balustrade? Try as he might, he couldn't remember: too many fragments of his memory reflecting only glimpses, like the shards of a broken mirror. He would have to take more care in future, much more care.

He pressed the 'speak' button on the phone.

'*Diga*,' he said, snapping it out, the bored exec tired of being disturbed.

'He's surfaced.'

An old man's voice, as dry and dusty as the track that led up to the villa through the stunted shrubs and cut-back pine. Coming across clear and loud, as though calling from Can Pau's down on the beachfront instead of the frozen climes of Scotland's capital.

'Who's surfaced?'

'Who do you think?'

Billy didn't need to think – he knew. What he didn't know was how come the chick was still wearing her bikini. He could only imagine that she'd put it on again after, just before he chased her from the bedroom out on to the patio. He hoped so, anyway. Either that or he needed his head examined.

He could hear the impatient rattle of the old man's breath in his ear. 'Costello?' he said. Making it a question.

'I want him finished, Billy, taken care of.' Jack Rankine was a man whose obsessive breath of life was a succession of limitless wants. 'I want you on the next plane out.'

4

'*Mañana*, Jackie-boy.' Billy smiled to himself, imagining the snarl on the old man's lips. 'I've a few loose ends need tying up. Well, one in particular.'

'Tomorrow, then. I'll have Dodds meet you at the airport.'

'When did Costello get out?' Billy asked.

'Nine, ten days ago. I've had Dodds on his tail from the moment he walked out through the gates.'

'He been busy?'

'First week he just sat in his flat picking his nose. Went out twice, once to visit his parole officer, once to buy food.'

'And now?'

'Now he's working for Jay Johnstone,' the old man sighed.

Billy laughed. 'I bet that makes you happy.'

'I want you back here, Billy. Fast.'

'Costello – what's he doing for Johnstone? Pimping?'

'Working as a bouncer in a wine-bar.'

'How the mighty have fallen.' Billy swigged from the bottle, smeared the sweat from his stinging eyes. A man could evaporate in this heat, if he wasn't too careful; just fade away in a cloud of steam. He said, 'What about the deeds, Jackie-boy? You had them drawn up yet?'

'They're here on my desk. All they need is signed.'

Where the dusty track climbed through the shrubs to approach the villa, there was a wooden plaque on the whitewashed wall to the left of the wrought-iron gates. Villa Rancor. That would be first to go. Then do something about the décor inside. Shoot down the flying ducks on the wall, paper over the bloodstains. Then think of a new name.

Rankine said, 'You still there?'

Billy said he was.

'Aye, well, don't forget your snowshoes.' The old man cackled and hung up.

Billy returned his attention to the girl. Sandra. Her of the freckles and peelie-wally skin. Maybe they hadn't made it to the bedroom after all. Had done it on the floor in front of the spitting log-fire. Him taking her from behind, both hands on her saddle as she moaned, '*More, Billy, more,*' ramming herself on to him, then shuddering as she came again and again and again.

Yeah, he could imagine it like that – easily.

He just couldn't remember doing it.

CHAPTER 2

He couldn't see their faces. They wore riot gear. The black visors of their helmets reflected only his own image, small and thin and cowering, naked in the corner of his cell.

Four of them. Looming over him, menacingly, anonymous. He could see eight more tiny reflections of himself, one in each of their shiny black boots. He felt like laughing.

'Want to share the joke, Costello?'

He couldn't tell which of the screws had spoken.

'Think it's a laughing matter, do you?'

They were taking it in turns.

'Out only ten days, Joe, and you're back inside?'

The one on the left now.

'And you find that funny?'

Joe must have nodded or laughed or told them to stick it. He watched as the tiny images of himself grew and grew as their boots swung in, as though in slow motion. He felt no pain. Maybe this was the action-replay.

His vision cleared.

The first one said: 'Should've listened to your supervising officer.'

The second one said: 'Should've told him about the job, Costello.'

The third one said: 'Should've read the conditions of your licence, Joe.'

The fourth one said: 'Should've thought about "recall".'

There was blood on their boots. He looked down at his body. It was covered in lipstick, running glossy and slick.

Suddenly, bells clamoured throughout the hall. Cons began to shout and batter on their cell doors. A voice, loud and unintelligible, came out over the PA.

'Joe, are you there?'

Of course he fucking was – where else was he going to go?

'Let me in, Joe. We have an appointment, remember?'

He wanted in so bad, the screws could let him in.

But the screws had vanished.

Joe tugged on his jeans, stumbled to the door. He fumbled with the chain and turned the mortise, massaging his gritty eyes as he held the door ajar.

'Sorry,' he muttered. 'Totally forgot.'

Robert Denbigh-Jones smiled. 'Heavy night?' he asked, squeezing past Joe into the dark narrow hall. 'Kitchen or sitting-room?'

'Kitchen.'

Joe closed the front door and followed Denbigh-Jones into the kitchen. 'Coffee?'

Denbigh-Jones settled his battered briefcase against the leg of one of the stools and sat down at the table without removing his heavy black overcoat. There was a dusting of snow on his thick dark hair.

'Just the business,' he said. 'White and two sugars.' He was a portly, red-faced man in his mid-forties, who spoke with a soft Welsh lilt, sharpened at times by a pure guttural Scots: originally from Cardiff – he had told Joe at their first meeting in HMP Saughton – he had remained in Edinburgh after graduating from the university. The most beautiful city in the world, he called it. He smoked continuously and smiled often. But there was a steely hardness, too, Joe had noticed, that glinted deep beneath the murky green waters of his eyes.

Denbigh-Jones pulled out a pack of Marlboro. 'Do you mind?'

Joe shook his head, not trusting himself to speak just yet, the remnants of the dream still clouding his mind. He switched on the kettle, spooned four measures of Continental Roast into the cafetière, washed and warmed two mugs under the tap.

Denbigh-Jones lit up, vanishing behind a cloud of smoke. 'Sorry we had to meet here, Joe, but you know how it is. Too much chance you'd bump into a few of your former fellow inmates at the office.'

'You think I'd start something?'

'Not you, no. But with some of the other parolees, better not to risk it. How are you settling down?'

Joe found an ashtray in one of the cupboards, slid it across the table to Denbigh-Jones. 'I'm managing,' he said.

'Any problems?'

'Nothing I can't handle.'

'Well, remember, Joe – as your supervising officer, that's what I'm here for. You have a problem you can't handle, don't be afraid to ask. Better I'm involved from the beginning, than have something blow up in my face. Understand what I mean?'

'Like I said, nothing I can't handle.'

'Good.' Denbigh-Jones did not look wholly convinced; he dug in his briefcase, brought out a sheaf of papers. 'Have you managed to get out much?'

Joe shrugged. 'I go to work, I come home. That's about it.' He switched off the kettle and filled the cafetière.

'How is the job?' Denbigh-Jones asked. 'You plan to stay there a while?'

'It's all right. Keeps me out of jail.'

'As long as it does. What exactly are your duties there?'

'General barwork, you know, serving customers, handling change, collecting glasses, that kind of thing.'

'Have they ever asked you to watch the door?'

'You mean, like a bouncer?'

'Mm,' Denbigh-Jones said.

Joe shook his head; perhaps too emphatically, he thought. 'Nah,' he said. 'They know better.'

'Because I could never allow that, Joe, no way. You know as well as I do that bouncers offer inviting targets to any pisshead with something to prove. One complaint of excess force by a member of the public to the police and that would be you, son – recalled to finish the rest of your sentence. Remember, you don't even have to commit an offence – your licence can be revoked, in the public interest, merely for giving serious cause for concern.'

'Don't worry. The public can sleep easy.'

'Glad to hear it,' Denbigh-Jones smiled. 'And the manageress, I understand, is a friend of yours?'

'We grew up together. She used to live across the street.'

Denbigh-Jones shuffled through a sheaf of forms, found what he was looking for. 'That's right. Rae Connell. I see she visited you at Saughton a few times.'

'Why go through it all again? I told you all this when I started the pre-release programme.'

'So you did, Joe, so you did. But you're not my only parolee and sometimes I need to refresh my memory. Would you mind if I had a word with Mz Connell?'

'I would.'

Denbigh-Jones's smile faltered. 'Why's that?'

Joe depressed the filter and poured the coffee. 'I don't think it's any of your business,' he said. But he was thinking about the dream, clinging still.

'Should've told him about the job, Costello.'

'You have her down here as your only friend, Joe. Also, she happens to be your present employer. If I'm to judge what kind progress you're making, it would help to talk to her.'

'White and two sugars.' Joe handed him the mug of coffee. 'How about you give it a couple of weeks, then talk to her? Give us both a chance to settle.'

'Thanks.' Denbigh-Jones held the mug in both his hands, blew at the steam. 'Okay,' he said, after a moment, 'a couple of weeks it is. Have you been to visit your father yet?'

Joe slumped at the table, absently stirring his coffee. 'Yesterday,' he said.

'And how was he?'

'Insane. The Sister said it was one of his bad days. He hardly said a word the whole time I was there, and when he did, it was only to deny I was ever his son. Same old story.'

Denbigh-Jones exhaled heavily, stubbed out his cigarette. 'Give him time, you never know.' He glanced again at his papers. 'What about your ex-colleagues on the force, Joe? You ever see any of them?'

'Past tense, the lot of them.'

'I see. And you've never considered contacting any of them?'

'Why should I?'

Denbigh-Jones sighed. 'Joe. You were put away for a crime you said at the time you did not commit. You are an ex-cop. People don't change that easily.'

No, never easily. But they change. And Joe had changed, was changing still. Walk out of Saughton Prison for the first time in a year and a half and you tend to see the city in a different light. You find yourself looking at things more, not just looking but *seeing*. Buildings you'd never noticed before, there since the days they'd take you down off the Mercat Cross and break you to pieces on the wheel. Or the way the sunburst clouds leap off the twilight skyline like the world was on fire. Or the beautiful people, the snappy young posers sitting in their flash new motors talking into phones, hoping you'll notice and envy their fragile affluence. And the kids: all permed hair and baggy jeans, heavy fringes shielding shy, sullen eyes, or laying on the grease and looking sharp through scowling narrowed eyes. Skateboards and mountain-bikes. Skintight cycling shorts and slash-kneed jeans. Observing people – the matter of life – no longer through a cynical copper's eyes but the eyes of a man who's lived in the dark too long and knows he will never return. As though you had to lose part of your life in order to appreciate the rest of it. People so involved in the big issues of life, of survival, they are blind to the little things of which life is made, and made enjoyable – the trivia of existence so often taken for granted by those who have never been forcibly removed from normality. Being able to walk down streets, to go into shops and pubs and restaurants. To listen to people talk of everyday things, planning tomorrows that will be better than all their yesterdays. To have the choice. To be able to drift with the eddies and currents of life, to improvise, to follow new ways with a will and to enjoy every fresh experience as though it were your last. Yes. So much new to take in, so much old to remember. First couple of days he'd spent walking the streets, waking up excited as a kid on Christmas day, heading uptown, taking his time, getting to know the city he had known yet never known. His city. But staying away from all the old haunts, the pubs he used to frequent before-shift, on-shift, after-shift, drinking the empty hours away. No going back to the way things were. The past was past. Now he would cross the street if he had to, taking the long way round. No longer needing the alcohol, the forced camaraderie, the cheap laughs. That was the old way, lying like dead skin behind him, shed in the midnight chill of endless nights in solitary. A hard lesson learnt. Forgive and forget. Adapt and survive. He wouldn't make the same mistake as his father, end up broken and twisted by hate, life a bitter taste at the back of his throat. No. There were many ways to live a life.

He was finding out.

* * *

11

He tugged his gaze away from the window, ran his fingers through his hair. Denbigh-Jones watched him patiently, the trace of a smile on his lips. The art of conversation, he had once told Joe, was often one of the most difficult aspects of release for a convict to overcome: it took time to throw off the shackles of institutional doubt and rebuild one's self-confidence.

How much time? Joe wondered.

He chose his words with care and spoke with a soft intensity he hoped would pass for sincerity. 'I told you already, what's past is past. It's all behind me. I've done the time, now all I want is left alone. Is that too much to ask?'

Denbigh-Jones held up the palms of his hands. 'Okay, Joe, I'm sorry. But I do have to ask.'

'Ask away, but don't insinuate.'

'Point taken. Now, about Christmas . . . have you anything lined up?'

'I hadn't really thought about it.'

'Okay, no problem, neither have I. Always tend to leave it till the last moment.' Denbigh-Jones glanced at his watch, returned his papers to his briefcase. 'Just be sure to let me know if you decide to leave the city.' He stood up, drained the rest of his coffee, consulted a small pocket diary. 'We'll meet again two weeks today – here, if you don't mind.'

Joe said he didn't.

'Any problem with that, you know my number. Any problem with *anything*, in fact.' Denbigh-Jones peered out the window and shook his head at the sombre grey world beneath an overcast sky from which powdery snow continued to fall. 'Another front on its way, the forecast says. All we bloody need. Still . . .' He proffered his hand.

Joe closed the front door behind him and stood there for a long time, wondering.

Did Denbigh-Jones suspect?

Or did he know?

'Should've told him about the job, Costello.'

Dreams, he thought.

As if the real world wasn't enough.

CHAPTER 3

Where the hell was Dodds?

Grace McEwan sighed and lit up another cigarette, letting the match burn slowly down to her fingers before she dropped the dying flame in the ashtray.

Look at her.

Twenty-one today and what was she doing? Sitting on her own in a wine-bar full of posers, waiting for the trouble to start. Typical. She glanced at her watch for the second time in as many minutes.

Where the hell was he?

Business was already picking up: couples mostly, coming in out of the snow, stomping their feet inside the doors before heading towards the bar. It was a Couples Only night. Which meant the bouncer on the door had naturally had to give her a hard time before letting her in. Coming across as though he'd lose his job – if the manager walked in and saw her sitting alone in the corner near the door – when all he really wanted was to get in her pants. Obvious by the way he kept looking over now, trying to catch her eye. She swirled the ice in her Pernod with her finger, then sipped it absently as she looked out over the bar.

She'd been here once before, she recalled – three, maybe four, years ago. It'd been different then, a real pub, a local full of character and characters, with a blazing log-fire and lots of wee rooms and some of the hardest clientèle you could find in the city. The kind of place you could get anything you wanted if you knew the right person. In its own way, a warm, friendly place, part of the community.

But all that had long disappeared. Now it was a wine-bar called Posers and was painted and carpeted in pastel shades of cream and blue. With marble-topped tables on wrought-iron stands, and plastic ferns and plants in baskets hanging from the walls. Cheap plaster busts of Rabbie Burns lining the top of the gantry, lit by twee fox-glove lamps on tall brass poles. Yuck, double yuck. Burn the place down, Grace thought, and come the morning, she'd have done the world a favour.

It was also Golden Oldie night. Which meant the jaded DJ behind the console was dusting off all the old favourites; peeling back the years to expose cold memories and faded dreams. For Grace, a succession of birthdays amidst a succession of faceless foster-parents. A confusion of memories all slurring into one big fat nothing. Good, bad, indifferent – what did it matter? They'd all been the same: a constant, bickering reminder of her failure to conform. Never letting her forget their sacrifice, ignoring her needs as they silenced her demands. Discipline, they'd say, that's what she lacked. A little discipline in her life, that's what she needs.

But what did *they* know? What do they ever know?

She took another swallow and felt the yellow mellow slip down her throat and kindle the fire inside, quiet the jangling nerves. Slide deep to the quick where the wounds heal slow. She crushed out her cigarette, grinding it angrily into the ashtray.

Look at her.

Twenty-one today and here she was almost dripping tears in her drink. As though the burden of all her years was about to break her buckled back. Jesus.

And where the hell was Dodds, she wanted to know?

A party would have been nice. Some decent music and wild dancing, a few friends to get a good crack going. Get totally mortalled and trash the place stupid. Or even a buffet-banquet, she thought. Plates and plates of those tasty little delicacies and fluffy puff-pastries that melt in the mouth stretching off into the white table-clothed distance. Start at one end and nibble her way to the other, with sombre-faced waiters in crisp penguin-suits wheeling in trollies of champagne slammers and bowing so low that their trousers split. The image making her giggle now and think again of Dodds.

It had to be the suits. Dodds always wore these sharp double-breasted suits with tapered waists and baggy trousers he thought

14

made him look the man about town he tried so hard to be. Didn't realise he looked like a teddy-bear with clothes on. She wondered which it would be tonight – the shiny shark-grey or the creamy woollen one. If he came at all, that was.

Though he'd sounded pretty definite yesterday, she thought. When he'd explained about the job he wanted doing and paid half the money in advance, there'd also been a note of excitement behind his jumbled rush of words, she recalled. Something about promotion, the big picture. Which would be good news for her only if he ever found the courage to ditch his glaikit wife and set up home with her. Though Grace certainly wasn't going to hold her breath waiting.

A few presents would've been nice, too. Or even one. But Dodds wasn't exactly the most thoughtful man in the world. Or the most romantic. Like, he'd be in her door a couple of minutes and that was it, she'd be flat on her back with her legs in the air. Talk about finesse. She'd tell him, how about a little conversation first? Or a quiet drink? Or even a little foreplay to get in the mood? But that wasn't Dodds. He said he couldn't help it, like it was something in his genes. She'd ask him why he couldn't keep it there, and he'd call it 'unbridled passion'. Grace wasn't too sure what the hell to call it.

Men.

She took out a match and struck it. Sat hypnotised by its flame until she dropped it dying into the ashtray. Looked up to find the bouncers' heavy dark eyes on her legs, just lapping her up. Obviously he had nothing better to do than ogle the talent. Typical. He flashed her a hopeful smile but she looked right through him, pretended he wasn't there. She sensed rather than saw him turn away towards the double swing-doors as a stream of snow-covered couples pushed noisily into the bar.

A birthday cake would have been nice as well, she thought. With some of that thick chocolately icing her Nan used to let her lick from the bowl after. The smell of the cake in the oven invading the whole house, Grace hardly being able to wait till tea, drooling her way through the afternoon, having to sneak upstairs every once in a while to light a few matches just to calm herself down.

Like she was having to do now, waiting for Dodds to show, for the trouble to start.

She wondered what form the trouble would take. When she'd asked him yesterday, he'd told her not to worry, just to do what she did best, what he was paying her to do. That he had everything under control. That if she saw him in the bar, she was to ignore him and use the disturbance to sneak through the back. A diversion, he called it. Grace had let her jaw hang for a moment to show him how impressed she was.

She struck another match.

'Been stood up?'

The bouncer.

Who didn't look much of one, now she came to think of it. Tall, yes; wiry, yes; but not a patch on Arnie Schwarzenegger. Leaning over her now, with one hand on the back of her seat and the other on the table. A question in his come-to-bed eyes.

'Bog off,' she told him.

'Only trying to be friendly,' he replied.

'Well try it somewhere else.' Hoping Dodds would hurry the hell up.

And then suddenly he was there, standing like a monolith in the centre of the floor, looking around with his red lips curled. He spotted her in the corner and swaggered across.

'This guy hassling you, doll?'

The bouncer came away from the table, held up his palms. 'Sorry, pal – couples only.'

Dodds said, 'I am a couple. Anyway, I ain't here for the pleasure, I'm looking for Joe Costello.'

The bouncer said, 'Any particular reason?'

'I've a message for him. From a friend.'

'I don't have any friends.'

Dodds took his time, brain on overtime. 'One concerned about your sense of humour, Joe,' he said eventually, towering over the bouncer, dwarfing him.

'I don't have one of them either.'

'That's what they always say about cops,' Dodds grinned, 'but I don't believe it. Wear a suit like that and you have to have a sense of humour.'

The bouncer cocked his head and frowned at Grace. 'What was the name of that film?' he asked, his tone pleasant, sincere. 'You know the one – where the gunslinger swaggers into the saloon and calls the homesteader at the bar a dirdy yeller dawg?'

Dodds stared in disbelief. Then he smiled. The way flesh does when you slice it with a razor.

*   *   *

Grace couldn't get over it.

Sitting in the blackness of the cleaner's cupboard and trying to breathe as little as possible of the stale, musty air laden with the smell of polish and disinfectant, the scene replayed itself vividly over and over again in her mind.

It was mental. She couldn't get over it. The way that bouncer who didn't look like a bouncer at all just stood there and took it. Dodds powering in punches and the guy just stood there spitting out blood, buckling eventually under the deluge of blows, falling to his knees and then to the floor, finally curling to a ball as the boots swung in, offering no kind of resistance, if any at all.

It didn't make sense.

And the look in the bouncer's eyes just before the first blow landed – that was another thing. Staring right in her fucking eyes. Grace sitting alone in the corner, trying to pretend she wasn't even there and the guy looks right in her eyes and sort of shrugs his eyebrows as if to say *Que sera, sera*. Trying to be cool in front of the ladies even though he's about to get his head staved in.

It didn't make sense.

Bouncers were paid to fight. To sort out trouble, if not to start it. They were supposed to defend themselves. Some guy comes in and starts a rammy, the bouncer's supposed to come over and beat seven colours of shit out of the guy before throwing him out on the street a bloodied mass of pulp. Give the rest of the punters a little entertainment. Not curl up in a little ball on the floor and wait for his bones to break. And then there was Dodds.

Yes, Dodds.

Who said he loved her and wanted to leave his wife and kids and set up home with Grace.

Who only opened his mouth when he wanted to lie or stuff it full of breast.

Who paid her coin to light a few fires but couldn't even remember her birthday.

Dodds.

Recalling now the emptiness, the almost overwhelming nausea she had felt as she watched him pummel and pound the bouncer's motionless form. In the quiet of the cupboard, and over the accelerating beat of her heart, she could still hear his fists and the sounds they made as bone met flesh, and bone met bone.

Sickening her now as it had sickened her then.

Glad she had left when she did, squeezing through the throng of bloodthirsty gawkers to pass unobserved down the corridor to the Ladies, and then through the door marked STAFF ONLY to the small cleaner's cupboard under the stair, she now sat waiting impatiently for the big luminous hand to edge its way round to the time Dodds said it was safe to come out.

Getting close now.

Thoughts already turning to the task ahead as anticipation coursed through her veins, jangling every nerve in her shivering frame. Christ, she was wound up. Like a clockwork toy about to explode with one more turn of the key. If she wasn't careful, the cleaner would come in in the morning and find bits of Grace sliding down the walls. Come unstuck, and she'd end up like that bouncer. Which was not a happy thought. So she searched and found the box of matches in her bag, took one out and struck it. Breathed in the acrid sulphur fumes as she watched the flame crawl towards her shaking fingers.

Calm down, she told herself. Be cool. Like ice. Ice and fire, Grace and Danger. The Ice Queen and the Dragon Queen.

She giggled nervously in the dying light.

Licked finger and thumb and extinguished the flame. Peered at the luminous dial of her watch. Twenty minutes. Which was 1200 seconds. Which was . . .

Fuck it.

She slid back the bolt on the door and crawled out into the corridor. Strained her ears for a trace of sound as she let her eyes adjust to the paler darkness of the corridor. Reviewing the floor-plan in her mind.

To the right was the kitchen. To the left, the door marked STAFF ONLY which opened on another corridor: right to the bar, and left to the fire exit. Her exit.

Better check that first.

Then find something to jam all the doors open, create a good flue: because fires, like people, need oxygen to live.

Okay. Let's go. Do the Ice Queen.

She slung her bag across her shoulders and made her way to the door marked STAFF ONLY. It opened noiselessly on a corridor faintly illuminated by a clear night sky visible through the skylight. She let the door close softly behind her before moving cautiously towards the fire exit, exactly where Dodds had said it would be.

She'd taken only a few tentative steps before a sudden sound stopped her dead in her tracks.

18

She could hardly breathe. Could feel her heart pulsing, croaking like a frog in the back of her throat. Couldn't move. Eyes bugging out like stone-cold marbles. No. Please, she thought, not now. Don't piss yourself now. Hold on. There has to be a logical . . .

A hissing sound. Coming from her left. Like running water. From behind the door marked . . .

Gents.

Christ, what a fool, she thought, as the pent-up breath exploded from her lungs. What a stupid, scared little baby. Frightened of a few bloody urinals. Almost wet your knickers, Ice Queen, standing there like a gobstruck wean in the shadow of the bogeyman. Almost left a steaming calling card. Christ.

Still cursing herself, she pushed into the Ladies and relieved the pressure. Lit up a cigarette and sucked it dry in a couple of drags. Hand shaking so hard she had to guide it to her mouth. Thinking, never, no never again. Get out of here and that's it, no more fires. No more creeping round in the middle of the night, scaring the shit from your system. You're getting too old, it's time to move on.

But knowing it was only wishful thinking.

She rose and left the washroom, no caution now as she approached the fire exit. Seemed simple enough: all you had to do was slip the bolts at the top and bottom and then kick the bar. And the door would open. Simple.

Satisfied she had a line of retreat, she turned to make her way back down the corridor to the bar. It was then that she saw it. And for the second time in almost as many minutes, stopped dead.

Up in the corner, over the door to the bar. Seemingly innocuous, a little red light in a little white box, flashing on and off every time she moved.

Feeling the sudden anger rise inside her.

Anger at Dodds.

No alarms, he had said. Who we talking about here, he had said, Jay bloody Johnstone or someone who knows how to run a business? He had said.

She should have known. Never trust a word Dodds says. Her fault.

Aware now that she had set off the alarm the moment she poked her head into the corridor. Sending silent bells ringing down at the local cop-shop. Don't panic, she told herself. Keep calm.

She panicked.

Ran to the fire exit. Slipped the bolts. Stepped back and kicked the release-bar.

Nothing happened.

She kicked it again.

Nothing happened.

She launched her whole body at the door.

Still it would not budge.

Wild thoughts assaulted her mind as she struggled for the calm that would not come. Sue the bastard. Take him to the cleaners for endangering human life. For contravening the terms and conditions of his licence. Inoperative fire-doors. Someone could fucking die. Jay bloody Johnstone. Cheapskate supreme.

She attacked the door with renewed and desperate frenzy.

It could have been a rock.

The first frustrated sob broke from her lips as the wail of a siren cut through the sound of her fears.

CHAPTER 4

A s snowflakes sank like down from the overcast sky, blanching
the Royal Infirmary forecourt outside his window, Joe
Costello studied his face in the mirror over the washbasin and
cursed the senseless beast of modern bureaucracy that had brought
him here.

'Christ, when I was a kid,' he told George O'Brien, who shared
the two-bed ward with Joe, 'a kicking was just a kicking, something
that happened to almost everyone once in a while. No big deal. All
you did was crawl on home and take a few days off work until
the swelling and bruising disappeared. Nowadays, it seems, it's all
flashing blue lights, ambulances, hospitals and police.'

'In other words, questions,' O'Brien wheezed. He was a slight,
bald man in his early fifties who had just sacrificed one of his lungs
to cancer. He lay on his bed, in dressing-gown and slippers, smoking
roll-up after roll-up.

'What it means,' Joe said, fingering the shallow cut over his
swollen right eye, 'is these days you just can't have your head
kicked in in peace. You can be lying there in a coma with your
brains dribbling out and there'll be some nosy kid in a uniform
who wants to know the exact sequence of events that led to your
present condition. As if you can remember or even give a shit.'

O'Brien chuckled. 'It's the modern form of torture, Joe. They're
crafty, see. Why take you down the station and sweat you under
the lamps when they can slam you in a ward and make you eat the

hospital food? One day of such tasteless slop and even a politician would be forced to tell the truth.'

'Observation, the doctor said.' Joe winced as he gently probed the puffy swelling beneath his left eye. 'I told him if he didn't fetch me my clothes he could observe me walking out into the snow in his hospital fucking pyjamas.' There were two more cuts on his cheekbone, now neatly stitched, where the Stone Age Man's heavy gold ring had torn parallel gouges in his flesh. Christ, he looked a mess. Eyes, bloodshot, lips burst in several places, and the cap from one of his front teeth missing. He looked like a semi-assembled Robo-Cop with its face-mask off.

'He'll be off searching for a strait-jacket,' O'Brien said, lighting up a fresh cigarette, dissolving into a fit of coughs.

Footsteps echoed down the main corridor. O'Brien hastily pinched out his roll-up, and was still wafting ineffectually at the thick cloud of smoke over his head when the very serious young doctor walked in carrying Joe's clothes. He dropped them on Joe's bed, sniffed the air suspiciously, frowned at O'Brien, but said nothing. It was a battle he had lost already.

'What's the verdict, doc?' O'Brien asked, nodding towards Joe. 'He going to live?'

The very serious young doctor tapped the tip of his pencil against his teeth and studied Joe down the length of his nose. 'There's good news, Mr Costello, and there's bad news.'

'Tell me the good news.'

'There's a Miss Connell at Reception, waiting to take you home.' The doctor's smile was as tight as a nervous tic. 'However, there are also two policemen outside who want to talk to you. Shall I send them in?'

'Give me a minute.' Joe glanced at George O'Brien.

'Okay, I'm going, I'm going. You think I like the sight of blood and grown men crying?'

O'Brien and the doctor left and the door slowly hissed shut.

There's never any trouble – that's what Rae Connell had said when she phoned him up last week saying she was in a bit of a predicament and could he help her out. As a favour, she added: just work the door for a couple of nights until she could find someone else. That's all, a week at the most, she said.

He'd had to tell her sorry, he was through with all that, he couldn't take the risk.

'Risk? What risk?'

'Of trouble.'

'You've never been scared of trouble before, Joe.'

'I've never been on parole before either.'

'Joe, please – I wouldn't be asking if I didn't need your help. You're the only person I can turn to, trust.'

Okay, so Joe suspected Rae's emergency wasn't quite the emergency she made it out to be. That she was just trying to help him out and save his face at the same time. She knew him well enough to know that he'd never accept charity but would always help a friend in need. So . . .

So Joe relented. Thinking it wouldn't do him any harm, might even do him some good.

'You won't regret it, Joe,' she said. 'You'll get double-time and a taxi home and all the drink you can throw down your throat in as long as it takes me to ring up the tills at the end of the night and maybe sack a few staff for the hell of it. How's that sound?'

Like trouble, he'd wanted to say. But kept his reservations to himself and told her, aye, it sounded fine. Then turned up prompt at eight the next night and stood around the rest of his shift earning the easiest money he'd ever earned. A piece of piss, he'd told her later, as they sat sipping drinks after everyone else had left.

'You looking for the job?' Rae had asked.

Joe had laughed.

But a week later he was still there, and beginning to enjoy himself.

Until Stone Age Man waltzes in, does the pogo on his face and puts him in hospital and in trouble with the law.

Detective Sergeant Bob McInnis strode up to the bed with a broad smile and shook Joe's hand. 'Good to see you, Joe. How're you feeling?'

'How I look.'

'Like shit, huh?' McInnis dragged a chair across and gingerly lowered his formidable bulk. In the almost two years since they'd last met, McInnis hadn't changed much. The tense air of a barely restrained aggression was still there, etched indelibly into the detective's taut, angular face, and the threat of sudden violence, Joe noticed, still lurked, simmering, behind those dark restless eyes. He watched as McInnis pushed large, blunt fingers through his greased-back hair and asked, 'Are they going to keep you in?'

'I'm free to leave the moment you're gone.'

'We'll try not to keep you.'

'We?'

McInnis jerked his head in the direction of the door and lowered his voice. 'Kerley,' he said.

Joe groaned. 'What's that bastard want?'

'You?'

'You mean he hasn't forgiven me yet?'

'For the business with the whore, I don't think he'll ever forgive you,' McInnis said with a wry grin. 'As for the rest, he reckons you got off lightly.'

'For something I didn't do?'

'You know the way his mind works: once a con, always a con.'

'And all I've heard for the last two years is once a cop, always a cop.'

'I would've come to visit, Joe – you know that.'

'Sure,' Joe said, 'I know.'

McInnis shifted uncomfortably on the chair. 'Was it hard?' he asked. 'The time inside?'

Joe shrugged but said nothing.

'You don't like to talk about it?'

'I don't even want to believe it happened.'

Footsteps approached along the corridor. McInnis rose from the chair and crossed to warm himself against the radiator beneath the window. Outside, snow continued to fall lethargically from the dirty white sky. As the door burst open, he said, 'Give us a call, Joe, we'll go for a drink.'

Detective Inspector Brian Kerley marched into the room, waggling a finger menacingly at McInnis. 'Associating with a known criminal is an offence, sergeant. You know the score on that.'

'Sir?' McInnis stared blankly at his superior.

Kerley ignored him, turned to Joe. 'So. We meet again. I always hoped we would.'

'I didn't know you cared.'

Kerley reddened. He hadn't changed much either, Joe noticed. Still the pinched grey face, the red-rimmed eyes, the hooked and broken nose, still the tight-lipped gash through which he let his poisoned breath escape. And he was still chewing gum with tobacco-stained teeth.

'Care about you, Costello?' Kerley sneered. 'Not a fucking chance.' He removed the clipboard from the end of Joe's bed and pretended to study it. 'What I do care about is crooked ex-cops poncing about my streets like they own them, getting involved in fights and fires while consorting with known criminal elements. All of which, correct me if I'm wrong, contravene the conditions of your licence.' Kerley looked up from the clipboard and added, 'Sadly, it appears, the doctor thinks you'll live.'

'Poor you.'

Kerley sighed dramatically as he replaced the clipboard. 'I see you learned nothing inside.'

'One thing I learned is never trust a cop. What do you want?'

McInnis stepped away from the window. 'Just a few questions, Joe, no big deal.'

Joe couldn't believe it. Here they were, giving him the good-guy/bad-guy routine. Mr Nice and Mr Nasty. Pinky and bloody Perky. Jesus!

'Is this official?'

Kerley said, 'You can answer the questions here or down at the station.'

'Am I under arrest or what?'

'We just want to know what's going on, Joe. Like what really happened last night.'

'Nothing happened last night. I fell down some stairs.'

'Was this before or after the guy came into the pub and kicked fuck off your face?' Kerley smiled at his own sense of humour. 'Before or after someone tried to burn the place down?'

Joe sat up. 'Someone what?'

'Very convincing, Costello.'

McInnis said, 'We think whoever picked the fight with you was creating a diversion so his accomplice could sneak through the back and hide in the cupboard under the stair.'

'Yeah? Well I was here all night.'

'How convenient.' Kerley's sarcasm was as subtle as a cosh.

Joe asked the extent of the damage.

'A broken kitchen window,' McInnis told him. 'It looks as though the firebug panicked when the alarms went off and bust his way out through the window. More glass outside than in.'

'The kitchen window?' Joe said. 'Even an anorexic worm would find that difficult.'

'You hear that, sergeant?' Kerley sneered. 'We better put out a bulletin on anorexic worms.'

'Was anything taken?' Joe asked, ignoring Kerley as though he wasn't there. If it wasn't that McInnis had once been his partner, Joe would have given neither of them the time of day.

McInnis shook his head. 'Not even the float in the till.'

'So how do you know it wasn't just an attempt at burglary?'

'We found another incendiary device – same as the last one. Which is why we're here, Joe.'

'You seriously think I'm involved?'

'No,' Kerley said. 'It's obviously just a coincidence that since you started working for Jay Johnstone two of his properties have been torched to the ground and an attempt made on a third. Nothing more than chance.'

'So charge me for being unlucky.' Joe, though, had to admit he'd had the same thoughts himself – last night as he lay awake trying to figure out why some Neanderthal he'd never seen before should want to come in and dance on his face. There were answers crowding the back of his mind, but none he wanted to hear.

McInnis said, 'If you can tell us about the man who beat you up, maybe we can get a line on his accomplice.'

'He had big fists. Hard fists. And boots. Look for man with bloodstained boots.'

'You're not being very helpful, Joe.'

'The doctor says I have a mild concussion. Temporary amnesia.'

'You remember that course we went on, five, six years ago? Part of that joint venture between the Fire Brigade and CID?'

Joe said, sure, how could he forget?

'And they had what they called a Psychological Profile of the Typical Pyromaniac, right?'

'Right.'

'You remember what it said about the heaviest concentration of pyromaniacs?'

'Between the ages of sixteen and twenty-five, wasn't it?'

'Sixteen and twenty-eight,' McInnis corrected. 'But with the highest concentration at the age of seventeen.'

'So?'

'So whoever the accomplice was, he was probably sitting in the bar last night. And he would've had to've come past you.'

'Last night was a Couples Only night. No single men or gay couples allowed. And no seventeen-year-olds, either.'

'What about women?'

'It's possible,' Joe conceded, suddenly recalling the girl who'd been sitting alone drinking Pernod in the corner. 'Though the profile – if I remember correctly – suggested most fireraisers are male.'

'I'm just keeping an open mind, that's all.'

'Or in Costello's case,' Kerley said, 'an open sewer.' He stood by the window now, hands in pockets, looking contemptuously out the window. 'Tell me, Dayglo, you wouldn't be entertaining malicious thoughts of revenge, now would you?'

'On the slimy bastard who had me sent down?'

For the second time Kerley's scrawny neck reddened inside his frayed shirt collar. 'On Jack Rankine,' he snapped. 'The man whose daughter we found dead in your flat.'

Joe sank back on the pillows with a sigh. 'I'm tired,' he said. 'Call the nurse.'

'A hearse is what you're going to need if Rankine ever catches up with you. A shovel and a hearse.'

'That's all over with, Kerley, forgotten.'

'Not for the likes of Rankine. Thanks to you he's now got his face to save. The moment he knows you're out on the streets, you better watch your back.'

'So why don't you tell him yourself?'

'Maybe I will,' Kerley said. 'Maybe I will.' He flicked his head at McInnis. 'C'mon, sergeant, let's go. Before this bad-cop stink makes me puke.'

McInnis made a what-can-I-do? gesture and followed Kerley from the room. He came back a few seconds later and asked who Joe's Supervising Officer was.

'Denbigh-Jones. Why?'

'I'll square last night with him, put him in the picture.'

'Thanks. But, Bob? Don't mention I was working the door. He'd smile me to death if he ever found out.'

'Only,' McInnis said, 'if you promise to be careful. Okay?'

'Careful of what?'

The detective shook his head woefully. 'I just hope it isn't as bad as I think.'

'Why, what do you think?'

'I think Jack Rankine is still very much on your mind.'

CHAPTER 5

The Edin Hill Hotel is West End Georgian New Town with a little Doric influence thrown in in the shape of the imposing sandstone pillars flanking the main entrance. Four floors – including the penthouse suite – seventy-two rooms, two restaurants, three function rooms, one lounge bar and the Café Romano, a small nightclub in the basement. Also in the basement, the new New Town Health Club – open to the public at exorbitant annual membership fees – which includes three glass-fronted squash courts, a heated indoor swimming-pool, two saunas, two Turkish baths and a jacuzzi.

Proprietor: Jack Rankine.

A bear of a man with thick grey hair, small black eyes and a silver-streaked beard, Jack Rankine climbed laboriously from the depths of his Rolls Royce Silver Cloud – with its telephone, bar, TV, chauffeur and smoked-glass windows – and grunted his way up the wide hotel steps to the canopied entrance where one of the hall porters already stood with the door held open.

Steps.

Jack Rankine had suffered his first attack two years ago – climbing steps. No Giant's Causeway, no National Museum, just a few ordinary steps leading out of Xanthos, the small nightclub he owned on George St. The street which – he'd tell anyone who'd listen – taken along with Princes St, constituted the richest square-fucking-mile in Europe: more money there, he'd insist, than in the Queen Mother's purse.

His second attack, more serious than the first, almost punched his lights out for good. It caught him late in the same day he heard that the wop Costello had been released from Saughton, as he lay panting on one of the chambermaids, hoping for a miracle, even half a one. But the only divine message he received was forget it, Jack, or die in excruciating pain.

Arterio Sclerosis was the diagnosis: a narrowing of arteries serving the heart. That was the bad news. And a few days later, while lying in the ICU at the Royal Infirmary with tubes sprouting from every orifice God had given him and even a few He hadn't, Rankine's doctor, a haemophiliac with a morbid sense of humour, had told him the good news.

'Well, Jack, the tests are in. It's not all bad.'

'No?' Rankine said.

'No,' the doctor told him, 'At least now we know you have a heart.'

Which had naturally depressed him for a couple of days.

The lobby was wide and deep, a subtle blend of natural light and designer dark, plushly carpeted. All panel and polish and pastel shades. An atmosphere of homely comfort and bright efficiency. The lofty ceiling elaborately corniced, the chandelier an explosion of jewels that would catch the sun on a summer's day and slice it into a thousand shafts of gently swirling light. On winter days a roaring, crackling log-fire blazed in the wide stone hearth beneath the broad sweeping staircase to the gallery. Armchairs were deep and sumptuous. Plants flourished in deep brass pots, their webbed leaves glossy and veined, looking good enough to eat. And all about the milling guests, the bustling staff; the working day, the holiday, in perfect fluid motion. Moments like these and Rankine could forget the pressures of the outside world and remain suspended, buoyant, caught in this gentle eddy by the banks of life. But never for long.

'Mr Rankine, Sir!'

Beth Friedman, his personal assistant, was waiting at Reception. She came round the counter, dressed in tight black jeans and a heavy-knit fisherman's jumper, and escorted him to his private penthouse lift. Her shoulder-length fair hair was scrawled back from her forehead and tied in a pony-tail, her manner brusque and business-like as ever.

'How was your lunch, Sir?' she asked, following him into the lift and turning her key in the switch. The doors closed with a hiss.

Rankine scowled. 'Barely edible,' he said, 'but still easier to digest that what I had to listen to. Is Dodds back yet?'

'Yes, sir. He's waiting for you upstairs.' As the lift sighed to a halt and the doors hissed open, Beth asked if there was anything else.

'Phone the airport and find out what time Billy's flight gets in. With the weather like this there are bound to be delays. William P. McCulloch, Beth – you'll find all the details on my desk.' Rankine strode from the lift then turned with an afterthought. 'Has the Christmas tree arrived yet?'

'About an hour ago. The Head Porter wants to know if you have any special instructions.'

'Tell him the same as last year.'

'Yes, Mr Rankine.' The lift doors closed and Rankine stalked along the deeply carpeted corridor to his office. The same as last year, yes, he thought, smiling inwardly. Except that this year he'd have a bigger and more beautiful Christmas tree than any other hotel in the city, and one with lights enough to drain the national grid. And when he ferried in the busload of orphans to open the mountain of presents he'd ordered, the press would be there in their hordes. The perfect festive front page copy:

Ho-Ho-Ho-telier Captures Orphans' Hearts.

And sickens Jay Johnstone's.

Dodds was staring out of the wide plate-glass window behind Rankine's desk when the old man walked in. The look of disdain on his face as he peeled off his overcoat evident even to Dodds.

'Something up, Mr Rankine?' he said, coming round the desk to take his employer's coat and hang it on the stand.

'Your time on this earth, you imbecile,' the old man snapped.

Dodds looked puzzled and hurt. 'I don't understand, sir,' he murmured.

'The story of your pathetic life.' Rankine stormed across to the drinks cabinet, poured himself a hefty measure of malt and drained it in one long draught. 'I give you a simple job to do, with explicit instructions even a child would understand, and what do you do? You blow it.' He sighed wearily and sank into the chair behind his desk.

Dodds flushed. 'Sir, I don't understand . . .'

'You know where I've just been? Having lunch with a cop who was called out to Posers last night. You want to know what he told me, Dodds, or should I have you put down right now?'

'I only did as you asked, Mr Rankine.'

'I told you to put Costello in hospital, did I?'

'Not in so many words.'

'Not in any bloody words. I said don't even let him know he's being watched.'

'I was only using my initiative, like you said.'

'I said that? I need my fucking head examined.'

'I'm sorry, Mr Rankine, I thought—'

'Aye, you thought. That's the problem.' Rankine rose with an effort, crossed to the drinks cabinet and poured himself another generous measure. Then lumbered over to the wide plate-glass window beyond which the world blanched softly beneath the ceaseless featherfall of snow. He turned his thoughts to Billy and the villa in Spain, a decision yet to be reached. The villa would be no real loss; it was, in fact, already becoming a burden, one which he could well do without. And the truth was, he needed Billy now – Dodds' unreliability had already convinced him of that – especially if he was going to finish what he'd set out to accomplish. But McCulloch was becoming greedy: today the villa, tomorrow what? The hotel? And when is enough ever enough? The answer, of course, was simply obvious: when you're dead.

Perhaps Dodds might yet have his use.

To the east the sky was already darkening as yet another cold front closed in. He hoped Billy's was a rough flight home.

'What about the girl?' he said, returning his attention to Dodds. 'What's her excuse?'

'Jay Johnstone must've installed alarms since I checked the place over. She said she panicked when she heard the sirens, had to break out the kitchen window. I don't know how much longer we can count on her cooperation, Mr Rankine, I think her bottle's burst.'

'For your sake, Dodds, I hope it hasn't. Because of your bungling interference last night, I've had to bring everything forward. Which means I want her out again tomorrow night.'

'I don't know, Mr Rankine . . .'

'Then you'd better persuade her, Dodds. I don't care how, just do it. Use your lonely brain-cell, or that manly charm you keep bragging about. Either way, it has to be done tomorrow. Properly this time, and no mistakes.'

'You want me to case the joint first?'

'Case the joint?' Rankine sneered. 'Christ on steroids, Dodds, what century are you living in? No, I don't want you casing any joints – in fact, I'd rather you just sat at home and smoked them. No, this time she knows the layout.'

'You mean the place she used to work? The massage-parlour?'

'And I thought your head was just decoration. Yes, Dodds, that is what I mean. And I want it fired just before midnight. Before your friendly firebug turns into a pumpkin and does another runner.'

'I could go along with her,' Dodds suggested, 'to make sure.'

Rankine dismissed the suggestion with a curt wave of his hand. 'You've done enough damage already,' he growled. 'Tomorrow, you chauffeur. Billy's flying in from Spain and I want you at the airport to meet him.'

'Billy McCulloch?' Dodds looked and sounded shocked.

'Anything wrong?'

'The man's a nutter!'

'You should get on well then. Anyway, Beth's got the details. I want him at ease, Dodds, so take the Roller and wear your uniform, and treat him like a visiting PM. In fact, no, treat him with a little respect. Make him feel like he's coming home.'

'Is he?' Dodds did not look happy. 'Coming home for good?'

'For good or evil, Dodds, home is where they bury your arse. You'd do well to keep that in mind.'

CHAPTER 6

R ae Connell turned out of the hospital gates, wheels suddenly spinning then skidding across the icy road. She brought the car back under control with consummate ease, pulled up behind a taxi at the red light, and sighed. 'Some days, Joe, you need a crutch,' she said. 'Others, a wheelchair. Today it's definitely a wheelchair.'

Maybe it was the eyes, Joe thought. Or the way she carried herself. Or her taut, unblemished skin over high cheekbones and determined slant of jaw. Or perhaps it was something deeper, a subconscious energy with which she charged the ether around her. Whatever it was, Rae Connell always reminded Joe of Annie Lennox. Which always managed to piss her off every time he mentioned it.

'What are you trying to tell me, Joe?' she'd say. 'I should eat more? I'm too skinny? Look. See that? That's fat. Annie Lennox doesn't have any fat.'

And Joe would tell her, 'That's skin, Rae. We've all got skin.'

So Rae would tug her hair and say, 'We've all got hair, too. But Annie's is short and fair, and mine is long and black. Her eyes are the brightest blue and mine the darkest brown. Where's the similarity?'

And Joe would wink and smile and change the subject. And sometimes even have to fight her off.

But today there were deep shadows beneath her deep brown eyes.

'Long night?' he asked.

'Long night, long day,' Rae replied. 'First bell this morning, I had Jay Johnstone in, climbing the walls because the polis had dragged him from bed to give him a little friendly advice. Seems what happened the other night was the last straw in the eyes of the law, and we can count no more on their assistance in times of need. I say big deal, so what? but Jay reacts like he's been denied a knighthood.'

'The ego has landed.'

'With a bump. Which reminds me, Joe – he wants you to come to his party tonight. So he can look you over.'

'That *will* be right.' A party was the last thing on his mind; bed and sleep was all he had planned for the next few days. Maybe even weeks. 'You know, Rae, I still don't understand why you work for him.'

'You work for him, too, remember,' she pointed out. 'Anyway, you'd rather I'd carried on working for Rankine?'

'You know what I mean.'

Rae sighed as the lights changed. 'Sure, Joe, I know. But you were inside and when Rankine discovered we were friends, that I was visiting you, that was it, I was out on my ear. When Johnstone came along and offered me the opportunity to get one over on Rankine, believe me, Joe, I jumped at the chance.'

They turned down Forest Road, skidded through a red light, the midday traffic on George IV Bridge light but lumbering beneath the sombre leaden sky. The snow had eased off slightly in the last half-hour but the radio warned of worse to come; odds on a white Christmas, the weatherman said, were shortening by the day.

Jay Johnstone, Joe thought, as they waited at the High Street lights. Rae's boss and current owner of six city-centre pubs, two night-clubs, three massage-parlours, a snooker-hall, a restaurant, two laundrettes, four cars, and a mansion in Colinton Village large enough to house at least a quarter of all the city's homeless. A man who'd fought his way up and out of the Niddrie he'd been born to, who had reputedly founded his small empire on the profits he'd made in the early Seventies, bringing large quantities of amphetamine sulphate into the country from Norway. Reputedly, because he'd never been caught, and had always worked alone. A man with a chip on every pore on his shoulders, a paranoid bully who bludgeoned his way through life with all the subtlety of a runaway truck. Joe could still recall the only two times they'd met – first when Joe was an aide assigned to Central CID, and then again six years later when he was a DS in Licensing. Both meetings had instilled in him a sudden, inexplicable urge towards violence.

Rae interrupted his thoughts. 'It's only a party,' she said. 'You'd be doing me a big favour.'

'I'm still recovering from the last one I did you.'

'I know. But there's something about me you just can't refuse.'

Which was true enough. Ever since they'd first become friends at school, Rae had always been able to bring Joe round to her way of thinking. Only once in all those years had he had cause to regret it.

She must have read his mind. 'How d'you feel, anyway?' she asked.

'Better.'

Or perhaps he should have said numb. Mind numb, body numb, looking at the world through a painkilled haze. Sitting there trying to think, to figure out a nice way to tell her he wouldn't be returning to work in the wine-bar again. That he couldn't afford another brush with the law.

The lights changed and they turned down the Royal Mile, taking it slow, the cobbles treacherous beneath the thin coating of snow. As they crossed the North Bridge and trundled down the High Street, Joe asked if the police were checking through Johnstone's personnel files for someone with a grudge motive.

'What files there are,' Rae said, 'they've been through twice already. The trouble is that most of Jay's businesses employ a lot of part-time and temporary staff, and not all of them go through the books.'

'Sounds like Johnstone.'

Blue lights flashed at the foot of the Canongate as police in yellow cagoules directed fast-congesting traffic. Two cars and a Corporation bus were scrunched together and skewed across the road as though locked in mortal combat. People stood in huddled knots, breath mingling as the passengers from the crippled bus stamped their feet and clapped gloved hands. As Rae waited to be waved on through, Joe said, 'There was a girl in the bar that night. Looked about twenty, sitting on her own in the corner, drinking Pernod. Did you see her?'

'I was busy working, if you remember.'

'Not bad looking, either, in a scrawny kind of way.'

'So you gave her the patter.'

'I asked her if she'd been stood up.'

'Original. What did she say?'

'Told me to bog off.'

Rae burst out laughing. 'I think you better get some practice in at the party tonight.'

'Which was when Stone Age Man walked in and went through the "You looking at my pint?" routine. Asked the girl if I was bothering her.'

'You think they knew each other?'

Joe shrugged. 'It's possible,' he said, trying to add flesh to the faint skeletal impressions left in his mind. 'What I do remember is seeing her a couple of times take out a match and strike it, then watch it burn down to her fingers. And she *was* small enough to fit in that cupboard.'

'You want to tell the police?'

Joe shook his head, immediately regretting the sudden motion. 'Hell, no. Most delinquent fire-aisers are male – male and white. I'm just keeping on open mind.'

'Aye?' Rae glanced at him sharply. 'Last week, all I did was mention Jack Rankine and your mind closed quicker than a rich man's wallet.'

'Aye,' Joe said heavily, 'but that's Rankine for you. He reaches parts of your psyche no other psychopath can.'

The traffic cop waved them through. They skirted the twisted wreckage, passed Holyrood Palace on their right, then headed up through Abbeyhill.

Rae was exactly three months and two days older than Joe. They had both been born and brought up on opposite sides of the same cul-de-sac off Easter Road, were both only children who found it hard to make friends. Inevitably, Rae had become the sister Joe never had, and Joe the brother Rae never had. They attended the same schools, the same classes, and got into the same kind of trouble as each other. In the evenings they would do their home-work together, then hang around in the street outside the corner chip-shop or down by the railway yards near the old steelworks where, at the age of twelve, they first played Doctors and Nurses together, you show me yours and I'll show you mine. Happy days then, curious, carefree and long. Evenings, Joe remembered, he could look across the street from his bedroom window and see right into Rae's. Sometimes at night she would leave her curtains open as she undressed for bed, then would challenge him on the way to school next day and call him all kinds of Peeping Tom pervert – though with a smile mischievous enough to have him back at his window for a week after that. At the age of thirteen, Joe decided he wanted to be a cop and Rae decided she wanted to be a nurse. At fourteen they lost their virginity to each other in a clumsy, fumbling, wine-soaked haze. Then, at fifteen, their lives were suddenly torn apart when Rae's parents moved out of the city to the village of Balerno in the shadow of the Pentland Hills. Dark days those, both of them lovesick and lost, Joe crying himself to sleep, unable to concentrate at school, leaving eventually to work in the local slaughterhouse. In the year that followed, they met only twice, both aware that that magic something between them, whatever it was, had gone. The next time they met was eight years later on a demonstration along Princes Street. Joe was a young PC on escort duty, Rae a student on a Business Management course at the local Polytechnic. After the demo they met for a drink and from that moment on their friendship had never looked back.

'Nothing ever changes,' Rae said, standing by the window of Joe's top-floor tenement flat, looking down on the evening rush-hour bustle of a street-lit Easter Road. She spoke wistfully, without turning. 'Not a bloody thing. The sins of our fathers, and their fathers, and their fathers' fathers . . .'

Joe placed two painkillers under his tongue and drank them down with the dregs of his beer. 'People change,' he said.

'You really believe that?' Rae came away from the window to stand by the fire, now glowing comfortably in the hearth. 'I mean, look around you, Joe, tell me what you see.'

'My house. My home. Things that are mine.'

'Crap. This is not *your* home, Joe, it's still your father's, your parents'. Nothing's changed in the thirty-odd years since you were born here. The same dark ceilings, the same gloomy wallpaper, the same grubby furniture . . . this flat's not a home it's a bloody museum piece, a shrine to the memory of parents you scarcely knew. A mother who died when you were young and a father who hated you from the moment you pulled on your uniform. A prison, Joe, that's what this is, a prison away from prison. Look at those pictures on the wall, or the framed biblical quotes. Or those fading photographs of the good old days before the war when the name Costello fronted almost every damn chip-shop on the north side of the city. What about that gilded Madonna in the alcove? Do you still kneel before its forbidding face every morning and night the way you used to as a kid? Do you hell.'

Joe knelt before the fire, picked a poker from the rack, and began pushing absently at the coals. 'Maybe I like it here. Maybe it gives me a sense of identity, security.'

'Like prison did?' Rae retrieved her untouched bottle of beer from the mantelpiece and swigged from it. 'Remember when I used to come up here after school and sit in this very same room, waiting for you to finish your homework? I'd sit in that seat by the window and watch your father. I don't think he ever spoke to me once in all the years I knew him. I'm not too sure he even knew I was there. He'd just sit in that chair where you sit now, and stare at the fire. And the only time he'd move or show any emotion at all was when he took hold of that poker and went down on his knees and stabbed at the coals. Just as you're doing now.'

Joe replaced the poker on its hook and climbed slowly to his feet. 'Something wrong with that?'

'I don't know, Joe. You're just not the same man any more. It's like someone's pissed on the flame of your life. I mean, where's my friend "Dayglo" Joe, the only guy I knew who had volume buttons on his clothes?'

'Still around somewhere, I imagine.'

'Locked away with the rest of your past, no doubt.'

'Like I said, Rae, people change.'

'Mmm . . .'

Rae began drawing patterns with her finger in the dust on the mantelpiece, deep in thought, her coal-black hair a curtain across her face. It was a pose he'd seen many times, one that signalled she had something to say but was running it through her mind, rehearsing it, making sure it came out right. Joe knew better than to interrupt.

'*Dayglo' Joe* – now there was a name he hadn't heard in years, now twice in two days. He'd earned it the very first day he was seconded to CID as a young, ambitious aide. He'd strode into the Squad Room – as proud of his plainclothes then as he had been of his uniform almost three years before – only for the DI to haul him up in front of the shift to explain the meaning of '*plain*' clothes.

'Joe, look around you,' the DI had said. 'We're all polis here and, in the line of duty, we all have certain reputations to uphold. And one of those, constable, is that we're not supposed to know how to dress. It's a reputation we're proud of, but it also has its practical side: when we're not working undercover, our *plain clothes* are meant to be just as much a uniform as our uniforms. We have to dress the way the public expects us to dress, so that when we make an arrest we are instantly identifiable. If we all went round dressed like that—' he said, indicating Joe's immaculately cut scarlet three-piece, his canary silk shirt and sunburst tie '—we'd have more suicides on our hands than the Crash of '29. I mean, prisoners would be *killing* themselves, Joe. No one would ever take us seriously again. So why don't you go on home and see if you can dig up something a little more discreet – a grey suit, for example. Oh, and Joe?'

'Sir?'

'If you can find one that doesn't quite fit, even better.'

From that day on the nickname had stuck.

Rae emerged from her silence, brushing the hair from her eyes with a comb of fingers as she looked him squarely in the eye. 'Joe,' she said, 'you have to let her go.'

'Who go?'

'Don't give me that, Joe, you know who I mean. Karen.'

'You mean just forget her?' Joe snapped back harshly. 'Forget we were ever in love, forget all the good times, forget she was brutally murdered the day before the wedding?'

Rae bit her lip as she shook her head. 'Two years, Joe, two years since she died. It's time you let her go, concentrated on what future *you* have. I mean, d'you think it would've made her happy to see you living like this? Look what it's doing to you, twisting you up inside. What you need is a holiday, to get away from all this.'

'Chance would be a fine thing.'

'Chance is,' Rae said, her sudden smile mischievous, taking him back through the years. She came away from the fire and sat on the arm of his chair, looping her arm round his neck. 'Johnstone's given me the use of his cottage on the West Coast over Christmas. I'm going up anyway, but I'd much prefer some company, and we could be back in time for Hogmanay.'

'The West Coast is wide and long, Rae.'

'Ardnamurchan.'

'The edge of the world? You want to spend Christmas on the edge of the world?'

'The westernmost tip of mainland Britain,' Rae said, laughing at the expression on Joe's face. 'Just you and the elements and me – and if you're lucky, maybe even a sheep or two. What d'you say?'

'I don't know . . .'

'It would do you a power of good.' Her fingers gently massaged the back of his neck. He could feel himself sinking, as though into a warm, hypnotic trance. 'It's what you need, Joe, to clean the cobwebs from your mind.'

'I'll think about it.'

Her lips brushed his ear, teasing. 'Maybe there's some way I can persuade you?' she suggested breathily, playfully, sending shivers through the whole of his body. 'Something I can do that will change your stubborn cop's mind?' Her hand slipped inside his shirt, moved coolly on his chest.

Two years, he thought. Two years since a woman had last touched his body. Then it had been Karen, now it was Rae: the only two women he had ever truly loved. He felt suddenly as though somewhere inside him a dam was breaking. Could feel the hairline cracks in the wall spread beneath the aching pressure. Christ, it had been so long. Far too long.

He said, 'Remember the time we first made love, the night your parents were away?'

'Remember it? I'm still sore from it!'

'And we drank that bottle of wine your father had been saving for his wedding anniversary?'

'Aye, and then you took advantage of me.'

'Not the way I remember it.'

'I was a young and innocent virgin and you seduced me.'

'Did I hell! You had to grab my hand and force it up your skirt.'

Rae laughed and grabbed Joe's hand. 'You mean like this?'

'Yeah,' Joe said, 'like that.'

A few minutes later as she led him through to the bedroom, he wondered: Christ, without her, where the hell would I be now?

CHAPTER 7

Fucking typical.

Brilliant sunshine over the whole of Europe, but the moment the plane crosses the Tartan Curtain it's suddenly pissing snow. Flying into the swollen banks of cloud like passing from day into night; from Gerona on the Costa Brava to Edinburgh on the Costa Faeces, like descending from heaven to hell. Typical. Welcome home, William P. McCulloch.

Billy collected his bags and passed quickly through the busy concourse. Look for a guy in a chauffeur's uniform, Rankine had said. A big guy with bog-brush hair and the kind of face that makes Ben Nevis look pretty by comparison. Name of Dodds. He'll probably be standing by the departure gate, Rankine said.

He wasn't.

He was out on the pavement arguing with a cop. Drawing attention to himself. Pointing at a glistening Roller on the double yellow line, winding the cop up rotten. The cop already reaching for his notebook.

Billy turned and headed angrily back across the concourse to the bar. He ordered a pint and took it over to a window seat where he could watch the cop and the moron on the pavement outside.

The cop was stabbing the moron's chest with the stub of his pencil, emphasising a point he was trying to make. Because the moron was a moron, he was smiling. Probably saying what did he give a shit for, his boss would pay the ticket anyway. Which

43

would wind the cop up even more, make him ask twice as many questions. Like, who is your boss? Or, who you meeting off the plane, and why's he here, business or pleasure?

And the moron telling the cop the truth. Because he was a moron. Because he was the perfect kind of moron with which Rankine liked to surround himself.

What the hell was he doing here? Billy wondered. Here, when he could be lounging by the side of the pool with a beer in his hand and a headful of something mellow, just buzzing away to the sound of the breeze ghosting through the trees? Here, when he could be watching the fishing-boats head out to sea, or tasting the pine on the air as he relaxed on a bed of buoyant dreams. Peace and quiet. Time and space. To dredge his riddled memory and figure out once and for all how the girl Sandra ended up dead in his pool.

Instead, no, he was a million miles adrift, looking out on a sea of slush and snow beneath a bruised and battered sky, watching grey people shuffle their weary chains through a grey and disconsolate world. Watching in particular the cop as he turned and walked away, leaving the moron smiling for a moment on the kerb before he, too, turned and made for the main entrance.

Billy leaned back in the soft, dark leather, as the Rolls swept past Gogar and hissed along the Glasgow Road. He turned on the TV and caught the local evening news. Politicians were still fighting amongst themselves and getting nothing done, manipulating lives for their own sordid ends; idiots were still falling down mountains or getting trapped on cliffs; firms were still shedding jobs like seasonal fur. And so it went on, a bleak, relentless portrayal of a country dead in its head and dying on its feet, too pathetic to do anything but whimper and whine and sell itself short to the men in the suits who couldn't touch nothing without turning it to shit.

Home of the brave? Billy thought. More like home of the slave.

He punched the button and opened the bar, poured himself a triple dram and threw it down his throat. Then hammered on the partition window.

The moron said, 'Yes, Mr McCulloch?' Watching Billy warily in the rear-view mirror as the window slid down.

Billy slipped his arm around Dodds' neck, pressed the blade of his knife gently into the flesh below his ear. The car almost left the road, swerving wildly across the lanes.

Billy said, 'Think you're pretty hard, huh? Think you've got muscles in your shit, huh?'

Dodds tried to shake his head without impaling himself on the knife. Sounds came from his throat, strangled sounds. The car still careering across the road but losing speed now as Billy eased the pressure on the big man's throat.

'Rankine's top man, eh?' Billy said. 'So smart you have to draw attention to yourself, start winding up the polis when all you have to do is park the fucking car and stand there like the dumb shit you are?'

'Hey, wait a minute—'

'Screw the nut,' Billy snapped, increasing the pressure of his forearm for emphasis. 'Just screw it shut and drive.' He released his hold on the moron and sank back.

Dodds drove. He had to slow as a bus pulled out, switch on the wipers as a soft snowy rain began to fall. To their right Saughton Prison loomed dark and solemn beyond its forbidding walls.

Dodds said, 'Brings back memories, eh, Mr McCulloch?' His voice hoarse, his tone reconciliatory.

'Aye,' Billy said, with dripping sarcasm. 'The only reason they build the walls so high is to stop me trying to get back in.' Billy pressed his face to the window now as they nosed along Gorgie road. There the Station Bar where he'd learned to drink and fight and puke on the pavement; there the old railway where they'd played chicken as kids, where Tosh had died like a fly on a windscreen, looking more like mince than chicken; there Ferranti's with its carpark, a joy-rider's dream but a rush-hour nightmare; there on the left, drab and grey as ever, the cobbled street he'd grown up in; and there behind, squeezed between church, school and distillery, Tynecastle Park, home of the Jambos, Heart of Midlothian.

'You like football, Mr McCulloch?'

'Aye,' Billy said. 'That's why I moved to Spain.'

On Saturday afternoons as a kid he'd scramble up on to the tenement roof with a couple of mates and watch the game from there. Those were the days of Alfie Conn, Willie Bald and Jimmy Wardhaugh, days when football was a game rather than a commodity.

Up past the Diggers and the cemetery – the Rolls losing traction on the hill for a second, sliding across runnels of slush into the centre of the road before Dodds regained control – down from

Dundee Street on to the West Approach Road, the Scottish and Newcastle brewery squat and anonymous behind a modest veil of mist, past the Sheraton and Caledonian Hotels, then east along Princes Street until Billy – who'd been searching the whole journey for some physical evidence of change since he'd been away – exclaimed, 'Jesus! What the fuck happened to the Palace?' Where the Palace Hotel had once stood on the corner of Princes and Frederick Street, there was now a gaping hole.

'Fire,' Dodds explained, as they waited at the lights. 'They reckon it was an insurance job.'

'Who reckons?'

'Anyone with half a brain cell.'

'So what do *you* reckon?' Billy sank back in his seat as Dodds pulled away from the lights without replying. A minute later they drew up by the canopied entrance of Rankine's club, dutifully patrolled by a foot-stamping commissionaire. Dodds climbed out and held the door for Billy.

Billy McCulloch glanced incredulously across the snowcleared pavement and said, 'You mean I've got to walk?'

CHAPTER 8

The multitude of cars parked carelessly along the semi-circular driveway looked as though they'd been tossed there by a passing hurricane. Spotlights lit up the sandstone façade of the house while floodlights bathed the ornamental battlements in an eerie unearthly glow.

Rae said, 'Jay believes every man's castle should be his home.' She continued driving around the drive, searching for a place to park as Joe gave up counting the number of windows splashing light across the lawns and said, 'So did Macbeth.'

'I wouldn't be surprised. Jay can't see the wood for the trees between his ears either.' Eventually Rae found enough space between a Rover and a Jaguar and filled it neatly. They strolled toward the house, neither of them in any particular hurry, Rae slipping her arm through his.

Joe said, 'I should've worn jeans. I'm going to walk in there and everyone'll stop talking to turn around and stare. I know it.'

'Do what I do at one of Jay's parties. Anaesthetise yourself.'

'Is that not dangerous?'

'Only if you wake up.'

Rae had decided on a green Tweed jacket over her bottle-green cashmere jersey, a silk red-and-black checked necktie, faded jeans, tartan socks and brogues. Her thick black hair tumbled free over her shoulders and glistened as they passed beneath the globular lamps interspersed between the low shrubs bordering the drive.

Joe, on the other hand, wore the same grey suit he'd worn on the day of his arrest. It was the only inconspicuous suit he had that wasn't covered in blood.

'Here we go,' Rae said. 'Don't say I didn't warn you.'

Jay was waiting to welcome them just inside the main door. He rushed forward and greeted Rae with a kiss on both cheeks before holding her out at arm's length, the better to admire her.

'Rae, darling,' he crooned. 'You look positively ravishing.'

Rae extricated herself from his grasp and introduced Joe.

Jay squinted up at him through blue-tinted shades. 'I've been hearing a lot about you, Joe – and none of it good. How's your face?' He held out his hand.

Joe shook it and shrugged. 'It's seen better days,' he said.

'I bet.' Jay looked him up and down. 'Nice suit,' he said.

'Likewise,' Joe lied.

Johnstone was wearing a baggy, woollen, cream-white two-piece suit, padded at the shoulders and tapered at the waist. It looked like something he'd maybe spent an hour throwing on. Beneath it he wore a white polo-neck sweater, and on his wrist a heavy gold watch. His soft and pink manicured hands were ringless, his blond-streaked hair greased back and tied in a tail.

Jay said, 'I've a good memory for faces, Joe, and yours is one I'm sure I've seen before. Can that be?'

'It's a small city.'

'The City of Coincidence,' Jay agreed. 'Small and cosy. Like one big happy family. Which is why I asked you along, Joe. We're all one big cosy family here, too.'

Jay ushered them through heavy double-doors off the galleried hall and down a shallow flight of deeply carpeted steps. The noise of the party rushed to meet them. As Rae walked on ahead, Johnstone caught Joe's arm.

'Rae says I can trust you, Joe,' he said. 'You think she got that right?'

'If you can't trust an ex-cop, who can you trust?'

Johnstone cocked his head and regarded him silently for a moment. 'She never warned me you had a sense of humour.'

Joe smiled what he hoped was a patient smile. For Rae's sake, he told himself. 'She told me you wanted to talk.'

'Damn right I do.'

'So how about now?'

Johnstone almost broke stride to stare at him. 'What, and miss the fun? Fuck no. Let's go join the party.'

Jack Rankine said, 'What's up with Dodds? He looked a little shaken.'

'Shaken but not stirred.' Billy watched Rankine's Personal Assistant cross to the wide mahogany bar that almost stretched the length of the room. She had a walk enough to hypnotise.

'I hope you've not upset him, Billy. He's a good man.' Rankine had paused at the entrance to survey the Clubroom floor like a laird looking over his land. Trying hard to impress.

'Upset him?' Billy said. 'I saved the moron's life.'

'You what?'

'I stopped throttling him.'

Ranking shook his head sadly. 'I need a seat,' he said.

'Good idea. Park your brain.'

Cigar-smoke hung like a sagging cloud over the few tight knots of members who stood with drinks in their hands, talking in low and earnest voices. Around the blazing hearth, relics in blazers and cravats dozed or read *The Daily Telegraph* in deep leather armchairs, only raising or opening their eyes to snap purple-veined fingers at the passing waitress. Beyond the wide windows, and against the crouching silhouette of the backlit castle, snow continued to fall from the starless black sky. Rankine led Billy to a couple of empty armchairs by the window.

'Who's the girl?' Billy asked, looking around for some service here. Dying of thirst already.

'Beth Friedman. *My* personal assistant, Billy – so keep your hands in your pockets. She's strictly off-limits.' Rankine glanced possessively across the bar.

'I bet,' Billy laughed. 'You shagging her yet?'

Rankine sighed. 'When will you ever grow up?'

'Because if you're not, how about putting in a word for me? For old time's sake?'

'Beth's the best PA I've had, Billy, and I don't want you scaring her off. I hope you get my drift.'

'What d'you think I am, a fucking snowstorm?' Billy looked around, trying to catch the eye of the waitress with the chunky-chicken arse and boobs way out to here. She was busy serving wine to some old fart over by the fire, bending low enough to make his glassy eyeballs pop. Christ, what a waste.

He whistled, called her over. She had the poutiest lips he'd ever seen. 'Pint of lager, gorgeous, and a Perrier for my old man.' She didn't even smile. He shook his head at Rankine and said, 'Christ, Jackie, what's a man got to do these days to make a woman smile?'

'Times change, Billy, times change.'

'You telling me? I ain't blind, you know.'

'We live and learn, Billy. Live and learn.'

'Aye. And some of us live better than we learn.' Billy swept the room with contemptuous eyes.

Rankine attempted to smile. 'You're not still mad at me?'

'You dropped me like a Sellafield brick, Jackie-boy.'

'It was your decision.'

'Don't give me that.'

'It was getting too hot. Something had to give.'

'So you gave me a one-way ticket to Spain,' Billy said. 'Great.'

'You also made the decision, Billy.' An edge to Rankine's voice as he leaned forward over the table. 'You agreed it was better for us both if you laid low for a while.'

'You didn't have to stop me getting work.'

'A year and a half on the Costa Brava – all expenses paid – and you're complaining?'

'I like my work.'

'I've noticed.'

'Yet you put the word out I was unpredictable, couldn't be trusted.'

'And so you were – strung out for days on that LSD, the way you were. There was no way of knowing what you'd do next.'

'So you bring in Dodds to take my place? That makes sense.'

'At least he does as he's told,' Rankine said.

'And Christ does he need to be told. I've seen more sense in a Hoover – a switched-off Hoover.'

'Which is why I brought you back, Billy. I need a pro.'

'Now you're talking.'

'I want this business finished once and for all. To sleep easy again.'

'You want him to meet with an accident?'

Rankine loosed a flash of yellow teeth. 'That's why we make such a good team, Billy. You and I, we think alike.'

Billy said, 'Yeah? When was the last time you thought you were a total arsehole?'

Rankine shot forward in his chair, his voice a venomous hiss as his finger punched the air. 'The day I pulled you from the gutter and gave you a job. You want to remember that, Billy, remember where the fuck you came from. You're not the only wee snot-nose for hire in this city.'

'Is that a threat, Jackie-boy?'

'A threat, a promise, and the truth.'

Rankine settled back in his chair as the chunky-chicken arrived with the drinks. She didn't even look at Billy, 'Your table is ready, sir,' she smiled at Rankine. 'Just go on through when you're ready.'

Fucking gold-digger.

Jewelled light from the crystal chandelier danced across the textured wallpaper as penguined waiters glided noiselessly between the tables. As they waited for the brandy and cigars to arrive, Billy leant back and stretched out his legs.

He said, 'I never killed a cop before.'

'Ex-cop, Billy. Bent ex-cop.'

'He still might have friends on the force.'

'Okay,' Rankine sighed, 'you want to renegotiate.'

Billy began making patterns in the salt on the tablecloth.

'I don't negotiate, Jackie-boy, I set the terms. Accept them, or look elsewhere. Like you said, times have changed.'

'You want the villa.'

Billy grinned. 'I think it's a bargain, Jackie-boy. Regard it as merely one more tax-loss you won't have to worry about.'

'I could get thirty of the likes of you for that price.'

'Then why haven't you?'

Rankine didn't reply.

The waiter arrived with two Armagnac brandies and two Havana cigars; he clipped each cigar as carefully as he would a mad dictator's toenail, then glided noiselessly away.

'You're right, of course.' Rankine reached inside his jacket, withdrew an envelope, and tossed it across to Billy. 'Hence, the deeds. Check them through if you like, but they're all in order. Made out to you.'

Billy stared at the hotelier in disbelief. 'Just like that?' he said. 'No argument? No wringing of hands, tearing of hair?'

'Just like that.'

Billy tore open the envelope and glanced over the paperwork. His forehead creased. 'I knew it was too good to be true.'

'The transference date can be changed,' Rankine said. 'The moment the job is done.'

'You wouldn't try to cross me, Jackie-boy?'

The old man said nothing. He looked tired, his face drawn and pale, his breath a rasping wheeze. A dried-out husk, Billy thought, of the man he used to know.

Billy said, 'Okay, so when do I start?' Eager now to get the job done before the old man passed away in his soup.

Rankine raised his head and stared at Billy through rheumy eyes. 'Soon as Dodds gets back. Johnstone's having one of his parties tonight, everybody who's nobody should be there – including Costello.'

'Alone, Jackie-boy. I don't want the moron hanging round my neck. It's not the way I work.'

'Take Dodds,' Rankine wheezed, 'or take the high road. I want this done my way.'

'Why not take Beth as well, make it a threesome?'

'Beth stays. She's not in the picture.'

'Speak of the gorgeous devil.' Billy watched her sway towards the table, admiring the way her breasts moved freely beneath her cashmere sweater. Late twenties, Billy reckoned, nearing her sexual peak. Experienced, he could tell, it was there in her smouldering eyes, and the way she stood with the tips of her fingers tucked in the pockets of her skintight jeans, emphasising the jut of her dinky wee bum.

Rankine waved a limp hand at Billy and said, 'Beth, this is Billy McCulloch. He's taking the villa off my hands.'

'That right?' she said, her voice as cool and empty as her eyes. 'Hi.'

'Anytime you want,' Billy grinned, 'come on over. Villa Rancor is at your disposal.'

'Thanks, but no thanks.' She turned to Rankine. 'What the hell kind of name is Rancor? Sounds like a contagious disease.'

'It was. One that almost killed me.' There was more life in the old man's cigar than in his voice.

'One of the country's largest catering companies,' Billy explained. 'At least it was until Jackie here sold up.'

'I never knew that.'

'It's history, Beth,' Rankine said. 'Ancient history.' Patting her hand as he changed the subject. 'Anyway, it's Billy's villa now. Well, almost. Just a few odds and ends and the paperwork to complete. You have some news?'

'Dodds called in. He's on his way.'

'Good girl. Wait for him in the lobby, dear, and let me know when he arrives.'

Billy watched her walk away, wondering how he could get her alone, away from the old goat. He said, 'Beth's right, you know. First thing I should do is change the villa's name.'

'First you have to think of one.'

'I already did.' The idea had come to him yesterday afternoon as he sweated in the shade of the pine on the hill behind the villa, watching the girl Sandra disappear beneath spadesful of the hard, sunbaked soil.

He popped his eyes at Rankine: 'Dunkillin.'

CHAPTER 9

An hour later and Rae was already feeling the effects of five anaesthetics, her eyes moist and glittering. 'Ask Jay what his favourite American Football team is,' she said, 'and he'll tell you The New York Dolls. Can't argue with that, Joe, he obviously knows what he's talking about. Ask him who he fancies in the Superbowl and he'll tell you Buffalo Springfield can't bloody fail.'

They stood near the door, looking down and across the three split levels that constituted the biggest sitting-room Joe had ever seen. In the centre of the lower level a coal-and-log-effect gas-fire glowed ineffectually beneath a tapering chimney which disappeared into the high ornate roof. There were plants everywhere, on every ledge and shelf myriad shades of green pushing from little pots and big pots, pots on pedestals and hanging-pots. Cheese plants and rubber plants and cacti of every size and shape. Verdure enough to compete with the Botanic Gardens, yet ample space still for the hundred or more guests already in various stages of alcoholic collapse. The music pounding from the large wall-mounted speakers seemed trapped firmly in the early Seventies.

'Lucky he doesn't support the Detroit Spinners,' Joe said. 'They went out to the Bengal Lancers in the play-offs.'

'That's what I mean – he's a minefield of information. Ask him a question and he'll blow his fucking arse off. I mean, look at him.'

Joe already was. He was watching the way Johnstone handled himself, down a level by the open patio doors, laughing at his own jokes as he chatted up a girl with bob-cut hair, a low-cut blouse and a high-cut red leather mini-skirt. All legs and eyes and a toucher, too, Joe noticed: every time Johnstone said something funny she had to lay a hand on his arm to stop herself falling off her stilettos.

'Who's the girl?' he asked.

'Eyes off, Joe, she's Jay's. Make a nice couple, eh? Jay and . . . well, whatever her name is. Go together like mistress and marriage. She works in one of his massage-parlours.'

'Where's his wife?'

Rae leaned back so her eyes could see over the rim of her glass as they moved sluggishly across the room. 'The woman in the corner over there? With the red silk – Christ, what is it, a ballgown – on? The one looking at Jay with murder in her eyes? Guess what.'

'And she knows about Jay and the girl?'

'Sometimes you act really stupid, Joe. I mean, what d'you think? They're just about fornicating under her nose and you ask if she knows. Christ. Tell me what it is you're drinking and I'll never touch it again.'

'Water.'

'On the rocks or on your brain?'

'You ought to slow down, Rae. The night's still young.'

'Sod it,' Rae said, slurring her words. 'A woman's allowed a drink.'

'Sure, but eat something first.'

'You know I can't eat on an empty stomach.' She squeezed his arm gently, then drifted off towards the bar.

Maybe Rae was right, he thought. A holiday, a week of isolation on the West Coast might do him some good. Give him time and space to sort things out in his head, decide what he was going to do next. Here in the city he felt surrounded, trapped and oppressed by the ruins of his past; too many reminders of what he had once been and what he was now.

He looked out across the dance-floor, over the grunting, grinding bodies gyrating to the Eagles' Hotel California, and wondered what the hell he was doing here. He didn't fit. He lived in a different world. Like the old days. Even though it was now two years since he'd last flashed a badge, he still felt that same sense of disassociation that every cop eventually comes to feel. Of not belonging. Maybe it was true what they said – once a cop, always a cop. Once your eyes have been opened to the sordid reality of the human condition and the sheer ugliness of civilised man's inhumanity to man, there's no turning back. The pettiness, greed and selfishness, the senseless violence and cheapness of life, the twisted perversions that you witness every day in the line of duty cannot fail but to instil in you a cynicism so deeply rooted that even the purest of your own emotions and motivations become suspect. Once you've lifted the stone and seen the vermin squirm, it's too late – only death will close your eyes to the world as you know it.

Vermin, Joe thought, such as Johnstone and his tatooed cronies. With their shell-suits and beer-guts and mean, empty eyes. Now standing round the man himself, laughing at his jokes as they eyed up the talent on the dance-floor and slopped their drinks on the carpet. A couple of years ago Joe wouldn't have been seen dead in such company. But people change. Rae was wrong: Joe *had* changed, and was still in the process of change. He just needed time. Metamorphosis was never easy, nor without pain or sacrifice. He was finding out.

A voice at his shoulder said, 'I don't think we've been introduced . . .'

Joe turned and smiled at the woman in the red silk ballgown. Told her no, they hadn't.

She said, 'I'm Andrea Johnstone, and this is supposed to be my party,' holding out her hand in such a way that Joe wasn't sure whether to kiss it or shake it or throw it back in the sea. In the end, he just shook it.

'Joe,' he said.

'Just Joe?' she asked, releasing his hand with a demure flutter of her long mascaraed eyelashes. She was in her early-to-mid thirties and had the kind of face Joe found curiously attractive – deep ponderous eyes and a wide, fleshy mouth which curled enigmatically when she smiled. The kind of face that makes you wonder.

'Just Joe,' he said, and wondered what she saw in a husband who saw nothing but himself.

'Are you one of Jay's latest recruits? He has such a quick turnover of staff I seldom have time to learn their names before . . . well, before they leave.'

'I'm a friend of Rae's, Mrs Johnstone.'

57

'Please, call me Andrea – no one else does.' There was a moistness in her eyes that was not all due to alcohol. 'I take it you've met my husband?'

Joe said, 'The man over there by the patio doors, talking to—'

'—bimbo in the minuscule skirt. Yes, that's him. It's our anniversary today. Twelve years – though God only knows how we've managed to last so long.' Beneath her long black lashes, moss-green eyes struggled for focus. Suddenly it seemed she had said too much. 'Well, I mustn't keep you all to myself. I'd better do my duty and circulate. If you'll excuse me?'

There were faces here he recognised, all distant past: from his life as a cop, from his life before. Faces that nodded at him, smiled at him, talked to him; others that stared, glared or hastily turned away. He didn't care. He passed through the sweating, jostling throng, riding conversational gambits as though punches. Let himself drift for a while on invisible currents, content to watch and listen.

There were other faces, too. Ones he felt he knew but couldn't place. Like the middle-aged guy with the florid face and glistening pate standing alone, like Joe, on the outside looking in, watching the couples dancing in the centre of the floor as he ran his pudgy finger around the inside of his grubby collar. Too short and fat to be a cop, too old to be an old friend. When Rae suddenly appeared at his shoulder he asked her if she knew him.

'What happened to your photographic memory?'

'I forgot to load the film.'

'Wylie,' Rae said. 'Wilberforce Wylie. Used to work for Rankine, now works for Jay once in a while – likes to call himself a private detective. If you wear a skirt, he'll follow you round.'

'Every time I look up, he's watching me.' In fact he was now pushing towards them through the jostling throng on the dance-floor.

'Maybe times are hard,' Rae giggled, hanging on to Joe's arm. Then she stood on tiptoe to whisper earnestly in his ear, 'Have you decided yet? About Christmas?'

'Later,' he said, regarding her affectionately, 'I'll let you know later.' Unable to commit himself yet, perhaps for the same reason that he'd still not told her he wasn't going to work as her bouncer any more.

'You better say yes, Joe Costello, or you can sleep on the floor tonight.' Again she rose on tiptoe, this time to kiss his cheek.

'Now I can leave you safely in the arms of lover-boy.' She swished away laughing as the bulbous private detective waddled across, dewlapped face running in sweat. He slipped Joe a card like a none-too-subtle backhander.

'You must be Costello,' he said, breathing hard, taking a handkerchief from his pocket and mopping his brow.

'Who's been talking?'

'You. Your body. The way you stand. The way you listen. Your restless eyes. Them and a million other little things only a trained observer might notice. And your suit.'

'What's wrong with my suit?'

'Nothing – on a bargain-rail at Oxfam. Nothing, if you don't mind people immediately thinking *cop*.' Wylie leaned forward and spoke breathlessly through his teeth. The kind of teeth that can chew an apple through a letterbox. 'Tell me, Costello, is it true what they say? Once a pig, always a pig?'

'About as true as once a dick, always a dick. Why?'

'Because if it is,' Wylie gasped, 'then I can give you what you want.'

Joe wondered what he wanted so much it had slipped his mind for the last ten years. Something the corpulent PI wanted to sell. 'Tell me,' he said. 'What do I want?'

'Not a what but a who.' Wylie trying to be as enigmatic as possible without talking in code.

Joe couldn't think. He couldn't be bothered. Instead he tried to remember the name of the song now blaring out across the dance-floor. The Stones. An early one . . .

Wylie glanced over his shoulder, scanning the room for moment before hunching close as Cassius to Joe. 'Think of a name,' he wheezed, 'that begins with Jack.'

'That's it, that's the one.'

Wylie seemed surprised. 'It is?'

'Yeah,' Joe said, 'Jumping Jack Flash. What a song.'

Wylie said he wanted to talk. Somewhere a little more private. What the hell, Joe said, glad for an excuse to leave the orgiastic atmosphere of the main room. After stacking a couple of plates with food from the buffet-table, the bulbous PI led Joe out into the entrance hall and down a wide, curving flight of stairs to what was obviously the recreational room.

The swimming-pool was sunk in the centre of a blue-tiled floor as long as the width of the house. The far, south-facing wall was a fortune in plate-glass window looking out across a paved patio and sloping garden, both now lying beneath a virgin blanket of floodlit snow. Lounging around the pool were several partially clothed couples with drinks in their hands, while in the water a few more couples, naked, had found another use for their hands.

Joe followed Wylie down to the far end of the room and up the open-plan stairs to the gallery bar, a garish mosaic of black gloss and mirror overlooking the pool.

'Look at that,' Wylie said, indicating the bar with one of his laden buffet-plates, before placing them both within easy pigging reach. 'Who says money's not a substitute for taste?' He then grunted himself on to one of the stools and angled it so he could keep one eye on his food and one on the girls in the pool. Joe, meanwhile, was trying hard to imagine Johnstone working out in the fitness room he'd glimpsed downstairs, or doing fifty lengths of the pool. Andrea, on the other hand . . .

'To business, Joe,' Wylie said, tearing at a Tandoori-chicken drumstick, chewing as he spoke. 'I'm talking Jack Rankine. Are you interested?'

'Should I be?'

'Word has it you're not the best of friends.'

'Rankine is history as far as I'm concerned. A closed chapter.'

'I can serve him to you on a platter, Joe. His head in a sweet and sour sauce.'

'For a price, no doubt?'

'Call it a wee investment for my future.' Wylie started on the pink salmon, shovelling it direct from plate to mouth.

Joe glared into the red, perspiring face. 'What future?' he said.

Wylie sighed, wiped his lips and shook his head. 'You just answered my question, Costello. Once a cop, always a cop. Always looking to make a crisis out of a drama.'

'I'm not into blackmail, Wylie.'

'Who said anything about blackmail?'

Joe said, 'What've you got on him? Love-letters? Dirty photos?'

'Maybe I made a mistake. Am talking to the wrong man. The Joe Costello I heard about is a man of patient ears. Who always listens and weighs the facts carefully before he acts.'

'People change.'

'So maybe I can't trust you after all. Let's drop it and move on. Look at it from another angle.'

60

Wylie, Joe was learning, was a man of many angles. You could see it in the restless beady eyes, how they flitted from selfish thought to selfish thought. Now devouring the well-built woman climbing naked from the pool.

'Jesus, would you look at her?' he wheezed. 'I've seen cats with less fucking fur.'

Which was only a minor exaggeration. Joe found himself wondering if Andrea stripped off down here when Jay was out being important in the city and she needed to burn off a little excess energy. Aye, he could imagine it, her long graceful body ploughing effortlessly through the water, her—

Christ, he was getting as bad as Wylie.

Who had now torn his feasting eyes away and was saying, 'Rankine's flipped, Joe, everyone knows it. You only have to look at the man and the way he's changed in the last two years. Barely recognisable. He used to pride himself on his appearance, have his beard trimmed every week – now it's like a bird's nest stuck to his chin. He's become reclusive, obsessive and paranoid. Locks himself away in his Penthouse Suite and plays God with the lives of those who surround him. Or cross him.'

'Meaning?'

Wylie had to wait until only half his mouth was full. 'Meaning Jay Johnstone. And what with this mega-big deal that Jay's lining up he can't afford to get mixed up in anything that might scare his investors away. Which means he wants Rankine off his back and is willing to pay to make sure it happens. He just doesn't want to get his own hands dirty.'

'Which is where I come in?'

'Put it this way: Jay knows all about you – the Vass enquiry, Karen's murder and the trial. He knows there's no love lost between you and, the way he sees it, you'd make a powerful ally.'

'Poor Jay.'

Wylie's eyes became slitted crescents as he shook his head with feigned regret. 'You know why I think most cops are stupid, Costello? Because they let their ideals outweigh their common-sense. Idealists are nothing but tools, romantics to be used by realists. And then when they find themselves trapped like dogshit on a pavement between scheming politicians and a fearful public, they wonder why they get no respect. Why nobody likes them.' The private detective paused to catch up with his breath.

'There a moral to the story?'

'Yeah,' he panted. 'Nobody likes dogshit, Joe, but it still gets stepped on. That's the moral. You got stepped on, you should've learned the lesson. You've seen the way you thought life was and the way it really is. Now you have a choice: remain stupid the rest of your life, or plug in your brains and use what you've learned to get what you want.'

'A week ago I was doing just that.'

'Sure. Staring at the walls. Feeling sorry for yourself. Letting all the injustices eat away at your mind. Feeling angry, feeling helpless, feeling dead. You think I don't know?'

'I know you don't know.'

'But on a more specific level, what you want more than anything else is to go back to the way things were. Be a cop again. Clear your name.'

'You're in the wrong profession. You ought to be a—'

'Mind-reader. I know. But tell me I'm wrong.'

'You saying now you can clear my name?'

'I don't know yet that I can trust you, Joe.'

'I scratch your balls, you scratch mine?'

'You're getting there.'

'Correct me if I'm wrong. You're saying we've got Rankine and Johnstone already at each other's throats and if we work together and play them off against each other, we could end up the right side of a lot of money. Am I right?'

'In a manner of speaking.'

Joe climbed off his stool with a sigh and laid a heavy hand on the private detective's shoulder. 'Well, in a manner of speaking,' he said softly into Wylie's ear, 'I don't give a shit. I don't believe you can help me and even if you could I doubt I would ask. And one more thing – if I clock you again I might take it in mind to plant you in soil and leave you to find your own fucking roots.'

Wylie jerked round like a startled guppy. But before he could summon the breath to reply there was a shout from across the pool.

'Hey, what is this? Sleuth's Corner or what?'

Jay swaggered up the stairs and slung an arm around each of their shoulders.

Wylie fingered his collar again and glanced at his watch. 'Christ, is that the time? I got work to do.' He wriggled out from under Jay's arm and lumbered away.

'Such a conscientious worker,' Jay said. 'You two know each other?'

Joe shook his head. 'We just met.'

'Lucky you.'

'He works for you?'

'Nothing I couldn't get a ten-year-old to do. Tonight he's making sure no-one runs off with the swimming-pool.'

'You had him check me over.'

'No offence, Joe, but I like to know who's working for me. Anyway,' – Johnstone waved his arm expansively about him, taking in the pool, the house or maybe even the rest of the world – 'whatcha think of it? Pretty grand, eh?'

'Nice party,' Joe replied.

'Yeah, yeah. I mean the house, man, the house.' Trying hard to impress, Joe realised. The bigger the ego, the more you have to feed it.

'Mm . . . big,' he said, tossing it a minnow.

'Big? Man, you've a way with words. This is more than big, Joe, it's unique. Not another house like it in the city.' He led Joe across to the window. 'See that one over there, behind the trees? That's where Graeme Souness lives. Guy must be loaded but lives in a place half this size. And that house over there? The white one with the turrets? President of I forget which bank. Has to have the place patrolled by fucking security guards – probably takes his work home. Then further down the hill there towards the village, you get all the doctors, accountants and lawyers, maybe even a politician or two. Monied people, Joe, who don't know the meaning of hardship. People who look down their noses at someone with sweat on his brow and dirt on his hands. Who think money is a right, rather than a reward.'

Joe yawned. 'You wanted to talk?'

Johnstone looked at him askance. 'Christ, times and places, man. Is this the time to talk shop? In the middle of a party? I mean, any minute now the pool's going to be alive with jiggling flesh. Follow the crowd, Joe, and you'll surface in the deep end with half a dozen beauties eating your clothes off.'

'Maybe you should feed them,' Joe suggested.

'Are you crazy?'

Joe beginning to think he was.

'I mean, this little get-together, you want to know how much it set me back?'

'Five hundred?'

Jay said, 'Where the hell you been living, man? Five hundred times ten and you might be close. You think I want to spend that kind of money just to sit and talk shop? If you can't take the pace, take a look around upstairs, see if you can spot the wife. Keep her company for a while. She's a bit like you, Joe, doesn't appreciate parties.'

Joe said, 'I feel like I know her already.'

'You do?' The smile faded from Johnstone's face as he regarded Joe thoughtfully for a couple of seconds. 'Yeah,' he said eventually, 'Isn't life strange.'

CHAPTER 10

The Dragon Queen moved cautiously in the darkness, from the first-floor bathroom window through which she had entered to the landing at the top of the stairs where she paused for a moment, alert for any sound as she let her eyes become accustomed to once familiar surroundings.

She heard the slow dripping of a tap in the bathroom. Wind buffeting shutters somewhere further along the street. The somnolent ticking of a clock. The hammering of her heart.

Nervous? The Dragon Queen?

Never.

She stifled a giggle. Then, satisfied she was alone, set to work.

Four doors led off the hall, four poky little cubicles where the 'business' was done. She checked each one, drawing the curtains in the two with windows before switching on her torch.

Little had changed. A few of the posters tacked to the walls were new, the lightshades in all four rooms, and the carpet in one. The pervasive smell of stale sweat and grubby sex, however, still clung to the nicotined walls and shabby furniture, bringing back memories almost too sordid for her to contemplate. Ugh. To think she had worked here for five months, twenty-three days, two hours and seven minutes . . .

Not that she'd been counting . . .

She shook the thought from her mind and, moving purposefully now, passed swiftly through each room, gathering together sheets

65

and towels, piling them beneath the long drape curtains in the rooms to the front and rear. Two of the sheets, she left in the hallway at the top of the stairs. Then she opened the windows a crack to admit the cool night air.

Air to feed the hungry flames.

Lucky flames.

From her woollen-knit shoulder-bag she removed a box of firelighters and a box of candles. Earlier this afternoon she had spent an hour carefully boring holes through the centre of each firelighter, wide enough to accept the two-inch stubs of candle. These she now inserted into the holes before positioning them beneath, but not smothered by, the linen she had piled in each room. Then she returned to the hallway and, getting into the rhythm of it now, tore the remaining two sheets lengthwise into strips. These she used as trailers, laying them along the hallway floor, connecting the four cubicles. Then, after one last check to ensure all the doors would remain open to ease the passage of air, she went softly downstairs.

Downstairs consisted of a small reception and waiting area, a room at the back for 'specials' and a poky, dingy, dusty little office where she had worked ten, sometimes twelve hours a day for a wage a two-legged flea could have carried home. Forced on to one of those employment schemes set up by the government to conceal the true level of unemployment, she had found herself one morning sitting across the desk from Jay Johnstone, listening to him say, *Not to worry, dear, this is all strictly legal, the position you applied for is strictly a secretarial one, so we strictly won't be asking you to do anything you don't want to do.*

Which, she later learned, was all strictly bullshit.

She began in the Reception area, closing the blinds and pushing what furniture she could back against the walls, scattering papers and magazines haphazardly across the floor. From the bathroom airing-cupboard, she fetched an armful of linen and constructed – again with the aid of the delayed-action firelighters – an artistic bonfire by the central dividing wall. Outside, the wind squalled, whistling under the front door, every now and then flicking at the pages of a magazine on the floor. Air-flow good, she thought, and turned her attention to the windowless office at the back. She switched on the light and walked round the desk to sit in the swivel chair to renew an old acquaintance.

Lest it be forgot.

She swivelled.

This room, too, had changed little. Like it could have been yesterday and not almost six months since the day she told Jay to stick his job arsewise and walked out on to the dole where they don't try to force twenty-year-old girls to suck fifty-year-old cock or face a slashing.

Taking her time, she went through each of the drawers, emptying their contents on to the desk but finding nothing worth even a second glance. Typical. If Jay Johnstone was anything more than the pervert he was, he was a cheapskate; and this place – Mama's Massage-Parlour – was the cheapest of his sleazy empire.

Next she turned to the three-drawer filing cabinet, emptying the contents of the top two drawers – all the precious records Johnstone had ordered her to index – out on to the floor. Let him try and explain that to the loss adjusters.

In the bottom drawer she found, as she knew she would, a selection of spirits and mixers, and half-a-dozen glasses, kept there for the special guests on a freebie. The plainclothes cops, for instance, who came in regularly every month 'to check the place over' and spend an hour with one of the girls in the room next door; local councillors from the Licensing Department; and Jay Johnstone's slobbish business friends – paunchy builders' merchants, scaffolders and stonemasons. Peasants.

Ironically, she recalled, the only officials who had continually refused the freebies were those from the Fire Department. Still, it would be a crime to waste such a fine selection.

Eeny, meeny, miny, mo.

The tequila had it. She shoved the bottle in her bag, then decided, no, what she needed now was something not far akin from a couple of hefty slammers just to soothe her racing pulse. So she half-filled a glass with tequila and ginger beer, sat down again behind the desk; slammed the glass off the table, then slammed the foaming liquid down her throat. God, that was good. So good, in fact, she immediately mixed another; dispatched that, and mixed another. Glanced at the phone. Dodds had said to give him a ring the moment she got out; had given her the number of his new portable phone. She found the number in her purse, and dialled. Dodds answered on the second ring.

She pinched her nose and said, 'Is that the Wan King? I'd like to order a banquet for two.'

'Wrong bloody number, hen. Try opening your eyes when you dial.'

As the line went dead, she burst into a fit of giggles, then almost choked herself to death when the third tequila slammer hit the back of her throat. Through streaming eyes, she glanced at her watch. Okay, plenty of time. Dodds had said he wanted the building fired at midnight on the dot. The two-inch stubs of candle she had tested this afternoon took between twenty and thirty minutes to ignite the firelighters. Then say five to ten minutes before the flames took hold and began to climb the walls. An hour at the most. Which left her time to play with – and maybe just one more slammer for the road.

But before that, a little more work.

First, she switched off the valves for the sprinkler system and disconnected the fire alarm. Then, fetching the fire-extinguisher from the Reception area, she used it as a battering ram against the dividing walls. Five minutes later, she had punched several holes through the plaster, exposing the wood beneath. Now the fire would spread from front to back that much quicker.

She returned to the airing-cupboard and dragged the last bag of linen through to the office – probably still the same linen she had spent hours every day ironing and folding, ironing and folding, getting all that ever-so-valuable work-experience that would stand her in such good stead the next time she applied for a job as an astronaut. As she tore the sheets into strips, she imagined she was tearing Johnstone's nerves from his spine. That brought the smile back to her face. She laid the strips along the corridor from front to rear.

Okay, what next?

An accelerant, perhaps. Something to add a little more urgency to the proceedings. She remembered the tins of paint and the bottle of thinners she'd seen in the cupboard under the stairs. She carried them through and placed them on the desk alongside the bottles of spirit, already in her mind's eye seeing the bright blue flash and dancing flame. Feeling now the familiar thrill of excited urgency hammer through her veins, driven no longer by need but burning desire. She glanced at her watch: time to call Dodds again.

He answered on the fourth ring. She could hear his car-radio in the background, someone whistling out of tune. He wanted to know if that was her playing the silly bitch, phoning him up earlier, asking for a carry-out.

'You think I've got time for games?' she demanded. 'With the whole fucking place about to go up in flames?'

'So what do you want? It's not midnight yet.'

'That's what I wanted to ask. You said midnight on the dot.'

'So?'

'So is midnight on the dot the first stroke or the twelfth?'

'Jesus bloody Christ, Grace!'

'Well?' she smiled.

'My kingdom for a woman with brains,' Dodds sighed. 'You listening?'

'Of course.' To his every sacred word.

'The sixth stroke, Grace, the sixth. Got that? Not the first, not the last, but the little piggy one in the middle. Okay?'

'Thanks, Dodds.'

'Now don't bother me again until you got something I want to hear.' The line went dead.

The sixth stroke. Who'd believe it?

She sat back in the chair and swivelled.

An artist paints a picture, first thing she does is light up a smoke and admire her finished work: a little self-appreciation never hurting anyone.

So she fished in her bag, brought out the makings and rolled one up, the smell of the firelighters and fuel on her gloves like perfume to her nose. Poured herself a final slammer, then leant back in the chair and blew smoke at the ceiling. Yeah, like that, try and let the muscles relax.

Try being the operative word.

For this was the chair where Jay always sat when he honoured the place with his presence. This was where he'd sit, with his fat arse slopping over the sides, beergut spilling over his trousers, hard-on jumping in his flies like one of those trick spiders you pump full of air and they leap across the table and scare the living shit from your bowels.

And he'd keep looking at it and frowning, shaking his head as though it was some strange phenomenon he didn't understand and couldn't control: him the poor stud a slave to women's desires, too much a gentleman to deny any poor girl a night of endless orgasm. Jay bloody Johnstone.

Who couldn't keep his groping hands to himself, or form a sentence without loading it with insult or innuendo. Jay bloody Johnstone.

Who would pay for the things he had said, but mostly for what he had done.

Most certainly for what he had done.

With a sigh that doused still smouldering emotions, she stubbed out her cigarette and gulped down the final slammer. Felt it ricochet off the walls of her brain.

At last.

She pushed the metal filing cabinet up against the back door, jamming it into place with the overturned desk – Rule Number Seven: never make things too easy for the firemen.

She collected together the bottles of accelerant and, moving from room to room, soaked all the trailers and streamers in spirit, careful to keep the liquid away from the delayed-action firelighters. When she'd finished downstairs, she turned off all the lights, lit the candles in each room, then hurried upstairs with the three remaining bottles. Three minutes later, and in the darkness of the room at the back of the house, the flare of the match was as bright and hot as the gleam in her eyes.

Once more she smiled.

Let the play begin.

'Who was that?' Billy asked as Dodds returned the phone to his pocket. 'The firebug?'

'Aye.'

'Problems?'

'Nuh.'

'You shagging her?'

Dodds said nothing.

They sat in one of Rankine's Audis, the heater on full, the radio down low, Billy whistling as they waited. Every few minutes a taxi would rumble past, turn in through Johnstone's gates and spill its passengers on the steps of the porch. In the last ten minutes he'd counted thirty-seven arrivals and no departures. It could be hours yet. He sank back in his seat and sighed.

Money. That's all he could see. Each side of the road, tucked away behind snowladen hedges and trees, tall iron gates and jagged-glass-topped walls. Properties that either whispered money, suggested it or stated it. Except Jay Johnstone's, of course, which screamed it.

It stood there, the largest of them all, behind its short semi-circular drive lined with trees, with its Tudor-Gothic-what-the-fuck façade, fancy Doric pillars and floodlights, crenellated battlements and tall, white windows. Billy could look back at his days as a postman and try to work out how many million years on double time it would take before he could afford a downpayment on a house like that. He could also waste his time.

Dodds sat like Medusa's lover in the passenger seat: apart from the one-word directions which had brought them here, he had remained stonily silent throughout the journey. Billy, however, was still buzzing from the four pints and half a dozen brandies he'd swallowed at Rankine's Club.

'You ever kill a man, Dodds? Look him right in the eye as you do the deed?'

Dodds said it wasn't his job, he was only Head of Security at the hotel. Someone needed a little roughing up, sure, okay, Rankine only had to say the word. Like with that ex-cop, Costello. Then it could be fun. But killing? – no, he could leave that for the likes of Billy.

'What d'you mean, the likes of me?'

'Heidbangers. Bamsticks. Mental bastards.'

Before Billy could reply they were suddenly bathed in light, both men sinking down in their seats as a white Mercedes came up the road behind them and turned into Johnstone's drive. Followed a minute later by a dark blue Volvo crammed with laughing faces.

'So morons do have feelings,' Billy said, straightening in his seat once the cars had passed. He took out his knife, opened it out, began cleaning his nails.

'All I ever hear is Dodds do this or Dodds do that,' the big man sulked. 'No one bothers to tell me what's going on, all I ever hear is rumours.'

'Rumours of what?'

'Rankine. His daughter. The cop, Costello.'

'You want to know what happened.'

'I want you to put that fucking knife away. It's making me nervous.'

'Stress kills. You ought to relax more, chill out.'

'Relax? When I don't know what's going on?'

'Ignorance is bliss, they say.'

'Yeah? Is that why you're always smiling?'

Billy's movements were a blur, one hand jerking Dodds' head back by the hair, the other flashing up towards the moron's face, streetlight glancing wickedly off the blade. Breath rattled ragged in Dodd's throat.

Billy's voice was a guttural hiss. 'You ever see that film *China-town*? With Jack Nicholson as the private eye?'

'Not my nose, Billy, not my nose!'

'What, then? Your balls?' The knife flashed again, the blade slicing through Dodds's trousers, plunging into the seat between his legs. Dodds choked on a scream as, again, headlights from behind filled the car with light. Billy released his grip on the moron, withdrew his knife and inspected the blade. No blood. Shit, he was losing his touch. When the car had passed, he said, 'You better learn a little respect, moron. It'll keep your nose on your face and your balls between your legs.'

'I only want to know what's going on!' Dodds whimpered.

'You got any booze in this car?'

Dodds shook his head.

'We shoulda took the Roller.' Billy peered at the moron. 'You ever hear rumours about me?'

'Nothing! Honest!'

Billy sighed. 'What's a man got to do to be talked about these days? In the old days, all you had to do was kill someone once in a while. You know, for a reason, to set an example. Do it with a little finesse, the personal touch. Put an axe in their napper or a sword up their arse. Keep the punters talking. Now it seems you have to kit yourself up in combat gear, go out on a rampage with a semi-automatic rifle and take out half a fucking street or shopping-mall. I mean, where's the point in that?'

Dodds wasn't saying. He was fingering the hole in his trousers, muttering something about his new fucking suit and how the wife would kill him. Billy, meanwhile, was keeping one eye on Johnstone's front porch, watching the latest arrivals stagger up the steps. As they entered, a man came out and stood there smoking for a while, looking, it seemed, right into Billy's eyes.

Billy said, 'Is that him?'

Dodds squinted through the windscreen. 'I thought you knew him.'

'People change.'

The moron shook his head. 'It ain't Costello.'

'You can be so sure?'

'Look at his face – the mark of Dodds is missing. No black eyes, burst lips, nothing.'

As he spoke, the man on the porch flicked his cigarette-end into the snow and returned inside.

'Okay. Go back to sleep.'

Dodds said, 'I heard Costello was engaged to Mr Rankine's daughter.'

Billy sighed. The moron never gave up. Questions, questions, questions. Like a bloody kid. He sighed again. What the hell, what harm could it do? He said, 'One of Rankine's partners got himself killed and Costello was one of the cops on the case. That's when it started, that's how he met Karen.'

'And they got married?'

'*Would've* got married if Costello hadn't shot out her eyes.' Billy studied his nails, then began again his knife-tip manicure.

'You what?' Dodds only had eyes for the knife.

'They were living together. Lovebirds. In one of those new Yuppie flats down the Stockbridge Colonies. Rankine went round to see her the day before the wedding, found her lying on the floor, bullet holes for eyes.'

'Costello?'

'Who else? She was going to turn him in, call the whole thing off, the wedding, everything. When they searched the flat the polis found more than £20,000 under the floorboards. Money Costello couldn't account for. Karen must've found it and threatened to turn him in. So he killed her.'

'The bastard. How long did he get?'

'The polis,' Billy said, 'have a way of looking after their own. They rolled-up their trousers, danced a little dance and shook a few hands – and suddenly what do you know, the procurator-fiscal decides there's insufficient evidence to prosecute Costello for murder. So they bang him away for eighteen months and call it justice.'

'And now he's out again.'

'And working for Jay Johnstone. A fact guaranteed to get right up Rankine's nose.'

Dodds frowned, obviously a sign of deep thought. He said, 'I walked in and found my daughter dead on the floor, I reckon I'd feel the same way as Mr Rankine.'

Billy studied the nails of his left hand. Satisfied, he began on his right hand. The moron's eyes remained locked on the blade. 'You ever seen a dead body, Dodds?'

'I never seen a live one.'

'Like woken up to find a girl dead in your swimming-pool and you don't know how she got there?' Show the moron what kind of mental bastard he was really dealing with here.

Dodds yawned. 'Not recently, no.'

'Man, you've never lived. Happened to me the other day. There she was, naked as the way she was born to be, floating face-down in the pool, and fuck me if I can't remember how the hell she got there.'

'Did you know her?'

'I might've done, in the biblical sense. But that's it, you see – I can't remember.'

'Yeah?' Dodds yawned again.

'You're not interested.'

'I don't want to know.'

The moron still sulking. Christ. Rankine had surrounded himself with wet-noses.

Billy said, 'So tell me about Beth. She have a boyfriend?'

Not so far as Dodds knew.

'She a dyke?'

Not so far as Dodds knew. And thank Christ for that.

'Women,' Billy said, 'when they act all snooty like that, what it really means is their pants're so hot they have to be cool or burst into flames. Like they're interested but they want you to work for your supper.'

Dodds wanted to know if Billy was an expert on anything other than sex and violence.

Billy said, 'What else is there? I'm a man, ain't I?' Headlights lit up the interior again and a black BMW nosed into Johnstone's drive. Billy folded his knife and returned it to his pocket. He smiled as he felt the moron relax beside him. 'I mean, it's violence that makes the world go round. Not politics. Not peace and love, or money or God – just pure sex and violence, the pleasure and the pain, the survival of the fittest. The way nature intended it. Fuck, if everyone lived in perfect harmony, think what a bore life would be. Politicians would have to earn an honest living. Rape would lose its meaning. People would end up killing themselves just to put a little excitement back in their lives. No, Dodds, there are only two true meanings of life. Sex and violence.'

'You really believe that?'

'Of course,' Billy said, glancing disdainfully at Dodds. 'I believe anything I say.'

CHAPTER 11

Joe made his way up the broad sweeping staircase, stepping carefully over sprawled couples glued at the mouths, the sound of the party gradually receding behind him. It wasn't so much the music – now some heavy beat booming that reminded him of the incessant crashing of machinery in the prison workshop – but the lack of air. Passive smoking was one thing, passive choking another.

Upstairs the décor and furnishings were much the same: blended by design, pastel paintings on the walls, a few hanging tapestries and carpets deep enough to break a lawnmower on.

Jay had said, his parting shot, 'You sure we haven't met before?' the look in his eyes like it was somebody else in there looking out, not Jay at all. Putting Joe off balance for a moment so that all he could do was stand there looking dumb as Jay reached up to tweak his cheek and said, 'Enjoy yourself, Joe, there's a good boy.'

There was a door at the end of the passage, slightly ajar, leading into a quiet room bathed in a soft pool of lights. The sound of classical music came to him on a breath of fresh air. He knocked softly and entered.

Andrea Johnstone stood leaning against French windows looking out over the balcony. She turned as he approached and he noticed the glossy tracks sparkling on her cheeks. She looked at him through eyes that showed no surprise, no embarrassment.

'Ah,' she said, 'you again.' She made her way slowly across the

75

room – placing her feet carefully, as though on a catwalk – to a box of tissues on a low table against the wall. After dabbing delicately at her eyes she crossed to the piano, where she arranged herself carefully on the stool and asked, 'What d'you think of it so far?'

When Joe shrugged, she said, 'No comment is comment enough. What's your name again?'

As he told her, he let his eyes sweep the room. It was a woman's room, a sanctuary, obviously hers, full of pastel shades and delicate lace, deep wingbacked chairs and fragile ornaments. A small hand-loom stood against one wall beside it a sewing-machine and stacked on shelves above were hundreds of rolls of wool in a hundred different shades. She ran a fingernail along the spotless keyboard, stopped at middle C.

'Joe Costello . . .' she mused. 'I feel I ought to know you.'

'Your husband hasn't mentioned me?'

'He tells me nothing. To him a wife is nothing more than a piece of domestic furniture. So tell me.'

'It's a long story. Some other time perhaps.'

Andrea said, 'There'll be other times? You don't know Jay. You wait. Five or ten minutes he'll be wondering where I am, then send one of his minions looking for me. If you want to stay on his good side you better go back downstairs.'

Joe said, 'Do you mind?' and crossing to the French windows, went out on to the balcony. Below him, lights from the lounge spilled out across the snow-covered lawn which sloped away into a darkness broken only by the shadow of a gazebo and the pale silhouettes of the skeletal trees bordering the garden. And there beyond, climbing like a mountainous rolling wave, the Pentland Hills rose silvery-grey in the pale moonlight. After a while he felt Andrea's presence beside him.

'You're not like the others, are you?' she said softly, a speculative tone to her voice. 'I mean, like the other people Jay has working for him. There's something different about you.'

He could smell her perfume, a subtle musky scent that, again, he found curiously attractive. Danger, he thought with a smile – pheromones at work.

She said, 'What's so funny?'

'I was thinking about this guy I just met – name of Wylie. You know him?'

'The silly wee man who calls himself a private detective? I doubt he could detect his privates if he tried.'

Joe found himself laughing. 'So why does Jay use him?' he asked.

'He's just another little pet to keep him amused, to remind him how much smarter he is than Jack. Do you know Jack Rankine?'

Joe said aye, he'd heard the name.

'Wylie's just one more of Jack's employees that Jay has managed to headhunt in the last couple of years. All because Jack and I had a thing going once – before Jay came along.' Andrea shivered. 'Shall we go back inside?'

He followed her in, admiring her poise, the way her body moved beneath the dress, filling out all the right places, suggested but did not reveal. 'I think you made the right choice,' he said, watching her cross to a mahogany cabinet lined with bottles and pour a large gin and tonic.

'The right choice would have been to walk out and leave them both to their macho posturing. They're both as bad as each other, totally paranoid. I mean, look at Jay. The man's a lunatic. He talks to himself. I wake up in the middle of the night and he's strutting up and down in the darkness talking to himself. Putting on funny voices, like two sides of a conversation. It's scary, I tell you, sharing your life with a split personality.'

'You think he's schizo?'

'I mean his personality split ages ago. Ran off with a pint of lager and has never been seen since.' She glanced up suddenly as the door banged open. 'Hello, Jay. How's the party going?'

Johnstone came strutting into the room. 'You're neglecting our guests, Andrea darling.'

'Joe's a guest. I was telling him about the ghosts.'

'Well maybe you ought to go downstairs and play the hostess with the mostest before there's another fucking ghost around the house. Like yours, if you see what I mean?'

Somewhere in the house a phone began to ring.

'There's no need to talk like that, Jay.'

'Andrea . . . darling?'

'Okay, I'm going. See you, Joe.'

'Joe says goodbye, dear. He says he really enjoyed meeting you. Now go on and leave us to talk, there's a good girl.' As Andrea walked stiffly towards the door, he added, 'Oh, and darling? See who's on the phone, will you?'

The door slammed.

'Ghosts,' Jay said. 'Whatever next?'

Jay was running away at the mouth. He said, 'Life was simple then. No worries, no nothing. Pick up your packet Friday afternoon, home for a quick bath then straight out on the town. You had to be in the pub back of six if you wanted to get your quota in, those were the days of early closing. Mind that? Half ten and out on the street, looking for someone to give a kicking? Heading up Lothian Road, hoping to catch a few of the Bar-Ox boys, pay them back for just being alive? And every now and then ending up in the cells, coming up to court Monday, the £5 fine making it all worth while, then having to phone the boss and say it was something you ate, don't worry, you'd be back on Tuesday. You remember that?'

Joe said, 'Not quite like that, no.' He watched the razorblade go chop chop chop, efficiently cutting and then shaping the small white mound of powder. Jay leaning forward over the mirror, actions automatic, mouth on automatic, small bald patch on his crown a glistening bloodless pink.

'What I'm saying is I think I was a happier man then.'

'You still seem to enjoy your money.'

Jay worked the razor with practised ease, splitting the coke in two, stretching out the lines long and thin, taking his time, artist at work, all part of the ritual.

'Yeah – but I have to work hard at it. That's what I'm saying, Joe. I never used to have to work to enjoy what I earned, I just did it. When it was gone it was gone and never mind, there's always going to be a Friday at the end of the week. But now, what do I have to look forward to? I'm rich enough to do anything I want except go back to the way things were.'

'Give it away.'

'Joe, they don't *let* you give it away. I did that, the wife'd have me committed. Say I wasn't of sound mind. And you know what? The courts would agree.'

'It can't be all bad,' Joe said.

'What I'm saying, Joe, is big money is a big target. Suddenly it's like you're a piece of shit with all these flies queuing up for a little taste. More friends than you ever thought you had or even wanted. People wanting this off you, that off you, but in the end always wanting.' Jay extracted a fifty from his wallet and, rolling it into a tube, took a line up each nostril with a flourish. Then he leant back with a sigh, and said, 'Sure you don't want one, Joe? Put yourself at ease?'

Joe shook his head. 'You still bringing it in yourself, or do you hire mules now?'

Johnstone's smile faded from his face. 'I don't think I heard that,' he snapped, giving Joe the eye – not the weird, vacant look, but the one supposed to see right down into his soul. 'Or if I did, I heard it all wrong.'

'Old habits die hard.'

'So they say. But people who go round making wild accusations don't die easy either. Especially ex-cops.'

Joe said, 'You want to get to the point?'

'Point?'

'Rae said you wanted to talk. All you've told me so far is how much money you have. Okay, I'm impressed. You've got so much money your pockets hurt. Now what?'

'Rae tells me I can trust you.'

'Question is, can I trust you?'

The humourless smile returned to Johnstone's face. 'I'd like to help, Joe. I know what you've been through. It's not easy. It takes time to learn how to trust again.'

'Prison has that effect.'

'Fuck prison, man, I meant your time as a cop.' Jay flattened each nostril in turn, clearing each with a couple of hefty sniffs. 'Anyway, what do you say?'

Jay's mind was obviously working faster than his mouth. Joe said, 'Say about what?'

'Working for me.'

'You mean I passed Wylie's clearance?'

'Like I said, Joe, no offence.'

'Offence taken.'

'Christ, what d'you want me to do? Go down on bended knees and beg? How many times do I have to tell you I'd like you to come and work for me?'

'And how would that look on my CV? From cop to con to working for a dope dealer in two easy years.'

Johnstone jerked like a puppet to his feet, his voice raised and thick neck reddening as he stabbed the air with his index finger.

'Ex-dealer, man, ex-fucking-dealer.' He strode across to the drinks cabinet, angrily poured himself a malt. 'Okay,' he said, 'okay. You're winding me up. A man's got to have his fun. He doesn't drink, he doesn't smoke, he doesn't like a little toot for his snoot, no wonder he can't relax, has to wind somebody up for the fun of it.' He tasted the whisky, savoured it and sighed, turning back to Joe. 'Okay, so you've seen the intelligence files. Big deal. That was all in the past. It was strictly the times, man, the times. I was young and ambitious and the money was easy. So what? I was a businessman. A merchant born in a nation of merchants. I was supplying a demand – and demand, as any businessman will tell you, is not subject to the law, it is the fucking law. Ask the Government. Ask the people selling arms to our enemies. Ask the CIA. But no, you don't want to do that, you'd rather take a shot at me because I'm more your size. Small fry. A guy who made a few pennies from his youthful folly and then has to spend the rest of his life taking this kind of crap from narrow-minded has-been cops who want to massage their principles in public. Yeah, well let me tell you something, Mr Joe Costello. All that time you spent studying the files down at Criminal Intelligence, did you ever see a conviction by my name, or one trumped-up charge that stuck? Did you?'

'A few D & Ds, I remember, and a couple D & Is.'

'There you go. So I got drunk and incapable a couple of times, so what? At that age, who doesn't?'

'The DS had you under surveillance for almost two months.'

'And what did they come up with? Nothing. Tore my house apart and all they found was some talcum powder and baking soda. Which naturally they took away for expert analysis. But drugs? The only drugs in my house at the time were the ones strictly affecting their heads.'

'You make a good case.'

'You know why? Because in this country a man is innocent until proven guilty.'

'And sometimes even innocent after proven guilty.'

'There you go, man, my point exactly. You should know.' Johnstone sniffed, clearing his nostrils again before sitting next to Joe on the sofa. 'Which is why I want to help you. Call me a Good Samaritan, a man who hates to see injustice. Rae says you're innocent, okay, I'll believe it. Let's see what we can do to clear the whole mess up.'

Joe returned the vacant smile. 'In exchange for what?'

'You continue to work for Rae.'

Joe stood up. 'Thanks, but no thanks. What happened the other night almost put me back inside.'

'Fuck, Joe, that was strictly an accident. Could've happened to anyone.'

'And the fires? Were they all accidents too?'

Jay dismissed the suggestion with a vague wave of his hand. 'Someone with a grudge,' he said lamely, 'that's all.'

'Is that what the police think?'

'The polis, Joe, I've had up to here. I don't ever want to see another one as long as I live.'

The door opened and Andrea sauntered into the room. Jay stared at her through boggled eyes as she went across to the cabinet and poured herself another gin and tonic.

He said, 'How's the party, dear?'

Andrea replied without turning, her voice as cold and detached as his. 'You better hurry, darling, or you'll miss the orgy in the pool.'

'You're right,' he said, grinning at Joe, 'I better.' He swept the mirror, razorblade and small white packet into the drawer of the ornate occasional table and rose to his feet. 'We'll talk later, Joe, okay? After you've had time to think it over.'

'Sure,' Joe said. But thinking, No way, not a chance. Find Rae and get the hell away from here. Breathe some air that was cool and clean and didn't stick to the back of his throat like bile.

Johnstone stopped by the door and turned to his wife.

'Darling? Who was that on the phone?'

'Phone? When?'

'Twenty minutes ago, remember? I asked you to get it.'

'Oh that!' Andrea said, swirling the ice in her glass with a silver swizzle-stick. 'That was the police, darling. Something about a fire in one of your massage-parlours.' She flashed her husband a brilliant smile. 'I think they want you there right away.'

CHAPTER 12

' I told him no.'

The road was a thin dark ribbon through a crystalline world of white. The near-full moon was the light at the end of a long dark tunnel, a shining silver coin glimpsed sporadically through spindly fingers of skeletal trees. A bridge took them across the ringroad and the road became a lane as the snow-burdened hedges closed in.

'And what did he say?'

'Nothing. That's when Andrea walked in and told him about the fire.'

Rae said, 'I wish I'd been there.'

'Where are we going?'

'Short-cut.' Then, 'Right again here.'

Joe guided Rae's Metro between the slush-filled pot-holes as she sat half-turned towards him in the passenger seat. 'You sure?' he asked. He'd almost had to pour her into the car.

'Course I'm sure,' she said, peering out the window at the looming grey shadow of the Pentland Hills. 'You ever been up there, Joe?'

'You mean walking?'

'Don't sound so surprised – a lot of people do it.' She rested her head on his shoulder and sighed. 'I used to go with my father. He loved it up there. Then with George. He didn't. Did I ever tell you about George?'

'Many times.'

'He was the lawyer. A rotten, stinking bastard. He didn't like anything I liked, he just wanted someone young and pretty to hang on his arm at all those boring fucking parties he went to.'

Joe said, 'Left here, or straight on?'

'Straight on and we'll come to the reservoirs.'

'You want to go skinny-dipping?'

'That will be right.' She yawned and snuggled in as best she could with Joe continually having to change gears. 'God, I'm tired.'

'I wanted to thank you . . .'

'Thank me? For what?'

'For, you know . . . earlier this evening. For being my friend.'

'Christ, Joe, forget it. We all need a little intimacy now and again. We're human, you know. Man needs woman, woman needs man. Nature's law.'

Joe said, 'Yeah?' Concentrating on the road, deciding he pre-ferred the sound of her voice to the sound of his own thoughts.

'Bloody aye. When I needed someone, you always came. Tonight you needed someone, so what's the big deal? That's what friends are for, Joe. Someone to trust.'

'You're pissed.'

'Damn right I am.'

For a while the only sound, that of the fan-heater and wheels sloshing through snow. Joe glanced in the rearview mirror. Couldn't tell – houselight or headlight – at this distance. Perhaps just a trick of the light. With an almost full moon now reflecting off the flickering snowscape of water and trees, what did he expect?

'You're very quiet tonight.'

'Sober is all.'

Rae laughed. 'You had your chance. All that free booze and you choose to drink spring water . . . you're either insane or following doctor's orders.'

'I go into the lion's den, I don't go in drunk.'

'You see Jay as a lion?' Rae asked.

And there it was again, caught for an instant in his peripheral vision, the flicker of a light in his rearview mirror. But gone the moment he focused.

'Am I wrong?' he asked.

Rae hesitated, thinking it over. 'A cornered rat is more like it now,' she said finally. 'Though, when I first knew him, started working for him, he was more like a lapdog, you know – friendly,

84

always seeking praise and recognition for the bones he'd bring home. And horny as a terrier, of course.'

'Were you ever lovers?'

'It's nothing but wishful thinking on Jay's part. He's just happy to let everyone think what isn't going on *is* going on, and maybe wind up his wife a little at the same time.'

'And you don't mind?'

'If people get the wrong impression? Why should I? It gives me an edge.'

'And not just a few curves either,' Joe said.

'Tonight,' Rae giggled, 'flattery will get you anywhere you want.'

Joe slowed as the road narrowed and turned.

'What's the matter?' Rae asked. 'Is there someone behind us?'

'I thought I saw headlights.'

'Anyone out here at this time in the morning would have to be mad.' Touching his arm as she laughed. 'Talking about mad, what did Wylie have to say for himself?'

'He said he can give me Rankine on a plate.'

'I wouldn't be surprised. You know he used to work for Rankine? He left about the same time I did – though not on good terms, I heard. Spent a month or two in hospital.'

'And now he's working for Johnstone, trying to find out who's behind the fires?'

'A two-year-old could tell him the answer to that.'

'Yeah?' Joe said, concentrating on the car's traction as the road climbed, hugging the northern lip of the reservoir, opening out as they reached the top and the hedges fell away behind them. Fifty feet below them on the left, the reservoir was caught like a sheet of smoked glass stretched across the narrow, steep-sided glen. The moon shimmered in its reflection.

'Rankine,' Rae said, sitting up now, searching for her cigarettes. 'Who else.'

'You have proof?'

'I don't need proof, Joe, just a few grains of common-sense. They've been at it ever since you went inside and I left Rankine to work for Jay. It's like some kind of warped-personality war. Rankine hears of a property deal Jay's been lining up for months, so he steps in and pays way over the odds and snatches the deal from under Jay's nose. Next thing you know, Jay's hired himself a dumper-truck and deposited a couple a tons of horseshit on

Rankine's hotel steps. It's all a game. One-upmanship. Rankine buys the latest model Merc, next day Jay's driving a brand new Porsche. Okay, no harm done, you might say – but they use people blatantly for their own petty ends. Regard their employees merely as pawns in their game, all ultimately dispensable. Only now, recently . . .' Rae trailed off, plugging her mouth with a cigarette.

'You think they're no longer playing games?' Joe suggested.

Rae exhaled in a sigh. 'I don't know if they ever were,' she said. 'All I know is this feeling I've had since the fires first started.'

'That it's out of control?'

'That it'll end in tears.'

Suddenly they were bathed in light as headlights filled the rearview mirror, the sound of the horn shattering their sense of warm isolation.

Rae said, 'There's a passing-place up ahead.'

'Man must be in one hell of a hurry.'

The car behind – an Audi – almost kissed the Metro's rear as it flashed its lights and hooted even more impatiently. Joe touched his brakes and watched the Audi back off a yard.

'There,' Rae pointed.

Joe slowed, indicating, and pulled off the road, rolling to a halt a few yards short of the steep embankment, headlights reflecting off the water, illuminating the far bank of the reservoir. He switched off the engine and turned to watch the Audi go past.

Only it didn't go past. It pulled in behind them, horn blaring, twin-beams dazzling. Five yards off, revving wildly. Two indistinct shadows behind the windscreen.

'What the f-' Joe said, before the roar of the Audi's engine drowned out his voice as it came off its marks, slewed across the icy surface and crunched into the side of the Metro.

Metal screamed. Rae screamed. Joe would've screamed but he was struggling with the ignition, trying to get his feet to the pedals as he yanked on the steering wheel to control the spin as the Audi strained on spinning wheels, forcing them slowly, inexorably, towards the edge.

'My God!' Rae gasped, knuckling her teeth. 'He's trying to kill us!'

The engine caught. Then stalled. Joe's fingers scrabbling at the ignition. The moonlight glinting lethal as a razorblade on the icy waters below. Rae, screwed round in her seat, mouth open, eyes wide. Disbelief. Her words lost beneath the screech of rending metal. Joe's movements instinctive.

But slow, too slow.

Years of training now rusty, unnatural. *Don't flood the engine, Christ, don't flood it.* The engine suddenly catching, Joe piling up the revs as the Audi reversed.

'Get out!' Joe yelled. 'Jump!'

'I can't!' Desperation tearing at her lungs as she struggled with the door. 'It's . . . jammed!'

'The window!' he shouted, gunning the accelerator.

But all traction lost.

The Audi surged forward again and hit them with a raw and brutal force that burst the air from his lungs and bounced Rae's head off the dash with a dull and sickening thud. She grunted and flopped back, deathly silent as Joe fought desperately to drag air back into his own aching lungs.

'Rae!' He leaned across and tried to force the door. 'Come on, Rae, come on!' Became tangled in the seatbelts, unable to move from behind the wheel.

Trapped, as the Audi reversed again on spinning wheels. Everything moving too fast, no time to think, to act.

His mind screaming. *He should've followed his instinct, trusted intuition. He'd seen the headlights, godammit, he'd seen them twice! He should've* thought – *this time in the morning, he should've fucking* known!

The Audi's gears clashed, giving him a moment's respite; time enough to find the gear and depress the clutch. His mind racing now, seeking escape. Scenting it.

The Audi, poised, a snarling beast on a flimsy leash.

First gear engaged.

Joe's hands sweaty on the wheel, slipping, as the Audi jumped forward again. The Metro's wheels skidding wildly in the churned snow as though motivated by Joe's rising panic.

No go.

Too slow.

Not enough traction.

The Audi accelerated. Impact. Slamming Joe's face into the steering wheel. Catching the door on the passenger side, spinning the car round and back amidst the screech of protesting metal. The horizon tilting, headlights blinding.

Excruciating pain. His face on fire. Blinding pain. His teeth . . .

Forcing his eyes open.

Rae . . .

The Metro teetered on the brink, its bonnet slowly rising. Rae's head lolling about on her shoulders, blood running thick from a large open gash in her forehead. The Audi facing them head on, steam rising from its buckled bonnet as its engine raced. One of the headlights gone, the fender crushed.

No, please . . . not Rae!

Joe struggling weakly with the door. Glancing up to see . . .

To see the Audi leap from its block and hurtle towards them.

One final effort . . .

But too late. All too late as the Audi collided head on and catapulted them, tumbling, over the edge. Into a stroboscopic world of black and white: a whirligig of white snow and black water rushing up to meet them.

Then the white disappeared and all that was left was icy black as the car slid quickly beneath the surface.

Pockets of air still rose bubbling, distorting the moonlit mirrored surface. Billy glanced at his watch. It was now five minutes since the car hit the water and Dodds was still standing there white-faced, with his slack jaw hanging and whole body ashake. Trying to come to terms with his first murder and not doing very well. He kept saying they should've waited until Costello was alone, that killing innocent women was not in his job description.

'Scruples,' Billy said, almost breaking his lips in a sneer, 'are for those who can afford them. Everyone dies in the end, what the hell does it matter they die a little early?'

'But innocent women, Billy?' Dodds stared at the glossy water, shaking his head in disbelief.

'Think of it as saving her from a lifetime of washing skidmarks from her old man's underpants. As if you're doing her a favour.'

Dodds didn't seem convinced.

Billy was patient. He felt the way he always felt after a good slaying: better. So he was patient with the moron and took his time to explain a few of the niceties of murder. His first murder, he told Dodds, was the one that still brought back the warmest memories. He was nineteen then, wore his hair long and tripped out to Led Zep, Floyd and Beefheart. When he wasn't eating his head on hash, he was out of his head on acid. And when he couldn't get acid, he'd try THC, speed, mescaline, mushrooms,

STP, downers, triple-dexies, black bombers, brown and clears – in fact, anyfuckingthing he could lay his hands on. When times were very hard he'd sink a bottle of the low-flying bird, go out and rip some bastard's face off. For the hell of it. So he wouldn't die of boredom.

It was during one of those hard times when supplies were getting low that Billy committed his first murder. The guy who lived up the stairs should have known better than to play his music loud at three in the morning when burnt-out acid-heads were trying to find a quiet corner in their minds in which to sleep. Loud music was okay, no complaints. But loud *disco* music?

So Billy had gone up the stairs and asked the guy nicely, 'Turn down your music or I'll blow your fucking kneecaps off.' The guy laughed in Billy's face. 'You and whose army?' he said, then slammed the door, nearly pulping Billy's snoot.

An hour later the guy answered his door again. This time there were three men standing there, dressed to kill in black balaclavas. They tapped his head and took him down to a waiting car. As they drove down towards Holyrood Park, Billy tied the guy's hands behind his back. When he came to, Billy forced a tab of acid down his throat. The guy started crying. Billy told him to stop. The guy cried even more. Billy cut off the tip of his nose with a Stanley knife. The guy started screaming. Billy had to gag him to shut him up. They drove up the Queen's Drive, as near as they could get to the Salisbury Crags. Then they kicked the guy screaming all the way up the Crags. When they reached the top they took him by the ankles and hung him over the edge so he could see what the city looked like upside down and far below. They took it in turns to sit on the guy's ankles. Billy told the guy about life, the life he'd soon be leaving. Told him a few of the many things he'd learned so far. About manners. About respect. About the way he was going to die, splattered on the rocks a hundred feet below. Three hours Billy lectured his hallucinating captive audience, by which time the guy'd gone quiet, save a whimper or two or three. Then, as the first light of dawn broke up the night, Billy tired. He told the guy, 'I hope you've learned your lesson,' and the guy said he had. He said it a thousand times, he'd learned his fucking lesson, would Billy now let him the hell go. What could Billy do? He obliged. He said, 'Have a nice death,' and let the guy go all the way to the bottom. Then they all went home to bed. And that was the last time he was ever kept awake by some small-minded bastard who couldn't take a hint. See?'

Dodds hadn't taken his eyes from the water the whole time Billy was talking. 'Did you hear that?' he said.

'Hear what?'

'I dunno. A sound. From down there.' Dodds pointed down towards the point of the Metro's entry, close to the bank.

Billy played the beam of his torch along the snow-covered rocks and boulders that formed the lip of the bank fifty feet below. He said, 'You keen enough to climb down, take a look?'

Dodds shook his head vehemently. 'It could've been air, you know. Bubbles.'

'Or even a fish farting.' Billy looked at his watch. 'Okay,' he said, 'it's time. Let's go.' He walked back to the car and gave it a cursory inspection before climbing in.

Dodds followed hurriedly, the relief evident on his face. 'Time?' he asked, sliding behind the wheel.

'For what we in the business call an *après-kill*. What you call getting rat-arsed.'

CHAPTER 13

Joe stood over the open grave with a handful of soil, oblivious to those around him. As large flakes of snow seeped from the lowering sky, tears streamed down his cheeks, his face set hard as the frozen earth on which her coffin lay.

Never any trouble, she had said. And now she was dead.

Someone pushed past. Earth clattered on the coffin lid. A hand rested for a moment on his shoulder. Jay Johnstone nodded once, grimly, then moved off towards Rae's parents to offer his respects. Joe remained where he was. Rooted as an oak as the wake of black-clad mourners continued to flow around him against a background of murmured condolences and choking tears. People spoke to him in sorrowful tones but their soft words melted like the snow upon his face. He dared not speak nor even meet their eyes as his fist clenched and clenched and clenched on the cold damp soil.

'Joe?'

The last straggle of mourners were picking their way carefully across the snow towards the line of cars. Rae's father laid a hand on his arm. They stood alone beside the grave. Stuart Connell was a broad man with a broad flushed face below flame-red hair. A trawlerman turned taxi-driver, Leith born and bred, he was a man of few wasted words:

'Let her go, Joe.'

Red hair. Her father had red hair and hers was black. Like her mother's. Her mother had wept openly as she tossed earth in the

91

grave. As had her father. To throw in the soil was to let her go. Yet Joe could not let her go. She was still there in his mind, alive and vibrant. The sound of her laughter still ringing in his ears. To let her go was . . . was . . .

Stuart Connell took Joe's hand and gently prised it open, held it out over the grave. 'Let her go, Joe, let her go.'

Soil clattered on wood.

Joe wept in Connell's arms.

It had stopped snowing. To the south and west there were even pockets of blue between the shifting banks of cloud. Mourners trudged in straggling groups through ankle-deep snow, back towards the chapel and the string of cars along the drive. As Joe approached, Johnstone climbed from his Porsche to lean on its door. 'You all right, Joe?' he asked. 'Comfortable back at the house?'

Joe said, all things considered, aye.

He'd been staying there as Johnstone's guest since the night Rae died. Four days, was it, or five? He seemed to have lost all sense of time, drifting in and out of deep dark holes of sleep, caring little if it was night or day, caring nothing for Andrea's soothing attention or Jay's magnanimity, craving only the drugs the doctor brought, the ones that lowered him gently into the comforting darkness where nothing ever happened or hurt.

'Stay as long as you want, Joe, you're my official guest. The wife gets on your tits, let me know and I'll get a divorce. Okay?'

'The doctor leave those pills?'

'Sure. Ask the wife.' Johnstone looked around distractedly. 'You going to the wake?'

'Later,' he said. First, there was something he had to do.

'Okay. If you want Wylie to pick up clothes from your flat, just give him the nod. And see if you can sober him up. He seems to have taken it bad.'

'And he calls himself a pro.'

Johnstone removed his glasses, and massaged his eyes. 'Don't be hard on him, Joe. His heart's been ripped to shreds. Poor guy was in love with Rae. Strictly from a distance, of course.'

'Yeah,' Joe said, 'of course.'

Jay glanced at him, squinting. 'You sure you're all right, Joe? Maybe you ought to—'

'I'm all right, I said.'

'Then I'll let you get on.' Johnstone was halfway into his Porsche when Joe grabbed his arm.

'First we talk.'

'Look at the time, man. I'm late already.'

'I want to know what's going on between you and Rankine, Jay. I want the truth. Now.'

'Joe, you're tired. You've had a hard day. Nothing is going on between Rankine and me, nothing.'

'Rae is dead, you call that nothing?' Joe felt his voice rising, could do nothing to stop it. 'You want to know what her last words were? She said anyone with a grain of sense would know Rankine was behind the fires.'

'She did, heh?' Without his glasses, Jay blinked like a mole in sunlight. 'You want to know something, Joe? Rankine never let's go. Once he gets an obsession in his head, he'll follow you down the very hoists of hell to exact his retribution. Twelve years I've been married to Andrea, and twelve years I've had that bastard on my back every way I turn.'

'And this is all because he thinks you stole his woman? Crap, Jay, and you know it.'

Johnstone sighed and replaced his glasses. 'Okay, so there was a sum of money involved. But that's history, Joe.'

'And so is Rae.'

'Okay, you're the shit-hot cop,' Jay sneered, 'why don't *you* find out who killed her? Or have you forgotten how?'

Joe shook his head, suddenly overcome by a weariness that threatened to buckle his knees. Like a punctured tyre, his anger deflated. 'First thing they teach you is keep an open mind,' he said, hearing the empty echo of fatigue in his voice.

'And for all these years I thought it was how to bend your knees.' Jay turned the ignition and the Porsche snarled into life. 'Aye, well you keep an open mind. I've got to head back down to the massage-parlour, talk to the loss adjusters and put up with a load more veiled accusations. If it wasn't for the girl the police say was seen leaving the building shortly before the fire, I'd probably be sweating under *their* lamps by now.'

'They have a suspect? A girl?'

'They're going through my personnel files right this moment. Reckon maybe she used to work for me.'

'Will they find anything?' Joe discovered he didn't really care; all he wanted was the comforting blackness of sleep.

'Hell, you know what it's like,' Johnstone shrugged. 'Turnover of staff in those places, I'd be clearing more tropical rainforest than McDonald's if I kept a record of them all.' He glanced at his watch and sighed. 'Anyway, I have to shoot. I'll be stopping through in Glasgow tonight, so make yourself at home. You need anything, just ask the wife. I'll be back tomorrow and we can talk then. Hey, and Joe? Mop up Wylie if you can.'

Joe watched the Porsche growl towards the cemetery gates, then turned and walked slowly back up the hill, towards the eastern wall of the cemetery.

Three words carved in stone. Apart from the memories, all he had left. He knelt and dusted the snow from the headstone, using a gloved finger to expose the inscription.

Karen Anne Rankine.

They'd met in the Preservation Hall, a blues night, the way it happens in corny films, eyes meeting through a haze of smoke across the crowded bar. Joe had strolled in halfway through the set, ordered his pint, then turned to lean against the bar.

When he saw her, he was suddenly alone in her presence, oblivious to everything around him. As though the rest of the hall and all the people in it had just crumbled to dust and blown away on a breeze.

She was one of two backing-singers in a six-piece blues band. Dressed in a black and green body-stocking, she moved to the rhythm with an almost hypnotic, sensuous ease. Her wild orange hair seemed to leap like flames and, in the glare of the spotlights, the hazel chips of her eyes glittered like gold in devilment. And her voice – what a voice! As clear and vibrant as a mountain stream, it seemed to permeate his every pore, reaching deep inside him to pluck the chords of his heart, filling the emptiness there with light and warmth . . . and something else he wasn't too sure of. And when their eyes did meet eventually through the smoky haze, it felt almost like a physical bonding. She grinned. He grinned. They both grinned until their lips hurt. When the set was finally over, Joe pushed towards the stage and Karen pushed towards the bar, and after meeting halfway, spent the next few minutes struggling for the words they knew they didn't need to say.

It didn't matter she was Jack Rankine's daughter.

It made no difference that Joe was a cop.

Neither then, nor later, when they discovered the awkward truth.

Because it was love, and love is blind.

And six months later she was dead.

He removed the flowers lying shrivelled in the snow, arranged the fresh ones he'd bought this morning. She had been buried in sunshine, he recalled, a warm summer's day in July. He remembered it well, not a cloud in the sky as he looked out through the bars of his poky little cell in Saughton's remand wing. He remembered also the fury that had raged inside him, and the half-dozen screws they'd needed to drag him down to the digger for trying to attack the Governor after he'd refused Joe's request to attend the funeral. So, that night, nursing his bruises alone in the midnight chill, he had given her a burial of his own, laying her to rest in the cold, dark depths of his mind, along with all the precious memories. For he had known then, as he knew now, that to face them any longer, whether in the dark of night or light of day, would mean the end of life.

For him, and most certainly for someone else.

He heard a car approach, sounding its horn, but paid no heed. He knelt there, as he'd knelt there the day he was released from Saughton, the words going round in his head, the meaningless words that would never bring her back, the apologies that were far too late, the words of love that fell like tears on ears of stone.

Again the car-horn sounded.

One day, Karen, he promised her. One day someone would pay.

He climbed slowly to his feet and crunched through the snow, down to the road. Then immediately wished he hadn't.

'Hey, fuckteeth! Costello!' The pinched grey face behind the wheel of the Escort was Detective Inspector Kerley's.

'What do you want?'

'Your arse in parsley,' Kerley said, with a flash of his tobacco-stained teeth. 'Get in.'

Joe remained by the side of the car. 'This official?'

'Should it be?'

'You're here for a reason.'

'I think, therefore I am. How about you?'

'I came to bury a friend.'

'But not to praise her? I hear you and Rae were good friends, Joe.'

'We grew up together.'

'*Very* good friends, I heard.'

'You still working Vice or is it just a hobby now?'

'Someone dies under suspicious circumstances – you know how it is – questions have to be asked. Like where were you on the night in question.'

'You serious?'

'No, I just came to try out a few new jokes.'

'You're saying Rae's death was no accident?'

'What a clever boy.' Kerley had a sneer sour enough to curdle milk. 'You should've joined the police.'

Joe said, 'Rae wasn't suicidal. If she had been, I'd have known.'

Kerley raised his eyebrows in evident disbelief. 'We have a witness says she left Johnstone's party with a man. That she was far too drunk to drive.'

'You have a description of the man?'

'Aye. He wore trousers.' Kerley settled his sluggish, red-rimmed eyes on Joe's. 'Maybe you can help me there – seeing as you and Connell arrived at the party together.'

Joe shrugged. 'Rae was her own woman. I never even saw her leave.'

'You any witnesses? Who saw you at the party after she left?'

'When did she leave?'

Kerley shook his head wearily. 'You were a good cop once, Costello. Till the Cosmo Vass enquiry. Then something must've went snap in your brain.'

'Yeah, you took me off the case.'

'Me?'

'Yes, you. Bum-tonguer Kerley. You used your influence with the CI, had him withdraw me from the investigation. You've been after me ever since the day I caught you juicing the tom.'

'That's always been your problem, Costello, you're too fucking righteous. You think I was the only cop on her slate? Christ, half the bloody squad were dipping their wicks, and you had to make a show out of me. So 'course I used my influence, 'course I got you removed from the case. And you know what? When I saw you go down, I laughed. I laughed myself sick.'

'You always were sick.'

'Sick, maybe, but not bent.' He paused to unwrap a stick of gum and slot it in his mouth while his eyes swept back and forth among the huddles of overcoated mourners still congregated by the line of cars. 'Something's going on here, Costello. I know it, and you know it. Rae Connell did not die by accident. When they fished her out of the reservoir, she was still wedged in the passenger seat.'

'You've dredged the reservoir?'

'For the driver?' Kerley sighed impatiently. 'We both know the score on that.'

'If not an accident,' Joe asked, 'what then?'

'Murder?' With a hopeful glance at Joe.

'Why not misadventure?'

'Because murder has a better ring to it. Especially if you consider all the evidence.'

'You've started using evidence?'

The detective dismissed Joe's comment with a curl of his blood-less lips. 'Evidence such as the two sets of car-tracks, the damage to the rear of the Metro and the flecks of paint we found on the bumper, the broken headlight glass, the single set of footprints we found climbing the bank, the two sets of footprints we found at the top of the bank, the anonymous phone call that called us out . . . what more do you want?'

'You off my back.'

'One day, Costello. When you're back behind bars.'

'You don't want to hear my alibi?'

Kerley's smile was less than gracious. 'Yeah. I heard you managed to find one. Something about a fight at the party.'

'It's all a little hazy,' Joe said, returning the smile.

'I bet. But awfully convenient though. I mean, if it wasn't for the fight, I'd swear you looked like a man who just stepped out of a car-wreck. Strange, isn't it?'

'You're trying to tell me something.'

'Give the boy a great big hand.' Kerley switched on the ignition and turned the heater on full. 'A bit of friendly advice, that's all, from one side of the thin blue line to the other.'

'What's a few convictions between friends, eh?'

Kerley scowled. 'The DCI reckons you're trying to play the hero and clear your name. Me, I don't give a shit. I think you're guilty as hell, and just hope I'm there when they finally haul you in. Because all the sympathy you have on the force is not going to help you one little bit if I find your arse in shit. You know what I mean?'

'I didn't know you cared.'

'I don't.'

'So why're you here?'

'I like funerals. They remind me of my childhood.' The detective pulled on his Rally-style driving-gloves and started the car. 'Tell me,' he said. 'A question I've had at the back of my mind every time I hear your name. Why her eyes, Joe, why shoot out her eyes?'

Before Joe could reach him, the car shot away.

'Read about it in the papers, you said,' Rankine sneered, tossing the paper on to Billy's lap. Again he winced in pain as he drew in breath, and wondered briefly if he should call his doctor; it had been like this since he awoke first thing this morning. But he shrugged the thought aside; there were more important things on his mind. 'Okay – so show me. I must have overlooked it the fifty thousand times I've read it already.'

Billy ignored him. He was concentrating on the black-clad mourners congregated in small groups by the row of glistening black hire-cars. He swept the binoculars back and forth, searching for a face he recognised.

'Leave it to Billy, you said.' Rankine sat huddled in his overcoat in the corner, cocooned in hat, scarf and gloves. The Rolls was pulled off the road a quarter of the way along the circular drive, Rankine and Billy in the back, Eddie the chauffeur ensconced behind the smoked-glass partition.

Billy sat up straight, focusing on the man descending the slope who wore tinted shades beneath his trilby. 'The man himself,' he said, 'Jay Johnstone.'

'What's he doing?' Rankine suddenly just as alert.

'Getting in his car.'

'Is Costello with him?'

'Look,' Billy said, 'I told you not to worry. Just because there's no mention of the pasta-gnasher in the papers doesn't mean he's still alive, Jackie-boy – they just ain't found his body yet. Take my word for it, he's just one more fucking pollutant in our drinking water. Probably lying at the bottom of the loch with his eyes bugged out.'

'I wish I could believe it.'

'You will.' Billy followed the progress of Johnstone's Porsche along the drive until it disappeared through the tall wrought-iron gates, before resuming his observation of the mourners. He said, 'Christ, and the polis, too . . .'

'Where?'

'In the blue Escort . . . see? Talking to some guy – looks like another cop – bent down by the window.'

'Let me see.' Rankine grabbed the binoculars, trained them on the Escort. The images leapt towards him. What could the police want here? he thought. Rae Connell's death had been reported as an accident, so why the presence? Then he saw the driver's face and relaxed. Kerley. Good. The man was doing as he'd been told. But the other man talking to Kerley with his back to the binoculars – who was he? Why the long earnest conversation? And there was something about the man's stance which disturbed him; was somehow familiar? Or the shape of the head, and the way it . . . His attention was suddenly attracted by an even more familiar form making its way slowly down the steps.

'So, Mr Wylie,' he muttered, 'we meet again.'

'The private dickhead?' Billy grabbed back the binoculars.

Rankine's breath laboured up his throat like an old woman carrying her shopping upstairs. He said between gasps, 'I don't like it, Billy, I don't like it. I thought you warned him off.'

'Fear fades,' Billy said, 'as fast as broken bones mend. Maybe I ought to have another wee word with him, remind him of those two happy months he spent in hospital. What d'you say, Jackie-boy?'

'I still don't like it,' Rankine repeated. His skin began to crawl beneath a sudden prickly sweat. He flicked the intercom switch. 'What's with the heater, Eddie?' he demanded. 'It's like a fucking sauna back here.'

'Sorry, sir.'

Rankine loosened his scarf and opened the window, gulping in the cool, fresh air like a long-distance swimmer.

Billy nudged him and said, 'Look at the slob – he's drinking from a hipflask now. Can't even wait till he gets to his car.' He turned to Rankine. 'And you're worried about him? A guy who can't walk fifty yards without sucking on a bottle?'

'So what's . . . what's he doing there?' Concentrating on his breathing, having to force the words out.

'How the hell do I know?' Billy took up the binoculars again. 'Maybe he's a hearse-chaser now. Who cares?'

Rankine rummaged about in the built-in drinks cabinet below the TV, the effort bringing runnels of sweat to his brow. Maybe he had left some pills there, in case of an emergency. His trembling hands scrabbled among the bottles. He watched two of them fall, as though in slow-motion, and roll across the floor. As he bent to retrieve them his vision clouded red. He groaned. Blood hammered in his ears. Something heavy, and ominously vague, fluttered in his chest as his breath rasped ragged through teeth clenched tight. Palpitations. The doctor had mentioned palpitations. *Tachycardia.* Runaway heart. Nothing too serious.

If you happen to be in Intensive Care.

'Billy?'

Billy wasn't listening. He was leaning through the window watching the man in the rumpled suit talking to the cop in the car. Then the man straightened up and walked away as the cop drove off. The man walked towards Wylie, his face suddenly larger than life in the binoculars. Instantly recognisable. 'No,' Billy groaned. 'It can't be.'

Rankine was doubled over, clutching his chest, fighting for breath. 'Billy . . .'

'Costello,' Billy hissed, oblivious, his attention still fixed on the two men now watching the Escort make its way slowly down the drive. 'The fucker's still alive.'

The name hit Rankine like an electric shock, jerking him back against the seat, eyes abulge. His bluish-grey lips moved soundlessly as spittle dribbled down his beard. The world seemed to crash about his ears. Something punched him in the chest, something hot, something hard, crushing him in its vicelike grip, twisting him like a rag, squeezing, churning, mashing every jangling, vibrant nerve in his body. He could not move. He could not speak. He could not breathe.

As though from a great distance, and through rose-tinted eyeballs, he saw Billy slowly turn and stare.

Smiling.

CHAPTER 14

Returning home from the wake, Joe asked Andrea to turn into the gates of the Royal Edinburgh Hospital. That is, if she wasn't in a hurry to get home.

'Hurry to get home for what?' she said with scarcely concealed bitterness. She pulled smartly into a space in the carpark and, killing the engine, shot him an awkward smile. 'Would you like me to wait or are you signing yourself in?'

'Come along if you want,' Joe said. 'Meet the father of my sins.'

'He's in here?'

'He was last week.'

Andrea nodded towards the back of the car. 'What about him?'

Wilberforce Wylie lay sprawled across the seat with his pudgy pink hands clasping a hipflask possessively to his belly. He was snoring loudly.

Joe said, 'What about him?' and walked towards the entrance.

Andrea caught up. Joe led the way down the anonymous corridors of the Andrew Duncan Clinic, heading for the shop in the main part of the hospital. As they walked, they passed a seemingly endless stream of harassed-looking nurses and whistling porters weaving through a continuous procession of bowed and slipper-shuffling patients. In the shop, Joe bought a box of Jaffa Cakes and a six-pack of Penguins.

'Are you hungry?' Andrea asked.

'Not me. My old man.'

'Where is he?'

Joe glanced at his watch. 'Right now, he'll be upstairs by the lift, waiting for the food trollies to arrive.'

'You know your way around,' Andrea observed, as they waited for the lift.

'I worked here once,' Joe said, 'on a case. Back when I was a Det Con, still wet behind the ears. It was my first ever capture – a guy they called the Night Prowler.'

'One of the patients?'

'We thought so at first. But then he turned out to be one of the night-shift doctors.'

Andrea shuddered. 'It makes you think, doesn't it?'

It certainly does, he told her. The Night Prowler had been terrorising the hospital for weeks, dressed in black right down to the slit-eyed ski-mask, preying on the night-shift nurses, dragging them into darkened recesses and empty corridors at knifepoint, forcing them to suck on his rock before taking all their clothes and making off. Joe had been one of a team of detectives assigned to the case, had spent each night dressed as a porter, patrolling the corridors, polishing floors, collecting rubbish, hanging round the all-night canteen, checking doors and windows, chatting up the nurses.

One nurse especially.

Doreen, from County Armagh. She worked in Ward 10, the security ward where they hold the criminally insane awaiting trial. A woman with a sparkle in her eyes to set any cold man's heart on fire. Married, though, with two kids, and a husband in oil. No matter. Joe had been happy to follow her around and share the laughter in her eyes. Until one night he was walking her back to her ward from the ADC and asked her to wait while he went to the gents. And came out two minutes later to see her feet being dragged round a corner.

'So what happened?' Andrea asked, as they entered the lift.

Joe punched the first floor button and the lift doors closed. 'The guy resisted arrest. And after the trial, Doreen never spoke to me again. Too much violence in me, she said.'

'Was she right?'

'At the time, maybe yes.'

The doors opened and there he was, Aldo Costello. A slight man with thinning grey hair, long at the back. Dark eyes shadowed by a craggy brow. Sunken cheeks. Grey slacks, pink shirt, long cardigan and faded leather slippers.

'Biscuits!' he said. 'Just what I like. Biscuits.'

'Hi, Dad.'

'And Jaffa Cakes, too.'

Joe handed them over. 'This is Andrea, Dad.'

Aldo peered and Andrea smiled.

'What does she want?'

'She drove me here.'

'You forgot how to drive?' Aldo studied the box of Jaffa Cakes as though it was counterfeit.

'She's a friend.'

'She a cop, too?'

'I told you, Dad—'

'Dad nothing. Two years you don't visit. Nothing.'

'I was here last week but you wouldn't see me. Remember?'

'The *boys* wouldn't see you.'

'They don't like cops either?'

'They don't eat cops.'

'Can't we sit, Dad?' Behind him, the lift-doors closed.

'Going down,' Aldo said, checking his watch. Then, 'Sit and what?'

'Talk.'

'Talk about what?' Aldo glanced suspiciously at Andrea.

'Things. You know. What fathers and sons are supposed to talk about. Family.'

'The day you put on that uniform, you disgraced the family.'

'*You're* my only family, Dad.'

'So me you disgraced.' Aldo cocked his head and listened as the lift returned. 'My own son a fascist. Wearing the same cop uniform they wore the day they dragged us away, your own family. Huh.'

'I told you already, Dad – I'm not a cop any more. I'm just me, your son.'

'Once a cop, always a cop.'

'Like once a father, always a father?'

The lift arrived and a bearded kitchen porter pushed a loaded food-trolley out into the corridor.

'Food,' Aldo said, licking his lips. 'I have to go.'

With that, he turned and followed the trolley towards the ward at the end of the corridor.

Andrea looked at Joe, eyebrows raised.

'Quick visit,' she said.

'That,' Joe told her, 'was one of the longer ones.'

After dropping off Wylie at his flat on the Pleasance, Joe asked Andrea if she'd mind driving back across town to his Easter Road flat to pick up some much-needed clothes.

It felt strange.

As though by mistake he'd entered someone else's private little world. One to which he could no longer relate. He thought of what Rae had told him the morning of the party, about the flat being a museum-piece, a shrine to people he had never truly known nor would ever get to know. A prison.

He *had* changed, he realised, as he packed what few clothes he had into a small brown suitcase. Nothing momentous or palpable that he could put his finger on, just a growing sense within, that in the last few days he had turned an important corner in his life, and there was no turning back. Tomorrow night Jay Johnstone returned from Glasgow. They would talk. And Joe would listen – not the old Joe, but the new. Decisions would be made.

And somewhere along the line, a balance redressed.

Andrea was locked deep in thought on the journey home; she didn't speak until she had angled the car into the garage and switched off the engine. There was concern in her voice as she turned in her seat to study him.

'You're not planning anything stupid, are you, Joe?'

'Stupid?'

She cocked her head the way Johnstone often did, as though it helped her see more acutely the lies she clearly anticipated. Her eyes were moist, her composure cracking, her face like the wall of a dam about to break under pressure. 'Like revenge?' she said, her tone half-question, half-accusation.

'Hell no,' Joe told her, forcing a laugh as he shook his head. 'Sleep and more sleep is all I plan.'

She didn't seem convinced.

Coffin-black.

He sees his father's acne-pitted face, twisted in silent pain, float-ing towards him through the drifting fields of moonlit plankton. Mouthing the soundless words of an endless refrain. '*This is how they died. Beneath ice-cold waters in the midnight chill, this is how my parents died. This is how they died . . .'*

He can't breathe. Around him the water swirls, as cold as a dead man's heart. He feels only his aching lungs, bursting and about to rip.

He can't move. Is pinned to his seat, jammed against the steering wheel. The pressure increasing as the car pitches into darkness as deep as the sleep of the dead.

He is alone. Cut off from the rest of the world. His struggle for survival passes unnoticed. The final rejection.

He is blind, but for the flickering images that flash before his mind's eye. Images of leering faces, taunting; of loving faces, laughing. Nameless faces, hordes of them, passing like lustrous ghosts through dark rooms and prison cells, summer days and wintry nights, before disappearing back into the blackness from whence they came. Gone. He is alone again.

Ice.

Now he is ice. Can feel the creeping numbness steal away his strength, defraud his will to live. Engulfing him in a comforting sense of resignation. *Just breathe, Joe, breathe. One little breath to take all your cares away. One little breath . . .*

But somewhere deep inside still burns the fire of resistance. Fuelled by fear, fear and anger. Anger that someone should try to kill him, fear they might succeed.

Kill him?

Kill *them!*

Rae! He has forgotten . . . she is there, somewhere close in the darkness, slumped unconscious, water creeping up her nose and into her mouth. Already breathing water.

Panic takes control. Arms flail sluggishly in the current, numb fingers searching blindly in the dark. He tries to recall . . .

Impressions. Of the car's rolling tumble towards the water – embedded like shards of glass in his mind. Of Rae strapped into the passenger seat, being tossed like a piece of soggy lettuce, limp and unconscious. He touches something soft.

She is still in the seat beside him.

Suddenly the car jolts to a standstill, slamming him against the steering wheel, almost driving the breath from his body. He fights back the panic that will kill as quick as a greedy grab of breath. The noise in his ears at fever pitch, the pressure on his lungs unbearable.

Fire.

Now he is fire. Every nerve and fibre in his body ablaze. Demanding oxygen.

His fingers seek her face. Slip easily into her open mouth. Something fast, small and slimy wriggles out between his fingers, flashes away into darkness. He recoils in shuddering disgust.

Suddenly there is light. Twin beacons glowing softly in the gloom. Drawing him like a moth to source. His face passes through the seaweed of her hair. Still her eyes entice, sucking him closer. Her hands clasp the back of his head, guiding his lips to hers. They close. They kiss. Her breath, rank and cold, steals through his teeth like a thief in the night. It has the taste of a thousand years. He pulls away, repulsed. Her eyes, bulging white orbs, bore into his. She is telling him something. He doesn't understand. He wants to understand. But he is drowning. And she is dead.

Cell-dark.

He was sitting upright in bed, breathing hard, damp sheets clutched fiercely in his fists. Sweat stung his eyes, running in salty runnels to his mouth.

Disorientated.

Something rising from the pit of his stomach. A word. No, not a word – a name.

Footsteps echoed down the hall, the heavy ringing gait of the night screw doing his rounds, scuffing seps on the catwalk and swinging his keys. Slowing as he approached Joe's cell . . . stopping.

The name . . . whose name?

The door opened and Joe blinked in the sudden harsh light. Rae's voice soft and full of concern.

'Joe? Are you all right, Joe?'

She stood anxiously at the end of his bed.

'Joe?'

He squinted, blinking through the tears. 'Who . . . ? I thought . . .'

'I heard a yell, Joe.'

Not Rae. *Andrea*. Which meant . . .

'I heard you yell.' She came round the bed. 'I thought I better . . .'

Not a cell. A room.

'Andrea?'

'Yes, Joe. Are you okay?'

Was he?

'There was a name . . .' He didn't know how to finish.

'Just a nightmare, Joe. Don't worry. It's over now.'

'She kissed me. She was trying to tell me something, a name.'

Cool hand on his brow, caressing.

'Forget it, Joe, it's all over.'

But it would never be.

'I tried to pull her free but she was stuck. Her eyes were open, and there was something in her mouth. Trying to get out. I couldn't breathe. I had to get air. I pulled her arm but it . . . came away in my hands. I tried to . . . I tried . . .'

'We know you did, Joe. You did everything you could.'

'Her eyes, God, her eyes . . .'

'Forget them, Joe, you have nothing to fear. Go back to sleep now.'

'Sleep . . . yeah. Back to sleep.'

CHAPTER 15

Typical. Dodds was late. 'Meet you in the Reference Library at half-twelve,' he'd said, 'Don't be late.' It was now back of one and Grace was tired and bored and getting more pissed off with every passing minute. She'd been in the Central Library since it opened this morning, moving as she always did from room to room, exploring every little corner from basement to attic, pulling out books at random, searching for that special spark that would light the fire of her imagination and send her off on one more adventurous voyage of exploration through the archives. That was how she pictured herself, a valiant seeker of knowledge, a lone pioneer of the labyrinths, with a world of experience and endless possibilities at her fingertips. Although there were days when she resented being forced to return to the dull, predictability of mainstream life when the library closed, today was not one of those days. She felt uneasy, somehow threatened, yet couldn't put her finger on it.

It had been with her since the night of Jay Johnstone's party, the night she had gleefully torched the massage-parlour and burnt for ever the loathsome memories of the time spent working there. And there, she believed, amongst the dying embers and skeletal remains of the massage-parlour lay the cause of her unease: the damp, cool ashes of her need for revenge.

Perhaps that was it: now that her craving for retribution had been appeased, she felt hollow and drained. Soulless. In limbo. What she needed now was direction. A goal in life rather than a life in gaol.

Which meant cutting herself free from Dodds. Something easier said than done.

The Reference Library on the top floor was her favourite room. What she liked most was its airy sense of light and space, the high domed ceiling, the tall elegant arches and book-lined alcoves. She would spend the first hour or so prowling the alcoves in search of inspiration: inspiration which, more often than not, depended on her mood. Then, having found a title, she would carry the book to one of the tables in the centre of the room and begin her journey of discovery for the day. See where it took her.

Earlier this morning, for instance, she had spent exploring the General English History section; had found an interesting book there, entitled *A Dictionary of Superstitions*. In it she had discovered that you mustn't poke your neighbour's fire until you have known him seven years or been drunk with him three times. She would remember that.

Now, however, she was no longer in the mood. The place was almost too quiet, she thought. Term was over and the students had better places to be, hence the almost tangible silence that seemed to hang like a shroud from the high, ornate ceiling. A few of the tables around her were occupied, old men reading the *Financial Times*, academic types poring over leather-bound volumes, a Goth up front sleeping with his head on his hands, snoring.

She herself sat with her chin in her hands and watched the young librarian with the short fair hair and ever-so-serious eyes file away cards in the bank of drawers at the far end of the room. He wasn't that bad-looking either. A bit on the wimpy-intellectual side, perhaps, but he had a tidy wee bum encased in jeans tight enough to make her wonder. But as much as she had wondered, in the whole time she'd been there he had only looked at her once. Shy was not the word. And God, look at the shoes. Brogues. Brogues said more about a man than his dick in his hand. She sighed and returned her attention to the notepad in front of her, on which she had written a list of priorities. Visualise your needs, she had read somewhere, and they become easier to attain.

1 (a) Tell Dodds to take a running fuck.
  (b) Take his money first, then tell him it's over.
2 Find somewhere else to stay.
3 Become a nun.
4 Then pray for him to die in excruciating pain.

So many choices, she thought bitterly, she could hardly decide. She glanced up, startled, as the door at the far end crashed open, exploding the air of studious calm. She watched open-mouthed as Dodds staggered in and stood belligerently searching the glaring upturned faces. She buried her head and tried to hide behind her hands, but too late. His voice boomed and echoed across the cavernous room.

'Hey, doll!' he yelled, 'I'm home!'

Grace shrank as Dodds was shushed by a chorus of serious, puckered mouths. As usual he was impervious.

'Hey, Gra-cie!' he sang, 'Daddy's ho-ome!'

Grace grabbed together her belongings, stuffed them in her shoulder-bag and, fuming, strode stiffly between the tables, passing Dodds without a glance, taking the stairs two at a time. He came running out after her.

'Hey, don't tell me you're in a huff,' he said when he caught up.

She took the stairs three at a time.

'Okay, I'm late,' he said, 'I'm sorry.'

Grace stormed past the security desk, out on to the street.

'I couldn't help it, doll, I couldn't get away.'

Whining at her heels like a lovesick puppy.

She turned to confront him with balled fists clenching. 'You want to know the difference between you and a toilet, Dodds? Toilets don't follow me around after I use them.' She turned angrily on her heel and headed left towards the High Street, lunch-hour traffic heavy through the dirty grey ridges and rivers of slush, wind plucking at the blouse beneath her leather jacket.

'Look,' he said, catching up and grabbing her arm. 'I brought you the money.'

'And you're drunk again,' she hissed, pulling her arm free.

'I only had a couple,' he told her. 'Look, let's go for a drink and I can give you your money. That's what you want, isn't it?'

She wasn't too sure any more. 'Dodds, it's time we had a talk.'

'Sure, doll, whatever you want.' He pointed at the pub across the road, on the corner of the Mound and the High Street. 'How about Deacon Brodie's?'

They crossed at the lights, entered the pub and while Grace found the only vacant table upstairs by the window, Dodds elbowed his way through the crush at the bar.

The place was mobbed, a riotous assembly of office-workers

having their annual Christmas piss-up: party-hats and streamers, flying beer-mats and poppers, shrieks of laughter, song, and loud raucous cheers. Grace watched them smile and joke and rib one another in genuine camaraderie, and felt deep within her a sudden twinge of envy; wanting to belong, but knowing she never could.

Yet there was hope, she thought. The real Deacon Brodie – the inspiration for Robert Louis Stevenson's *Dr Jekyll and Mr Hyde*, and after whom the pub had been named – had managed to satisfy the demands and desires of both sides of *his* character: respected Deacon of Wrights and cabinet-maker by day, redoubtable burglar by night. Not for long, sure – he had died, ironically, on the same Tolbooth gallows whose drop he had improved only a short while before his arrest – but at least he had tried.

'Why the painful face, doll, something wrong?' Dodds set the drinks down on the table, pulled up a chair.

'I was thinking,' she said.

'Poor girl.' He gulped at his pint of lager, halving it in seconds. 'What about?'

'Dr Jekyll and Mr Hyde. How there's a bit of each of them in all of us.'

'You spend too much time in that library, doll, I think it's affecting your head.' Dodds leant back in his chair and surveyed the bar. A woman at the neighbouring table thrust a paper hat on his head and screeched with laughter. Dodds glowed like a kid and leaned towards her, giving her the patter. Grace turned to look out of the window and watch the punters wade through the swamps of slush on the High Street below.

Dodds, she thought, was a good example. A married man with two young daughters and a respectable job in a city-centre hotel, he had a Mr Hyde inside that liked to hurt: with words, feet or fists. All he needed was a few drinks to become that mean and snarling beast. You could watch the pints go down and almost see the dark hairs sprouting on the backs of his hands, see his mind submerge to its primordial form, an organ whose sole function was to procure satisfaction for the basest of his most ignoble instincts.

As it was trying to do now, with the bubble-headed blonde at the next table. Suddenly Grace decided she'd had enough. She gathered her bag and rose to her feet. Dodds looked guiltily round.

'Hey, doll, don't go,' he said. 'I was just being friendly.' He reached in his pocket and withdrew an envelope which he tossed magnanimously on the table.

'Count it,' he said, 'it's all there.'

She did, and it was. She put it carefully away in her bag.

'You going to smile now?' Dodds asked. 'Show your old man how happy you are to see him?'

'You ever do that to me again and I swear to God I'll burn your house down.'

'Wassamatter, doll?'

'You.'

''Cos I'm a wee bit late? Christ, grow up, will you. This is the big picture we're living in now, a grown-up's world with grown-up problems. You think you have it hard, you don't know nothing. I got problems right now would make your pubes turn grey. Hey, sit down, doll, for Christ's sake.'

She obeyed, but remained perched on the edge of her seat, bag on her lap, ready for flight.

'That's better.' Dodds patted her hand. 'This guy, Billy, I was telling you about? A fucking nut-case. The whole thing's getting out of order. I mean, breaking a few legs here and there, I don't mind, but killing an innocent woman? I think maybe I'm outta my depth, doll, way out.'

Grace wasn't sure she heard it right. She leant across the table and hissed: 'What d'you mean, killing an innocent woman?'

Dodds seemed startled, sobering up immediately. 'Did I say that? I don't think I did.'

'I heard you. You said—'

'A slip of the tongue, doll, forget it.' Dodds gulped at his pint, then hastily continued. 'I was telling you about Billy, this wide-boy partner of the boss's I got to work with. Real name's William P. McCulloch, but his friends call him bastard. Flew in last week from the Costa del Fuck-knows-what, all black suits, suntan and shades . . . and guess who has to go meet him at the airport? Yours bloody truly.' He glanced at Grace to see if she was keeping up.

She said, 'William P. McCulloch – what's the P. stand for?'

'How the hell would I know? Anyway. So there I am, driving back into town and suddenly the next thing I know, I've got a knife in my neck and this guy climbing the wall in my ear, telling me what a big-shot he is and how if I mess around with him I'm going to end up worse than sliced salami. Then he tells me to pull over. So what do I do? I pull over. He gets out and says, "wait here," and then goes into this off-licence while I sit wondering what the hell I should do, cos the boss has told me

113

to watch this guy every step of the way and not let him out of my sight.'

'There a moral to this story?' Grace yawned with great exaggeration.

'You want to wait till I'm finished?' Dodds, serious now, and frowning. 'Where was I? Right. So I decide to stick with the crazy and follow him into the offie just in time to see him open a can of Special and drain it. The guy behind the counter, a fat guy with more chins than hairs on his head, starts flapping and squawking, saying he hopes Billy's going to pay for the can he's just about finished. Billy just looks at him and says, "Fuck no." Then he opens another can, takes a couple a swigs, puts it down and picks up another can. By this time the fat guy's popping eyes all over the shop and threatening to call the polis. So Billy opens another can and says cool as you like, "See here, porkie, it says on the label *10% extra FREE*." He says, "They put FREE like that in extra-big letters so slugs like you can fucking see it." He says, "So that's what I'm doing, porkie, I'm taking my FREE 10%. And if you want to argue about that I'm going to come round that counter and cut your fucking nose off." Then he picks up a four-pack and wanders out. And that's Billy for you, doll, the kind of problem I could well do without.'

Grace yawned again. 'So why don't you trash him,' she said, 'like you did that woman?'

Dodds reached across the table, grabbed her wrist and squeezed until she gasped. He said, 'I'm going to tell you something, doll, which you're going to keep to yourself or end up the same way she did. Am I getting through?'

Grace winced beneath the pain but said nothing.

'Good,' Dodds said. 'Because I want you to understand it had nothing to do with me. It was an accident. It was Billy, trying to be the big-shot. We just wanted to warn this guy but things got out of hand, and the woman . . . Christ, doll, d'you think *I* like it?'

Grace tried to summon up the courage. Listening to Dodds's monologue she had already made up her mind. She had all the words ready, the right words. But now he was saying he'd been party to a murder. Laying his guilt off on her. A secret shared suddenly becoming one more chain to tie her down. Realising now that he would never let her go. That knowledge kills.

Dodds said, 'I can't stop thinking about her, doll – she's on my mind from the moment I wake till the moment I sleep. I get nightmares. I wake up sweating. I've started drinking first thing in the morning. Even that don't make it go away. Doll, help me will you? Say you believe me. Please?'

Grace stood up and shouldered her handbag. 'I need a pee,' she said.

'But you do believe me?'

'Sure, don't worry. I'll be back in a sec.'

Two minutes later she came out of the Ladies and ran down the stairs. No more, that was definitely it, end of story. Dodds wanted to get involved in murder, that was his problem, not hers. They had conspiracy laws these days that could put her away for years. Accessory after the fact. Failing to report a crime. Lock her away in Cornton Vale and throw away the key. Christ, what a fool she'd been.

She was almost through the door to the street when Dodds's heavy hand on her shoulder swung her around. His mean eyes blazed.

'Going somewhere, doll?'

'I feel sick,' she stammered, 'need some air.'

His fingers dug painfully into the side of her neck. 'You were running out on me, doll.'

'I wasn't, Dodds, honest!' A cry broke from her lips as his grip tightened on her neck. Pinpoints of light shimmered across her blurring vision.

'The truth, doll.'

'Okay, I was, I was!'

'That's better.' He loosened his grip, his smile as tight as a rubber band about to snap. 'Now, you were saying?'

Her words clambered out over struggling breath. 'It's over, Dodds, we're finished. Go back to your wife.'

'You can't do this, doll, I won't let you.' His eyes struggled for focus as his fat lips trembled. 'You and me, we're a thing, till death us do part.'

'Or at least till your wife finds out. You want me to give her a call, let her know what's been going on these last few months?'

She gasped as his fingers again bit deep into her neck.

'You don't understand, doll,' he whined. 'I need you.'

Something snapped inside her head. Enough was enough. With all the force she could summon, she brought her knee up hard between his legs. 'No,' she said, as he collapsed writhing and moaning to the floor, 'I kneed you.'

She turned and pushed through the door and emerged gratefully on to the street where there was air and light and what pathos there was was aseptic and clean and packaged in lies she could swallow with ease and just as soon forget. She waved down a floating taxi.

'Where to, love?'

'Anywhere,' she said. 'Just the hell away from here.'

CHAPTER 16

J oe Costello awoke late and confused, sunlight dappling the curtains, at first wondering where he was, then why he was there. He lay for a while listening to the strange sounds of the unfamiliar house, allowing his jumbled thoughts the time to assemble. Somewhere from the depths of the house came the sound of a Hoover, while outside, steel rasped on tarmac as someone shovelled snow from the drive.

Andrea called it The Pentland Room. She had put him in there because of the subtle shades of green and mauve: they aided convalescence, she said. It was a light and spacious L-shaped room, almost a self-contained flat, with a small, open-plan kitchen-area and bar-top forming the base of the L. Most of the furniture was pine, and the pictures on the walls were pastel scenes of the Pentland Hills in summer. A week ago Joe could've stood at the south-facing windows for hours, letting his mind ramble free as he looked out over the rolling hills. Now, however, he could look out and see only the shadows of memories too dark to contemplate.

He climbed laboriously from bed and, after rummaging through various kitchen cupboards, breaking a tea-cup, spilling half a carton of milk on the floor and stubbing his toe, eventually broke his fast on a cafetière of Javanese coffee.

Someone had slipped a note under his door. He fetched it on limbs that creaked and groaned like the deck of an ancient galleon. Andrea. She had gone into town, would be back later in the afternoon. If he needed anything, he was to just ask the maid, Janine.

Maids and all, he thought. La-di-da.

He poured a second cup of coffee and, in bare feet and dressing-gown, made his way along the numerous corridors and downstairs. He lost his way only once.

The maid Janine was in the main kitchen, slaving over a hot crossword. She jumped when he entered, almost biting through the pencil between her teeth.

'Oh!' she cried. 'You shocked us something awful!' She was a plump, full-breasted woman in her forties, with a wide, fleshy mouth in a kind, round face. Blushing, she wiped her hands on her apron, then held one out. 'You must be Joe.'

Joe wasn't going to argue. He shook her warm, doughy hand and asked where the swimming-pool was.

'Better follow me,' she said with a smile, and led him out through the scullery and down the back stairs, then along a plain, whitewashed corridor to a door at the far end. It came out beneath the gallery bar overlooking the pool, where Joe and Wylie had had their little falling-out.

'You'll find trunks and towels in the cubicle at the far end,' Janine said, 'and I switched the sauna on earlier, just in case. That's it over there, the pine door with the small window.'

Joe thanked her and she scurried away.

The surface of the pool was like a sheet of plate-glass. He found a selection of trunks in the cubicle and pulled on the least garish, a pair of lime-green boxers. As he did so, he studied himself in the full-length mirror.

His whole body, it seemed, was a battlefield of cuts and ripening bruises that ached and burned and throbbed every time he so much as breathed. The old bruises, shades of grey – the fresh ones, shades of purpled black. His face was almost unrecognisable: left eye almost closed, the skin of his right cheek grazed, both lips cut and swollen. His jaw was stubbled with five days' growth and felt like something wooden nailed to the bottom of his head. Movement was slow and painful.

Beyond the glassed walls the world appeared as crisp and brittle as china. Skeletal trees reached out of the crusted snow towards the glazed blue sky where the pale disk of the midday sun hung shimmering. Like Joe, too weak even to cast a shadow.

He dived into the pool. The first few lengths he swam like a rusted wreck, his muscles screaming in protest at every tortured move he made. He concentrated only on propelling his body successfully from end to end. Twenty minutes later, he lay gasping on the tiles like a beached whale. Then, on legs of rubber, he staggered the length of the pool to the sauna. There, stretched on pine, he simmered, sweating the poison from his pores. Fatigue rolled in on waves, crashing on the shores of his consciousness. Eventually, he submerged into a sleep, once more turgid with dreams.

Awoke sometime later to the touch of hands moving softly on his back.

He existed only beneath the pressure of her fingers.

'Why the police?' Andrea asked. They were in the gym, a narrow, low room of mirrors and pine, tucked away below the gallery bar. A few weight-machines against one wall, an exercise-bar along the other; the third was thick plate-glass overlooking the garden. He lay face down on the padded bench, prisoner to her professional touch.

'The police?' It was hard to think. The last few days it seemed he had been waking from dream to dream, as though lost in a Dickian time-slip. 'I don't really know. It just seemed natural at the time.'

'How did your parents react?'

'My father? Like someone'd passed a few thousand volts through his brain.'

'And your mother?'

'She died when I was young.'

The pressure stopped. 'I'm sorry.' Then started again. Kneading the muscles at the base of his neck.

Joe said, 'The luck of the Costellos.' He watched Andrea in the mirrored wall as she concentrated on his spine with sure, professional hands.

'You make it sound like a curse.'

Luck, he had often thought – not least in those cold, dark hours of his incarceration – was as inherent in genes as the colour of one's eyes. The difference between good and bad luck dependent only on one's own perspective. A run of bad luck – examined closely in the midnight chill – can easily seem a curse.

'Sometimes that's how it seems.'

119

Beyond the plate-glass window powdery snowflakes fell in swirl-ing, disconnected eddies. Like one of those paperweights, Joe thought. First you shake it. Then you shake it again. When you get fed up shaking it, you take it apart to see how it works – and it's never the same again. Which, in a way, was like opening up the past to understand the present.

Andrea said, 'And your father's still not forgiven you.'

'Sometimes he has good days. When the moon is full.'

'Has he always lived here?'

'He was born here. His father came over in his teens with some French firm to work on the Forth rail bridge, and stayed on once the construction had finished. There was already quite a large Italian community here then and more opportunity for work than there was back home.'

'Do you remember your grandparents?'

Joe shook his head. 'They both died during the Second World War. My grandfather in the seas off Donegal, my grandmother of a broken heart.'

'They were interned?'

'Aye,' Joe said, 'You can imagine it, how dangerous they were: both in their sixties, with their son, Aldo, still in his pimply teens. Suddenly it seemed that running a couple of chip-shops down Leith was a severe threat to national security.'

'Did your father ever talk about those times?'

'For a while it was all he ever talked about. Watching his father die – squashed beneath tons of steel as the ship, crippled by torpedo, capsised – I'm not surprised. Spending God knows how long in the water before he was rescued, and then the rest of the war interned on the Isle of Man – I'm still not surprised. Then returning home after the war to find his mother had also died and that the family business no longer existed – well, what does surprise me is that he doesn't hate the people, the country that did this to him and his family.'

'Rae once mentioned something about a vendetta,' Andrea said. 'Bad blood between Rankine and your father . . .'

'You want to know why? Because it was Rankine who grassed his folks to the Special Branch when they began rounding up all the Italian nationals. I don't know all the ins and outs but I do know they were rivals even then. When the Edinburgh mobs took to the streets and started burning and looting Italian stores and res-taurants, it was the likes of Rankine who threw the first stones.'

Andrea said, 'All the time I knew him, Jack never once talked about his past. Like he was a spoiled child, over sensitive to criticism, possessive even about secrets no one wanted to know.'

'Like the fact he was more a fascist than ever would be the people he informed on. He told the police my grandparents were fascistoni, that the back of their shops were used for subversive purposes and that my father ran messages to other clandestine units. Can you believe that? I mean, my grandfather – who fought alongside the British in the first war and had the medals to prove it, an ardent Socialist and member of the Italian Anti-Fascist Federation – suddenly being interned as a Fifth Columnist?'

'And your grandmother as well?'

Joe's laugh was humourless. 'There were quite a few women and children who escaped internment – but not the Costellos. Rankine made sure of that. And when my father returned orphaned after the war it was only to find the family business gone, taken over by . . . you want to guess who?'

'I don't need to,' Andrea said, concentrating on her hands as they kneaded his back, working his muscles like a wedge of potter's clay. She asked what his father had done next.

Joe said his father never talked about the years following his return to the city; as though life for him only really began again when he met Joe's mother, Gabriella, who had come over after the war. They met at the dancing and were married six weeks later. By the time Joe was born they already owned a small chip-shop on the Southside and the flat on Easter Road. For the Costellos, things were looking up.

'Do you remember your mother at all?'

'The same way you remember a childhood dream, I suppose – more a sense of feeling than an actual visual memory. A good feeling, warm and . . .' Joe's voice trailed off into a groan as Andrea began to work on the minefield of bruises down his side.

'You said she died . . .'

'There was a fire one night, she was working late and was overcome by the smoke. When the frier went up, she didn't stand a chance. Later, when the inquiry into her death discovered certain fire regulations had been ignored, insurance was denied and my father's licence revoked. He became a twisted and broken man.'

'Did he blame that on Rankine, too?'

'Of course. But again, maybe with just cause. Although my father would never substantiate his claims, I've heard since that when the business began losing money, there were rumours of extortion and intimidation, and that was about the same time Rankine stepped in and offered to buy my father out. Next thing you know, the place is up in flames.'

'Sounds familiar,' Andrea said.

'Doesn't it.'

'When it comes to apportioning blame, Rankine and your father seem to have a lot in common.'

'Yeah?' Joe raised himself to his elbows. It took effort. He felt like a piece of used chewing-gum stuck to the bench. 'Rankine sits secure in his penthouse suite while my father ploughs a frenzied furrow along a psychiatric ward corridor?'

'Mm,' she said, her fingernail absently tracing a soft circle around a pale crescent-shaped scar on his back. 'And you, Joe? Do you harbour desires for revenge?'

'I thought I would come out of Saughton,' he said, 'and that would be it, end of story. Make a new life for myself free from the chains of the past. But some people just never let go. They want you to pay and pay and pay.'

'Don't I know it,' Andrea murmured, as somewhere far off a telephone rang. 'Relax,' she added, 'it's probably only Jay. Phoning from some plush hotel in Glasgow while his secretary takes something down.'

'In shorthand?'

Andrea smiled. 'She'd need a very short hand, I assure you.'

The phone continued to ring.

Joe said, 'It might be important.'

'You're right,' she said with heavy sarcasm. 'Executive orders from the man at the top: don't pack the Union Jack swimming-trunks, pack the tartan ones. Policy decisions of national importance: don't forget the suntan oil and the kingsize pack of condoms.'

'You're going away?'

'He didn't tell you?'

'Maybe he meant to tonight,' Joe said, swinging his feet to the floor, stretching. 'He said he wanted to talk.'

'Which means he'll probably offer you another job. He doesn't give up easily.'

Joe asked where they were going.

'Skiathos,' she told him. 'We go every year, sometimes for a week, sometimes less.' Sighing heavily, she added: 'But mostly it depends how long we can stand each other's company.'

122

'Greece, huh? Lucky for some. Is it hot?'

'Sometimes it's kind of warm. Once, I think, they even had snow.'

'Just once? Lucky bastards. When do you go?'

'Jay's got some kind of heavy meeting tomorrow, potential investors flying in from God knows where to look over plans and maybe sign a contract or two. If all goes well, we'll fly out in the evening, change at Gatwick.'

'You don't like Christmas here?'

'Jay doesn't.'

'You mean all the goodwill is too much for him?'

Andrea smiled for a second time but shook her head. 'I think it's probably because he's an orphan.'

'He is?'

'Mm.'

'Lucky bastard.'

Jay chalked his cue with the air of a professional and said: 'Watch this, Joe, you might learn something. Black into that pocket there, and see how I screw the cue ball back off the cushion with a little left side and bottom to set me up for that easy red into the corner. Here goes . . .'

The cue-ball leapt off the table and rolled across the floor, coming to a halt between the drinks cabinet in the shape of a globe and the deep and faded red leather sofa.

Jay said, 'And that's what happens if there's chalk on the cue-ball: you get a little kick. If this was a professional game, I'd've called the referee over and had him clean the ball before I took my shot. As it is, I'll just take it again. Okay?'

Why not? It was his table. Joe yawned, returned the ball to Jay.

'Hey, Joe? I'm not boring you, am I?' Jay didn't look up as he prepared to take the pot again, sighting along the cue.

Joe yawned again. It was his own fault. Andrea had warned him, 'He doesn't talk business at the table. No, soon as he's finished throwing food down his throat, he'll say something he's seen in one of those pompous old films – like, *What say we gentlemen retire to the study for port and cigars while the lady of the house gets on with her work.* Wait and see, Joe – he'll probably even challenge you to a game of snooker.'

Which is exactly what happened.

This time the cue-ball stayed on the table but caught too much of the black, sending it ricocheting off the side cushion to split the pack of reds.

Jay shook his head ruefully. 'I must be losing my touch. A few years ago, I'd've cleared the whole table from a position like that. You want a shot?'

Joe leant over the table, pocketed an easy red, followed it with the black, coming back up the table for a long red over the corner pocket but playing it safe, dragging the cue-ball back to nestle against the top cushion. Jay looked on in open-mouthed silence, his dark frown deepening as the muscles twitched in his neck.

Jay said, 'Aye, well that's enough of that, I think. How about we get down to business before the wife comes moping in? I hear she gave you a massage this afternoon.' He threw Joe a long, piercing glance. 'You still okay?'

Joe replaced his cue in the rack. 'She's got good hands,' he said.

Johnstone cocked his head and nodded thoughtfully. 'Mm,' he said, holding Joe's gaze, letting the silence say all the things he dared not voice. Then he smiled and crossed to the drinks cabinet. 'But if you want hands that know what they're doing, come down to Feelings and try some of the girls there. I'm talking *real* massage, Joe, where anything goes. And for you it's a freebie, on the house.'

'The kind of place they smear Raspberry Ripple all over your body and lick it off?'

Jay looked up from mixing his drink. 'You've been there?'

'I bust a place like it once. Could've opened up an ice-cream parlour, the amount of chocolate topping they had. Banana splits, a speciality.'

'I keep forgetting. You must have bust a lot of places.'

'At least two of yours. You don't remember?'

'A cop's a cop – who looks at faces?' Jay held up his glass. 'You want one?'

Joe shook his head.

Jay said, 'You don't drink, you don't like parties, what the hell do you like? Girls?'

'I prefer women.'

'Yeah? Well, we all have problems. Me, I like a bit of fresh meat for my rotting vegetables.'

'I like a woman I can talk to.'

'Talk to? What the fuck for? Gag 'em and shag 'em, that's what I say.' Johnstone tasted his drink, nodded appreciatively. 'You want me to fix you up while we're away? Send along a wee festive chicken to warm your Christmas cockles?'

'I'll be busy enough.'

'You're not thinking of doing anything stupid, I hope. Like going after Rankine alone.'

Joe shrugged.

'Because I've got all the trouble I need,' Jay continued, 'without getting mixed up in another fucking murder investigation.' Jay set his glass down on the edge of the snooker-table, scooped up the black-ball. 'See that, Joe? That's a crystal ball and it's showing your future – the way things stand right now. You need all the help you can get.'

'Meaning what?'

'Work for me.'

'You're offering me Rae's job?'

'You think you could handle it?'

'No.'

'Nor do I. You're not that kind of guy, Joe. Nine-to-five, sitting behind a desk shuffling papers, that's not your *forte*. It's why you became a cop, right?'

'I liked the uniform.'

'Sure you did. And the unsociable hours and shite pay.'

'There's more to life than money.'

'There is? Why didn't anyone tell me?'

'You were probably in a meeting.' Joe rose wearily and crossed to the window where a sallow moon in an inky sky cast indistinct shadows across the sloping snow-banked lawn. Without turning, he asked, 'If not Rae's job, what job?'

'What you're good at. Protecting the innocent from the forces of evil.'

Joe turned back to the room. 'You want a bodyguard?'

'You think that's funny? After what happened to Rae?'

Joe was trying to imagine throwing himself in front of bullets aimed at Jay.

He said, 'Money can't buy you life, Jay. I doubt you have enough to put even a deposit on mine.'

Jay sighed and shook his head. 'Shit, if only Rae could hear this. Joe, do me a favour. Look around you, use your eyes.'

Joe looked around, using his eyes. He saw a room full of

cliché. Dark oak panelling and book-lined walls, and a wide mahogany desk by the window. A deep-pile burgundy carpet and crushed-velvet drapes. Paintings in oil, in elaborate frames: of fat ugly bastards on sleek white horses; of ashen-faced matriarchs, haughtily unamused. Subdued lighting and artful shadows. Around the crackling log-fire, worn leather armchairs deep enough to lose your arse in. And, as centre-piece, the full-size snooker-table, green baize bathing in the splash of the low, overhead light. All that was missing was the moosehead on the wall.

'Well?' Jay said. 'Can you see it?'

'See what?'

'Money. Anywhere you care to look, that's what you're looking at.'

'Image,' Joe said, 'is all I can see. The *colour* of money.'

Jay looked hurt, vulnerable. As people who surround themselves materially do, when their costly defences are breached by the unimpressed.

'What I'm saying, Joe, is humour me. Name your price. Think about it over Christmas and give me an answer when I get back.' Johnstone's tone was one that Joe hadn't heard before, one he couldn't immediately place. But coupled with the bovine look in the businessman's eyes, Joe suddenly understood: he was trying to say please.

Joe shrugged and said he'd give it some thought.

Johnstone pulled out his wallet, extracted a thick wad of notes, slapped it down on the snooker-table. 'Call it a retainer, Joe, no strings attached. Go on, take it – if not for my sake, for Rae's.'

Joe hefted the wad in his hands. A thousand, maybe two. 'For Rae, then,' he said, and pocketed the money without bothering to count it.

'Good man.' Johnstone rounded his desk and flicked through a large appointments diary until he found what he was searching for. 'One last thing, Joe. The polis. Detective named Kerley. You know him?'

'We've met.'

'After the funeral, so Wylie said. What did he want?'

'He said he liked funerals and couldn't wait for mine.'

Johnstone nodded pensively. 'Because he's been sniffing around Posers the last few days, asking a lot of pointed questions – mostly concerning you. Is there something going on I don't know about?'

126

'I got him into trouble once, that's all. He's just got a long memory.'

'Wylie also said it was Kerley who had you removed from the Cosmo Vass murder inquiry.'

'For a drunken PI, Wylie suddenly seems to know a whole lot about everything.'

'And you, Joe? What do you know that you're not telling?'

There it was again, that piercing, hungry shark-eyed look that was supposed to send him into spasms of fear. Joe shook his head and smiled wryly, then crossed to the window and peered up at the moon. Johnstone, however, was not about to give up.

He said, 'How about the fact that it was Kerley who was first on the scene after Rankine discovered his daughter dead in your flat? Or the fact that he was the one who discovered the money under the floorboards? Or the fact that he was the arresting officer and one of the main prosecution witnesses at your trial? These little coincidences ever cross your mind, Joe?'

'A thousand times a day, every day I spent inside.'

'And?'

'And nothing.'

'Keeping that famous open mind of yours, Joe?'

'Why don't you ask Wylie, if he knows so much?'

'I did. And you know what he said? He said Kerley's in Rankine's pocket, has been for years.'

'Give the dog a bone.'

Johnstone looked hurt, sad-dog eyes widening behind his blue-tinted shades. He paced up and down behind his desk for a minute, head bowed by the weight of thought, then seemed to physically pull himself together. 'You know what I think, Joe?' he said eventually. 'I think we better let things cool off over the Christmas period. Not give anyone the excuse to do something rash.'

'You're the boss.'

'Now that's what I like to hear.'

CHAPTER 17

Billy hammered on the door, the sound echoing across the deserted street.

'Just talk to her?' Dodds asked, concern tugging at the corners of his eyes and mouth.

'Isn't that what I said?'

'Aye, but—'

'Aye but nothing. Just a few friendly words, that's all. Put her in the picture.'

They stood outside a derelict-looking house on a derelict street of a derelict scheme, stamping their feet as they waited, surrounded by darkness and silence. The night was cool and sharp, the sky clear and moonlit, the snow crackling beneath their feet.

'No one home.' Billy peered suspiciously at Dodds. 'And you said she'd be here.'

'Maybe she just popped out,' Dodds suggested with little conviction.

'And took your brains along for the ride, no doubt.' Billy pounded the door again. Nothing. No sound from within, no sign of light escaping around the boarded-up windows. 'Let's try the back.'

Billy led the way, placing his feet cautiously as he skirted the building, careful to avoid the broken concrete slabs and rusted fence-posts sticking out like jagged spears from the twisted wire-net fence. Moonlight splashed on a jungle of bin-bags, weeds and broken slate. The back door rattled on its hinges when he knocked.

He turned to Dodds. 'Kick it in.'

Dodds hesitated. For a moment it seemed he was about to argue, then with a shrug and a sigh, he launched himself at the door. The lock burst at the first attempt and Dodds went sprawling inside. Billy walked past him into the hall, flicked a light switch. Nothing happened.

'So what does she do, eat a ton of carrots each day or what?'

'Candles,' Dodds said, picking himself up, dusting himself down. 'In the room at the front.'

'Candles, eh?' Billy felt his way along the hall until he came to a door. It swung open to his touch. He nodded Dodds through and a few moments later a match flared. Soon the room flickered in a candlelit glow as shadows swayed across the walls.

'Cosy,' Billy said, 'I don't think. What's upstairs?'

'More of the same big nothing.'

'So check it anyway.'

Dodds took one of the candles and lumbered out of the room. Billy heard his heavy tread tentatively take the stairs.

So, this was where the firebug lived. Couldn't be better, he thought. Not a living soul within a quarter of a mile, no friends or relatives dropping by unexpectedly, no nosy neighbours poking their nebs through twitching net-curtains. In other words, no witnesses. If only all his victims had been so considerate. He began searching the room.

Not that there was much to search: a single mattress on the floor to the right of the fire and below the boarded-up window; a black nylon grip, overflowing with clothes; a bag of coal and some tinderwood to the left of the fire; a mantelpiece piled with books and boxes of candles; a threadbare carpet the colour of shit in the centre of the floor; an upside-down orange-crate supporting a stack of women's magazines, a brand-new Walkman and an untidy heap of cassettes of bands he'd never heard of.

The bed, he noticed, was perfectly made: sheets and blankets smoothed flat, the corners tucked in, as neat and coolly inviting as a hospital bed. Or a prison bunk. He stripped back the bedclothes to find spotless sheets and nothing stashed under the pillows. He heard Dodds trudge down the stairs.

'Well?'

'Maybe she's out on the town,' Dodds said, scratching his chin, 'celebrating with all that money I gave her.'

'Or maybe she's found herself a new boyfriend, eh?' Billy lifted the nylon grip and emptied its contents on the floor. Knelt down and held up a pair of pink skimpy knickers. 'Christ, Dodds, you never said you were shagging a midget.'

'And no one told me you were a pervert,' Dodds snapped.

'Pervert, am I now?' Billy pressed the knickers to his face and sniffed. 'Ah,' he sighed, 'the smell of cunt. Ain't no smell like it. Like rubbing your face in the morning dew. What did you say her name was?'

'Grace. Now put them back.' Dodds stepped forward a pace, frowning so hard his eyebrows met on the bridge of his nose.

'Grace, eh?' Billy leered, again pressing the panties to his face. 'I'd certainly like to grace her cunt. Maybe we should hang around till she gets back. Play two's up for a while.'

Dodds snatched the panties from Billy's grasp, stood there like a colossus, casting long quivering shadows as the muscles strained in his fat red neck.

'I could get tired of you, McCulloch. So tired I might snap your fucking neck.' His sledgehammer fists clenched at his sides.

Without taking his eyes from the moron, Billy rose slowly to his feet and slipped his hand nonchalantly into his pocket, where his fingers closed on the haft of his knife. Mildly, ever so mildly, he said, 'You ever wonder why your lovebird has so many candles lying around the place?'

'I'm warning you, Billy!'

Fucking amateur. Only amateurs warn people.

He said, 'It means you ain't giving her enough of what she needs, needle-dick.'

Dodds came at him like a two-year-old would. Billy ducked under the wildly swinging fist, came up behind the overbalanced Dodds, forearm locking around the fat red neck. His knife glinted like flame in the candlelight as he pressed the blade to the moron's cheek.

Dodds froze.

Billy froze.

It was as though someone had paused the film. Stillframe.

The sound of their breath ragged, the wind whistling beneath the doors, the rattle and bang of corrugated-iron along the street. The two of them locked together like Sumo wrestlers, immobile, gathering strength to break the deadlock. Billy could feel it gathering momentum inside him, the bloodlust. The rush of blood to his head, the tingling skin, the loosening of his bowels . . . all primary symptoms of his killing urge. It would be so simple.

131

Too simple.

He released the moron and with a sudden violent jerk sent him slamming against the wall. The bloodrush reached his brain. He watched his knife go to work through a pinkish haze. Like it wasn't in his own hand but someone else's. Slashing at the sheets and blankets on the bed, stabbing the mattress to death, shredding the clothes to ribbons, ripping the magazines to tatters. The Walkman exploded against a wall. Cassettes burst beneath his feet. Books flew off the mantelpiece.

Moments or minutes later Billy found himself standing in the centre of the room, pulse racing and breathing hard as Dodds, cowering in the corner, watched him fearfully with bugged-out eyes.

'So,' he said, closing away the blade of his knife with a loud, hollow click, 'where was I?'

CHAPTER 18

It was a day of heavenly flatulence. As low wispy clouds scudded across the whiplashed sky, gale-force winds ripped through darkened city midday streets, whisking dust and paper into chaotic frenzy as the populace battled, scrunched and bowed, against its sudden ferocity. Where scaffolding clung to sooted façades, tarpaulins flapped and banged in manic bursts, like prisoners battering on a closed cell door. The wind sang, it crooned, it moaned and screamed; it whispered and wailed and drove all things mad.

Joe felt mad. That special kind of insanity described by Henry Miller: 'To be joyous is to be a madman in a world full of sad ghosts.' U2 blared from the quadraphonic speakers. Mad, totally mad. As he drummed the wheel in time, waiting for the lights to change, the car-phone rang. It was Jay, wanting to know where the fuck his Porsche was.

'Right here, Jay, on the end of the phone. You want to speak to it?'

'Christ, what is it? The whole fucking world's gone mad. You steal my wheels in the middle of the night and now the wife's skipping about the house packing, singing love songs in her nightie. Has someone spiked the drinking water or what?'

'The wind, Jay. It has that effect, blows away the cobwebs, clears the mental clouds. Can't you feel it?'

'All I can feel is a pain in my heart where my Porsche used to be. You going to bring it back or do I call it up stolen?'

133

'Call it what you like, Jay, I'll be back in an hour.'

'You better be.'

Joe could hear the sound of running water in the background. 'Careful, Jay,' he said. 'Wash it too fast and it might fall off.'

'Seeing as you've already got the car, you can drive me to the conference.' Jay was thinking as he washed. 'That way I can get tanked up for the flight tonight. Aye.'

The lights changed. Joe drove like a hunchback around the Barnton roundabout, phone clamped between shoulder and chin, Jay's voice tinny in his ear.

'You still there?'

Joe said he was. Smiled at the blonde in the Fiesta as he passed with a racing change of gear.

'You better take care, Joe.'

'Don't worry, I'm fine.'

'I mean the fucking car, man. Mess it up and you mess me up. Understood?'

'Roger, Juliet. This is Charlie One, out.' Joe replaced the handset with a smile.

Kids, he thought, grown-up kids with toys.

'Of course,' Wilberforce Wylie said, 'the trouble with free-running oscillator-type radio-transmitters operating on FM is, Okay, you can listen in on your car radio or whatever, but it also means so can anybody else who happens to be passing or living nearby, twiddling their knobs trying to find Radio Forth. It's what we in the trade call "compromised security".'

Joe said, 'Get away?' They were in Wylie's first-floor office, the private detective spilling over the chair behind his desk, fat fingers laced across the broad expanse of his waistcoated stomach. His mood also expansive.

'Okay, you say, why not use the Air Band frequencies? They're higher and because you need to have a suitable receiver, offer less chance of compromised security. All well and good, Joe, but you start using transmitters and suddenly you find you have a host of other determining factors to consider. For instance . . .'

In the fierce heat of a Calor gas fire on full, Wylie's office stank like the bowels of a corpse left rotting in the sun. Joe crossed to the window, opened it and looked out across the Pleasance to the Salisbury Crags rising clear and lethal against the eastern sky. Across the street, and beyond the new Southside Division Police

Headquarters, Arthur's Seat was etched in black and white, a crude stalking beast crouched against the horizon. Joe, in no particular hurry now that his mind was made, was content to let Wilberforce Wylie rattle on in his effort to impress.

'. . . and not only that but you have to consider the environment, Joe, the surroundings. What kind of obstacles you have between your transmitter and receiver. Some places you can maybe transmit half a mile, others, like certain parts of the city centre where you have tall buildings crammed in close, that kind of thing, you can maybe only transmit a hundred, maybe two hundred yards.'

Joe said, 'Two hundred yards? Gosh.'

Woken by the sound of wind-buffeted shutters in the early hours of the morning, and unable to return to sleep, Joe had felt rising within him an urge, as sudden as it was inexplicable, to mount the wings of the gale and ride it till it dropped. To leave all to chance, and laugh in the fearsome face of fate. So while the sombre city whistled and snored, he'd taken Johnstone's flame-red Porsche and burned along the city bypass, out over the Forth Road Bridge, into the country, accelerator to the floor as he headed north.

Wylie said, 'So you can see why I prefer the line-powered room-transmitters. You don't have to worry about changing batteries, or low-quality transmission or reception because they get their power from the telephone line you attach it to and operate over any distance as long as there's a telephone there.'

A few miles south of Stirling he'd cruised past a squad-car at 140, palming his horn and relishing with childish glee the momentary glimpse of the driver's open-mouthed surprise. Naturally, it gave instant chase – but even with its siren wailing and indignant flashing lights, it was nothing more than a poodle yapping at a greyhound's heels. It clung for half a mile before sinking without a trace in his rearview mirror. He left the M8 at Stirling and found an all-night café on the far side of town where, after parking the Porsche behind a high screen of trucks, he devoured the biggest meal he'd had in a week. The exhilaration of the morning still clinging like a persistent dream.

Now, even with the window open the stench of stale sweat and whisky mingled with garlic and cheap talc was still sharp enough to choke on. Joe took a deep breath and said, 'Rae told me you used to work for Rankine.'

'So?' Wylie said, immediately on the defensive. 'We both did.'

'She also thinks – *thought* – that Rankine is behind the fires.'

'So what's new? I already told you that myself.'

'You also said you could give me Rankine on a platter.'

'I said that?' Wylie waggled his chins, then brought out a handkerchief and mopped his running brow. 'I think you must've been dreaming.'

'Maybe I was,' Joe said, letting it go for the moment. 'But the guy who came into Posers and redesigned my face, he was no dream.'

Wylie laughed. 'A nightmare then?' It was like watching a horse whinny.

'Stone Age Man, Wylie, the proverbial brick shithouse. With blond highlights in his hair, dressed sharp in a shiny suit and heavy gold rings on his fingers. You know him?'

'Acts like he just got thrown off the set of Taggart?'

'Worse.'

'Sounds like Dodds. Runs security for Rankine out at the Edin Hill Hotel.'

'Dodds,' Joe said, filing the name away. 'Is that his surname?'

'Does a monolith have a Christian name?'

Joe indicated the glass-fronted cabinet behind the door, where shelves of innocuous-looking gadgets were displayed like jewels on a crushed-velvet base. 'You ever use those line-powered room transmitters when you worked for Rankine?' he asked.

Wylie seemed taken aback, his adam's-apple bobbing like a float between collar and lowest chin. 'Let me get this straight, Costello. I didn't work for Rankine, he was a client. Like Johnstone is a client. And both of them pretty small fry compared to others I have on my books. Industry, that's where the real money is.'

'You didn't answer my question.'

'Dear me. I must be going senile.'

'What kind of work did he engage you to do? The Peeping Tom variety? Marital infidelities?'

'Nothing of the sort,' Wylie said, indignation spluttering from his lips. 'Straightforward business, that's all. Any more than that, I'm not at liberty to say.' A buzzer sounded on the stair. Wilberforce Wylie grunted to his feet and wheezed to the door. 'Client confidentiality, you understand. Excuse me a moment.'

As the private detective tortured the boards on the stairs, Joe flicked through the appointments diary on the desk; it was full of fancy doodles and blank white pages. The drawers of the desk were locked, as was the steel filing cabinet against the far wall. The plants on top needed water, and the room needed dusting. The air, heavy as a cosh, needed nothing less than freedom.

Joe crossed to the glass-fronted display cabinet which Wylie had earlier described as his 'salesroom'. Guaranteed to impress even the least gullible of clients, the PI had said, though the appointments diary painted a somewhat different picture. Its doors were unlocked.

On the top shelf of the unit reposed an assortment of miniature and sub-miniature transmitters and receivers, some concealed in desktop- and pocket-calculators, some in ballpoint pens; others in power-sockets, telephone-sockets and 13-amp adaptors. On the next shelf down were room-transmitters and telephone-transmitters, from the size of a compact lighter to cigarette-pack size; a 'recording' briefcase; voice-activated amplifiers in shiny black boxes, with switches and sockets and small grey jacks. On a lower shelf, the tools of counter-surveillance: electronic sweeping equipment, hand-held radio-frequency detectors, body-worn detectors; telephone monitoring and scrambling equipment; and in pride of place what Wylie had described as a 'state of the art' FM-AM spectrum-analyser, a fancy device of switches and dials and digital displays, meters and buttons, sockets and plugs and red winking lights: in fact, more tiny knobs on it than on the benches of the House of Commons.

Toys.

And in the wrong hands, dangerous toys. Hearing still the murmur of voices downstairs, Joe turned his attention to the back of the flat.

In the small back-room overlooking the cobbled courtyard where Joe had parked the Porsche alongside the PI's rusting black Beetle, there was a two-bar electric fire, and an armchair with matching footstool facing a large flat-screen TV. On the coffee-table beside it, a Betamax VCR struggled for space with a pile of well-thumbed hard-core porn magazines and several moulding cups of coffee. The uppermost magazine, Joe noticed, bore the intriguing title: *Rampant Donkey Fuckers*. He was about to investigate further when he heard heavy footsteps on the stairs. When Wylie lumbered wheezing into the room, Joe was again by the window, looking out at the Crags.

'Business?' he asked, turning back to the room.

'As if I haven't got enough on my books already,' Wylie sighed, flopping breathlessly into his chair and wiping his sleeve across his brow.

'You're right. All those fancy doodles and blank pages.'

'Bloody snoop,' Wylie sneered, slamming the diary shut and glowering at Joe.

'Call it professional curiosity.'

'Well you're not a cop now, Costello. Maybe you never were. Anyway I got a brain here that works better than any diary I ever seen, one that nosy ex-cops can't read any time I so much as turn my back for a second.'

'You keep all your records there, too?'

Wylie found a half-bottle of Grouse in a drawer, poured what little was left in a dirty plastic beaker. It disappeared in a gulp. 'What do you think?' he said breathily.

'That there's probably plenty of room.'

'Very funny.'

'But some things you just can't keep in your head. Am I right?'

'Where's all this leading, Costello? I think I must've lost you back there – like the moment you waltzed in uninvited with all these questions. They burning holes in your mind, or what?'

As a detective Joe had always been taught that too many specific questions can reveal specific areas of ignorance. That during interrogation it was vital not to let the suspect know exactly what you didn't know. So he decided on a different tack.

'I need to know if I can trust you,' he said in a milder tone. Then smiled inwardly when he saw the glimmer of greed spark deep in Wylie's eyes.

'You mean my proposition?'

'It's tempting, I have to say that.'

'We're both on the same side, Joe.'

'Sure. But I need to think it over. Make a few plans.'

'So what do you want to know?'

'The conversations you pick up from your bugs,' Joe asked, 'do you record them?'

Wylie snorted. 'You think I want to sit for hours on end in some dank, dripping basement with headphones for ears? Of course I record.' He glanced obliquely up at Joe. 'Why? What do you have in mind?'

Joe shrugged and, crossing to the display cabinet, lifted out the spectrum-analyser, weighed it absently in his hand. It was heavier than its weight in brick. 'You keep copies of those tapes?'

'Hey, careful, Joe! That's a fortune in your hands there!'

'Well, do you?'

'What do you think? I'm a total incompetent?' The detective's eyes were fixed firmly on the analyser. Again he asked, 'Why?'

'I'd have thought the recordings would belong to the client.' Joe now enjoying Wylie's obvious discomfort.

'They get the originals, sure.'

'And you keep the copies, I suppose – just in case.' Joe watched the sweat break out on Wylie's forehead as he bounced the device in his hand. 'Do you keep them here?'

Again Wylie snorted his derision. 'Are you crazy? A kid could break in here.'

'What about all this equipment?'

'Insured. Replaceable. Anyway, the place is wired. And seeing as I live upstairs, I'd know if anyone broke in.'

Joe replaced the spectrum-analyser upon its velvet throne, could almost feel the fat man's relief. 'You use any of this gadgetry for Johnstone?'

'Christ, Joe, what d'you think? He's a professional paranoiac. The only man I know who's got a diploma in delusion. Has me down at his house every Friday afternoon to sweep the place clean. Follows me round from room to room, just to make sure I'm not working for *them*.'

'Of course,' Joe said, 'you wouldn't dream of leaving a bug around to find "accidentally", now would you?'

Wylie's small round eyes narrowed to slits.

'No, I thought not,' Joe continued. 'You must have plenty enough work already.'

'You're damn right I do. And I'd like to be doing it now.'

'Of course.' Joe made to leave, then turned at the door, Columbo-style, for one last question. 'How about Rankine? You still do a few odd jobs for him? For old times' sake?'

Wylie just sneered.

Downstairs, Joe lingered long enough to price a few of the second-hand TVs displayed in the window of the electrical repair workshop below Wylie's office, before collecting the Porsche and heading back across the city.

Jay said, 'Like it, huh?'

'For a twelve-foot extension to my penis,' Joe replied, 'it's not bad.'

'Why?' The guard frowned suspiciously. 'Who's asking?'

'A cop with a sense of humour. Tell him I'm in the bar.'

Rae had once told him a joke about a commissionaire. Not a good joke, but better than a punch in the nose. A guy called Joe Costello applies for a job in a hotel. The manager tells him to go downstairs and fill in a questionnaire, so Conscientious Costello goes down and kicks fuck out of the old boy in uniform on the door.

The Belford Lounge was a quietly rippling pool of hush beneath a high, elegantly corniced ceiling. Dust-motes danced in the weak rays of sunlight that seeped through the tall arched windows, making mirrors out of the glass-topped bamboo tables scattered strategically about the lounge. Beneath one of the windows, a huddle of bespectacled, middle-aged ladies giggled over their long drinks, while a couple of suited businessmen pored over a spread of papers nearby. Further along the bar from Joe, a lone American rode his stool as he wrote postcards and engaged the bow-tied barman in tourist-talk. Carols oozed like festive balm from hidden speakers.

Once in Royal David's City . . .

Joe could vaguely recall his sixth or seventh Christmas when, as the most tuneful and angelic-looking boy in the nursery, he had been elected – no, *commanded* – to sing the processional solo at the end-of-term Parent's Day service. He could recall needing more prompts than Ronald Reagan. And that his voice kept cracking. But what he remembered most clearly of all was the sense of utter despair as the uncontrollable warmth trickled down his legs. That and the tanning he received as soon as he got home.

Goodwill to all men . . .

Wilberforce Wylie was obviously planning a little goodwill of his own. At the party, he'd said about Rankine: '*I can serve him to you on a platter, Joe. His head in a sweet and sour sauce.*' Which meant Wylie had some kind of incriminating evidence against the hotelier, evidence that could be used either to put the black on him or slam him away for the rest of his natural. And the odds were on that whatever Wylie held over Rankine was recorded on tape.

Perhaps, Joe thought, he should pay a midnight visit to Wylie's office. See what he kept hidden among his Y-fronts.

And what kind of work, he wondered, had Rankine employed Wylie to do? Surveillance was the most obvious answer – but surveillance of whom? Business partners like Cosmo Vass? Or rivals like Jay Johnstone? A lover, perhaps, or lovers? The possibilities were endless. So what information – or indiscretion – had Wylie inadvertently overheard that could prove so damaging to Rankine? A crooked deal, perhaps, or some sexually deviant act? Again the possibilities were endless. What Joe couldn't understand was why Wylie had waited until now. Why hadn't he made his move on Rankine before? *'Call it a wee investment for my future,'* he'd said. So why share it with Joe, why tell him at all? Why all the intrigue?

Joe shook his head, as though the motion would hurl all the questions and doubts from his mind. It didn't. He took another sip of his Highland Spring Water.

Games, he thought. Kids with toys playing games. Wylie as Bogart as Marlowe. Enveloping himself in an enigmatic veil as he talked from the side of his mouth, hoping the sum of his allusions would equal the sum of a tangible reality.

There were other questions still nagging his thoughts. Like who told Rankine that he'd be working at Posers the night Dodds came in like a Joe-seeking missile? Or that he was going to be at Johnstone's party the night Rae died? If the feud between Johnstone and Rankine was as acute as Rae had made it out to be, then surely each would have a spy in the other's camp. Did Wylie fit that role? Could he still be working for Rankine, passing on whatever information the old man wanted? It was certainly possible. And worth looking into.

Then there was the question of Detective Inspector Kerley. Was he just following Rankine's orders, or playing some devious game of his own? Acting together, they were a formidable foe – as Joe had discovered once before, too late and to his cost. But if there was some way to lever them apart . . .

Joe's thoughts were suddenly interrupted as a huge fist bunched his collar and jerked him from the stool.

The fist belonged to Dodds.

CHAPTER 19

'So,' Dodds said, lowering Joe back on to the barstool, 'you found your sense of humour.'

Joe rubbed his neck and smiled.

'Because that's what I call timing,' Dodds continued. 'There's a comedian up the stair with a punch line just for you. Maybe even a couple.' The words reeling from his mouth on whisky-laden breath. 'Are you going to come quietly or do I have to break your nose?'

Joe decided to go quietly.

'What's the PS stand for?' Joe asked, as the lift-doors closed.

'Penthouse Suite.' Dodds glared at him through rheumy half-bottle eyes as he turned his key in the lock.

'And this button?'

The lift sighed past the first floor.

'Emergency stop – why?'

The lift sighed past the second floor.

'Because' – Joe smiled as he jabbed the button – 'I think I'm going to puke.'

'You wha—'

The lift shuddered to a sudden halt as the point of Joe's elbow sank deep in the big man's kidney, choking the words in his mouth. Dodds stared at him in pained disbelief. Somewhere in the distance a bell started ringing.

One of the first things you learn as a cop is how to subdue with minimum force. And one of the first things you learn as an ex-cop in prison is how to finish a fight before it's begun – using maximum force. You learn because you have to, because it's the only way to survive. Hit first, hit hard, and hit where it hurts. Then hurt them so much they'll never look at you again without remembering that pain. Either that, or spend the rest of your sentence bending over for the 'B' Hall Baron.

So when Joe closed on Dodds he moved with practised, precisioned ease, picking off targets as they presented themselves, hitting them with unrelenting accuracy, fists slamming in like machine-powered tools. One minute Dodds was squared up to Joe, with his shoulders back and chin thrust out, the next he sat crumpled in the corner, his face a bloodied piece of jelly in his hands.

Joe yanked back the big man's head by his hair and spoke softly in his ear. 'First, I'd like to thank you for coming along today and giving me this wonderful opportunity to talk to you.'

'You're mad,' Dodds said, his strangled voice crawling over broken lips.

'Mm. And in the spirit of such a festive occasion, I thought we'd play a game called Honesty. It's really quite simple. I ask you a question and you tell me the answer, and if I think you're lying I break two of your bones, and if I think you're telling the truth, I break only one. With me so far?'

'Fuck you, Costello.'

'Question Number One – you have five seconds in which to answer: last Saturday night, were you, or were you not, driving a white Audi up by the Clubbiedean Reservoir? Please answer yes or no.'

Dodds stared at him in total bewilderment.

'I'm going to have to hurry you . . .'

'Fuck you, Costello.'

Slap. Dodds's head ricocheted off the wall of the lift. Bending back the security guard's hand, Joe forced him to his feet. 'Wrong,' he said. And with a jerk and a twist he broke Dodds's wrist, slamming him against the doors with a loud metallic clang. The lift rattled against the walls of the shaft. Dodds slumped to the floor in a tangle of legs, stunned as though a slaughterhouse cow. 'Try again.'

'Fuck you.' A moan. With a hint of defiance.

The alarm bell stopped ringing. The sound of voices on the floor above and below.

'Oh dear,' Joe said. His fingers stabbed through the air.

Dodds screamed.

'I'm blind!' Half-true. His right eye hung halfway down his cheek, attached only by a few knotted chords of bloodied optic flesh. 'I'm fucking blind!'

'Not if you get to a hospital in time.' Joe slapped away Dodds's groping hand and took the optic chords between two fingers. 'Not if you tell me what I want to know – now.

'Okay, okay!' The words spilled out in a panicked rush. 'I was in the car. But I wasn't driving. I didn't want anything to do with all that. I didn't know he was going to do it. I'm not into that, I'm not—'

'Who, Dodds? Who was driving the car?'

'Billy was. I thought he just meant to follow you. I didn't want nothing of murder.'

'Billy who?'

'McCulloch, Billy McCulloch. The boss brought him over from Spain. He's got a villa there, on the—'

'Why bring him over?'

'For you. To get you.'

McCulloch. The name tolled in the back of his mind like a distant bell. A warning bell.

Now someone was shouting at them from the floor above, asking if they were all right.

'Why does Rankine want me dead?'

'You killed his daughter!'

'Where is he now?'

'Hospital. Private one, somewhere outside the city.'

'Which one?'

'I don't know. They don't tell me anything any more.'

The terror on Dodds's face confirmation enough.

'What's wrong with him?'

'He had an attack. A mild one.'

'And McCulloch? Where's he?'

'A hotel, I don't know the name. Somewhere on the Southside, one of the one's the boss used to own.'

The voices upstairs becoming more persistent. Time to move.

Joe said, 'Next time I see you, Dodds, better hope you're in a coffin.' He removed the lift-key from the security guard's chain, turned it in the Penthouse lock. The lift jerked, then climbed. As they passed the third floor, the voices receded.

The TV reporter was in the middle of his second take. '. . . and it appeared as though the children from the Marshfield Home would have to do without their Christmas party this year until local millionaire, hotelier Jack Rankine, heard of their plight. He immediately stepped in and offered the services of his Edin Hill Hotel, free of charge.'

Out of shot, the Marshfield Children's Choir waited nervously for their cue, gathered in three ranks in front of the Christmas tree. Guests and staff looked on, as kneeling newspaper photographers flashed off films in the dimmed soft light of the lobby. Behind the reporter, now in full flow, the lift-doors opened on a hiss. A man emerged. A tank of a man in a torn and ragged uniform. Dodds. He staggered out, clutching his face in one bloodied hand, the other crookedly outstretched as he weaved, sobbing, across the floor.

'. . . and now the Marshfield children have a personal message for Mr Rankine, who was unfortunately taken ill earlier this week, and is still recovering in hospital. It is a message of thanks to the man who has—'

The first scream was that of a little girl over whom Dodds tripped; the second from the boy upon whom he landed. The third and fourth, shrill harmonies from the first two girls to spot the dangling eye. A chorus of screeches and screams followed, as Dodds climbed unsteadily to his feet and stumbled, roaring, like a wounded bull through the scattering ranks of the assembled choir. Panic ensued. Breaking into pandemonium as the big man crashed into the base of the Christmas tree, causing a shower of brittle, brightly coloured baubles to fall like popping bombs of glass. As guests and staff rushed forward, the tree swayed. Then, like the mast of a ship crippled on mountainous seas, the sway became a list, slowly gathering momentum until it crashed upon the seething surface of upturned chairs and faces.

There were delays because of the wind. They sat in the Departure Lounge watching planes struggle along the runway and push themselves stubbornly into the evening sky as they waited for their shuttle-flight to be called.

'We could always take a train,' Andrea suggested, her tone

inferring she would rather go by rail. She sat beside Joe, absently ripping a beermat to shreds.

'And miss the connection? Hell, no.' Jay beckoned the barman and ordered another drink; his third in thirty minutes. 'You want one, Joe?'

'You want me to drive the Porsche home drunk?'

Jay said, 'And a glass of mineral water for my driver.' He didn't ask Andrea. They weren't speaking – except to snipe at or insult one another. The atmosphere at the bar, tense; Joe uncomfortable between them. The drinks arrived and Jay paid as though under extreme duress.

Jay's business meeting at the Conference Centre had been a success: agreements reached, contracts signed, hands shaken. 'Two hundred thou, Joe – as good as in the bank,' Jay had said when Joe arrived to pick him up. 'How's that for an afternoon's work, eh?' The drinks session after the meeting, it appeared, had been an even greater success: Joe had to pour Jay into the car. Then stop twice on the way home so Johnstone could puke down the side of the door.

'Like I said, Joe, sorry to turf you out the house. But you know how it is with these security firms, they like to do things their own way.'

'Sure, no problem.'

Andrea said, 'I told Joe he could use the cottage over Christmas if he wanted.' She turned to Joe. 'I left the keys and stuff in the Porsche, just in case.'

Jay said, 'He doesn't want to, I already asked. He's going to be busy, he says.'

'Busy doing what?'

'Why don't you ask him.'

She did.

Joe shrugged. 'This and that,' he said, glancing at the clock, wishing Traffic Control would hurry up and call their flight.

'Look,' Jay said. 'He can't wait for us to leave.'

'Can you blame him?'

'He's been floating around all day with a glaze in his eyes and a smile on his puss. Says it's the wind. Me, I think it's love: he's got a lady lined up for this evening. Wants to try out the recliners in the Porsche.'

'Shut up, Jay. There's more to women than just a poke in a Porsche.'

'Since when?'

'Since the day the last troglodyte died.'

'See, Joe? The moment she starts losing an argument, it's out with the fancy big words.'

'You're sick, Jay.'

'You're damn right I'm sick – sick and tired of your continual bitching. I work hard all day, come home with a deal worth more than two hundred thou – and do I get any thanks in return? Not a chance. I just get a hard time.'

'Last time you had a hard anything, folk were still walking round in flares.'

'Women, eh, Joe?' Johnstone said, shaking his head in disbelief, as their flight was called. 'You just can't believe a word they say.'

Twenty minutes later, and with a sense of relief, Joe watched their plane climb laboriously into the windlashed sky. When it was no more than a speck in his eye, he collected the Porsche and returned to the city and the emptiness of his Easter Road flat.

Midnight came and went. He sat in his father's chair, poker in hand, watching the frenzied dance of flames that reflected the state of his own emotions, every now and then kneeling to stab intently at the glowing coals.

Billy McCulloch.

If he concentrated hard enough on the fire he could still see McCulloch's face the way it had looked almost six years ago when they'd faced each other across the Sheriff's Court as the one-year sentence was read out: McCulloch, contorted by hate, screaming at Joe, swore his bloody revenge.

It all seemed so obvious now.

CHAPTER 20

Waverley Station.

People coming, people going, all with a bustling sense of purpose and direction. Even those who sat on their luggage in the centre of the concourse, watching the Arrivals and Departures board with tired, wistful faces – they still had somewhere to go and a reason for going. Unlike Grace, who now felt herself trapped in limbo, not knowing which way to turn.

'*Passengers awaiting the arrival of the Inter City from Aberdeen are reminded that the train is now running approximately twenty minutes late . . .*'

She stared dejectedly into her third cup of lukewarm coffee, stirring it absently as she wished her life away.

She wished she'd never met Dodds. Wished she'd never taken his money. Wished she'd never worked for Johnstone. Wished she hadn't started those fires. Wished Dodds hadn't told her about the woman. Wished things were just the way they used to be . . . But most of all she wished she'd remembered to take the money.

Arriving home from a lousy party in the early hours of yesterday morning, she had noticed the tyre tracks in the snow and the confusion of footprints around the house but, in her slightly addled state, had thought little of it. Only when she discovered the back door hanging wide from its one remaining hinge, had she realised she'd had uninvited visitors.

Looking back on it now she could smile. Especially at the way she had stepped nervously down the hall, placing her feet ever so carefully so as not to make a noise, yet at the same time calling out in a tremulous little voice, *Is there anyone there? –* the way they always do in horror films when the woman's just about to die of too much cleaver in her skull. Aye, she could laugh now, but at the time the only reason she didn't mess her pants was because she was holding it in forcefully with both her trembling hands.

And yes, now, sitting in the populated warmth and security of the café, she could reason things out reasonably without bursting into torrents of tears. Because that was yesterday and today was a brand new day: one full of people and motion and light and noise, and with no dark, silent rooms to magnify the sounds of her fear.

And no money.

'Passengers awaiting the arrival of the Inter City from Aberdeen are reminded that the train is now running approximately thirty minutes late . . .'

At first she'd thought it was burglars. But then burglars don't hang around derelict schemes looking for loot. Nor do they smash a shiny new Walkman to pieces when it could fetch at least fifty under the table. So she had eventually arrived at the only conclusion that made any sense:

Dodds.

Dodds had obviously fallen into something far too deep, and was now out of his depth or up to his neck. The big picture, he'd called it, whatever he meant by that. Nevertheless, he'd made a mistake. A big mistake. Had had one swallow too many and let it slip to Grace about some woman's murder. And now he'd either decided to, or been ordered to, silence her.

Hence the destruction of her squat.

She tried to imagine herself dying under the hand of Dodds, tried to envisage his flat eyes squinched in his broad twisted face, watching the spark of her life slide like the sun behind the clouds of her eyes as he dug the stubs of his fingers into the pliant flesh of her neck.

But it didn't work, the image failing to materialise with solid conviction. Thug maybe, but murderer? She shook her head.

The police, she thought: she could always go to the police.

But tell them what? That she'd burned down four of Johnstone's properties because he'd made obscene advances towards her? That a married man she was having a scene with had paid her damn good money to start the fires, and that that same man was now involved in a murder and trying to kill her?

Nah, she decided, not a chance. She took one step inside a police station and it would be bye-bye Grace, hello Cornton Vale for the next God knows how many years. Better to work this one out on her own.

First she needed money.

Which meant she had to return to the squat. In her panicked dash to get as far from the house as possible, she had forgotten her secret stash, her 'mad money'. All the money she'd accepted from Dodds was now wrapped securely in a couple of poly-bags and shoved up what was left of the wastage pipe under the sink in the kitchen. Unless Dodds had already found it.

Either way, he'd be waiting for her.

'*Passengers awaiting the arrival of the Inter City from Aberdeen are reminded that the train is now running approximately forty minutes late . . .*'

But she had no choice. The money was her only hope. Her ticket out of limbo. Without it, she might just as well throw herself at Dodd's mercy.

Which was not a pleasant thought.

Tonight, then, under the cover of darkness.

CHAPTER 21

'**Y**ou imbecile!'
Jack Rankine's voice was brittle and dry and floated on a
raft of sighs.

Billy McCulloch stood by the window of Rankine's private room,
staring out across the hospital grounds and the snowthatched cottages
of Dalmeny to the slate-grey Firth of Forth beyond. The two great
bridges – road to the left, rail to the right – framed the view, their
distant Fife Approaches disappearing into a hazy shore mist beneath
a lowering dark sky. Billy's mood was also dark and lowering.

He turned away from the window and regarded Rankine with a
look of contempt. 'You haul me across from Spain to do a specific
job,' he said, 'and what happens? I end up a fucking wet-nurse,
going from one hospital case to another.'

Rankine lay semi-reclined on the bed, his drawn and jaundiced
face set against the pillows like an ancient papyrus in a clipboard
frame. Beside the bed, a cardiograph winked and blipped alongside
enough sophisticated electronics to silence the fears of even the
most hyper hypochondriac.

'I left you in charge and look what happens.' Rankine said,
waggling the newspaper in front of Billy's face. 'Front bloody
page. *Security Guard Runs Amok At Children's Christmas Party –
Hurt*. Brilliant,' he sneered. 'I couldn't have done better myself.'

'Leave a loaded gun about, it's going to go off. Employ a moron
like Dodds, what can you expect?'

153

'Where is he now?'

'The Royal Infirmary. They reckon they can save his sight but not his intelligence. He'll carry on being a vegetable for the rest of his life.' Billy glanced around the room. 'You got anything to drink here?'

'Does it look like a hotel?' Rankine sneered.

'All those shares you own in this place and you can't even get waitress service? Maybe it's a mental hospital you should be in.' Billy swept his eyes around the room, taking in the TV and video, the ensuite bathroom, the carpets deep enough to shine a man's shoes. 'Anyway,' he added, 'it does look like a hotel.'

Rankine said impatiently, 'So how much did Dodds tell Costello?'

'Nothing you need worry about. Seems Costello was only interested in whoever was driving that car.'

'You.'

Billy grinned. 'The price of fame.'

'Does he know where you're staying?'

'Dodds said he told him nothing.'

'In other words,' Rankine said, 'everything he knows.'

'Which must've kept Costello busy for at least a second or two.'

'You better leave your hotel. Stay with friends or something.'

'Friends?' Billy shot him a look of disgust.

'No, of course. Stupid suggestion.'

'You're right.' Billy began pacing up and down. 'Anyway, why leave? Let Costello come to me.'

Rankine frowned, tugging his unkempt beard. 'I don't like it, Billy. This is not what we planned.'

'Neither was Dodds cracking up.'

'I think you better tell me the rest of the bad news,' Rankine sighed.

'With Dodds we have a problem. The terminal kind. It seems he's let it slip to the firebug that he was somehow involved in murder. And now she's run out on him.' Billy had already decided not to mention their visit to the squat the other night; didn't want the old man bursting his valves just yet.

'Will she talk?'

'Well, she's not the kind to forgive and forget. Look at what she's done to Johnstone already.'

'You know where to find her?'

Billy nodded. 'I know where she lives. I think I'll take a run up there tonight, see what I can do to shut her up. Maybe it'll help jog my memory.'

The old man regarded him in puzzlement.

'The girl in the pool,' Billy explained. 'Remember? Sandra the student, the one I buried behind the villa, took two fucking hours to dig just a few feet down. Her of the peelie-wally skin and black-string bikini.'

'I told you before – I don't want to know.'

Billy wasn't listening. He said, 'I even dream about her now, wake up in the middle of the night and can't get back to sleep. Just because I can't remember what happened. It's driving me crazy.'

'*Driving*?' Rankine shook his head wearily on the pillow, every other breath now a sigh. 'I thought bringing you over, that would be it, problem solved. Now I have more problems than ever.'

Billy went round the bed and tapped the LCD display on the cardiograph. 'See that green line, Jackie? You just concentrate on keeping it alive and jumping, and I'll handle the rest. First the girl, then Costello. Then we can sign a few deeds, okay?'

Rankine sighed and closed his eyes.

'Mentone House Hotel, can I help you?'

'Room 104, please.'

'Putting you through.' Joe counted fifteen rings before the receptionist came back on the line. 'Sorry, sir, there's no reply. Would you like to leave a message?'

Joe asked when Mr McCulloch was due to return. The receptionist said she was sorry but maybe he had the wrong number, Room 104 was registered to a Mr & Mrs Mitchell . . . what was the name again? McCulloch, Joe told her, William P. McCulloch. Hum, she said, no Mr McCullochs registered at the moment, but we do have a Mr P. Williams in 211, could you have mistaken the name?

Joe said, No, but thanks anyway.

Room 211.

Newington is Southside, the southside New Town. It is split down the centre by Minto Street, a wide and now treeless avenue lined by large Georgian townhouses, which drops like an arrow to the south. To the left and right, narrow secluded lanes lead off through tree-shrouded portals to sleepy suburbia land, kingdom of the Volvo Estate and two-car garage. Most of the Minto Street townhouses are now exclusive hotels or up-market B &

Bs advertising 'SATELLITE TV IN EVERY ROOM.' Mentone House Hotel sits back off the main thoroughfare, at the top of a short steep drive.

From the mouth of the lane where he was parked across the road, Joe could keep one eye on the main entrance, the other on the three workmen now climbing into a blue van at the top of the drive. He watched the van reverse down into the main road, then head off up Minto Street into town.

He'd give them ten minutes.

You wear a pair of scuffed steel-capped working boots, faded and torn jeans hanging halfway down your arse, a Fuck The Poll Tax T-shirt and a tool belt slung as low as a Lee Van Cleef holster, you have to whistle lecherously at anyone vaguely resembling a woman or risk being called a poofter. As a time-served joiner on a 714 there are certain unwritten laws to observe. So when the chambermaid passed him on the second-floor corridor he turned and whistled after her. She smiled, shaking her head as she unlocked the door to Room 212. A solid woman in her late twenties, with dark-brown hair beneath a starched white cap. Sparklers for her eyes.

Joe tried the door to 211. It was locked. He said, 'Do us a favour, would you, doll?'

'I just cleaned in there, I hope you're not going to mess it all up.'

'Check the windows, the gaffer said' – Joe stepped back so she could unlock the door – 'then shoots off down the pub with the rest of the boys an' leaves me here. Great. Nothing I like better than spending my lunch hour checking windows when I could be down the pub getting paid to get pissed.'

The chambermaid pushed open the door and stood aside.

Joe winked. 'Marry me, doll. You won't regret it.'

She smiled again briefly. 'That's what my husband said. And he was lying too.'

Joe wondered what the P. stood for. He couldn't recall seeing it on any of McCulloch's records or files, and it certainly wasn't mentioned during the trial six years ago. Maybe it was a recent touch of vanity.

William P. McCulloch – aka P. Williams, Mad Billy, Billy Wee, and Billy the Chib – travelled light. One black suit hanging in the wardrobe, a couple of round-collared white shirts neatly folded on the shelf, four pairs of green tartan cashmere socks, one pair of black slip-ons, two pairs of boxer-shorts and a copy of the latest *Playboy*. Either he was a man of few needs or was not planning to stay very long. Joe checked the pockets of the suit, found only a few balls of fluff.

Yes, it all seemed so obvious now.

Joe went across to the window, opened it wide and checked outside. Vines climbed the wall on either side of the window and several feet below the sill there was a narrow ledge that skirted the building. No sign of the workmen's blue van. He left the window open and turned back to the room.

Billy McCulloch. A name Joe had come across time and time again in the Cosmo Vass murder inquiry. Indelibly linked to Jack Rankine – whom he worked for – and thus to Cosmo Vass via Rancor, the catering company upon whose board both sat as directors. Joe could look out the window across the railway, beyond the grounds of the Blind School, and point out the house that had once belonged to Cosmo Vass; the same house where Cosmo's wife had discovered his mutilated body in the cellar.

Joe crossed to the dressing-table between the two windows and began going through each of the drawers. Four were empty, but in the centre one he found a folder stuffed with papers, which he scanned briefly: they appeared to refer to a transference of deeds for a villa in Calella de Palafrugell, from Rankine to McCulloch. As yet unsigned. Interesting. A few scribbled notes and doodles, and the name Dunkillin circled in red.

Cosmo Vass had been the third victim of the man the media had dubbed *The Acid Killer*. Post-mortem investigation revealed that he had been first injected with a large but non-lethal dose of LSD and then tortured for several hours. The killer had apparently used most of the tools in the cellar workshop: sanders, drills, planers, chisels, hammers, saws . . . all while Vass's head had been gradually crushed between the tightening jaws of the workbench vice.

Joe checked the underside of each drawer, the back of the dresser and wardrobe, the lining of the curtains, the pelmets, and the carpet in each corner. Then started on the wall-pictures.

The Acid Killer had initially come to the public's attention four years earlier, when his first victim had been found at the bottom of the Salisbury Crags, with both his hands and feet tied. There, too, a large but non-fatal dose of LSD had been discovered in the victim's bloodstream – but no apparent motive for murder. The second victim followed a year later – a well-known local dealer and junkie, found floating face down in the Union Canal. He, too, had been bound hand and foot, tortured, and pumped full of LSD. Again the murder seemed motiveless and again the investigation remained unsolved.

Joe moved across to the bed, searched under the mattress, the pillows, the sheets. Finding nothing, he drew out the suitcase that was under the bed. It was unlocked. In the left side pocket, he found a bunch of photographs. Mostly of a girl in her late teens, with pale skin and long blonde curls, posing with a crooked smile by the side of a pool, part of a house – no, villa – in the background. In most of the shots she wore a black string bikini; in others, nothing at all. Joe returned the photos and moved on.

After the death of Cosmo Vass, the murder squad drew up a psychological profile of the killer – yet it matched no one drawn into the net of possible suspects. Whilst the killer had exhibited in his handiwork most of the common traits of psychopathy, he had not yet, it seemed, crossed the threshold of reason into murderous insatiability. And so the case remained open. Even now, more than two years later.

Joe walked through to the bathroom.

Yes. Billy McCulloch. A name he had come across during the investigation, yet had always ultimately ignored. Why? Because he didn't fit the profile. The McCulloch he knew then was nothing more than a small-time Gorgie wideboy, a postman-turned-dealer with a liking for petty violence. Nothing extraordinary there. He spent time inside: first time up when he was still in his teens, three years for attempted murder; then later, for dealing, three months; then once for B & E, six months; and once for reset, nine months. When he next hit the streets a free man, it seemed he'd turned his back on his criminal past and was trying to make a go of it. Somehow he managed to get a clerking job with the Post Office and two years later had a postal round of his own. Six months later a man on McCulloch's round was seriously wounded when someone ran a sword through his letterbox. Joe got the case and it took him less than a week to capture McCulloch: traces of the man's blood were found still on the sword hanging over McCulloch's fireplace. Billy then went for a year behind the big stone wall. The next time he came to the court's attention, he was already working for Rankine's corporation. The charge was extortion, but he walked on a technicality. After that, he seemed to have disappeared completely.

Dodds had mentioned Spain. And Joe had found the deeds to a villa on the Costa Brava, and photos of a girl by a pool, overlooking a bay. Spain.

Why should McCulloch move to Spain? And how could he afford that kind of lifestyle? It was obviously Rankine's villa, but why should he sell it to Billy? And where had Billy got that kind of money?

Puzzled, he opened the bathroom cabinet. Nothing there but a bottle of painkillers and a pack of condoms, seal unbroken. It would be interesting, Joe decided, to find out exactly when McCulloch left for Spain. He turned his attention to the toilet.

There were no guns in waterproof bags in the cistern; in fact, nothing but water. He was on his knees, feeling round the back of the toilet-bowl base when he suddenly heard the liftdoors open and footsteps approach along the corridor.

As his fingers closed on something small and hard, taped to the niche at the back of the bowl, the footsteps halted outside the door.

Keys jangled.

Joe was already in motion.

CHAPTER 22

Billy sat at the crowded bar, trying to hang on to his thoughts as he nursed his third pint of something not very special. It wasn't easy: there was a darts match on behind him and the pub was heaving, and already there was the distinct smell of trouble in the air – the away team was winning four sets to three. He glanced at the wall-clock again, but it was still too early to go visit the girl, the firebug, Grace. So he sat and wondered.

He wondered if she was as pretty as Dodds said she was. He wondered if his car was safe outside, and if he really cared. He wondered how long he would have to use it before he got the Audi back from its repair and re-spray at the garage. He wondered what he would do if Rankine croaked before signing over the deeds of the villa. He wondered how the girl, Sandra, ended up in the pool instead of his bed. In fact, he wondered about anyfuckingthing he could think of so he wouldn't have to think about Joe Costello.

He'd seen it once on TV. One of those documentaries with David Attenborough creeping through the jungle and talking very softly so as not to wake the viewers. This one was about a special kind of wasp – big fucker, too, not the kind you want to find just the head of in your half-eaten picnic sandwich.

What was special about these wasps, Billy recalled, was that they like to lay their eggs in those things caterpillars turn into before they burst out moths – cocoon-like things, but with some fancy Latin name he could never remember – so that when the

161

wasp-eggs finally hatched they already had a built-in food supply waiting for them. They would then feed off the insect until they were big enough and strong enough to bite their way out.

Which was kind of how Billy felt right now. As though, sometime in the recent or distant past, Joe Costello had laid his eggs in Billy's bloodstream and now they were eating him inside out and getting bigger and stronger with every passing day.

Especially today.

From the moment he'd returned to the Mentone House Hotel – after wet-nursing the old coffin-dodger all afternoon and making arrangements for his Christmas convalescence in the cottage he owned in the village down the road from the hospital – he'd been able to think of little else but Joe fucking Costello and the missing bottle he'd taped behind the toilet before leaving his room this morning.

So as not to lose it.

Now he was looking at a year's supply down the drain. Not the kind of crap you could buy on the street a fiver a tab and spend half the trip wondering if you just hallucinated or did that poodle really piss on your shoes – no. Billy was talking the real thing here: liquid semtex, MacAllans thousand-year-old. The kind of stuff that hits your bloodstream one second, then blows off the top of your head the next; punches you out of your shoes and sends you into orbit. No *wondering* about it.

And now it was gone.

So Billy had gone downstairs and asked one of the chambermaids if anyone had been in his room that afternoon. She said, yes – she had. He said, Anyone else? And she opened her eyes wide: Oh there was someone else, one of the workmen, a joiner, who went in to look at the windows – why, was something wrong? Billy asked what the joiner looked like, did he have dark hair, sleepy kind of eyes and a large bushy moustache? And she said, yes, that was him.

Which was why Billy was trying very hard not to think of Joe Costello right now, in case he did something he might later regret.

Like kill him too quickly.

The memory of that morning six years ago, when Costello kicked down his door and hauled him away, was still clearly etched in Billy's mind. He would still, even now, go over it again and again and try to work out exactly what it was about Costello that had worked its way so deep beneath his skin. At one time or another he'd been captured by must've been half the polis in the city; but none of their faces had ever stuck in his mind, nor their attitudes wound him up, to the extent that Detective Sergeant Costello's had.

Perhaps it was the words Costello had used, the sanctimonious tone of his voice as he prepared to put the cuffs on Billy who was standing there naked and shrivelled against his sitting-room wall as PCs and WPCs wandered in and out, smoking and laughing and generally tearing his place apart. Costello had said:

'Turn around, McCulloch, nose to the wall, hands behind your back. You want to know something, McCulloch? The only difference between you and a piece of shit is the shit's got more brains. I mean, any self-respecting turd who'd just run his sword through some guy's groin, the first thing he'd do would be clean the blade, wash away the blood. You, on the other hand, not only forget to wipe it clean, you hang the fucking thing like a trophy on the wall for all your peasant friends to come and admire. Feet back and spread your legs. If I imagined for a moment you were capable of stringing two intelligent thoughts together, I'd regard you as dangerous. As it is, you're nothing but a streak of diarrhoea running down this city's leg and I'm the man with the tissue who's going to wipe you clean away. I said hands behind your back, Skidmark.'

Like he was Clint fucking Eastwood, Billy remembered thinking as the cuffs closed tight on his wrists: had probably stayed up the whole night rehearsing the speech in front a mirror. Then it was: 'Turn around, McCulloch, leave your feet where they are, shoulders back against the wall. Sharon!'

The plain-clothed cunt who'd been taking pictures of the sword wandered over. 'Sir?'

'Ever seen one as small as that, Shar?'

'Never, sir, thank God.'

'Why not take a couple of snaps, keep them to remind you how lucky you are?'

The cunt smiled and began taking pictures. Which was when the mist came down in Billy's mind and the next thing he recalled was the boots flying in and then later coming to as he was being dragged down the stairs to the car.

Looking back at it now, and in the light of recent events, it was as though Costello had been put on this earth solely to torment him. To wind him up to such a point he didn't know what he was doing. Fucking up Billy's life by just *being* there.

Suddenly there was a shout and the sound of smashing glass. Billy looked up, becoming slowly aware of his surroundings again, as though waking from a dream.

A woman screamed. Tables overturned. A man staggered blindly with his face in bloodied hands. Bodies surged and fists flew. The local darts team had lost.

This was more like it, Billy thought, a little home entertainment. His chib slipped comfortably into the palm of his hand. He held it pressed against his thigh beneath the table as the fight spread like fire down the far side of the bar. There were more shouts now as glasses and darts arced across the room. A barstool crashed through one of the windows. Another woman screamed as a dart pierced the side of her neck. A tumbler smashed against the wall behind Billy's head, showering him in glass. A fat man reeled into his table, sent Billy sprawling. So he buried his blade in the fat man's buttock and then pulled himself free. Bottles exploded on the gantry. More screams added to the pandemonium. The barman slammed down the phone with one hand, picked up a baseball-bat with his other. Time to leave, Billy thought, time to leave.

Still with his knife by his side, he pushed towards the door. Someone barred his way and sneered something offensive. Someone collapsed to the floor, holding his punctured chest. Someone shouldn't have opened his big fat mouth when Billy was in a mood.

Billy continued towards the door.

Seven or eight years ago, Joe Costello had walked into the same bar Billy McCulloch was now leaving. He'd stopped off at the first pub he came to, needing a drink, needing it fast, needing it strong enough to overpower the stench of decay and taste of death clinging to his palate like a stiffening corpse.

The old woman had been lying in her high-rise flat for more than a week, no one willing to say exactly how long. Maybe she had tripped over the flex of the two-bar electric fire which had burnt off her face, or maybe her knees had given way as she climbed out of her chair to switch over the TV. Whatever. She ended up with her face in the fire and had burned, melting like a candle until the meter ran out. As soon as the pathologist and ID Branch had ascertained accidental death, Joe had burst from the building on a rising tide of nausea and headed for the nearest anaesthetist, which happened to be a bar round the corner with graffiti-scrawled, pockmarked walls, and a mosaic of pavement-pizzas and broken glass outside: the same bar in which Billy had been drinking for the last hour and a half.

Joe remembered his impression of walking into a war-zone, the bar basic under dim lights, the barman resenting having to climb down off his stool, slouch over to take Joe's order. Joe just about to order a Famous Grouse when a voice behind him says, 'You're Costello.' Joe turned to look in liquid eyes squinting at him. 'You and me, pal, the same class. The Academy, mind?'

It had been a big class. Joe shrugged, not in the mood for the sakes of Auld Lang Syne.

'I'll buy you a drink,' the guy said. Rab, Tam, something like that. His body short and square, hard and brutal as an executioner's block. Used to sit at the back of the class and fart a lot, Joe recalled.

So he said, 'It's okay, pal, I'm just having the one.'

'I said I'll buy you a drink.'

'Thanks all the same.' Turning back to the bar to order the low flying bird, changing his mind, telling the barman, No, make it a double. A heavy hand on Joe's shoulder suddenly whipping him round.

'I'll buy you a drink.'

Joe found himself looking down his nose at six inches of sharpened steel. The guy's breath in his face almost as rank as the old woman's body. So he shrugged again and said, 'Thanks, Tam. I appreciate it.'

'Rab.' The bayonet disappeared and Rab paid the barman. Joe took two heavy swallows. Rab said, 'See?' Then returned to his seat and didn't even look up when Joe left just a few minutes later.

So that now, when the barstool crashed through the window on to the pavement outside, Joe wasn't exactly surprised – he merely sank lower behind the wheel of the Porsche and waited for McCulloch to emerge.

Which he did, just a few minutes later, spilling on to the pavement amidst a crowd of people as eager as him to escape the police whose sirens could now be heard approaching. Joe watched him saunter across the road to his car, a dirty red Capri, and climb in. When Billy pulled out, Joe followed.

Up the hill several hundred yards behind the bar there were Streets, Crescents and Loans, Terraces and Groves, Gardens and

Drives. Pleasant-sounding names for nothing more than a network of bleak, deserted roads binding the fabric of the run-down scheme together. Here and there a patch of mud-churned grass, a tree perhaps, a wind-bowed barrier of neglected shrubs.

No sign of people or cars.

Billy McCulloch appeared to be in no hurry, the Capri crawling along the pot-holed road and slowing at every corner. Looking at street-names, Joe realised. He switched off his lights and continued to follow at a distance.

Suddenly McCulloch braked and climbed out, leaving the Capri idling behind him. A hundred yards further down the hill, Joe pulled quickly into a short driveway shielded by a snow-capped fence and, with craning neck, watched Billy walk up the road, placing his feet carefully to avoid patches of ice and mounds of slush, and then cautiously approach the door of a semi-detached on the brow of the hill. Joe could see that the windows of the house were boarded. McCulloch glanced around once, then knelt to peer through the letterbox. A minute later, he returned to his car, backed it off the road into the shadow between two dilapidated houses, and switched off his headlights.

Joe sank down in his seat and waited.

The street off which he'd parked was lightless, wide and lifeless. Either dark holes behind paneless windows or boards for windows. A ghost estate and communal junkyard: beneath a crusted canopy of snow, rusting hulks of tyreless cars, discarded prams with buckled wheels, ripped up paving-stones strewn, like the aftermath of a riot, across paths and cratered lawns.

Who was McCulloch waiting for, Joe wondered. Who in their right mind would choose to live in a place like this? Dodds, the security guard? One of Billy's old-time cronies? Or was it a trap and Joe the bait? He tried to think back: was it possible Billy had seen him leave the hotel?

He recalled with humour the moment the chambermaid walked in and found him halfway out the window and ready to jump. He wasn't too sure who was the more surprised. She asked what he was doing and he told her 'checking outside for signs of rot'. She told him she had to lock up now as she was off for an hour, and Joe said, no problem, he was finished here anyway. His pulse was still racing almost twenty minutes later.

But he had left the hotel to return to the Porsche, and had sat there waiting for almost an hour and a half before McCulloch returned. And even then, Joe had barely recognised the man as the Billy he'd known before. Bomber-jacket and jeans had since given way to a black suit and tie. And he'd put on weight, his face and body now much rounder than the mean, lean, gaunt-looking man he had last seen screaming revenge across the courtroom floor. Gone also the long, untidy hair, the pitted unshaven face; replaced now by a widow's peak, cropped short, and a pitted shaven face.

Perhaps McCulloch had noticed Joe following, had recognised Johnstone's Porsche in the sporadic light of the cloud-dogged moon. Or maybe he was merely clairvoyant. Joe smiled at his own paranoia and gave up wondering. Settled down to what might be a very long wait. Surrounded by snow on this mid-winter night, he let his thoughts drift to the island of Skiathos in the warm Aegean Sea.

By now Jay and Andrea Johnstone would be sitting in some *taverna* overlooking an empty beach washed by gently lapping waves. Jay would be gorging on chips with ketchup, while Andrea sampled the local Moussaka. Poor Dimitri or Kostas would be run off their feet trying to bring Jay's beer faster than he drank it, while Andrea would be sipping Metaxa and making big round eyes at anything in trousers just to wind Jay up a bit and have some fun. Give it another half-hour and Jay would be up on the table, doing his Zorba the Greek impressions and continually falling over.

Joe yawned, deciding he was quite happy where he was. Well, almost: as his stomach rumbled, he wished he'd stopped to buy some food; as his bladder pressed, he wished he'd brought an empty milk bottle. Then something moved on the periphery of his vision and all thoughts of discomfort evaporated as he froze.

A dark silhouette, small and slim, moved slowly up the hill, working from one block of shadow to the next, stopping every now and then to look around. As the silhouette passed fifty feet away, moonlight glanced briefly on a bracelet, on sharp, delicate features inside a duffel-coat hood, before the moon slipped back behind the cover of cloud.

McCulloch was waiting on a woman. His woman? Joe wondered.

She came to the house Billy had checked out earlier. She glanced around again. Then almost ran round the side of the house, disappearing into shadow. A few moments later, McCulloch hurried across the road and vanished into the same bank of shadow.

Joe climbed from the Porsche.

CHAPTER 23

She'd been drinking, Billy could tell. He could smell the aniseed on her breath when she answered the door.

Grace McEwan said, 'Then I s'pose you better come in.'

She was tiny. Like a delicate figurine. The sharp bones in her angular face casting pockets of shadow as she regarded Billy askance, head cocked, peering at him through the copper-coloured sweep of her fringe.

'Aye,' Billy said, 'Your boyfriend couldn't make it. He's sort of indisposed.'

'He's not my boyfriend, never was.' She led Billy down the lightless hall to the room on the left where, already, candles flickered, weeping pools of wax on to the flaking paint of the mantelpiece. 'Sit where you like,' she said, with a listless wave of her childsize hand.

Where you like was the shredded mattress against the wall. Billy grimaced. Then hitched his trousers and lowered himself down.

'Had visitors?' he asked conversationally, sweeping his eyes around the room. Nothing had changed in the forty-eight hours since he and Dodds were last there. Obviously this was the first time the waif had returned.

'Aye,' she said. 'Like you, the unvinvited kind.'

He nodded towards the books strewn across the floor. 'Read a lot, do you?'

'What's wrong with that?'

'Nothing,' Billy shrugged, 'if you know how to read.'

'I can read.'

'So where's *The Joy of Sex*?'

'I don't read fiction.'

'Hey, that's really funny. I like that.'

Grace ignored him. 'So what's the crack?' she asked. Gripping the mantelpiece with one hand, she continued to watch him sideways, her other hand clasping her oversize duffel-coat to her pimple-size chest.

'You going to sit down? Or will I walk out of here with a crick in my neck?' He watched her shrug her fragile bones, then fold herself neatly on to the pile of cushions. He said, 'Nice-looking girl like you, what I can't understand is how you can live in a place like this.'

'Same as any place else,' she told him, 'you breathe in, you breathe out.' She curled her legs beneath her. 'You said you had some news.'

Fuck. If she had the nails, she'd have been sitting there buffing them. Flashing him looks of boredom over her knuckles.

He lobbed her a smile loaded with all his boyish charm. 'In the olden days they'd chop off the heads of messengers bearing bad tidings.'

'Just what I need – some bad news to pick me up.'

'It's about Dodds . . .'

'Don't tell me – he's still alive.'

Billy said, 'Sadly, yes. In hospital.'

'What happened?' Then, 'No, forget it, I don't want to know.'

'He's a moron, that's what happened.'

'I thought you said you were a friend of his . . .'

'A loose interpretation. How long've you known him?'

'Coupla months, why?'

'You talk much? You know, lying here together, pillow talk?' Billy watching her eyes narrow, realising he'd moved too soon.

'None of your business, mister whateveryousaidyournamewas.' Indignant now, pointy wee chin thrust forward. 'What *did* you say your name was?'

'Billy. Maybe Dodds mentioned me.'

Seeing from the look in her eyes he had.

But the waif composed herself well, frowning now, slowly shaking her head as she said, 'Doesn't ring a bell. You work with him or what?'

'Or what.' Climbing in stages to his feet, dusting himself down. 'Place like this, I bet you could have the wildest parties and none of your neighbours would ever complain.'

'Neighbours? What neighbours?' Anxiety grating her voice.

'Mm,' he said, crossing to the mantelpiece, 'That's what I thought.' Examining the bottle of Pernod like it was vintage Château Lafite, as he asked, 'Dodds tell you about the woman?'

Oh eyes of innocence. Almost enough to melt Billy's heart.

'What about what woman?'

'I've been trying to picture it . . . you know, you and Dodds together on the shagpit there. And I can't. My mind won't accept it. You lying with your legs in the air and the moron pounding the marrow from your bones, I wonder how you're still alive. How you ain't covered all over in bruises. Or maybe you are?'

Jumping to her feet now. 'Out!' she cried, 'Go on, leave!'

'Or what? You'll call the police?'

'I don't know nothing about any woman. Dodds never told me anything, he'd just come in that door and throw me on the bed. God's honest!'

'Princess, if that were only true.' He reached across to lift her chin with his finger. 'But you see, I spoke to him this morning. He was still on a high from the operation and told me everything. Said he was drunk when he told you about the woman, that you walked out on him. Went for a pee and never came back.'

He watched her shoulders sag as his words hit home. Tiny hands still clasping the duffel-coat to her chest, her narrow nothing waist. 'Fucking ignorant,' she muttered, 'never could keep his fat mouth shut.'

Billy rested his hands on her shoulders, looked deep in her eyes. 'You're telling me?' he said. Then prised open her fingers without much effort. Her hands fell like tassels to her sides. He undid each of the buttons, taking his time, watching her eyes as he did so. Then with a flick of his fingers the coat slipped off her shoulders and fell to the floor.

'So what happens now?' she said, defiance cracking in her voice. 'You going to take off your clothes and disgust me to death?'

Such a shame, Billy thought, as he undid the button of her jeans and pulled down the zip. Like the girl Sandra he'd found dead in the pool and couldn't remember how she got there. A criminal waste. Still, it had to be done. He edged the jeans slowly down over her hips, snagging her panties with his thumbs on the way,

171

then let them slip to the floor as his hands moved softly over her buttocks.

She shivered, but still remained motionless. In her eyes, a confusion of emotions, of which fear was the foremost. Billy smiled. Then ran his hands up under her jersey and blouse to cup her breasts.

'No bra,' he said, mocking surprise as he tugged jersey and blouse up over her arms.

'Fancy that,' she sneered. Then spat in his face.

He knocked her sprawling to the floor. Her cunt winked up at him from its sparse dark bush. Blood seeped from the corner of her mouth. She groaned.

'I think what we have to do,' he said, trying hard for the moment to control his temper as he smeared the spittle from his face with the back of his hand, 'is talk about it. See if we can't work something out.'

Joe was fifty yards from the house when he heard the scream. It ripped the calm of the night to jagged shreds, propelling Joe from a walk to a sprint. He slipped and fell, picked himself up and continued, deafened by the blood-rhythm beat of his heart and the echo of the scream reverberating in his ears. A man's scream, he was sure of that. A scream of pain, extreme pain, trailing off into a gargled groan.

Billy's scream, he hoped.

He dived into the shadow by the side of the house. Waited, listening, as he tried to regulate his breathing.

Silence.

He edged cautiously through the slush, down the side of the semi to a back garden wild with weeds. The fences between the houses were bent and crippled. Dark shadows with moonlight eyes scurried amidst the entrails of snow-covered bin-bags, across shattered slates and broken paving-stones, the débris of a council's economic warfare.

The back door of the house stood open, hanging on a solitary hinge. He was already moving towards it when suddenly he heard footsteps. He threw himself flat behind the bin-bags, landing awkwardly on something hard and sharp. Had to bite back a cry of pain as he watched the bent and awkward form of Billy McCulloch hobble, muttering, along the side of the house and across the road to where the Capri was parked.

172

Joe allowed himself a soft groan as he gently massaged his ribs, exploring the damage. Nothing serious, he told himself, hoping it was true. He could feel the sticky warmth of blood beneath his shirt.

McCulloch, meanwhile, had unlocked the boot of the Capri and lifted out two large jerricans which he now carried, still hobbling, back to the house.

The back door scraped shut as far as its hinge would allow, and a few moments later Joe heard the soft rumble of voices.

What now? Joe wondered. He was thinking about jerricans: large jerricans, full jerricans. The kind you keep in the boot of your car in case you run out of . . .

Petrol?

Billy was careful not to splash his shoes or clothes, keeping well away from the fire in the hearth, shaking out the last few drops on the slashed cushions by her head. She watched him with pleading Roger Rabbit eyes as she struggled against the cords that bound her hands and feet.

He kicked her again in the groin. She choked on the gag but lay still.

'Not so brave now, are you, princess?'

Women.

All the fucking same. You try to be nice and what do they do? – take advantage of your pleasant disposition. Give them an inch and they soon want twelve. Well, that was it – no more. No More Mr Nice Guy McCulloch. Teach her a lesson she won't forget for all eternity.

He tossed the jerrican aside and stood over her, hands on his hips.

Look at her. Look at her now. Like a plucked fucking chicken. How could he have thought her attractive? All angle, skin and bone as she lay there, sprawled across the floor, blood on her lips, seeping from her nose where he'd hit her, hard, a backhand blow, the fury of which fired him still.

He said, 'There was this girl, a student, couldn't have been much older than you. And *she* was pretty, had a bit of meat on her bones, something a man could get his hands on. But she was stupid, she must've said the wrong thing, because next morning she woke up dead in the swimming-pool. Someone had left an axe in her back. She probably died quite quickly, never felt a thing. You, on the other hand, are going to die slowly. In terrible pain. So think about it, princess, was it all really worth it?'

Her eyes narrowed in reply, her nostrils flaring, teeth bared like fangs as she snarled behind the gag.

Billy laughed. Then took the second jerrican out into the hall, through to the kitchen, where he doused the sideboards and units and, as he backed out, the floor. Then he went upstairs, moving slowly from room to room, having to feel his way in the blackness to avoid the ripped-up floorboards. He splashed the Four Star liberally as he went, then finally backed down the stairs.

'Still here, princess?'

She had squirmed across the floor and was trying to cut her cords on a blunt table-knife she must have had hidden somewhere. 'Naughty, naughty,' he admonished, clicking his tongue as he took the knife and put it in his pocket. 'That's cheating.'

He glanced at his watch, wishing he could stay a while, wanting to make the most it. But he had other fish to fry. Joe Costello and Dodds and, once Rankine signed over the deeds, maybe pop him as well, make it a nice round figure. Then ride off into a Catalan sunset with a high in his head.

What more could any man want?

'Well, princess,' he said, shooting his cuffs, 'I have to love you and leave you. It's been nice, but it could've been nicer. Don't take it personally.'

The firebug squirmed and kicked her legs.

'Sorry?' he said. 'I didn't quite catch that.'

She made strangled noises through the gag.

'You're right,' he said, taking a box of matches from his pocket. 'Not quite poetic justice, I agree, but justice nevertheless – live by fire, die by fire. Your own personal barbecue.'

He picked up the jerrican and backtracked down the hall, sloshing petrol. Opened the back-door and stood on the step.

'Have a nice death,' he called.

Then struck the match, dropped it to the floor, and ran.

One second Joe was watching Billy dash from the house to the Capri – trying to decide, stick with Billy or see what's going on inside – the next he was looking at a conflagration, huge tongues of flame shooting out of the door to feed greedily off the air.

His actions were immediate, instinctive.

In a couple of bounds he confronted the wall of flame belching from the blazing door, the heat already intense on his face. For a second he stared at the gaping mouth of flame then, bracing himself, filled his lungs with air, and threw himself inside.

Around him the hallway blazed. Unseen objects hissed and popped and trailed their fiery tails as they fell. The immediate intensity of the heat like a debilitating body-blow as he blundered, forearm across his lower face, through the doorway on his left.

Kitchen.

Flames climbing the walls.

Water? He tried the taps. Nothing. Disconnected. Which meant the gas was also disconnected.

He hoped.

Eyes now stinging from the thick curling smoke. Move, he told himself, no one in the kitchen, *watch your step but keep on moving*. He retreated back into the hall, the carpet afire, the banisters afire, throat on fire.

He heard sounds above the roar of fire, human sounds, choking sounds. From somewhere down the hall. He moved towards them, beginning to choke himself now as he tried to ignore his skin's blistering pain.

Sweat ran down his face in swollen rivers, almost blinding him as he stumbled towards the end of the hall, stairs to the right, a door to his left, hoping she wasn't upstairs, knowing he'd never make it back through the bank of ravenous flame, but she wasn't, she was lying in the room to his left, not a woman but a girl, Christ, in the middle of the floor, naked and bound, surrounded by a closing ring of fire, moving, not much, but moving, the whites of her eyes barely visible but able to focus as he lifted her from the floor, her body so light he almost lost his balance as he pushed blindly through the palling smoke towards where the door should be, driven now by a force inside himself but beyond himself, the physical Joe ready to drop, to sink to the floor, to rest just a little minute, the tiniest of minutes to regain his strength, but the other Joe, the new Joe, driving him on through the scorching flame into the hall, across the smouldering furnace floor, bouncing off the walls, lungs ablaze, weakening with every scalding breath of the acrid fumes, blind now, staggering blind, every step a thousand coughing, choking miles on leaden legs, buckling now like girders, as he fell and fell and fell . . .

. . . into the cool night air, landing heavily on the concrete path, the impact and the weight of the girl exploding the breath from his scalding lungs as he doubled-up, choking, wretching, coughing in uncontrollable spasms, trying to turn himself inside out as the girl rolled from his chest to kneel by his side, her frail body heaving in its bonds as a stream of thick black liquid oozed from her mouth.

Air.

CHAPTER 24

Still coughing and choking and trying to find breath, Joe carried the girl, now wrapped in his leather jacket, down the hill towards the Porsche as, behind him, masonry crashed and wild flames leapt, licking thirstily the jet-black sky. The girl looked back over his shoulder, her liquid eyes ablaze. She weighed next to nothing in his arms.

'Can you stand?'

She nodded weakly. Then noticed the Porsche and suddenly regained her strength. She began struggling in his arms, kicking out so wildly he had to drop her in the snow.

'What the—'

'You bastard!' she croaked, springing to her feet, backing away from Joe. 'You think I'm getting in there?'

'You'd prefer to stand out here in the freezing cold and wait for the police and fire brigade to arrive?'

'More than I want to step in Johnstone's fucking car with a complete total stranger!' Her tone and stance defiant, her fists clenched, ready to swing.

Joe shrugged, climbing behind the wheel. 'Suit yourself,' he said, turning the ignition. Even above the growl of the motor he could hear the wail of distant sirens.

'Hey! Where're you going?'

'Somewhere I'm appreciated. Can I have my jacket back now?'

The girl was on the brink of tears. She looked back at the burning house, then at Joe, then in the direction of the sirens, then back at Joe. 'Okay,' she said, 'I'm sorry. I appreciate it, you saving my life. I do.' But she still stood there, knock-kneed and forlorn, shivering so violently her teeth rattled.

'If you don't get out of that cold, you're going to get frostbite.'

She took two steps towards him and raised her fist. 'And you'll get a fat fucking lip if you don't tear your pervy eyes offa me.'

Joe held open the passenger door. The sirens were loud now, only minutes away. The girl, propelled by their urgency perhaps, climbed in and slammed the door. She refused to look at him. Joe backed out into the road.

'There another way out of here?' he asked.

'First left, first right.' Her voice cold and distant, detached.

They came out on to Niddrie Road just as a fire-engine flashed past, followed quickly by two squad cars. They were too busy speeding to give the Porsche a second glance. Joe headed into town.

'I suppose now you're taking me to Johnstone, right?'

Joe shook his head, concentrating on the road. The girl continued:

'He found out about the fires and now he wants to pay me back.'

'Johnstone's in Greece. He doesn't know who you are, or probably even care.'

Silence for a while. Then, 'So where're you taking me?'

'Hospital.'

'No way!' she cried hoarsely, looking at him now, 'no bloody way! It's nothing serious, I tell you – just a few minor burns, *that*'s all. Nothing I can't handle.'

'A doctor, then.'

'Doctor, hospital – what's the difference, they're still going to ask more bloody questions than I'll ever want to answer. 'Fore I know it, the polis'll be on my neck saying I burned down the house, headlines in all the fucking papers. Then I'll wake up dying one night with psycho-Billy's hands round my neck. So forget it, mate, whatever you said your name was.'

'Joe,' he said. As he approached the roundabout at Cameron Toll, another fire-engine went screaming by. He turned up Dalkeith Road.

'Charmed, I'm sure.' She twisted the rear-view mirror round so she could study her smoke-blackened face. 'Fuck, what a mess.'

'You always swear so much?'

'When I'm nervous I swear even more' – licking her finger to smear the soot from round her eyes – 'and fuck am I nervous. You got something I can clean my face with?'

'Try the glove compartment.'

'Just what I need, a glove.'

As she rooted around among the maps and envelopes, Joe asked, 'Is there anywhere you can stay? Friends, family?'

She threw him a look of disbelief. 'You think I *chose* to live in that sewer?' She had found a chamois-leather, used it now with gobs of spit to wipe her face. 'What about you? Haven't you got somewhere we can go?'

'We'll try my flat.'

'Then what?'

'Get you some clothes.'

'About time too.' Conscious of her semi-nakedness now, tugging down the hem of Joe's jacket to barely cover the tops of her thighs. 'Joe, eh?' she said, ruminatively, after they'd passed the Commonwealth Pool and were heading down the Pleasance. There were no lights, Joe noticed, behind Wylie's office windows. 'And you work for Johnstone, right? Is that where I've seen you before?'

Joe shrugged. 'I get around.'

'Man of fucking mystery.' The girl tossed the chamois back in the compartment.

'What's your name, anyway? Maybe you'll feel a little more relaxed once the introductions are over.'

'Relaxed? What's that mean?' She crossed her legs and hunched even deeper into Joe's jacket. 'Okay. You can call me Grace or Guinevere, depending how you see yourself. Where'd you get this anyway?' – meaning the Porsche – 'Johnstone give it you, or did you steal it?'

'Aye. Saw the keys hanging in the ignition, thought just what I need. What would you have done?'

'First, I'd've learnt to drive.' Grace sighed, shaking her head at the button-mushrooms that were her knees. Then lapsed into a silence that took them down Holyrood Road, through Abbeyhill, down on to Easter Road. Joe slowed as he passed the cul-de-sac where he lived, glancing up first at the lightless windows of his flat, then at the line of cars parked against the kerb. He almost missed the red Capri.

It was along the end of the cul-de-sac, its bonnet protruding

from the shadowed entrance of Arnott's, the builder's merchants.
A faint rooflight glowed in its interior.

Joe punched the accelerator.

'Christ!' Grace yelled. 'What was that for?'

'Change of plans.' Joe touched sixty, thankful for the grit on the
road as he checked the rearview mirror. 'That was your friend,
Billy,' he said, 'waiting outside my flat.'

'For you?'

'Who else?'

'He after you, too?'

Joe nodded, checking the mirror again. They were alone on
the road.

'Great. So now I have to sit here naked for the rest of my
life.'

'I'll think of something.'

'Aye? Like what?'

'You have any suggestions?'

Grace chewed her bloodied lip. 'I read this book once,' she said
after a moment. 'About the Samurai and how they used to believe
if you saved someone's life, you became responsible for them for
the rest of yours.'

'You want to go to Japan?'

'Fuck, anywhere – so long as it's abroad.' She frowned across
at Joe, her voice dropping, deadly serious. 'Even England,' she
added.

Joe thought maybe the shock had addled her brains.

Joe thought maybe the shock had addled *his* brains. Driving
aimlessly around for the last twenty minutes, trying to decide
what to do and where to go, and the solution was there in the
car all the time.

'There's an envelope,' he told Grace. 'In the glove compartment.'

The young girl – girl, woman, he couldn't yet decide – caught
the tone of his voice and scrabbled around among the maps for a
moment before coming out with a large buff envelope. Written on
the front, in Andrea's looping scrawl, it said: 'Joe – in case you
change your mind.'

'This the one?' Grace asked.

Joe flicked on the dashlight. 'Open it.'

'So what have we got?' Like she was opening a Christmas present.
'A map of the West Coast, a tourist brochure for Ardnamurchan –

180

Jay Johnstone was obviously suffering from the throes of festive magnanimity. First, he'd let Joe drive him out to the conference centre – a vast new Euro Complex on the west side of the city where men in suits and serious expressions could meet similar men in suits with suitably serious expressions – and now he was saying:

'It's yours till we get back. The only condition, that you pick us up from the airport. I'll give you the flight-times later. Think you can manage that?'

'I'll try.' Joe pulled in by the canopied entrance to the Conference Centre – a pentagonal neo-gothic shrine to smoked-glass and chrome – and waited with the engine running.

'Good.' Jay checked the tilt of his glasses in the sun-shield mirror, smoothed his hair, and glanced at his watch. 'The meeting shouldn't last more than an hour; the drinks, another two or three. Pick me up, say, four-thirty. Okay?'

'Have a nice day, sir.'

Kids, Joe thought.

Kids with toys. At least a hundred of them running amok, spilling out of the Warrender Suite into the lobby, screaming and laughing, chasing one another around the base of the sparkling Christmas-tree that towered, almost touching the domed skylight, over guest and wild-eyed child alike. One group of children danced excitedly, bobbing, tugging and weaving around the red-girthed maypole of a white-bearded Santa, while another waded and kicked through the multi-coloured sea of hastily torn and discarded wrapping-paper. Carols oozed like balm from the PA system as moist-eyed matrons stood around in pairs, arms folded, watchful as mother hens; and guests, too, looked on, drawn perhaps by the noise and the fevered air of excitement, or the presence of the Scottish Television film crew struggling with their equipment through a swamp of tiny clinging hands. Inside the main entrance, and beneath the tinselled banner *The Edin Hill Hotel Welcomes The Marshfield Children's Home*, the commissionaire, replete in all his gold-braided finery, conversed with a uniformed security guard, while another stood leaning with his back against the reception-desk, scanning the lobby with listless eyes. Neither of them looked anything like Dodds.

'Not due on for another half-hour,' the guard at the desk said, his watery eyes washing over Joe. 'If he ain't already legless, that is.'

'Drinking a lot these days, is he?'

wherever the fuck that is – and two keys for a door that must be at least eighty-foot high. What's it all mean?'

'Somewhere to go. A cottage. Mine for Christmas.'

'In Ardnamurchan?' Her voice rising as she studied the map. 'But that's the edge of the world! Or as the brochure puts it: 'The westernmost point of mainland Great Britain'. Nothing there but sheep and fucking mountains.'

'You're right. But also no psychopathic hitmen there to burn you out of house and home.'

'Sheep, mountains and rain. And probably mice as well.'

'A warm fire, clean clothes, hot food, a bath . . .'

'Bath? Did you say *bath*?'

Grace slept as Joe drove through the night, the road north as quiet and black as the glens through which it wound.

Before leaving the city he had bought an assortment of salves and creams, plasters and bandages from an all-night chemist and then, once out of the city, had pulled into a lay-by and climbed out, leaving Grace to clean and bandage her burns. Just beyond Stirling he had stopped again, this time at an all-night garage to fill the car and buy food and drink, and a couple of tartan blankets in which Grace now slept, gently snoring, curled in a ball on the semi-reclined passenger seat. After leaving the garage she had turned her back on Joe to stare out the window, sinking into a deep thoughtful silence as she watched the shadowed world flash by. Joe, too, with thoughts of his own, had welcomed the silence.

Persons unknown equal motives unknown. Once you know all the players, you can work out the play. In every successful investigation there is always a turning point, a single factor, a development upon which any resolution depends. A fulcrum. A clue. Something or someone around which or whom the whole investigation turns. Depends. It might be a single fibre found beneath a forensic microscope that places a possible suspect at the scene of the crime. It might be a witness who doesn't realise the importance of what they have seen or heard. It may be a stray comment heard on a bus, a magazine on a coffee-table, something seen on TV. A look in someone's eyes.

The unknown quantity.

Grace.

Driving now through pockets of rain, the road was like a

glistening slug's track in the headlights, climbing through close dark forests still stiff with snow before heading west across rolling barren hills where the silvery moon made glinting mirrors from the fleeting lochans; the names on the map, Glen Dochart, Ben More, Crianlarich . . .

He had recognised her immediately. Even with her blackened, blood-smeared face, wild eyes and sooted hair, as he carried her from the burning house to the car . . . the girl he had seen striking matches in Posers the night Dodds came in and restructured his face.

Grace it was who had attempted to set fire to Posers that night, and who had later succeeded with the massage-parlour on the night of the party. But how did she connect with Rankine? Through Dodds or Billy? Or was it something to do with Johnstone? And why did Billy McCulloch want her dead? Because she was a liability? Because she knew too much? Or merely because McCulloch liked to kill?

Questions, questions, questions, he thought angrily. More bloody questions than answers. Though there was one solution that sprang readily to mind: first use Grace to implicate Dodds in the murder of Rae, then use Dodds to implicate Billy, and Billy to implicate Rankine. The Domino Principle. It might work, he decided, but only if Grace could put the finger on Dodds, and only if Billy didn't find them both first.

Which were two too many ifs for this time in the morning. And there was still the matter of Karen's death to clear up. Joe sighed, as the burden of the last six days seemed suddenly to weigh heavily upon him . . .

Bearing north-west now, Joe drove through wailing squalls of wind-driven rain, passing Tyndrum – dead to the world – the road climbing again through deeper glens, Bridge of Orchy flashing by. Then having to slow as visibility dropped and fatigue set in, Rannoch Moor, the staccato hammering of rain on the roof hypnotic, the droning warmth of the heater inducing a trance-like drowsiness he was finding increasingly hard to keep at bay.

Eventually, he pulled into a lay-by, reclined his seat, and within seconds was fast asleep.

'Spooky,' Grace said, a few hours later as they dropped into Scotland's most infamous glen, the first streaks of dawn now blanching the bruised and swollen sky. Drizzle seeped through layers of mist stretched like gauze across the foot of the glen, from glossy black rock on one side to scree-mottled slope on the other, the towering silhouettes of the snow-capped summits looming like shadowy spectres over the narrow twist of road, closing out the sky. 'Definitely spooky.'

Joe had to agree. This wasn't the first time he'd driven through Glen Coe, and he felt it now as he had felt it before, the almost tangible sense of history through which he passed. As though the hacked and broken bodies of the murdered Clan MacDonald had been absorbed into the fabric of the place and breathed yet in the swirling eddies of mist. As though, if he strained his ears hard enough, he might any second hear the fearful screams of women and children being pursued up the flanks of the glen by Campbell battle-cries, hounds and blood-running swords. As though the treachery of that fateful February night in 1692 had seeped like MacDonalds' blood into the unforgiving soil, never to rest until the taste of revenge passed bitter-sweet and blood-warm through their cruelly silenced lips.

'Like passing through the Valley of the Shadow of Death,' he told Grace, his voice almost a whisper. He had to concentrate on the slippery road now as it dipped and wound through a gully of sheer black rock, there the river in spate to his left, there the looming Three Sisters ahead, and there the first sign of life, a straggle of trekkies in bright-coloured cagoules stomping down the road.

Grace said, 'You can almost feel it, can't you . . .' and Joe said, 'Mmm . . . Look at those idiots.'

'Like they've nothing better to do than obstruct the traffic.' Her mood strange, as though subdued by the weight of the atmosphere, her problems nothing but dust beside the awesome timelessness of their surroundings. 'It's funny, you know, but I've only ever seen this place in black-and-white photos. In the old history books you find buried in the library you have to ask the guy on the desk to carry over because they're so damn heavy they'd break your back. Drawings of bearded, kilted men with daggers and swords chasing women with babies in their arms up the sides of the glen – freaky stuff. And I always wondered how-the-fuck-come you never see any colour photos – like Glen Coe in spring, with the sun bright on purpled hills and wee baby lambs frolicking their fluffy little arses in the air – why everything was always black-and-white.'

Joe said, 'Yeah?' glancing across at her, expecting more.

'Until now.' She flicked a finger at the windscreen, beyond.

'Look. Black and white. Anywhere you care to look, black and white. Maybe a wee shade of grey over there, and the mist, and the cloud . . . but everything else, black-and-bloody-white.'

'What about those cagoules?' Passing the trekkies as he said it.

Grace turning in her seat to peer through the back. 'See that? They waved. You know what I hate, Joe? *Nice* people. People who smile and wave and want to talk first thing in the morning.'

'You know what?' Joe said, flashing her a smile. 'You just called me Joe.'

'It's your name, isn't it?'

Joe thinking, Yes, but there are different ways of saying it. Waiting until he accelerated out of the corner until he said, 'You want to know something else? You've only sworn once since you woke up. Know what that means? – you're beginning to relax.'

'Relax, fuck.' She sank back in the seat and disappeared under the blankets. 'I'm just past caring.'

Loch Linnhe to their left was a sheet of corrugated iron, with the Ardgour hills beyond rising bleakly out of the low-lying mist. Ben Nevis to their right, dark and leviathan beneath its snowy crown, caught in glimpses as they approached Fort William. Grace emerged from her snug cocoon as Joe finally killed the engine in the carpark above the square.

'Hungry?' Joe asked.

'Was Billy a Hun?'

Joe frowned. He hadn't thought of McCulloch in hours.

Grace read his expression. 'King Billy, stupid. William of Orange. William as in Fort William – get the picture?'

'Now you come to mention it . . .' Joe climbed out and stretched, breathing deep the cool, sharp air. Although they'd left the rain behind them on the Ballachulish Bridge, the stench of the fire still clung to his clothes; had entered, it seemed, every orifice in his body. He said, 'You want to wait here?'

'Do I look like Lady Godiva? Christ!'

'I'll need my jacket.'

'You're welcome.' Contorting inside the blankets, she eventually shrugged it from her shoulders. 'Have you never heard of dry-cleaning?' she asked, passing it through the window. 'Or deodorant?'

Her moods, Joe was beginning to realise, changed faster than the Scottish climate. Or maybe with it. He flipped through his wallet, sighed, asked her what size she took, what clothes she might need. Five minutes later he said, 'You think I'm made of money?'

'I know Porschers don't grow on trees.'

An hour later, Joe returned, laden with carrier-bags. 'If they don't fit,' he told her, 'you can take them back.' She grabbed the bags, peering in each one, at first with suspicion, then with the makings of a smile.

'Hey, amazing, you did as you were told.' Emptying the clothes out on to the driving seat, opening out the t-shirts and jeans, the blouses, jumpers and jacket. 'Except the jacket. I said no belts or epaulettes and you bring me belts and epaulettes.'

'You can cut them off.' Joe had cleaned himself up in a hotel cloakroom, changed into his own new clothes, dumping the old ones in the bin. He still needed a bed, bath and shave but nevertheless felt almost totally refreshed.

And maybe, he thought, beginning to enjoy himself.

'Feel that leather,' Grace said, 'it must've cost a packet. Maybe I'll keep the belt and epaulettes after all.' Looking up at him through different eyes to say, 'Thanks, Joe.'

'Yeah, Happy Christmas.' He pointed at a wooden building shaped like a pyramid, and said, 'I'll meet you in the café upstairs.'

He had to look again to be sure.

She came towards him as though across a catwalk, laying it on thick, swinging her arms and hips up to his table to give him a full double-twirl before swaggering over to the self-service counter, grabbing a tray. Then turned suddenly to catch his eyes moving up her body, throwing him a wink forged in lecherdom. Joe just as suddenly returned his attention to the morning's *Scotsman*, thinking, shit, blushing at his age, what the hell next.

It was there on the Home News page, a couple of paragraphs squeezed in the right-hand column. Under the heading, *Police seek fireraiser*.

'You look worried.' Grace slid into the opposite seat, began transferring plates from tray to table. Sausage, egg, bacon, beans and chips; a portion of cheesecake; a strawberry mousse; scones and jam; a wedge of 'death by chocolate' cake; a pot of tea for two.

A typical Highland breakfast.

'We made the papers,' he told her.

'We did? Great.' Filling her mouth with chips. 'What's it say?'

'That a fire destroyed one house and severely damaged two others on the Bankburn Estate. That police are regarding the fire as "suspicious"; that they and the council were unaware that anyone was living in the condemned houses. And that anyone with any information should contact the police immediately.'

'That's all?'

'What more do you want?'

'A body count? Descriptions of charred flesh and scorched bone?'

'You're right. Billy reads that and he's going to know you escaped. Which puts you right to the top of his hit-list.'

'Look at me tremble.'

'One thing you don't ever want to do,' Joe said, his voice dropping as he leant forward over the table, 'is underestimate Billy McCulloch. He's a professional, Grace, he doesn't give up. He's killed four people I know of, maybe more. A lot more.'

'So why's he still walking the streets?'

Joe shrugged and shook his head. It was one more question to which he had no logical answer.

'So there are some things you don't know, eh?' she said through a mouthful of bacon and egg. 'Or perhaps you're just not telling.'

'In time, Grace, in time.'

Anger sparked in her eyes. 'Don't patronise me. I'm not a bloody kid.' Her tone softened slightly. 'Anyway, I trusted you.'

'You had no choice.' Joe said, pouring himself a second cup of coffee. He spooned in an extra sugar, adding: 'And *I'm* not running from the law.'

'Just Billy.' Her smile was tight but tepid. 'So why does he want to kill you?'

'It's a long story, one I'll tell you later.' He tapped the article in the newspaper. 'What's more important right now is why he should want to kill you.'

'Because I know too much?'

'About what?'

'Some woman who died. He was asking roundabout questions, trying to find out how much Dodds had told me.'

'How much *did* Dodds tell you?'

'Apart from the fact he wanted no part in murder, nothing.'

'Did you believe him?'

'In a way. He was drinking too much and I think even scared. He said he was way out of his depth.'

'He was, and he is.'

Grace glanced at him askance. 'You know Dodds, you know Billy, and you know all about the fires. You don't talk about yourself, you give nothing away. Scary. Then, on top of that, you know Johnstone so well that he lends you his Porscher, and gives you the run of his cottage in the middle of fucking nowhere. Scarier still. Especially since I'm sure I've seen you somewhere before.'

Joe stared into his coffee. 'I've been meaning to ask,' he said, without looking up. 'Last night, before the fire, I heard screams . . .'

'The bastard,' she said with a sneer, pushing aside her first course, and starting on the cheesecake. 'Guy's a fucking pervert. First he makes out like he's going to kill me, then he says like maybe we could work something out. I thought what the hell, rather a few minutes of yuck than a big endless nothing.'

'Okay, I can guess the rest.'

'You don't want to hear the best bit?' A wicked smile now teasing her lips.

'There's a best bit?'

Laughing now, choking on cheesecake. 'You should've seen his face, Joe. It was a scream – I mean, literally. There he was, his Ys around his ankles, me on my bended knees and his thingy like a shrivelled-up acorn twitching in my face. I mean, I almost burst out laughing there and then.'

'You can laugh about it?' Joe amazed by her resilience, learning something new about her every minute.

'He said, What you do, princess, is you put it in your mouth. So I said, Then what? And he says,' – tears running down her cheeks now – 'Imagine it's a Cadbury Flake.'

'So?' Joe puzzled, not quite there yet.

'So I did. I bit it as hard as I could.'

'You what?'

'Well, Christ, Joe – I mean, who *sucks* a bloody Flake?'

CHAPTER 25

Eight miles south of Fort William the Corran Ferry crosses the racing Corran Narrows to Ardgour, a peninsula of long extinct volcanoes that is almost an island, surrounded by lochs Linnhe, Eil, Sunart and Shiel. Now the front had passed the sky above the snow-dusted hills of Ardgour and Sunart was a postcard-blue, with the tepid sun blinding off the loch, the morning suddenly in sharp relief.

'It says here that the old pier was built by Thomas Telford in 1815.' Grace read from the brochure, bracing herself against the side of the ferry as it struggled across the Narrows. Joe squinted against the sun's glare, looking south down the loch, seeing the hazy silhouette of Lismore Island in the distance and wondering idly what it would be like to live in such beautiful isolation.

'Thomas who?'

'Telford. The guy who built the Caledonian Canal.'

'Ah,' Joe said, 'him.' There were only four other cars on the ferry but Grace and Joe were the only passengers to have left the warmth of their car for the cold of the wind and the lash of flying spray. Joe wondering now if he looked as ghostly white as Grace.

'It says sometimes the current here is so strong the ferry sinks and everyone on board dies a horribly painful death.'

'Yeah?' Joe trying to think of anything he might have forgotten to buy in the way of supplies. Worrying what he would do for money once he returned to the city.

'See? You're not listening, are you? Just patronising me again, like ignore me and I'll go away.'

'I was thinking,' he told her, 'that's all.'

'About what? How you can't wait to get rid of me?'

'That I should've filled up the tank before we left.'

'You're right, you should of.' Grace turned suddenly to lean over the side. 'Oh shit,' she said, retching, 'I knew that second cup of tea was a mistake.'

They came off the ferry last, turned south, the road clinging to the Ardgour coastline. Grace studied herself in the rearview mirror.

'You look fine,' Joe said. 'In fact, you look great.'

'You're just saying that.'

Joe said, 'No, it's true. You're a different girl—'

'There you go again. Patronising.'

'—woman. You're a different woman from the one I saw in Posers, the night you tried to burn it down. The night Dodds came in.'

Grace turned in her seat to stare at him. He kept his eyes on the road, the sun now glancing off Loch Linnhe to the left, the Glen Coe mountains dark towers in the distance beyond.

Suddenly she slapped her brow.

'I must be going senile,' she said. 'Of course. That's where I saw you before. You were the bouncer, the one I told to bog right off.'

'Steward. I was the steward whose teeth your boyfriend kicked in.'

'Boyfriend, fuck. The guy's a slab of brain-dead meat. I ever wanted a boyfriend I could of gone down the slaughterhouse and found a more lively one in the freezer.'

'He created the diversion while you sneaked through to the cupboard under the stair.'

'I was almost sick just thinking about it. Why didn't you fight back?'

A question Joe had asked himself many times since. 'Parole,' he told her lamely. Knowing it was more than that.

'Parole?' She let the word hang there between them as the road broke free from the shore to swing west through Glen Tarbert. Then she said, 'Of course. Dodds said you were a cop. An ex-cop. That you'd killed . . . oh fuck, his boss's daughter . . .' Grace breaking off to stare at him with a dawning apprehension.

'Brilliant. Here I am in the middle of nowhere, stuck in a stolen car with a woman-killer who used to be a cop. Thank *you* Lord.'

Joe smiled. 'She was my fiancée, Grace, and I didn't kill her. The charges were dropped.'

'Of course they were. You were a cop.'

'How old are you? Fifteen? Sixteen? You wear your cynicism well.'

'*Twenty-one*. And you wear yours like a shabby old raincoat.'

The silence stretched as far as the road, straight and empty into the distance. Joe, pushing the accelerator to the floor, watched the needle climb through the seventies, eighties, then the nineties. Holding the hundred mark, arms braced, hoping he didn't meet any sheep wandering across the road.

Grace was holding on to the underside of her seat, but smiling. 'Okay. I'm sorry. I believe you. You didn't kill your fiancée.'

Lifting his foot off the accelerator, Joe said, 'You sure now?'

'Dead sure.'

Joe slowed to a perambulatory sixty as the road narrowed to a single lane and Loch Sunart appeared, glinting, on their left.

Grace said, 'But you were still a cop.'

The hotel bar was small, low-ceilinged and dark, empty but for the pot-bellied landlord and a large Alsatian. A small tinsel Christmas tree stood on the bar and cards hung like banners from a piece of string stretched across its length. Diluted sunlight filtered through the dusty window at the far end of the room, barely warming the carpet-tiled floor. Grace ordered Chicken Kiev with chips and salad, and a Diet Coke, while Joe settled for a hamburger – no chips – and a glass of water.

'Where you going?'

Joe grinned, dropped the car-keys on the table. 'Don't worry,' he said, 'I'm only making a call.'

Wylie said, 'Where the fuck've you been, man? I've been trying to get hold of you for ages.'

Joe said, 'It's a long story,' and told him an edited version. When he'd finished, Wylie asked where Billy was now.

'Last I saw, he was sitting outside my flat.'

'You want me to check it out for you, Joe? Give it a sweep?'

'Aye. There's a broom in the cupboard.'

Wylie sniffed. 'Very funny.'

Joe said, 'Try the Mentone House Hotel. That's where he was staying yesterday.'

Yesterday? Joe thought. Was it only yesterday?

'Yeah? And what do I do then?' Wylie sounded like a petulant kid.

Joe said, 'All that fancy equipment in your office and you ask me that?'

The fat detective didn't sound convinced. 'I'll see,' he said. 'Where can I contact you?'

'At the cottage. If there's a phone, I'll call you tonight.'

'And a Merry Christmas to you, too.'

Grace said, 'It says here the Gaelic for Strontian means "Point of the Fairies".' Studying the brochure again.

'I thought Strontian was a metal.'

'*Strontium* is the metal, stupid. Apparently it's an element of Strontianite, discovered here . . . fuck, probably by the fairies. And you know what? They used to use it in fireworks. For the crimson flames.'

'I'd have thought you'd had enough flames recently to last you a lifetime.'

'I have, believe me.' A very small voice.

Their meals arrived and for a while they were silent as they ate, watched over by the drooling Alsatian.

'Who did you phone?' Grace asked, wiping her plate with a piece of bread.

'Guy called Wylie, a private detective.'

'Why do you need a PI? An ex-cop like you.'

'To find a few things out.'

'Like what, oh man of mystery?'

'Like why you should want to torch Johnstone out of business.'

'Easy,' Grace said. 'For the money.'

Joe waited.

'Okay, so I had my reasons. The money was just a bonus.'

'Who paid you?'

'Dodds. You going to bring out the rubber hose now?'

'That's an idea. You ever been behind the door?'

'A stroll at Cornton Vale – and you?'

'Saughton, for too long. What charge?'

'Fire-raising.' With a mischievous smile. 'And you?'

'Conspiracy.'

'Yeah? I never took you for a bent cop. Weird maybe, but not bent. So what did you do, if you didn't kill your woman?'

Joe sighed. 'They found some money I couldn't account for.'

'Why not?'

'Because I'd never seen it before.'

'How much?'

'Twenty thousand. Cash.'

'Someone wasted that much money just to set you up?' Shaking her head in disbelief. 'Sure.'

'Not just someone,' Joe said, 'but your boyfriend's boss.'

'Jack Rankine? Why would he do a thing like that to his prospective son-in-law?'

'Maybe I was getting too close.' Joe pushed back his chair. 'Shall we go?'

The single-track road into Ardnamurchan clings to the southern lip of the peninsula, crushed between the lower forested slopes of the hills and the jagged shore of Loch Sunart. Across the coruscating water, the tree-lined shore of Morvern and the isles of Risga, Oronsay and Carna; and there in the hazy western distance, the island of Mull.

'You know what Ardnamurchan is Gaelic for?' Grace still with her nose in the tourist brochure.

'Hangover?'

'No,' she giggled. 'It means "height of the great seas". Though I don't see why. I mean, they don't look high to me.'

'Maybe it was pygmies lived here then.'

'Maybe you're right.' She was quiet for a moment, content, it seemed, to stare out across the loch through the gaps in the trees. Joe was about to switch on the radio when she asked, 'Getting too close to what, Joe?'

'The truth? Or Rankine's daughter? I'm still not sure.'

'The truth about what?'

'A guy called Cosmo Vass. Used to be Rankine's partner and fellow director on the Rancor board. You've heard of Rancor?'

'Some kind of corporation, right?'

Joe nodded. 'Anyway, this was back when Rankine was trying to go legit, polish his public image. There was even talk of him going into politics.'

'Sounds like he had the right pedigree.'

'And enough low friends in high places to oil the necessary

palms. Still, it never happened. What did happen is Rancor. Under Cosmo Vass's direction, it soon became Scotland's fastest-growing fast-food and restaurant chain.'

'I didn't realise it was *that* big.'

'It isn't, not any more. When Vass died Rancor was bought over by CatCom, and Rankine pocketed a clean six mil, plus I don't know how many shares, and a seat on the board. Which was all very fortunate for our good friend Jack.'

'You mean because his partner died?'

'Exactly. It was no secret in the business world that Rankine was in favour of the merger and Vass against. Next thing you know, Vass is dead and the merger complete. Only Vass didn't just die, he was murdered.'

'And that's where you came in?'

'Aye,' Joe said in a light parody. 'Detective Sergeant Costello was then assigned the case.'

'You were in charge?' Impressed.

'Hell, no. Just a very small part of the Murder Squad.'

Grace said, 'I've never seen a real dead body before.'

'You wouldn't ever want to. And certainly not the body of Cosmo Vass. The guy was ripped to pieces.'

'Funny I never read about it.'

'You probably did. Remember the Acid Killer?'

'Vaguely. Some kind of sadist, wasn't he? Used acid to burn off people's faces or something.'

'Close,' Joe said. 'His speciality was the kind of acid that melts down your mind, not the skin off your hands. Lysergic acid diethylamide, commonly known as LSD.'

'That's right. He'd spike them up, then torture them. Give them the worst trip of their lives. How many did he eventually do?'

'Three we knew of. First, the guy they found at the bottom of the Crags; then a small-time dope dealer they found floating in the Union Canal with a fishing-rod up his arse.'

'Bum catch.'

'Then finally, Cosmo Vass. All three murders were apparently motiveless, the victims tortured, and each body contained large amounts of LSD. In Vass's case, the post-mortem revealed he'd taken at least three hours to die from the multiple wounds sustained. Worse, that he'd been conscious for most of that time.'

'Jesus,' Grace said, lapsing into thoughtful silence as Joe pulled into a passing-space and waited until the post-van had passed. 'So you think Rankine had something to do with Vass's death?'

'I thought it was all far too convenient, yes. One of the first things you do in any murder investigation is ask yourself, "who benefits?" Whether by chance or coincidence, it doesn't matter – who gains is the vital question. Even with the random killings of a serial killer; sometimes they get lazy and start poaching close to home.'

'So Rankine stood to benefit most?'

'Like I said, it was all too convenient. Rankine wanted out but Vass didn't. Then Vass was murdered, apparently by some maniac who picked his victims at random. Too much of a coincidence. I began thinking that if Vass's murder was not as random as it seemed, then it was possible the killer was somehow connected to Rankine. But it seemed I was the only one. Everyone on the squad knew there was something heavy between Rankine and my father, so they naturally thought I was just out for revenge. That I wanted Rankine involved for personal reasons.'

'So who did *they* suspect?'

'Any pinned-out junkie who happened to fall under their microscope. Last I heard, they had about fifty thousand suspects.'

'And they never caught him?'

Joe shrugged. 'I'm sure the files are still open.'

'But you couldn't prove it was Rankine?'

'He had an alibi. Anyway, it's not in his nature to dirty his hands when he can pay someone else to do it.'

'So what did you do?'

'Nothing. I was taken off the case. Too personally involved, they said.'

Grace frowned. 'I don't see—'

'I'd met Karen by then, Rankine's daughter. Corny it may sound, but it was love at first glance. For both of us.'

'So?'

'So Rankine made a big issue of it. He talked to my superior and said I was pursuing a vendetta. That I was only living with his daughter to investigate him. That I wanted to involve him in the inquiry because he was against Karen and me getting married. That I was a bent cop looking for a score, and only using his daughter to get at him.'

'And now you think Rankine put you in the frame to get you off his back?'

'That seemed the general idea: two birds with one small stone. Except something went wrong.'

'And Karen died?'

'Exactly.'

'You think Rankine was behind that?'

Joe shook his head. He'd ploughed this furrow a million times and still came up with the same conclusion. 'Not a chance,' he said. 'He loved his daughter, absolutely worshipped her. That's why he was so damned protective. I don't think he wanted her to marry *anyone*.'

'What about whoever planted the money? Maybe she walked in on him and splatto, next thing she knows she's dead.'

'And Rankine when he hears just accepts it? Says, Well, we all make mistakes, forget it, she was only my only daughter?' Joe shaking his head again, the same old furrow. 'I don't think so. The money could have been planted weeks before she died, Rankine just waiting for the right moment to tip off my superiors.'

'So who killed her?'

'A dead man,' Joe said, his face set hard as the granite hills through which they climbed. 'If I ever find out.'

The road broke away from the shoreline now to climb through desolate snow-speckled hills, a glimpse every now and then of iced-over lochans and shaggy-haired sheep. Clouds gathered on the horizon. For several miles neither of them spoke, each locked in their heads by the same combination of thoughts. It was Grace who finally broke the silence.

'Billy,' she said, 'You think Billy was the Acid Killer.'

'I'll tell you a wee story . . .'

'He was working for Rankine at the time, a nobody, a wee Gorgie wideboy who thought the world owed him a favour but wasn't going to pay. A chip on his shoulders some people call a head. First time I came up against him, he was a postie doing the rounds. One of the punters he delivered to accused him of poaching his giro, so next again day Billy rings the guy's bell, waits for the boy to start unlocking the door, then runs a fucking sword through the letterbox. Nice man. Second and last time up he did a finger for ABH and walked on a technicality. Not long after, he's seen flashing steel for Rankine and calling himself a "policy adviser".'

'Extortion?'

'By any other name, yes.'

196

'I don't understand. From all accounts, Rankine had more money than he knew what to do with. Why go in for all the hardarm stuff?'

'Why do some people want to rule the world, and others conquer Everest?'

'Because they're nutters; two coupons short of a toaster.'

Joe laughed.

'So Billy was Rankine's enforcer?'

'One of them. He was still a nothing then, a wideboy faster with his chib than he was with his brain. One among thousands on the streets. He got pulled a few times, sure, but nothing ever stuck, Rankine's lawyers made sure of that. Then a few years ago we fish that dealer from the canal and suddenly Billy's the shadow in suit and shades going all the places Rankine goes. A year later, Vass is found with his head in a vice and the Acid Killer hits the headlines again. Next thing you know, I'm going up the stairs for conspiracy while Billy's climbing on a sun bound plane with a wad in his sporran. You believe in coincidence?'

'If you knew all this at the time why didn't you say so?'

'Maybe my boss was right – I was too personally involved. I was in so deep everything became distorted. Looking for patterns to fit theories instead of theories to fit patterns. Billy was there the whole time, on the periphery of the investigation, to my mind nothing more than the wideboy he seemed. He didn't fit the psychological profile so I ruled him out. My mistake. It wasn't until I had a talk with Dodds that everything just fell into place.'

'You saw Dodds? When?'

'Just before he went into hospital. He was very helpful.'

'So, you paid him back.'

'Are you sorry?'

'I was just thinking, you and me, we're not really that different. When it comes to revenge.'

'Revenge is a poor man's dream. The first few months I was behind the door, the thought of it was the only thing that kept me sane. But then, I don't know, as the months became a year, the desire for revenge seemed to fade. Like a fire without oxygen. By the time I passed out through the gates, all I wanted was to pick up the pieces of my life and start again. Forget the past, look to the future.'

'So what happened?'

'Rankine happened. Rankine and Billy McCulloch.'

Coming down out of the hills Loch Sunart opened out again below them, the long smear of Mull on the horizon seemingly afire as the setting sun tinged the smokelike clouds in pink and gold. To the west, Ben Hiant, rising from the sea; to the east, Kilchoan, a scattering of houses squeezed between the hills and the bay. The ruins of a castle – Mingary, Grace informed him – to their left as they approached the village. They stopped to ask the way and were directed up a track to the right. The one right at the top, the woman said.

The track wound up through a cluster of modern holiday homes, all dark-stained pine around glint of glass.

'I thought you said it was a cottage,' Grace said disappointedly as they approached. 'Like a real butt-and-ben.'

Joe pulled to a halt in front of the building, killed the engine. 'You never seen an A-Frame before?' He hadn't either, but he'd seen pictures. Didn't care what it looked like, so long as it was warm and dry on the inside.

Neither made a move to leave the car, Joe leaning forward against the wheel as Grace chewed her lip.

'What I don't understand, Joe, is if Billy is the Acid Killer, how come he never spiked *me* up last night.'

Joe reached into his pocket and withdrew a small narrow bottle which he held up between forefinger and thumb, 'I found this taped behind the toilet in his hotel room. Yesterday, a few hours before he came to call on you. You want to try a wee taste, go ahead.'

'Acid?'

'Give it an hour and you'll be watching patterns crawl across the wall. Two hours and you'll be saying things like, *Hey, groovy – far out, man!*'

'Then what?'

'You're doomed. To a life wearing flares.'

CHAPTER 26

'We could always kick his door down,' Dodds suggested hopefully.

'Who's making the decisions here, you or me?'

'You are, Billy.'

'So shut it and let me think.'

Joe Costello was not at home. Two days since Billy had read the article in the paper, and two days now that Costello had failed to return to his top-floor Easter Road flat. Coincidence? Was it fuck. Three days was more than enough time to start jumping to conclusions – and more than enough time to find a man in the city if you knew where to look and who to ask. Except no one he spoke to seemed to know or care, and Billy himself was running out of ideas. Ideas and patience.

They sat in a small, draughty café on Easter Road, hunched over cooling coffees, Billy facing the street so he could watch for anyone entering or leaving Costello's stair. In the last two hours only the postman had come and gone.

Dodds said, 'Or we could try Johnstone's place again?'

'Yeah?' Billy sneered. 'And draw even more attention to ourselves?'

Johnstone's pseudo-majestic mansion in Colinton was the second place they checked. No answer when he phoned the first time, a message on an answering-machine the second and subsequent times. No cars parked out front the first day but a small red van sitting in the drive every time they had passed since. When Billy said fuck it in the afternoon of the second day and nosed the Sierra up the drive, a guy in a uniform and carrying a clipboard stepped from the van and ambled towards them. *J, & J, White* was the name painted on the side of the van, and below it, *Home Security*. Billy said, Who the hell are you? and the guy said, Who the hell are *you*? and it could have gone on like that all day if Billy hadn't felt his patience tearing at the seams. So he told the guy he was Johnstone's cousin just passing through and what the hell was going on that Jay needed fucking bodyguards posted round his house, was Salman Rushdie coming for tea or what? The security guard stared at Billy blankly for a moment before reading his reply off the clipboard. Something about Mr Johnstone being away on holiday, would Billy like to leave a message. Billy said, Yeah – tell him I never liked him any way.

Now Dodds said, 'Costello could still be in there. Just because all the windows are shuttered and the place closed up doesn't mean he isn't there. Him and the bitch.'

Billy smiled. 'Face facts, Dodds. Wherever they are, after two days of humping she won't be coming home to roost on you.'

'That man is dead. I get my hands on him, I tell you he is dead.'

'Hand,' Billy corrected.

Dodds clenched the fist hanging from the sling and said, 'One is all I need.'

'Fury of a moron scorned,' Billy laughed, reaching over to tweak the big man's cheek. 'You going to sit here moping all day or what? Go phone those hotels again, see if your boyfriend's checked in anywhere.'

Dodds glared at him through his one good eye, then sloped over to the phone on the end of the counter and began dialling. Watching Billy like a well-kicked dog from across the room. Since yesterday morning, when Billy had checked him out of the Infirmary – eyepatch, sling, bandages and all – the moron had been walking round with his face dragging the ground. More concerned that the firebug might be knobbing someone else than the fact that she might be blabbing about a murder. When Billy began jumping at conclusions and suggested she might be nuzzling nipples with Joe Costello, Dodds almost choked on his tongue. But at least, now, Billy wasn't getting bored.

Dodds returned, slumping into his seat with a sigh. 'He must be using another name. Or staying with friends.'

'Rankine says he has no friends, not since he went inside.' Billy wondered if he ought to check the hospitals again, let Dodds try all the hostels and bed and breakfasts.

Dodds said, 'What about relatives?'

Billy stared at the moron. 'You think I haven't already thought of that?' he snapped, wishing to fuck he had. Christ, what was happening, he was losing his touch.

'So?'

'He's got a father somewhere is all I know.' Billy dredging his memory now. 'He was mentioned at Costello's trial. Something about . . . a vendetta, if I remember correctly. With . . .'

Jack Rankine. Of course.

Rankine sounded weak on the phone, his voice hoarse, wavering. He said, 'You found him yet?'

'Maybe. You know where his old man stays?'

Rankine chuckled. 'That old fart? Hah! Course I know where he is, I put him there.'

'Where,' Billy asked, 'did you put him?' As though trying to persuade a child to remember.

'Ward 14. The Royal.' Rankine choked on brittle laughter. 'You think Costello's hiding out there? Under his father's bed?'

Billy hung up, returned to the table.

'Come on,' he told Dodds, 'let's move.'

'You know where he is?'

'No,' Billy said, 'but I know where he isn't.'

'Where's that?'

'At home.'

If home is where the heart is, Joe Costello was a heartless bastard. The flat was less a home than a mid-Forties-Fifties museum-piece. Cold and dusty, dark and musty, it offered sparse comfort and seemed little more than a makeshift shelter from the storm. The dark wood, the framed photos of people long dead stuffed in stuffy clothes in stiff postures staring grimly at the camera. One of the Sacred Heart. The tiled fireplace, the ashes in the grate, the silent clock on the mantelpiece, the dull brass ornaments, a statuette of the Madonna and child, the stiff-backed chairs, the grimy windows and threadbare carpet, the pile of old newspapers in the corner. A large black and white TV beneath a framed, embroidered picture of something not immediately apparent with the words

THOU SHALT FEAR THE LORD in large letters underneath. Looking around the room, Billy could see no sign of Joe Costello ever having lived here, as though the man existed only in the minds of others, leaving no visible mark as he passed through life. Certainly no evidence around of his days in the polis. No framed commendations or certificates on the wall, no medals for bravery, no crossed truncheons over the mantelpiece. Just plain fucking weird.

Dodds called from down the dimly lit hall. Billy found the moron in a small bedroom – as characterless as the rest of the house – going through a wardrobe.

'Look at all this,' Dodds said, pulling clothes from hangers, throwing them on the unmade bed. 'I mean, fuck, Billy, would you be seen dead in any of these?' Holding up a bunch of gaudy silk shirts with collars like elephant ears. 'Or this?' Holding up a puce-coloured three-piece, double-breasted, flared, with buttons all over the place and lapels wide enough to land a microlite on. 'Or these?' What looked like a job-lot of ties from Carnaby Street.

Billy shook his head, grinning. 'Well, well, well,' he said, 'the man's human after all.'

'Human? I've seen aliens with a better fucking dress-sense.'

'But feel the quality, man,' Billy said, fingering one of the black silk shirts. 'If it wasn't for the collars . . .'

Dodds flashed him a wary look from his one good eye. 'Hey, and look what else I found.' Reaching into the open bedside drawer to extract a thick five-year diary. 'Full of newspaper clippings, photos and stuff. Pictures of him and some woman. See?'

Billy glanced through the photos.

'Doll like that,' Dodds said, 'what the hell could she see in the likes of Costello? I mean, what a waste.'

'Karen,' Billy said, his voice dry. 'Rankine's daughter.' His pulse was racing, breath coming fast and jerky; he could feel a flashback coming on.

'You all right?'

No he wasn't. He sat down on the bed. Thinking, not now, Lord, not fucking now. But his heart already pounding out of control, vision going a little fuzzy round the edges.

Flashback.

'You look like you seen a ghost, Billy.'

Almost. Staring at the photo a second ago, of Karen and Costello lying on a beach somewhere hot, seeing her smiling eyes looking up at him, into him, through him, feeling the subtle shift in time, watching her shining eyes cloud, then blacken, to become small round holes suddenly seeping blood.

How he'd left her on the floor the last time he saw her.

Dodds said, 'Shit, Billy, you had me scared back there.'

Billy said nothing. He watched the snowflakes fall like puffs of cotton-wool against the windscreen, his brain charged by a million tiny electrical impulses, overloaded by the flood of incoming sensory data.

Flashback.

A hazard of the trade. He'd had them before, many times. But not for a while; since last summer, in fact. He'd been walking around the headland between Calella de Palafrugell and Llafranch – clambering over the rocks so he could check out the *chicas* basking naked by the shore – when the flashback came at him out of the clear blue sky, a seagull's shriek causing a little time-bomb of acid to explode in his brain, taking him back through the years to the first bad trip he'd ever had, down by the Leith Docks: seagulls, thousands of them, blackening the sky, screaming out of the dawn like pterodactyls, scaly talons dripping torn flesh and glistening blood aimed at his bursting heart, the ground beneath his feet like chewing-gum, every panicking step a lifetime long as the oily green water licked hungrily at the barnacled stanchions of the pier from which he was desperately trying to escape . . . The fear in the flashback as real as when it happened, he'd clambered hastily back across the rocks to the safety of the shaded *camino* where giant flying reptiles can't see the terror in your eyes.

'So what now?' Dodds said and Billy looked at him, stared at him, saw the pores on his face breathing, globules of sweat oozing out, like dewdrops on the moron's facial hair. Shit.

He said, trying to haul down a thought and keep it there, 'You have a father, Dodds? Any chance of that?'

Dodds was hurt. 'Course, haven't you?'

'Not so's I'd know. This father of yours, what does he do for Christmas? Visit you? Or do you visit him?'

'Usually he comes down, stays a couple a days, leaves just before I throw him out on the street. Why?'

'Christmas,' Billy said, concentrating now, 'is a special time. A time for families to put away their differences and all gather together. So what d'you think the chances are, Costello will go see his old man in hospital tomorrow? Maybe even take him out for the day?'

Dodds scratched his head. 'I dunno, Billy. The wife'd kill me, if I didn't show up all day.'

'You want to find Costello? Catch him in the middle of snogging your lovebird's snatch?'

'Okay. So what if he doesn't show?'

'Remember the fat PI? Wylie?' Billy smiled at the thought. 'We climb down his chimney and fill him full of the festive spirit. Then get him to sing a few carols.'

Dodds turned the ignition. 'You think he knows where Costello is?'

'Fuck no. But a man's gotta have some festive fun.'

CHAPTER 27

He awoke, body running in sweat. The room black as a womb but cold as ice. Black but for the narrow strip of light beneath the door, broken now by two restless shadows. Not knowing where he was, nor who it was who stood so quietly in the hall outside. Fear gripped his mind in its vice-like glove, paralysing him. Waiting for the rattle of keys in the lock, the heavy door to swing softly open on running shadows, masked faces, coming at him . . .

for him . . .

. . . with balled fists and vicious kicks and words of wisdom for his ringing ears,

How's it feel, Costello? Not so brave now, without your flat-tops by your side, are you? Think you're something special, do you? Think you're safe down here with all the beasts, eh? Think solitary can save you? Well, think on this, Costello. And this. And this. And this . . .

But the door opened without a key.

'Karen?'

'Who's Karen?' The figure approached the bed uncertainly, a dark silhouette in a halo of light. A sense of *déjà vu.*

Feeling his hackles rise. 'Karen?' But it couldn't be. Blinking, as he reached out to touch.

'It's me, stupid. Grace.' Taking his hand, clutching it to her chest. 'What did you think I was, a ghost?' Sitting tentatively on the edge of the bed.

Joe fell back on the pillow. A ghost, yeah, how stupid. Of course it was Grace. Who else? Recalling the fire now, the flight from the city, the leisurely drive here – two days ago? That long? – to the edge of the world. Falling into bed almost immediately, asleep even before he closed his eyes. Grace.

And yesterday, where had yesterday gone?

Thinking now, his hand still gripped by both of hers, how much she reminded him of Karen. Karen, too, had been small and slim. And moody. Her life either up or down, but never in between. No grey areas, everything sharply in focus, black and white. God, how the pain still hurt.

'Christ,' he said, still breathing hard. 'I was back inside. Down on the bottom landing . . . with all the beasts again.' Strands of fear like a broken web, clinging still.

'They put you in with all the perverts?' She massaged his hand as though it were frostbitten. 'What the hell for?'

'For my own protection.'

'Because you were a cop?'

Joe nodded. 'I'd have been mince in days if they'd left me on the landing any longer. Must've been at least half a dozen cons in the hall that I'd helped put there in the first place.'

'I'd've been terrified . . .'

'The first week there were mornings I was slopping out, I needed two hands to carry the pot along the hall. I'd look down and see half my bloody intestine there.'

She touched his brow with the palm of her hand.

'You want me to stay?'

A part of him said yes. A growing part. But his mouth said, 'I'll be all right.'

'Lucky you.' Grace rose from the bed, smoothed down her night-shirt and crossed to the door. 'If you need me again, just yell.' Her voice a cool echo in the sudden dark as she closed the door behind her.

Wind gusted, buffeting her window. The house had a whole family of sounds, special nocturnal sounds: the groaning and creaking of all kinds of wood; the moans of the whispering wind as it slithered under doors and whistled through keyholes; the tiny scratchings behind the skirting-boards that made her heart leap and miss its beat; the sound of Joe tossing and turning next door. It was like being stranded on a ghost ship, she had imagined last night: adrift and becalmed on the Sargasso Sea, Joe as the ship's Mate, and she the rebellious stowaway, out looking for adventure.

Mm.

She lay on her side, head propped in her hand, reading in the flickering candlelight. Trying to read. A part of her mind absorbing the words automatically as the rest of her mind worked overtime. Men. They just didn't understand. Like they were born on a different planet, spoke a different language. You had to spell it out for them, word by word, or they'd end up believing what they wanted to believe. Which was never to a woman's advantage, never had been.

Joe Costello. Said it was an Italian name. That his great or great-great-grandfather had brought over from some unpronounceable place in the north-west of Italy at the turn of the century. Came over to work on the Forth Rail Bridge, of all things. Joe certainly looked Italian, though, what with his dark, dark hair, and deep brown eyes that crinkled at the corners when he smiled. And his moustache: like Sacco – or was it Vanzetti – the Italian anarchist she'd read about in the library last week, the day before Dodds came storming in and later told her about killing the woman in the car.

What seemed like a lifetime ago.

He said he was thirty-one but looked thirty-five. Perhaps the pressures of incarceration had aged him. It had certainly aged *her*, the stroll she'd done at the Vale. She was mature for her age, her social worker had told her once. It didn't make her look any older though. Which was a bumful. Because Joe would probably see her as some snotty-nose brat complicating his life instead of as a woman, a woman with needs. Patronise her.

Except he hadn't done so yet.

She remembered the way he'd blushed when she'd caught his gaze lingering on her bum in the café the other day. Smiling now as she recalled her smile of the moment and the small but satisfying sense of relief she had felt that at least he was human in one respect.

Sure, he'd been a cop. But then who's perfect? Anyway, he didn't look like a cop, not any of the cops she'd ever seen. More like an academic, a university lecturer or something. The way he dressed, faded jeans and cowboy boots, heavy red jumper and Tweed jacket with leather patches on the elbows. Weird. Old enough to have been a freak in the early Seventies but he'd become a cop. The whole world broadening their minds at the time and there's Joe trying to narrow his. Okay, Grace wasn't going to criticise him for that; as far as she was concerned everything he had done in his life until the moment he crashed in and saved hers was fine by her. Destiny had brought them together and the power of Destiny was not to be sniffed at, nor dismissed as mere coincidence. No, there was definitely some strange power at work here. Joe had saved her life because he was meant to save her life. Though what she was meant to do next, she wasn't altogether sure.

She looked up as the door opened and light from the hall spilled across the pine floor, suppressed a smile as she squinted through the candle flame at Joe standing there in his boxer shorts, holding the door like he wasn't sure what to do with it.

'I changed my mind,' he said, looking sheepish.

'You took your time.' Closing the book, placing it next to the candle on the bedside table. Then sliding across to give him room.

'I couldn't sleep,' he said. 'The wind.'

'I warned you about the beans.'

'The wind rattling the shutters.'

'God, you're cold.' She snuggled in close, wrapping her arms around him. He smelled of smoke. Smoke and man. There was a small crescent-shaped scar on his shoulder-blade. She ran her tongue along its length, kissed it softly. Joe purred like a cat. No problem, she thought, and kissed it again.

'Joe?' she asked, squirming closer still. 'Do you believe in Destiny?'

But he wasn't purring, he was snoring.

Men.

CHAPTER 28

Scrunched into their jackets, hair blowing wild, they sat on the rocks below the lighthouse – the lighthouse that stood on the westernmost tip of mainland Britain – as leviathan waves, whipped into frenzy by the gale-force north-westerly winds, crashed against the rugged shoreline in explosions of icy spume.

Grace's mood had been subdued all morning.

During the half-hour drive from the A-Frame, she had turned her back on him and spent the journey looking out the side window at the barren, rolling snowscape. She had answered his attempts at small-talk with monosyballic replies, her thoughts imprisoned in a dungeon so deep behind her eyes, it seemed, that she couldn't even hear his voice.

Joe said, 'So what's the problem?'

'You,' Grace snapped. 'Crawling into my bed last night.'

'I'm sorry. I thought that's—'

'*Then* falling fast asleep. It's not normal.'

'No?'

'No.' She stared off into the distance, across to where the churning grey sea met the churning grey sky. 'You could at least have said goodnight.'

Joe said nothing. He'd woken this morning to the sound of smashing crockery in the kitchen below, wondering how he'd ended up in Grace's bed. Had lain there for a long while, breathing her scent off the pillow, thinking of Karen, thinking of Rae, trying

209

the power of telepathy to will her back up the stairs. Descending eventually when the smell of frying bacon became more than he could bear.

'Or maybe you think I'm too young.'

Joe shook his head.

'Or a virgin.'

'Nothing of the sort.'

'So now I'm a whore. Great.'

Joe looped his arm round her shoulders and, laughing, pulled her close. 'Grace,' he said, 'you are a very desirable woman. A little fucked up, sure, but still most definitely desirable. The moment I get you home—'

'Oh, so now I'm a little fucked up?'

'Sexually maladjusted is one way they put it.'

'One way who puts it?'

'The professionals. The people who draw up psychological profiles of the typical pyromaniac.'

'Me?' Incredulous. 'A typical pyromaniac?'

'Straight from the textbook. Not only sexually maladjusted but also inadequate.'

A seventh wave disintegrated on the rocks below, drenching them with its whiplash spray. They had to shout against the rising wind.

'How would you know? You were snoring enough for both of us.'

'And you've probably had only a limited contact with members of the opposite sex.'

'Crap!'

'And most likely you have problems developing and maintaining interpersonal relationships.'

'Go fuck yourself.' Grace broke away from the crutch of his arm, rose to her feet. 'Just because you read it in some fancy polis-manual you think it's true? That we are what we are because of rules carved in stone? Grow up, Joe.'

She turned and climbed towards the lighthouse.

They were in the Porsche, heading slowly back to the A-Frame through rivers of slush, Joe keeping the needle below thirty as visibility dropped with the sagging dark sky. Thunder rumbled, echoing flatly off distant peaks, no more than faint silhouettes in the lightning's flash.

'What else did it say?' Grace asked. When Joe took his eyes from the road to regard her quizzically, she added, 'That psychological profile burned into your memory.'

'Forget it,' Joe said, squinting through the windscreen now as the wipers battled against the almost horizontal rain. 'I was only joking.'

'So tell me.' Her humour was back, he could see, etched in mischievous lines at the corners of her mouth, glowing like coals in her eyes. 'Tell me all about myself.'

Joe didn't answer immediately. He was thinking of a line in an old Dylan song Karen had once used to describe him. *So easy to look at, so hard to define.* Thinking now, how well it suited Grace. And how easily Karen and Grace were now becoming intertwined, as though one in his thoughts and dreams. Past and present fusing into a molten confusion of long-suppressed emotion no longer smarting with pain. Realising now that he could think and talk of Karen in Grace's presence and not feel the unbearable longing that had always accompanied such thoughts. Smiling inwardly, he said, 'Where do you want me to start?'

'With my happy childhood.'

Headlights suddenly broached the brow of the hill. Joe braked, pulling neatly into a passing-place only moments before a red minivan sprang from the murk and passed with a flash of lights and blaring horn.

'Look, a Highland Cow!' Grace said, as a dark shape moved towards them along the fence by the side of the road.

'Highland Cow, hell,' Joe grinned, 'that's a Highland Pony.'

'It is?' Grace giggled into her sleeve. 'Better not send *me* out for milk in the morning, then.' She took a deep breath and wiped her eyes. 'You were saying? About my happy childhood?'

'Let me see,' Joe said. 'For happy, read miserable. You grew up in a harsh environment with inconsistent discipline and parental neglect, most likely in a broken home. You're quite intelligent but you probably did badly at school, what they call scholastically retarded – an underachiever. You were possibly fostered out – and if so, more than once – and have a history of delinquency. You either ran away from your homes or you burned them down. You probably thieved and burgled and drank more than necessary. How am I doing so far?'

'Keep your eyes on the road and I'll maybe live to tell you.'

Joe laughed and continued, quietly amazed by the sound of his laughter. 'Physically, you're a coward. You're self-conscious, intro-verted, aloof and seclusive. Most likely lonely and frustrated but you hide behind a façade of calm indifference and find expression only through excitement. You feel unloved and unwanted, have a low self-esteem yet crave recognition and power.'

'I do?' Said quietly, with calm indifference.

'And if you've ever had a job it was a degrading one that filled you with resentment and thoughts of revenge. You have no sense of remorse or responsibility for your actions – symptoms, perhaps, of a psychotic disorder or neurotic obsession.'

'Yeah?' Grace stared silently through the windscreen as they approached Kilchoan, driving slower than the rain running down the hill. As they turned into the track leading up to the A-Frame, she said, 'Is that it? You quite finished now?'

'Was I close?'

'Pal, you were close to dying.'

His father had once told him, 'Papa, that's what I am to you. Not Dad or Daddy, but Papa. You want a Dad, go find another one. If not, you call me Papa. Eh?'

It took Joe nearly twenty minutes to get through to the ward, another five before his father came to the phone.

Joe said, 'Papa?'

'Who is this?'

'Hey, Papa?' The line crackled.

'What you mean? My father is dead. You hear that, dead.'

'This is Joe, Dad. Your son, Joe.' He could hear a television in the background in the silence that followed. Some Christmas Day game-show special. Celebrity Bake A Sausage-Roll or something. That and a male nurse calling out names for medication, and the sound of his father's breath ragged in his ear.

'I ain't got no son. He's dead. You hear that? Dead.'

Joe said, 'Happy Christmas, Dad. They treating you well?'

Another silence followed. Joe watched Grace in the kitchen, pour off the juices from the chicken, return it to the oven. Caught a glimpse of potatoes, brown and roasting. Almost missed his father's reply.

'Warm turkey. They give us warm turkey and mushy peas. You imagine that? Mushy peas the likes of what your mother would never have let in the house. Carrots they find in a tin. Warm. They serve us food warm here so we don't burn ourself to death. You imagine that? Eh?'

'What about the tatties, the roast tatties?'

Aldo Costello sounded hurt. He said, 'They're my friends, you hear. I don't eat my friends.'

'So tell me about the gravy. You always liked gravy.'

'Gravy? Hah. You call water that don't even know what a turkey looks like, gravy? Eh?'

'Bacon? Chipolatas? Cranberry sauce?'

Again silence as the old man breathed into the phone. Grace was watching Joe as she thickened and stirred the gravy. She'd been quietly thoughtful since their return from the lighthouse, shooing Joe from the kitchen, telling him to light the fire, see if he could find a mousetrap somewhere in one of the drawers.

Joe said, 'How are the boys, Dad? Better?'

'Dying. Three times a day they feed us here, you imagine that? I ask the Sister, I say I need more food, I tell her I'm eating for three and she just smile. Too busy smiling to pull back her ears and listen.' The old man broke into a fit of coughing. Came back with, 'You taking care of the house, eh?'

Joe said he was. 'Soon as I get back, I'll come and take you out, Okay?'

'Back from where?'

'Ardnamurchan.'

'Never heard of it.' As though it didn't exist.

'West Coast, Dad. Edge of the world.' Joe smiled at Grace, watching him over the wooden spoon as she tasted the gravy. 'Man I work for has a cottage here. We should be back in a couple of days, Okay?'

'We? Whose we?'

'A friend, Dad, that's all.'

'That woman?'

'A different one. I think you'd like her.'

'Best thing you ever did, shoot that bitch's eyes out.'

'Dad!'

'I ain't got no son. He's dead, you hear.'

The line went dead.

They sat sprawled across the floor in front of the fire drinking Irish coffee, drinking more Irish – Bushmills – than coffee. The remains of the meal still lay on the table amidst a jungle of streamers and half-empty bottles. Candles flickered around the room as the tail winds of the storm whistled and moaned outside. James Bond in the shape of Sean Connery surfaced from dark waters, peeled off his wetsuit and adjusted his bow-tie.

Joe said, 'Badgers, I think.'

'Badgers?'

'"His boys", he calls them.'

'He's off his bloody tree.'

'They live in his stomach and eat all his food. Which is why he's always hungry.'

'Loopy.' Grace smiled, staring into the flames. 'Like his son.' She'd changed from her jeans into the black skirt and red pullover Joe had bought in Fort William. There was a glow to her skin now that wasn't solely down to the heat from the fire. She caught the direction of his gaze.

'Why the smile?' she asked.

'I was thinking,' Joe said, 'about something I read in a book once. How this guy's sitting in a hotel lobby or something, sizing up this woman who's just strode in the door and how he thinks she carries herself well, what with her "tight can and sensible breasts"'

'Yeah and?'

'I mean, what the fuck I'd like to know are "sensible" breasts? The kind that don't drink and drive and always wait for the green man? Or what?'

Grace giggled. 'Or the ones that like to stay in their brassières?'

'I couldn't help but notice—'

'Staring at them for the last half hour, I'm not surprised.' She sat up straight and thrust out her chest. 'Well?' she said. 'Are they?'

'Are they what?'

'Sensible.'

Joe frowned. 'I dunno.' Giving it some serious consideration. 'First impressions are often quite deceptive. I think I'd probably have to take them out – you know, get to know them better. Weigh them up a moment.'

'You want to weigh them?' Grace laughed, a rich gurgle rising as pure as water drawn from the bowels of the earth. 'Fuck, Joe – first you got to *find* them.'

Billy McCulloch said, 'You what?'

'Biscuits,' the old man said. 'For the boys.'

Billy shook his head. The old guy was gone, off his tree and

214

out to lunch. And he looked nothing like his son. Put the two of them side by side and you'd never guess they were father and son. Except by their dress-sense, maybe. The old man, Aldo, wore a cardigan stretched to his knees by something heavy in the pockets, what looked like potatoes. A pink shirt and grey trousers and worn leather slippers. Balding, with grey hair brushed back at the sides, and restless eyes that weren't as empty as they tried to appear.

Billy tried a different angle. 'Okay. So you don't know where he is, and even if you did, you wouldn't tell us because he's your son, right?'

'I ain't got no son.'

'That's right. So you can tell us where he is.'

Aldo said, 'The edge of the world.' Like it meant something.

'Is that why he can't come and take you out for a real Christmas dinner?'

The old man shrugged, eyeing Billy's hands with shrewd eyes. 'Biscuits,' he said, 'that's what I like. That's what the boys like most.'

'How about a festive feast, old man?' They were walking slowly down the corridor towards the main entrance where Dodds stood yawning, flexing the fingers of his slinged right hand. 'Think you could handle dinner in one of the city's most exclusive hotels? No expense spared?'

'The boys're always hungry,' the old man said.

A nurse bustled by, said, 'Hi, Aldo. You going home for the day?' The old man ignored her, turned to Billy.

'But biscuits is what I really like.'

The man was insane. Syd bloody Barrett.

Billy said, 'How about it, old man? And after dinner, as many biscuits as you can stuff in your pockets?'

'I have to speak to the boys first.'

'You do that. When you make up your mind, I'll be over there.'

Dodds said, 'You get anything?'

Billy said maybe. First they had to get the old man away from here, back to the hotel.

'What's he doing?'

'Fucked if I know.' The old man was pacing up and down – four steps, turn, four steps, turn – talking to a potato in his hand. Glancing up at them every once in a while.

Dodds said, 'The wife is gonna murder me.'

'I know how she feels.' Billy left Dodds gawking, returned to the old fuckwit.

'Made up your mind, old man? Offer's about to close.'

'No biscuits, no go.'

'Where the fuck am I supposed to buy biscuits on Christmas Day?' Billy pushed the old man back against the wall, pressed his face in close. 'Eh? You want to tell me that, old man?'

'No biscuits, no go.'

Billy glanced up and down the corridor. A couple of nurses down the far end walking away, a slippered patient hugging the wall and talking to himself, a kitchen porter pushing a food-trolley now disappearing round a corner. Billy rammed his forearm into the old man's throat, and hissed:

'Put it this way, you old fart – no go with me, it's no more biscuits, ever. You got that?'

Costello was having difficulty finding his voice. Billy released the pressure a fraction and continued:

'You might think you fool all these doctors and nurses here, old man, but you don't fool me. It takes one to know one and I don't know you.' Billy checked the corridor again, then told Dodds to fetch the car and bring it round the front here. He turned back to the old man. 'You want to see what crazy really means?'

See. There it was again. That sly sidelong glance. Not fear, but cunning in the old man's eyes. Not as vacant as he'd have you believe. Billy felt his knife grow in his hand. He let the old man see it. Right up close.

'Happy now?' Billy said, inserting the blade between the old man's fleshy lips. 'Or would you like a smile all across your face? Or your tonsils for Christmas dinner? Easy enough to arrange, Don Corleone – just say *no biscuits, no go* again. Yes?'

The old fart was making strangled sounds, teeth rattling on the blade. Again Billy eased the pressure on his throat.

Costello gargled.

'Sorry,' Billy said, cocking his head and cupping his ear. 'I missed that.'

'Okay,' the old man rasped, 'biscuits it is.'

'That's what I like to hear.' Billy returned the blade to his pocket, bunched the Don's collar. 'Okay, now's the easy part. You and I, we shuffle along to the main entrance, arm in arm, like we was father and son in deep conversation. Understand? You nod your head and smile your mental smile, I'll do the talking. When we get to the car, you climb in the front, I'll be right behind you. Any crazy moves and I'll rip out your spinal cord. Okay now? Let's do the shuffle.'

'Here we go,' the old man said.

Joe was being very considerate. Not the wam bam, that's it, ma'am, she knew from Dodds, but like she could see he was trying to please her, taking his time to warm her up, get that warm pulse flowing. And it was working.

'You like that, huh?' Stepping up his rhythm now, moving deep, deeper inside her. 'Huh?'

Like a gorilla, she thought, smiling to herself. With all that dark hair and grunting. And his black eyes on hers, watching. Intent as he moved inside her. Deep, private places. Like it never was before.

A strange, quiet man. Though sometimes neither strange nor quiet. A man of two moods: cold and distant, warm and distant. Who is he? Who is this man who can scream in his sleep yet smile at the day? Loving her now like it never was before.

But so serious.

'See that little black spot,' she said, 'up there on the ceiling?' Her eyes half-closed as she panted out the words. 'D'you think it's a spider?'

Joe, thrusting: 'You what?' Staring at her like she was mad.

'Ah . . . like . . . ooh . . . I been watching it for a while and it seems like it's moving . . . oh, that's nice . . . only then I look again and . . . aah . . . it doesn't seem to-ooh've . . . moved very much at all.'

Joe stopped. She could feel his whole length twitching inside her.

'A fucking spider!?'

'Aye, I know. That's why I mentioned it. Not everyone I know likes having spiders fall on their backs while they're busy making love. You know?'

'Tell me I'm dreaming.'

Grace grinned. 'See? Just up there, to the left of the lightbulb?' Bubbling into a fit of giggles as Joe slid his whole length deep inside her. God that was good. Giggles subsiding into snatches of breath and gasps of pleasure as he filled her again and again and again, driving the breath from her body, the world from her mind.

'Don't stop!' she yelled. Biting his shoulder as she rode the sensuous waves rippling through her body, growing with every plunge of his. Moving against him now, greedily. Wanting him deeper, wanting him. Wanting him, Christ, like she'd never wanted anything before.

Like it never was before.

CHAPTER 29

'And some booze,' Joe said, chopping onion and blinking through
tears.

'And now booze.' Grace stood by the kitchen door with her
head cocked and hands on hips. 'Why don't I just bring the whole
fucking shop?'

Joe grinned; he'd been grinning so much the last few days
his lips hurt. 'Good idea,' he said, 'and don't forget the condoms.'

'What, did the balloons run out?'

'Too small.' Joe scraped the onion from the chopping-board into
the frying-pan.

'I should be so lucky.' She zipped her jacket and disappeared, all
but her eyes, beneath its hood. Her voice muffled as she opened
the back door on the elements. 'I may be gone some time,' she
said solemnly.

'Not *too* long,' he told her. 'This man *needs* his oats.'

Wylie phoned a few minutes later, saying, 'He was here this
afternoon, Joe. Him and that ape of his, Dodds.'

'You spoke to them?'

'Are you serious?' Wylie's voice clung to the edge of panic.

'They hung around outside for must have been an hour, sitting
in their car across the road, looking up at my window.'

'They knew you were there?'

Wylie said not. 'Billy came across and tried the door, leant on the bell for a good five minutes. Then he drove off.'

'So what d'you think he wanted?'

'The tapes?'

'What tapes?'

'Tapes I was going to let you hear, Joe, soon as you got back.'

Joe said, 'The ones you've been blacking Rankine with? Those tapes?'

'It's not so simple, Joe.'

'Nothing ever is. Hold on a minute.' Joe dashed into the kitchen, turned down the gas beneath the frying-pan, stirred in the four chopped cloves of garlic, returned to the phone.

'You were saying?'

'The tapes,' Wylie said. 'They involve McCulloch as well.'

'And now he's looking for your blood.'

'What am I going to do, Joe?'

'Joe looked out the window, over the village of Kilchoan and across the bay to Ormsaigmore, a straggle of fishermen's cottages squeezed between hill and shore. Walking along the road, the tiny figure of Grace, heading for the shop. Only half a mile away and still he longed for her. Crazy!

He could hear Wylie's breath wheezing in his ear. 'D'you believe in God?' he asked.

'This is serious, man!'

'So is blackmail.'

'You don't understand, Joe. These tapes can put Rankine where he belongs. McCulloch, too.'

'Below sod and soil?'

Wylie said nothing.

Joe asked where Rankine was now, if Wylie had tracked him down yet.

'Easy.' Wylie sounded smug. 'You know Dalmeny, out by the rail bridge?'

'I've heard of it.'

'It's where he was born. I remembered he had a cottage out there, so it was the first place I checked. He wasn't there but a cleaner was. She said she was getting the cottage ready for Mr Jack's convalescence. Seems he had a couple of minor attacks last week.'

'Good,' Joe said, 'but not perfect. Where is he now?'

'In a private hospital just up the road from the cottage. Nurse I spoke to thinks he'll be there a few days more, at least.'

'And Billy?'

'Still at the hotel,' Wylie said grimly. 'That is, when he isn't sitting outside my door.'

Joe said, 'So why worry? It's Boxing Day. He'll be at the game. Or under the mistletoe with Rankine, playing hide the chipolata.'

'He came round once,' Wylie said, his voice cracking, 'he'll come again. Shit, Joe, what am I going to do?'

'What would Philip Marlowe do?'

They sat at the pine table in the cramped alcove off the sitting-room, elbows planted amidst the débris of the meal as they sipped on wine and talked in low, soft voices. Across the room, the fire crackled and spat, the only other sound.

Joe said, 'What they did, they marched them barefoot through the streets of Liverpool, loaded them aboard a luxury cruise-liner, the *Arandora Star*, fascists and anti-fascists alike, all bound for Canada.'

Grace said, 'But your father must've been no more than a kid then.'

'He says he wasn't the only one. He said when Churchill came out with his "collar the lot" directive, the authorities took him at his word. Enthusiastically. Didn't matter you were a kid or a crumblie, they put you in with the rest. Some they even dragged straight from hospitals and mental asylums.'

'So what happened?'

'Second day out,' Joe said, '2nd July 1940 and west of Donegal, the *Arandora Star* was torpedoed. For some reason no one can explain, she was armed, yet carried no markings and sailed lightless at night. What they like to call a legitimate target. Nearly 800 died, more than half of them Italians.'

'Your grandfather?'

Joe nodded. 'Him and almost half of Edinburgh's Italian community. My father was lucky. He was rescued by a Canadian destroyer and returned to Liverpool. Spent the rest of the war working on a farm on the Isle of Man alongside 14,000 other internees. He returned home to find Jack Rankine had stolen his father's business.'

'So that's how it started . . .'

'Any time after that, if something went wrong or worked out

badly, my father would blame Rankine. Even when my mother died.'

'Nice man,' Grace said softly, her face a flickering screen of shadows.

'He did his best,' Joe sighed. He told her of the long hours his father used to work down on the docks during the day, then scrubbing floors and washing dishes in a restaurant at night. Until the day came he'd saved enough money to open a chip-shop of his own.

'So where's the chip-shop now?'

'Gone. Replaced by a block of red-brick rabbit-hutches Wimpey call flats. What my father didn't know was the land actually belonged to a company called RanCor, Rankine's flagship at the time. When he found out later . . . well, it was like the straw that finally broke the camel's back.'

'Poor man.' Grace rose from the table and went across to stoke the fire. Joe began clearing the table.

Joe came awake suddenly, cold and sweating, and alone. He climbed from bed and padded out on to the landing, where he paused for a moment at the top of the stairs, looking down, watching Grace as she sat crosslegged and naked in front of the fire, striking match after match after match. She would take one from the household-size box, strike it with intense concentration, then hold it up in front of her eyes and watch it burn slowly down to her fingers, at which point she would take its tip and turn it upside down until the flame died. Then she would toss it into the fire and, as though in a trance, go through the motions again. Breaking the routine only to pick up the poker and stab at the coals. Joe returned to the bedroom, fetched the quilt from the bed and went downstairs.

Her eyes were thoughtful, her smile half-hearted, as he wrapped the quilt about her.

'Just like my father,' Joe said. 'I'd come down the stairs in the middle of the night and the old man would be sitting there in the dark, just like you, staring into the fire, seeing things in the flames no one else could see, I don't know, reliving memories no one else could ever share. Sometimes I'd be woken by the noise, I'd come down and find him in a silent manic fury, poker in his hand, stabbing the coals as though piercing the heart of demons only he could see. I'd say, "Papa, what's going on?" and he'd say, "Son, it's cold, go

back to bed". I'd say, "Cold, Papa? I'm burning here," and he'd
say, "Son, don't you feel it?" and I'd tell him, "Feel it? Feel what?"
and he'd look at me askance through kind of glazed-over eyes and
go, "The midnight chill, son, the midnight chill".'

'The midnight chill?'

'That's what he calls it, the time of night the nightmares come.
When you wake up gasping for air with your body running sweat
but cold as ice.'

'Like you did the other night?'

Joe said, 'Yeah. I never really understood what he meant until
I went inside, spent a couple of nights in the digger.'

'Digger?'

'Punishment cell. Read shite-smeared walls and cockroaches
so big you can see them lick their lips when they look at you.
Where punishment means they come in the door – five or six
screws at a time – with their shields up and truncheons flying. Shunt you into a corner and kick the holy living fuck from
your body.'

'Is that what you're dreaming when you wake up screaming?'

'Among other things.'

'And your father?'

'For him the midnight chill is the chill of North Atlantic waters,
of watching countless people drown, among them his father. How
many hours he survived in the water, he never has said. Only that
fire has the power to heal the coldness in his heart.'

'I know the feeling.'

Joe said, 'I thought I never would.'

'Like I used to feel fire offered me the only warmth I would
ever experience in life. Something I could rely on, like the only
way I could express myself, you know, emotionally. It became
everything to me, took me away from this dreary life, gave me
hope, excitement, comfort, money . . .'

'Past tense?'

Grace nodded. 'The night I was in Posers, it suddenly came
to me. Somewhere along the line I had lost it – you know, the
spark, the enthusiasm, the overpowering need. Maybe I lost it
the moment I started doing it for Dodds. For money. Like I was
somehow prostituting its power.'

Joe shivered. 'The taste of revenge, they say, is always bitter-
sweet.'

'Come here,' Grace said, opening up the quilt to wrap it now

223

around both their shoulders. She snuggled into the crutch of his arm and was then quiet for a while, deep in thought as she absently stroked his thigh.

'Joe?' she said eventually. 'What happens when we get back to the city?'

'Is that what you're worrying about?' He hugged her gently, kissing her hair.

'We go back now,' she said, 'and everything's still going to be the same. Nowhere to go and Billy out there somewhere, still trying to kill us.'

Joe said, 'I thought coming out here for a few days would help. You know, time and space to think, work things out.'

'My granny used to say running away from a problem never resolves it, only makes it worse.'

'Wise woman – but did she have a psychopath on her scent when she said it?'

'No, just a husband.'

'You can move in with me, if you like.'

She looked up at him, her eyes wide and serious. 'Is that a proposal?'

'A suggestion,' he grinned.

'Huh.'

He bent and kissed her pouting lips.

She said, 'And Billy? Is he going to move in to?'

'There's this cop I know, used to be my partner five–six years ago.'

'And?'

'I think I can still trust him.'

Grace was already ahead of him. 'You want me to grass up Dodds. To testify in court.'

'If we can connect him to Billy and Rankine, the game's over.'

'No way, Joe. No cops, no court, no nothing. I start talking and you know the score, I'll end up on a conspiracy charge, accessory after the fact. Either that or Billy will pump me full of acid and flay off my skin.'

'He'll do that anyway, unless we can take him off the streets. You point the finger at Dodds, I could almost guarantee you'd get immunity.'

'Almost's not good enough, Joe. It's like being almost alive.'

'You have a better suggestion then?'

Grace tugged at her lower lip. 'If your PI friend is right,' she said, 'then Rankine's now recuperating in his cottage in Dalmeny. What we do is go out there, wait till Billy shows up, then torch the fucking place and send them both to hell on a first-class ticket. That's what I'd do.'

'Murder.'

'Call it pest control.'

'Call it a lifetime under the screw.'

'Call it better than dead.'

The fire hissed and popped in the silence that followed, the hypnotic dance of its flames holding them both spellbound. Outside, the wind continued to buffet the shutters.

'We don't have to, you know,' Grace said after a while, her breath hot on his chest.

'Go back, you mean?'

'We could just stay here. Never go back, ever, ever at all.'

'We have to pick up Jay and Andrea from the airport,' Joe said. 'I gave my word.'

'Sod them. Let them get a taxi. Tell Jay we've sequestrated his cottage.'

'And do what?'

'Open up a chip-shop. Go into the family business. We could change our names and live happily ever after.'

'You want to know a secret, Grace? I hate chips. I loathe them. I wouldn't be sorry if I never saw a damn chip again.'

'But you're Scottish! I mean, how do you survive?'

'Deep fried pizzas, four times a day.'

'Ugh.' Grace punched him playfully, adding, 'I couldn't imagine life without a poke of chips.'

'You could if you'd peeled as many as I have.'

'I thought they had machines to do that?'

'In my old man's chippie, I *was* that machine.'

'Aye?' she grinned, her eyes flashing in devilment. 'Then peel away this cover, Joe, and give me the largest poke you've got.'

The storm had passed, the morning sky a bright blue dome edged by fluffs of wispy cloud. Grace was out, exploring the ruins of Mingary Castle, along the bay from the village, overlooking the Sound of Mull. She had awoken bubbling this morning, buoyant on a wave of youthful optimism. Joe on the other hand, feeling restless and with a growing sense of foreboding, had decided to stay and not taint her mood with his. After much pacing, he phoned the hospital for the third time and again the ward Sister told him no, his father had still not returned.

'Did anyone see him leave?' Joe asked.

'One of the staff-nurses saw him talking to a couple of men in the main corridor yesterday afternoon.'

'Could she describe them?'

'Is anything the matter, Mr Costello?'

'My brother said he was going to take my father out,' Joe said, forced to improvise quickly. 'I just wanted to make sure he did.'

'I think you can rest assured on that, Mr Costello. Is your brother by any chance . . . accident prone?

Joe laughed and said vaguely, 'Like father, like son.' But inside, a cold weight settled heavily in the pit of his stomach.

'Because,' the Sister continued, 'the nurse said one of the men wore an eye-patch and had his arm in a sling.'

With a clammy hand cold on his heart, Joe thanked her and hung up. He phoned Wylie. Again, for the third time that day, he received no answer. He slammed down the phone. Prowled the room like a beast incensed. Picked up a table-lamp, hurled it to the floor. Swung his foot and sent the coffee-table flying across the room. Weighed a heavy glass ashtray briefly in his hand, then flung it through the TV screen.

Grace returned from the castle, shrugged out of her jacket. She glanced apprehensively around the room, at the overturned fur-niture, the carpet of broken glass, Joe sitting in the armchair staring out the window, and the quiet, dark fury in her lover's black, black eyes.

'I've been thinking,' she said, crossing to sit on the arm of his chair and wrap her arm around his neck. 'What you said last night? About testifying? I'll do it.'

He shook his head. 'No,' he said. 'No.' Like he was try-ing to exorcise a demon. Her gaze settled on the half-packed grip.

'Joe, what's up? Why are you packing?'

'They've got my father.' The emptiness in his voice frightened her. 'The bastards've got him.'

'We'll go straight to the police, Joe. I'll testify, I'll tell them everything.'

'Not any more, Grace. It's gone beyond that now. What you

said last night, you were right. There's only one way to end this now – the way I should've finished it a long time ago.' He pushed himself from the chair. 'Get your stuff together, we leave in five minutes.'

Whatever you say, *sir*.

CHAPTER 30

Grace came with a shudder that seemed to contract every muscle in her body and rattle her very bones. Joe, considerate as ever, must have been holding back for he came too, just a few seconds later, twitching and jumping inside her, a weird kind of groan hissing through his lips as he collapsed on top of her. They lay that way, bathed in sweat, her fingers tracing patterns on his back until their breathing returned to normal.

She said, 'Was it good for you, too, darling?' – the way they do in the movies. But either he hadn't seen the movies or he didn't want to hurt her feelings. He merely grunted – maybe yes, maybe no, maybe just a grunt.

He'd been this way since she came back from the castle to find him packing. Cold and distant. Like a cop. Their mad dash back across the country, a headlong flight through the night, like one of those never-ending nightmares: Joe, with his face set hard in brutal lines, a mad demon, pushing the Porsche to its limits, propelled by his own silent fury. Answering her only in monosyllables, talking not at all. Like he was a different man, someone she had never met or slept with before. A stranger looking out through once familiar eyes. Weird, very weird.

Then arriving back at his Easter Road flat to find it trashed, torn apart. Taking it with a shrug of his shoulders, as though it was something that happened every day. He had left her then, amidst the débris of his flat, telling her not to move, to open the door to no one. Had returned late in the evening, looking drawn, haggard and drained.

'Did you try the hospital again?' she had asked.

'Yes.'

'No luck?'

'No.'

'What about Wylie?'

'Nothing.'

'You think they're holding your father at Rankine's hotel?'

'Yeah.'

'Is that where you've been all day?'

'Yeah.'

'So what're you going to do?'

'Sleep.'

And he had. The moment his head touched the pillow.

Now, as he raised himself from her and prepared to roll over, she said, looking deep into his eyes, 'Hullo? Is there anybody in there?'

He smiled, kind of. But at least he'd tried. She said, 'You always grunt like that when you come?'

He said, 'Grace . . .' and rolled on to his back.

Which was good a start as any.

She said, 'So you remembered my name.' Jabbing him playfully in the side.

'I need a favour.' His vocal cords rusty, not used to all this excitement.

'You just had one,' she told him.

But he was being ever so serious. The only glint in his eyes, reflections of the bedside lamp. Jesus. Black expressionless eyes. Building up to something. She could see him thinking, way back there behind them, working out how to say it so it came out right. Knowing what he was going to say even before he said it.

He said, 'I need you to set just one more fire.'

'What?' she said. 'Only one?'

Billy pressed the .38 Smith & Wesson to the old man's temple and told Dodds to move away from the window in case the bullet went through and through. 'Mind you,' he added, 'on second thoughts stay where you are. You could use the extra brains.' Dodds stared at Billy a moment through his unpatched eye then hurriedly left the room.

The old man, Aldo, was tied to a chair in the centre of Rankine's Penthouse office, looking up at Billy with lapdog eyes. Billy asked him if he'd ever heard of Russian roulette.

'Garibaldi, I've heard of,' the old man said. 'And Jaffa Cakes. Jaffa Cakes and Gypsy Creams. And Hob Nobs, I've heard of Hob Nobs.'

'Enough,' Billy snapped, wondering if this kind of insanity was contagious. He brought the gun round, pressed the barrel between the old man's eyes. It could have been a sausage in his hand for all the impression it made. Aldo squirmed in the chair so he could look past Billy and out the wide picture window where, against the sombre sky and towering over the rooftops, the castle was little more than a shadowy smudge behind the incessant fall of snow.

'So now you want to kill me?' the old man said. As though saying, 'You want another cup of tea?'

'Did I say that?' Billy ground the barrel into the bridge of the old man's nose. 'Did I?' Suddenly tired of all these games.

'You said Russian roulette. You said—'

'Enough!' Billy dragged across a chair and straddled it cowboy-style. 'Time's up, Costello. Either tell me where your son is or I'll air-condition your brains.'

'I ain't got no son.'

'Okay. Have it your way.' He took a handful of bullets from his pocket and began loading the chambers.

The old man wasn't that far gone. He said, 'Hey!'

'I know, I know – I'm only supposed to put one bullet in. But this is Scottish roulette. The same as the Russian version, only you load all the chambers except one. It ruins the suspense, I know, but it does save on laundry costs.'

Somewhere in the distance a bell began to ring.

Joe Costello burst through the Staff Only door, out into the lobby, his clothes and hair dishevelled, his face blackened by soot. The young receptionist – name-badged Moira – regarded him with startled eyes as he bent over the desk in a sudden fit of coughing. Through streaming eyes he could see guests and staff standing around in bewildered groups, unsure if the alarm was a practice run or the real thing. Joe ended their speculation.

'West wing!' he choked. 'Smoke all over the place! Get everyone out – now!'

The young woman reached for the phone.

'What're you doing?' Joe demanded.

'I have to call the Assistant Manager.'

'Where is he?'

'He just went up to his office.'

Joe forced a few more coughs, dragged his voice over the burning coals of his throat. 'You worry about the guests, Moira, I'll find the boss. Now hurry!'

As he ran towards the bank of lifts, he saw Grace crossing the lobby, heading for the entrance. Good, he thought. Now he could end it once and for all.

Dodds came running into the office as Billy cursed and slammed down the phone.

'I hope Rankine's insured.'

Dodds grunted. 'How bad is it?'

Billy said, 'You know what Joan of Arc's last words were?' "*How bad is it?*"' Billy rounded the desk. 'Where's the car?'

'In the basement.'

'Okay. It's in the basement. The car's in the basement.' Christ, he was beginning to sound like the nutcase tied to the chair watching them both with a smile on his fucking puss. Billy swung his gun round, centred it on the old man's face.

Dodds sprang forward. 'Are you mad? The place'll be swarming with cops any minute now.'

Billy thinking maybe he was mad. Had been standing next to these two too long. He let the gun fall to his side. 'Okay. So we take him with us.' He then began slashing at the rope with his knife. 'You hear that, old man? We're taking you with us. Try anything stupid and I'll shoot your potato. Okay?' The old man nodded, rubbing the weals on his wrists.

Billy crossed to Rankine's desk and began going through the drawers.

'Hey, what're you doing?'

'Minding my own business. You want to do something useful, go and start the car.'

'What about him?' Dodds said, nodding towards the old man now talking to the cheese plant in the corner.

In answer, Billy went over to the crazy Costello. 'Oh, and you,' he said, punching the old man full in the face, 'better lie down on the floor and not move a muscle.' The old man obliged.

Billy returned to the desk as Dodds made for the lifts.

* * *

By the time the lift came to a halt at the top floor of the hotel, Joe had already forced open the hatch in the roof. He slammed the HOLD button and hauled himself up through the hatch, out on to the roof of the lift. He found himself in the centre shaft of three, each separated from one another by a pair of concrete stanchions spaced far enough apart to allow access to engineers. The shaft to his left, he knew contained the Penthouse lift, where he'd had his 'little chat' with Dodds: it hung there fifteen feet above him. The one to his right, he wasn't sure: he could see doors above, but none below. There had been no third lift in the lobby. Perhaps from the Penthouse to the garage, he thought. Then cursed. If he'd overlooked something as simple as that, what else had he overlooked? Was saved from further self-recrimination by the sound of the lift on his right suddenly starting to rise. Knowing now that he had to change his plans, improvise. Think quick, act quick.

The lift passed the second floor, rising fast. The gap between the stanchions about two feet across; between the lifts, five or six. Would he make it?

Third floor and climbing. Ten feet.

What if there was someone inside? If it was a private lift, chances were that one of Rankine's retinue would be inside. Billy or Dodds – or maybe even his father. What would they make of the noise when he landed? Would they put it down to falling débris from the fire? Or climb up to investigate?

Six feet.

But then, Joe wondered, who would be going up in a lift when the whole building was being evacuated? Much more likely the lift had been called and would be taking someone down.

Three feet.

Yes.

Joe took two steps back, a deep breath, then threw himself across the gap. He caught his shoulder a glancing blow on the left-hand stanchion but his momentum was enough to carry him through. He landed heavily, awkwardly, skinning his forearm on a rivet as he scrabbled for a handhold, fingers reaching the closing on one of the cables; gripping it tight as he dragged himself towards the block.

The lift shuddered and came to a halt.

* * *

233

Billy stopped and looked back towards the lift. 'You hear that?' he said, his .38 appearing suddenly in his hand. He was midway between the lift and the Mercedes where Dodds stood waiting with the door held open. The old man, Aldo, halfway between them.

Dodds said, 'You're imagining things, Billy. Come on, let's go.'

Billy ignored him, began walking slowly back towards the lift. 'I heard something,' Billy muttered, 'so I did.'

He was twenty yards from the lift when he heard the sound again. He dropped to a crouch, listening. There it was again, a kind of scraping noise, followed by a human grunt. Definitely coming from the lift.

From *above* the lift.

'Holy shit!'

A pair of feet appeared, scuffed boots, as though from nowhere. Became a pair of legs, overalled, swinging, searching for a foothold. Billy frowned, hesitating – an engineer?

From behind him, Dodds hissed, 'Christ, Billy, put that gun away!'

Scuffed boots, overalls . . . now a tool-belt dropping into view. The hairs on his neck, tingling. Unsure what to do with his gun, feeling somehow threatened but not knowing why, he held it by his side as he rose from the crouch. Without taking his eyes from the swinging legs, he shouted back at Dodds, 'Get the old fart in the car. Quick!'

Aldo Costello still hadn't moved, as though someone had just removed his batteries. He watched as Dodds came away from the car and approached, squinting, through his one good eye. From beyond the street-ramp came the sound of multiple sirens converging on the hotel.

Now Billy watched as the man's torso came into view, hanging for a moment, face turned away. Tool-belt. What was it about the tool-belt? Why this weird feeling? Either the guy was a lift engineer or he was . . .

Joe Costello dropped to the floor of the lift.

'You!' Billy screamed, whipping up his gun, snapping off a round that missed Costello, missed the lift entirely, tore only a chunk of plaster from the wall nearby. As Costello dived to one side, Billy fired off another two rounds.

'This time you're dead, Costello, dead!' Firing again, but the bullet entering the lift, high and wide, the sound deafening as it hit the interior tin-plate wall, drowning the shouts of the old man and Dodds.

'You're mine, Costello, mine!' Exhilarated now as he stepped to the side and fired again. Costello was trapped, trying to squeeze his six-foot frame into the shallow corner behind the doors by the control panel, enough room there for a family of mice but not for a man trying to hang on to the rest of his life. Billy laughed. He laughed so hard his hand began to shake. Had to hold his gun hand with his other hand as he made his way slowly forward, approaching from an angle, seeing more of the target now, Costello hammering desperately at the buttons on the panel, trying to close the doors before the next bullet flew.

Ten yards. Billy wasn't going to miss from ten yards. 'You're dead meat, Costello.' Billy raised his aim for a headshot. Right between the eyes? Or one for each of his come-to-bed eyes? Or what about shutting that mouth for ever? Decisions, decisions.

Suddenly Costello shouted.

'Papa!' No longer trying to hide himself away but looking over Billy's shoulder. Crying for his daddy-oh.

Billy said, 'Say bye bye, Costello.' He'd made up his mind: the eyes had it. First the left, then the right. Same way he'd popped the woman, whatserface, Rankine's daughter.

'Billy, watch out!' Dodds yelled.

Watch out for what? Costello was trapped and unarmed, an easy target. Outnumbered two to one. Okay, behind him a moron and a Jaffa Cake . . . but no problem. Billy sighted along the barrel and took the pressure.

He sensed it the second he squeezed the trigger. Tried to fire and turn all in the same motion. But too late. The old man crashed into him as he fired and he collapsed to the ground in a tangle of legs as Costello's father collapsed on top of him, driving the breath from his body.

He looked up to see the lift doors close.

And the old man, Costello, grinning from ear to ear.

Billy ground the barrel of the gun into the leering teeth and pulled the trigger.

CHAPTER 31

The flight was delayed, the plane eventually struggling in against the wind more than two hours late. Joe waited at the arrivals gate, scanning the incoming passengers. He spotted Andrea, waved, and she came across, labouring under a mountain of bags.

'Am I glad to see you!' she said, letting the bags fall to the floor, sighing wearily.

Joe hoisted a couple of the bags on to his shoulder. 'Where's the man himself?' he asked, looking for Jay's swaggering gait amongst the final straggle of disembarking passengers.

'Forget him,' she snapped. 'Don't even mention his name.'

'He's not coming?'

'No.'

'You left him in Skiathos?'

'Not just in Skiathos,' Andrea said, 'but *Miss* Skiathos. Come on, Joe, take me home.'

They slashed along the city by-pass, the Porsche cutting through a sudden slanting rain, the slap of the wipers hypnotic as Joe brought Andrea up to date. She listened in silence as he told her about Billy and Grace, their flight to the cottage, Wylie's disappearance, and his father's kidnapping, rounding it all off with the events of the afternoon.

'You've been busy,' Andrea said curtly when he'd finished. An edge of bitterness to her voice.

Joe said, 'I'll drive you home and then be on my way.'

'Joe – I'm sorry. Hell hath no fury, and here I am taking it out on you. I didn't mean it like that.'

'What happens next is between Rankine and me,' he told her. 'There's no need for you to get involved.'

'Whether you like it or not, I am involved. And if you think I'm going to stay in that house all on my own, you're wrong. You and that friend of yours obviously can't stay where you are, so you might as well move in and at least keep me company. What did you say her name was?'

'Grace.'

'And she was the one who burnt down Jay's massage-parlours?'

Joe nodded, slowing as the slip road approached.

'Then there's a woman I want to shake by the hand.'

Joe dropped Andrea off at her house, leaving her with the two security guards on duty while he drove back across the city to fetch Grace. Expecting to find her climbing the walls, instead he found her scraping them.

'Anyone call?' he asked.

'Guy with one of those double-barrelled names. Something Jones.'

'Shit!' Joe exclaimed, 'Denbigh-Jones, my supervising officer. I was supposed to see him this morning. What did he say?'

'You're to call him back the moment you get in. Now.'

'Anyone else call?'

'Nah.' Grace smeared the fringe from her eyes with the back of her hand. 'You still think he'll call? Billy?'

Joe nodded. 'He'll want to gloat. It's his nature.'

'You're still worried about your father, aren't you?'

'I should never have gone to the hotel. It's only made things worse.'

'Only a fool would kill his hostage, Joe.'

'That's what I'm afraid of.'

Joe picked up the phone, dialled the Social Work Department, eventually got through to his supervising officer.

'No problem – this time,' Denbigh-Jones said, after Joe explained how he'd had to pick up his employer from the airport, had forgotten all about the appointment. 'Just don't let it happen again or I'll have to consider tightening up the conditions of your licence.'

Joe said it wouldn't happen again, adding: 'I could come in this afternoon . . .'

'All booked up.' Joe heard the thumbing of pages down the phone. 'How about we leave it till the new year,' Denbigh-Jones suggested, 'say the third? Ten-thirty or eleven.'

'Eleven.'

'And don't forget.'

Joe replaced the phone and wrote down the time and date of the appointment on the cover of the Yellow Pages. Grace was back scraping wallpaper.

'We made the papers again,' she said.

'I noticed. And there's something else – Johnstone's decided to stop over in Skiathos, has sent his wife back alone. She won't say it but I think she's scared Billy might make a move on her. She suggested we move in with her for a while.'

'Are you asking my opinion?'

'We're in this together, Grace.'

'Well . . . maybe she's right. It *would* be safer for all of us.' She cocked her head and thoughtfully studied the flap of peeling wallpaper she'd been working on.

'What else do you think?'

'I was thinking maybe a light blue or yellow here in the hall, brighten the place up a bit, make it less the funeral-parlour it is at the moment. What d'you think?'

Joe looked at her standing there, scraper in one hand, other hand cupping her chin, her small frame lost in his oversized dungarees. He could do nothing about the sudden glowing warmth in his heart, the smile that stretched his lips. 'I think,' he said, crossing to close her in his arms, 'you're amazing.'

Her face lit up. 'You do?'

'I seriously do.'

'Then you must've been drinking. You want to see what else I've done?'

'Can it wait?'

'For what?'

He scooped her up in his arms. 'For this,' he said, kissing the tip of her nose.

'Is that all?' Her breath hot on his neck and her hand hot on his skin as he carried her through to the bedroom.

'Just a taste of what's to come.' He laid her gently down on the mattress. 'What happened to the bed?'

'Legs on beds make me nervous,' she giggled, struggling out of the dungarees, lying there now in just her T-shirt and panties.

Joe pulled off his jeans. 'They do?'

'Things get under them,' she said, slipping the T-shirt over her head.

'What things?'

'Like monsters. Horrible slimy things with rows and rows of glistening teeth. You just never know when they're going to jump out and get you.' She teased her panties slowly down her thighs, lifting her knees to slip them over her feet as Joe removed the rest of his clothes.

'Okay,' he said finally, standing naked before her. 'No problem.'

'You don't mind? The legs off the bed, the redecoration?'

'I have a great respect for you,' he told her solemnly.

'I noticed. A growing respect.' She grinned as she took his hand and pulled him down on top of her. 'So come on, Joe,' she said. 'Give me some of that respect.'

Drizzle seeped from the night-blue sky as Joe pulled up in front of the Johnstone house. The security firm's van was gone from the drive, the white lawns sparkling in the wash of light cast down from the ground-floor windows. Andrea was waiting for them, notepad in hand, under the floodlit porch.

'Joe,' she said, after he'd made the introductions and carried the bags into the house, 'someone called for you. I think it was your good friend Billy.'

'He leave a message?'

Andrea consulted the small telephone-pad. 'He said what you did this afternoon was a very silly thing. He said he's having a lot of difficulty controlling his temper. He said if you want to know what happens when he loses his temper, go and ask Wylie.'

So Wylie was back; but back from where, Joe wondered. 'What did he say about my father?'

'That he's living on borrowed time. That his life now rests in your hands alone.'

'Thank God for that,' Joe sighed. The relief he felt was as heavy as the dark sense of foreboding which had cloaked his thoughts since the moment the lift doors slammed on the scene in the basement garage. His father was still alive. Billy hadn't gone wild and done something stupid, as Joe had feared he might;

he had realised that Aldo alive was a far better weapon than Aldo dead.

Joe hoped.

'Did he say anything else?'

'He said he'd phone tomorrow to name a time and place.'

'He wants to meet?'

Andrea nodded. 'He wants to make an exchange, he said. You for your father.'

Grace, who had been standing in the hall, looking down over the split-level sitting-room with awe-studded eyes, said, 'Don't go, Joe. Don't trust him.'

But Joe could still see clearly in his mind the look in his father's eyes as the old man threw himself at Billy, moments before the lift-doors closed and saved his life. It was a look he had seldom seen – and then, only years ago. A look in which glowed the first sparks of life. A fire rekindled in the old man's eyes.

'I have to,' Joe said. 'There's no other way.'

Wilberforce Wylie was still not at home.

Behind the new Southside Police Station on the Pleasance, Arthur's Seat was a snow-grey silhouette against the black overcast sky. The night streets quiet but for prowling taxis and their prey, the odd pedestrian wading through rivers of slush, now the rain had ceased. Joe rang the buzzer again and passed the time watching the reflection of the street in the Electrical Repair shop window immediately below Wylie's office. He saw no movement on the street behind, heard no sign of life from the building in front.

He rang the buzzer again and, not for the first time, wondered what the gross PI had been so busy doing the last couple of days that he couldn't get to a phone. As far as Joe was concerned, Wylie was still very much the Man of Mystery, whose place in the whole puzzle was still unclear, and whose allegiance and motives would only finally be dictated by the greatest amount of money on offer. And now, with Jay Johnstone temporarily out of the picture . . .

Joe was about to give up and return to the car when he noticed the corner of something white protruding from the letterbox. He pulled it out.

It was a card. A Christmas card. Unsealed. On the front it had a picture of a badger, a rabbit and a robin posing in the snow beneath a gnarled old tree. Inside, a Mrs J. Roberts wished Mr W. Wylie 'A Merry Christmas'. Better late than never, Joe thought, and pushed the card back through the letterbox. As he did so, the door swung silently open.

The street was deserted.

Joe pushed the door wide and, stepping quickly into the darkness, closed the door and snibbed the Yale. Felt around for a light-switch, found one on the left-hand wall, flicked it on.

The door into the electrical repair shop was locked. A passage led through to the back. Two doors there, both also locked. Which left the stairs. Joe climbed. The door to Wylie's office was open. He crossed to the windows and drew the curtains. Then switched on the light.

Hurricanes are destructive. They can make the monuments of Man look like Christmas stocking toys. They can rip trees from the earth and snap them like twigs. They can pluck up the sea and hurl it at the land. And, so it seemed, as Joe himself had recently experienced, they can creep up your stairs and lay your house to waste.

The only points of reference, the walls, the floor and the ceiling. Everything else in the room was devastated: in pieces, shreds and tatters, powder, splinter and crumb; the débris piled and strewn across the floor like the flotsam of a shipwreck beached upon the shore.

Furniture had been hacked, limb from limb: the armchairs, the tables, the cabinets, the desk. The carpet had been ripped from the floor, as had, in several places, the floorboards. Papers and books, files and folders, torn and crumpled, littered the floor. Framed pictures lay broken on glinting beds of glass. Cassette tapes everywhere, both audio and video, gutted. The TV in the corner, smashed and disembowelled, with its legs in the air like a dog floating dead in a Bangkok klong.

But no Wilberforce Wylie.

And no sign of all the fancy electronic equipment Joe had seen last time he'd visited.

Ask Wylie, Billy had apparently said. *Ask Wylie what happens when Billy has a tantrum.*

Except Wylie wasn't here.

He was upstairs in the small flat above his office. He lay naked, spreadeagled, pinned to the floor by six-inch nails driven through his hands and feet. His eyes protruded, as white and sticky as the white of a cream egg. His flesh hard as papiermâché, pockmarked

242

and punctured, spotted with blood as black as the crusty pool around him. Tiny screwdrivers, like acupuncture needles, were buried to their hafts around his knees and elbows. Other instruments of torture lay roundabout: a soldering-iron, a small transformer, wires of differing lengths and sizes, and a blood-encrusted pair of pliers.

And embedded in the floor between his head and his neck, an axe.

Joe phoned the police from a call-box up the road, by the Royal Commonwealth Pool. He told them about the body and where to find it; when they asked for his name, he hung up. Then he climbed back in the Porsche and turned into Holyrood Park, driving as far as he could up the Queen's Drive, before leaving the car to walk the rest of the way to the top of Arthur's Seat.

The city lay spread out below him like a dark, choppy sea of reflected shimmering lights. To his right, the Salisbury Crags, at the foot of which the Acid Killer's first known victim had died. And there, beyond, the dark silhouette of Calton Hill, its monuments and observatory. And there, to the south and west, the dark-grey shadow of the Pentlands looming over Colinton and the Johnstone's house, where Grace and Andrea now slept.

Joe stood there, oblivious to the biting cold and passage of time. His thoughts roamed from Grace to his father to Billy to Wylie to Rankine, and back again. Again and again, round and round. Until his mind became sluggish and he could think no more. He returned to the car and headed back across the city.

There was a car on the drive in front of the house. As he pulled to a halt, two men climbed from the car and walked towards him.

Detective Inspector Kerley said, 'Joseph Costello, we have a warrant for your arrest.'

Detective Sergeant Bob McInnis merely shrugged.

CHAPTER 32

'**C**harge him.'

'With what?'

Detective Inspector Kerley almost smiled. 'Parole violation, of course.'

'Do we have enough, sir?'

'We can place him at the scene of the crime, can't we?'

'Not directly, sir. ID Branch are running a check on all the prints they found but have so far failed to come up with anything positive. All we have is the Porsche.'

'The fucker's guilty as God, Bruce, and I want him.' Kerley peered through the peephole for a moment, turned back in disgust. 'Look at the bastard. Cool as you like. Feet on the bloody table, pretending he's asleep, not a worry in the world. Well, I tell you, Bruce, I'm going to have him. He's *mine*. I'm gonna nail him to the floor the same way he nailed Wylie.'

'He's been through it all before, sir.' Sergeant Bruce was unconvinced. 'He knows the score. I think we'll have to do more than just tickle his belly to make him roll over on this one.'

'Damn *right* we'll do more than just tickle his belly. What about the tapes?'

'You mean the Special Delivery?'

'Well, I didn't mean your personal Mantovani collection.'

'Audio Team are still working on them, sir. Seems they had to get in some special equipment to read the video. Two, three hours, they reckon.'

'Path report?'

'Ditto. Early indications, however, suggest he died from either shock or loss of blood, possibly both.'

'When, man, when?'

'Sometime between Monday and Tuesday night. Parrish said he won't commit himself further until he's finished the PM.'

'And where was Costello on Monday night?'

'I dunno, sir. Like I said, he hasn't said a word.'

'Okay. Let's make the bastard sweat. Put him back in number four. No access, nothing, without my authorisation. Got it?'

'Sir!'

'Oh, and Bruce?'

'Sir?'

'Has he been searched yet?'

'This morning, sir.'

'*Strip*-searched?'

'I don't believe so, sir.'

'Then jump to it, Sergeant. Who's the duty surgeon?'

'Spadefinger Sam, sir.' Bruce glanced at his watch. 'He's probably on his tenth pint across the road by now.'

This time Kerley did smile. 'You know, Bruce, some days I actually enjoy this work.'

From the living-room window of Rankine's Dalmeny cottage you could look out over the slate-blue Firth of Forth, the road bridge to the left, the rail bridge to the right, North Queensferry directly opposite on the coast of Fife. On clear days you could watch the subs and frigates, minesweepers and cruisers slide silently beneath the bridges to and from the Royal Naval Dockyard at Rosyth, or watch the oil-tankers manoeuvre for position at the off-shore terminal. Other days you could look out the window and see nothing but a hanging bank of mist almost thick enough to drink. Days like that and Billy could stand at the window and still be reminded of Spain: Calella, during the winter months, when the mist would roll in off the Med and smother the village beneath its clammy veil, yet never reach the villa tucked high and secluded on the headland. Days when he could look down over his world from the poolside patio and believe he was God.

Soon, Billy told himself, soon.

He returned to the tape-recorder on the table, inserted one of the last three cassettes and pressed Play.

'*Darling, I really think we ought to do something about the garden,*' – a woman's voice. In the background, classical music, playing softly – '*I mean, if we leave it any longer, people will start to talk.*'

'*What do you mean, start?*' A man's voice, it belonged to Cosmo Vass. Cosmo Vass, deceased, Billy thought with a smile. He punched the Stop button and, ejecting the cassette, loaded another. This time the voice was Jay Johnstone's.

'*Hey, Bobby, how's it going? Aye, no problem. Look, if I'm not there, start without me, okay? That's right. No, tell 'em anything you like but just don't commit yourself until I get there. Okay? Yeah, you too. Ciao.*'

Ciao? Billy thought. Shit, what a poser. The whole time Wylie had had his bugs in Johnstone's office, the only thing they'd ever learned about Jay was the size of his ego. That somedays he'd have to hire half a dozen porters to carry it around for him. Billy skimmed on through the tape.

'*Mm, Jay, now, put it in me now,*' – a woman's voice, grossly overacting. One of his secretaries, no doubt, sitting on his lap. Jay's voice now saying – '*What do you mean? It is in you.*'

Billy tried the final cassette. Again Jay Johnstone. This time the woman's voice was that of his wife. The bug obviously in the bedroom of their fifty-room Colinton castle.

'*Maybe you never looked close enough, Jay. If you get in close, they change. I've never seen eyes like that before. Almost carnivorous. Mmm.*'

'*What, like a hyena?*'

'*And bright enough to warm the coldest heart. Maybe even yours, Jay, if you could find it. Ten years, and I don't even know if you've got one.*'

'*You ought to be thankful for small mercies.*'

'*And yours is awfully small. I bet Colin—*'

'*Colin this, Colin that, it's all I've fucking heard since I made the mistake of letting you go to his dancing classes.*'

Billy punched the Pause button as Rankine shuffled into the room. What with him and the old man, Costello, both wandering round the house with directionless eyes, it was like living with a family of geriatric ghosts. Even Dodds seemed almost alive.

Over the last couple of days, Rankine's voice had degenerated to little more than a whisper – as though he could no longer summon the strength to strum his vocal chords. He said, 'Is it there?'

'Nah,' Billy told him, 'but listen to this. The joys of married life.'

Billy released the Pause button.

'*I do believe you're jealous, Jay.*'

'*You work hard enough at it, why the hell not.*'

'*Now it's my fault you feel insecure. To think I married you when I could've married a man. At least a man could get his trousers off. What a waste.*'

'*You want my trousers off, right, you'll get my fucking trousers off. Gimme those scissors.*'

'*Get them yourself. Anyway, I bet Colin doesn't have to cut his trousers off.*'

'*I'll show you. I'll give you Colin fucking Gunn.*'

'*Please do, darling. I can't wait.*'

Billy stopped the tape. 'See what I mean, Jackie? And *you* could've ended up married to her.'

Rankine's face was grim. 'You've checked all the tapes?'

Billy pointed at the pile of cassettes on the floor. 'What d'you think they are, decoration?'

'You must have overlooked them, Billy. Having too much fun with Wylie that you never searched the place properly. The tapes were there, they must have been there.' Rankine sighed as he lowered himself into an armchair.

'If they were, he'd've told me. He told me everything else.'

'How can you be sure?'

'He crossed his heart and hoped to die.' Billy tossed the final cassette on to the floor with all the rest.

In Saughton, hardly a day had passed without some imbecile finding a way to tell him, 'once a pig, always a pig'. Out on the street again, it was no different. The likes of Wylie and Johnstone going out of their way to remind him, 'once a cop, always a cop'. People too lazy to learn and change saying people can neither learn, nor learn to change. People who live in a world of comforting stereotypes, forced to paddle in the shallows of their minds for the rest of their lives lest they sink out of depth and drown. Weak people. Insecure people. Lazy people. All fearful guardians of an atrophying *status quo*.

And now they were saying, 'once a con, always a con'. More specifically, DI Kerley had said it. Again and again, from the moment they had brought Joe up from the cells to the Interview Room, to Kerley's parting shot almost two hours later:

'Okay, Costello, you want it the hard way, you can have it the hard way. Boys, take him back down and remove his clothes. Let's see how hard he really is.'

Joe sat naked on the wooden bench, legs outstretched, hands clasped behind his head, counting. The trick was to keep both body and mind focused on one single aim: stay warm. Ignore the freezing cold and concentrate on the sit-ups.

101 . . . 102 . . . 103 . . .

But it was hard to concentrate. And almost impossible to suppress the burning anger, or the growing concern for his father. Impossible not to speculate on the outcome of his predicament.

110 . . . 111 . . . 112 . . .

As far as he knew they had nothing with which to charge him. So the Porsche had been spotted near the locus – so what? There'd been plenty of other cars nearby. That was no criminal offence. Maybe by this time they'd found his prints in Wylie's office – but again, so what? The prints would not be fresh enough, would even perhaps have deteriorated by now, given the constant heat and dripping condensation in Wylie's office. Certainly not fresh enough to place him at the locus when the crime was committed – in Joe's mind, sometime over the last two days and probably no earlier than Monday.

125 . . . 126 . . . 127 . . .

And witnesses? If Kerley really had the witness he said he had, then Joe would've been lined up straight away, no farting about. No, Joe was sure, Kerley's questions had proved nothing but the DI's own ignorance. And by now, Andrea's lawyers would be on Joe's trail and he'd be out on the street in a couple of hours. So why worry? What else could go wrong?

142 . . . 143 . . . 144 . . .

Keys rattled in the lock. The cell-door opened and Dr Sam 'Spadefinger' Smith lurched unsteadily into the cell, squinting myopically at Joe through half-moon specs.

'My,' he exclaimed, opening out his black bag and removing a pair of surgical gloves. 'What a handsome specimen!'

*   *   *

Jack Rankine sat down on the edge of the bed and said, 'you're lucky to be alive, you know.'

Aldo Costello stood by the window, looking out across the Forth, hands in the pockets of his cardigan. He neither replied nor gave any indication that he was aware of Rankine's presence. In fact, he hadn't said a word since Billy had brought him out here after yesterday's fire at the hotel. Just stood in this room with its bolted-down windows and stared into space.

Rankine stroked his beard and continued regardless. 'Billy says if his gun hadn't jammed, you'd be lying three-eyed on the basement floor. And you know what? In a way, I'm glad his gun jammed. I wouldn't like you to have the satisfaction of a quick and easy end, a hero in your son's eyes. No. Much better this way. First watch your son die, then yourself. If you concentrate very hard, you may even see it coming – though I'm sure Billy's got a few ideas lined up, and you know the way he is, how he likes to stretch these things out, squeeze every last drop of pleasure he can from the simplest of acts.

'Mm. Billy. Mad Billy McCulloch. They should call him the Marquis de McCulloch, you know. Me, I'm an old man, Costello, older than you. I've been around, you might say, and I've seen a lot, perhaps everything there is to see in this cruel and thankless world. But there are times, I tell you, when Billy McCulloch frightens even me. I look in his eyes and I see something there, peering out, but it's not human, not even remotely. I sometimes wonder what I've unleashed upon the world, and was it really worth all the trouble.

'You read the paper this morning, that bit about Wylie, the private detective? That was Billy, all his own work. You can see he takes pride in what he does well. I like that in a man. On the other hand, did Wylie deserve to die like that – or does anybody – you might ask? In Wylie's case, most certainly yes. I was happy to pay him a little bit here, a little bit there, but the man got greedy. Blackmail is a dirty word in my book, a very dirty word. So you can see, he didn't leave me any other choice; he had to go. Still . . .'

Rankine's voice trailed off into a sudden fit of coughing. Tears came to his eyes, a gob of something heavy and warm to his mouth. He didn't want to spit it out in case it was blood; better not to know. Costello could have been hewn from stone for all the sign of life he showed. Rankine cleared his throat and wiped his beard.

'Perhaps in a different life, you and I, we could have been friends. We just started off on the wrong foot, as they say. Maybe that's what war does to people, makes them behave irrationally, do things they later regret. Me? Do I regret anything I've done? Not one bit. The way I see it, life is a game, and every game has its winners and losers. There is no such thing as a moral victory, and a good loser is a loser nevertheless. And I have never been a loser; I know only how to win. You on the other hand have lost almost everything you ever had . . . and tonight you lose it all. There must be a moral there somewhere.'

Still Costello did not move or speak.

What did it matter, Rankine thought? The old man was already watching the last day of his life. Tonight they would meet with the young Costello, and naturally there would be no exchange. A bullet in the back of each of their heads and that would be it, all over.

A car scrunched over the gravelled drive and a minute later Dodds walked in. He appeared almost sober, only his unpatched liquid eye revealing the truth. 'Where's Billy?' he asked.

'Out,' Rankine told him. 'Probably biting the head off the neighbour's cat to cheer himself up.'

'I don't like it, Mr Rankine.'

'So *you* go bite its head off.'

'I meant Billy,' Dodds said, shaking his head. 'Everything was fine till he came along. Now it's all a mess.'

'Which is a matter I'd like to discuss with you, Dodds.'

'Here?' Dodds nodded towards Costello by the window.

'Why not?' Rankine rubbed the palms of his hands on his trousers, began massaging his stiff knees. 'Dodds,' he said, 'how would you like to earn yourself some money? Big money?'

Dodds licked his slug-like lips. 'I think it might be my pleasure, Mr Rankine.'

'Or better still, a villa on the Costa Brava?'

'You mean Billy's?'

'It's still mine, Dodds. The deeds haven't been signed over yet.'

Dodds's eyes widened in dawning comprehension. 'You want me to . . .'

'Tonight,' Rankine rasped, 'we settle all old scores. Perhaps you have one or two that need settled?'

'Damn right I do.'

'Good. Do we have a deal?'

'We most certainly do, Mr Rankine.' Dodds held out his hand.

251

'Jack,' Rankine said, shaking Dodds's hand. 'Call me Jack.' He rose laboriously to his feet and slung a paternal arm around the young man's shoulder. 'Now, tell me about the hotel, Dodds. What sort of damage are we talking about?'

Aldo Costello continued to stare out the window as the two men left the room.

CHAPTER 33

They came for him mid-afternoon, just as Joe was trying to remember what eventually became of The Man in the Iron Mask. Two uniformed PCs, calling him 'sir', saying would he mind coming with them, DS McInnis would like a word. Joe took his time dressing, then followed them hesitantly up the stairs, puzzled by the apparent change in attitude and the fact that he wasn't being 'escorted' – as he had been on his previous session with Kerley. Perhaps Andrea's lawyers had found him already.

'Coffee, sir?' They stood outside the same Interview Room as before.

'Black,' Joe told him, 'with four sugars.'

'If you just wait inside, sir, DS McInnis will join you shortly.' Both men wandered off, leaving Joe alone to enter the room. It hadn't changed in the two or three hours since Kerley had lost his rag and called Joe all manner of scum. Two minutes later the PC arrived with Joe's coffee, leaving just as Bob McInnis entered. The DS closed the door and crossed to shake Joe's hand. His grip was firm, exuding warmth. Joe tried to read his ex-partner's eyes but, as ever, they were too dark and too restless. Instead, he watched as McInnis folded himself on to the facing seat and pushed large, blunt fingers through his greased-black hair.

'I won't waste time on pleasantries, Joe – we both know it's a wee bit late for that.' A ghost of a smile glided across his lips. 'I hear Kerley gave you the treatment this morning.'

Joe said, 'He never did like me.'

'Ever since the day you caught him pantless with that prostitute.' More than just a ghost of a smile now.

'How was I to know he'd take it personally? I was only doing my job.'

'As he was doing his.'

'Or trying,' Joe laughed. 'Christ, I can still see the look on his face when I kicked in the door and shouted, *'Police, you better come quietly!'*

Mcinnis grinned. 'It was probably the 'cuffs that did it, Joe.'

'All I did was ask him could he spare a pair. I mean, lying there spreadeagled the way he was, with the tom getting stroppy, what'd you expect me to do? Go back to the station and requisition a pair?'

'It was all anyone talked about for weeks in the canteen. No wonder he wanted you out.'

'And didn't he succeed.'

'The evidence was there, Joe. Like Kerley said at the time, justice in Britain must be seen to be done.'

'Seen to be done?' Joe said, making no effort to hide the contempt from his voice. 'It has to be seen to be believed.'

'Touché.' For a moment what looked like a pained expression lingered on McInnis's face but it disappeared just as suddenly, replaced by a brusque business-like manner as the detective spread a typed transcript on the table before him and studied it for a minute in silence. Eventually he levelled his eyes with Joe's. 'Let's talk about Wylie first, our good friend Wilberforce.'

'Aren't you forgetting something?' Joe indicated the video-camera bracketed high in the corner, and the switched-off tape-recorder and microphone on the table between them.

'This is merely an informal chat, Joe, nothing more. We just need to clear up a few points first, before . . .'

'Before what?'

McInnis appeared not to hear him. 'So,' he said, 'you're still claiming you didn't visit Wylie last night?'

Joe said, 'Sure, I went to see him. But there was no answer. So I left.'

'Why didn't you mention this to Kerley?'

'I wouldn't give him the satisfaction.'

'Okay. So you left immediately?'

'I had a pint in the Auld Hoose, thought maybe Wylie would be there. He wasn't. So I came home.'

'Joe, we worked together almost a year. I never lied to you then, and I ain't lying to you now. We *know* you were there – inside.'

'Can you prove it?'

'We could compare your voice-print with the tape of the guy who phoned it in. We already know you were out in Johnstone's car last night.'

'So?'

'So nothing. Except it was spotted near the locus. You see, the Desk-Sergeant here has a thing about Porsches – his daughter was killed by one. So when he saw it on his way to work, it stuck in his mind.'

'JJ1,' Joe said.

'That's the trouble with personalised number-plates: they're easy to remember. The rest was pure routine. So tell me now, off the record, was it you who called it in?'

Joe shrugged, thought what the hell, and nodded.

'And?'

'I found him lying there. Already dead.'

'We know. The pathologist reckons he died sometime on Monday. Probably late evening or night. You want to tell me where you were?'

'On the road.'

'Any witnesses?'

'Probably.'

'But you're not prepared to say?'

Joe replied with a shrug. 'So what happens now? You going to throw me back in the cell and pull out my nails?'

'For parole violation?'

'Isn't that the way it goes?'

McInnis leant back in his chair, fixing Joe with an expressionless stare that tried, but failed, to hide the motion of riotous thoughts within. Joe waited, unbowed by the weight of his former partner's look, patience and silence both being weapons he'd learned to use well during his time inside. Eventually McInnis leant forward again, gathering together the spread of papers on the table.

'Joe,' he said, the edge gone from his voice, 'there've been a few developments. Christ, I don't know how to say this.' The

255

detective shifting in his seat, obviously uncomfortable. 'Look, Joe, I'm sorry.'

'Sorry?' Joe said, his voice rising. 'Sorry about what?' Unable to control the sudden panic slamming through his veins as the phrase 'parole violation' continued to reverberate around his head.

'I should have believed you, Joe. We all should have.'

Joe leaned across the table and grabbed the detective's lapels. 'What are you trying to tell me, Bob?'

'Hey, Joe, easy!'

'Tell me what's going on, man!'

'While we were at Wylie's this morning, sifting through all the débris, a parcel arrived, Special Delivery. It was addressed in his own handwriting. He must have realised something was going to happen so sent them off for safekeeping.'

'Sent what off?'

'Tapes. A couple of videos, maybe half-a-dozen cassettes.' McInnis laid his hand on Joe's wrist. 'You want to let me go now, so I can breathe a little?'

'Okay, so breathe.' In the pit of Joe's stomach there was a cold spot. It seemed to be growing steadily, spreading through his body like a creeping anaesthetic.

McInnis said, 'I suppose you know Wylie used to work for Rankine?'

Joe shot him a pitying look.

'And that he kept copies of all the tapes he made?'

Joe said, 'He was using them to put the black on Rankine.'

'How do you know that?'

'He tried to get me interested.'

'Yeah, well his bank records suggest he's been at it since . . . since you went inside. Over the last couple of years he's bled Rankine like a leech. Almost £50,000 in all.'

'Get to the point.'

'Does the name McCulloch mean anything to you?' the detective asked. 'William P. – aka Billy – McCulloch?'

'Rankine's right-hand man. Does all the dirty work. Used to be a wideboy, a small-time nothing, fast with his mouth and faster with his chib. Now he lives in Spain, I hear.'

'We have it on the tapes, Joe – proof he murdered Cosmo Vass. You were right all along: Rankine *was* involved. And we can get him, too, as an accessory. In fact the call's already out.'

'Why not pick him up at his hotel?'

'Because he's gone. No one's seen him since – McInnis broke off to glance at Joe through narrowed eyes. 'You wouldn't happen to know anything about the fire, now, would you?'

'What fire?'

'That's what I thought. And your father?'

'What about my father?'

'You still see him?'

'Sure,' Joe said. 'I'll probably see him tonight.'

'How about returning him to the hospital? Get him off our Missing Persons Bulletin?'

'I was thinking maybe it's time he came home.'

'Joe, I'm getting a bad feeling about all this . . .'

'How d'you mean?'

'You're holding something back again.'

'My temper.'

'C'mon, Joe, I *know* you. You're the quiet, thoughtful one, remember? the cop who always thinks before he acts. I'm the loud and thoughtless one who always acts on impulse. You're cool and calm and slow to simmer and I'm brash and volatile and quick to boil. You control your emotions and put them in a bottle while I use a bottle to get them out. You're the ice, Joe, and I'm the fire, and that's why we made the best damn team the Squad has ever seen.'

'And look where it got me.'

'Maybe that was always your problem – you never really knew how to communicate. Always held yourself aloof, detached, isolated. Even when it came to the Vass inquiry. Perhaps if you'd shared your suspicions then, none of all this would've happened. Lone wolves, Joe, fight alone; they also win and lose alone.'

'What's to share, Bob? Last time I shared my suspicions, I was taken off the case and ended up inside.'

'Christ!' McInnis jumped to his feet and began pacing from bare wall to bare wall. 'I mean in the last few weeks since you started working for Johnstone there've been God knows how many fires in properties he owns. *Then* someone stomps your face to shit and the next thing you know, a friend of yours drives into the Clubbiedean Reservoir and drowns. All the forensic evidence suggests it was murder, but you think it was an accident. Strange, indeed, don't you think?'

'Or coincidence?'

'I haven't finished yet,' McInnis said, waving him down. 'Just a few days later, guess what? One of Rankine's security guards runs amok at the orphanage Christmas party and injures three of the kids. *Then* a derelict house burns down in Craigmillar and a witness recalls seeing a Porsche driving away. *Then* a private dick in Johnstone's employ is found dead and nailed to a floor. *Then* your father goes AWOL from his psychiatric ward. *Then* there's a fire at the Edin Hill Hotel. And *then*, to crown it all, you sit here now and try to make me believe you don't know what's going on.'

'What does it matter? Like you said, in a couple of hours it'll all be over.'

'First we have to find them. And you know what? I think you know where they are.'

'Me?'

'And I also think Kerley's right. You are trying to play the hero. Maybe even get a little of your own back at the same time.'

'You know what they say, Bob . . . Once a cop, always a cop.'

'Which is one good reason to hold you here until the whole mess is sorted.'

'But you won't.'

'No?'

'Because you owe me one. You and the whole damn force owe me one.'

'I've said I'm sorry, Joe – what more can I say?'

'That I'm free to go.'

McInnis sighed and shook his head. 'You are, you are, the moment you want.' Then he hesitated, looking down at the scarred table-top as though searching for the words he wanted to say. Eventually he shook his head again, collected the sheaf of papers and, without looking up, said, 'But first there's something I think you ought to hear.'

CHAPTER 34

Dusky-blue was the evening sky and dark the sliding waters of the firth, reflecting bright the shimmering lights on the northern shore, the road-bridge strung like a gaudy necklace across the Forth, the rail-bridge like a rusting fairground dipper. Aldo Costello sat close in front of the silent TV, humming tunelessly the *Neighbours* theme as he munched through a packet of Gypsy Creams and watched the Australian soap. Dodds was down in the village buying in supplies.

Billy said, 'Somewhere quiet, out of the way, where we won't be disturbed.'

'Down on the shore?' Rankine suggested.

'With people spilling out of the pubs or walking their dogs? Come on, Jackie-boy, the answer's obvious. Use your eyes. Look out there and tell me what you see.'

Rankine said, 'Fife is what I see.'

Billy sighed and shook his head, wished he had a tab of something handy, take the edge off his mood. 'You ever see that film, *The Thirty-Nine Steps*?' he asked.

Rankine frowned. 'You're not serious?'

'I checked it out this afternoon. It's perfect. Easy access from both sides, it's quiet, out of the way, no chance of being seen or interrupted. What more do we need?'

'A sense of the absurd?'

'A sense of drama, Jackie-boy. Something to remember the rest

259

of our lives. We set the time for midnight, just after the last train. By then, both stations will be deserted. We come across from North Queensferry, they from Dalmeny, and we meet halfway. After it's finished we head back here.'

'And him?' Rankine glanced over at Costello, hunched in front of the TV.

'The choice is yours, Jackie-boy. Mine not to reason why.' Billy stared out the window, feeling the first rush of excitement take to his veins. 'See that?' he said, pointing out towards the rail-bridge. 'The fall is long and the waters fast and freezing cold. Anyone fell in there, they wouldn't last a minute and wouldn't be found for days. If ever. Like a toilet, Jackie, just drop 'em in and flush 'em away.'

'The Forth *is* a toilet.'

'There you go then. So what's the problem?'

Aldo Costello suddenly began singing as he rocked back and forth on the edge of his seat. '*Everybody needs good neighbours . . .*'

'What the hell's he on?' Rankine demanded.

'About 100 mils of Librium, why? He too lively for you?'

'When you were out his afternoon, I asked him does he remember the war, like the day Italy sided with the Nazis and made him our instant enemy. And you know what he said? He said, "*War? What war?*"'

'Well, it was a long time ago.'

'I asked him does he still remember the day we stoned and looted his father's shop and burned down his uncle's restaurant. You know what he said? He said, "*All those biscuits. What a waste.*"'

'Like yesterday,' Billy said, 'you should a heard him yesterday. He said the best thing his son ever did was shoot out your daughter's eyes. Said it all came down to training, that he'd taught Joe from an early age: when peeling tatties, always go for the eyes.'

'Like he did with Dodds?'

Billy blinked. 'Yeah. I never thought of that. Maybe he's not as crazy as he seems.'

There is no faster communication process in the force than that which transmits gossip. As he accompanied McInnis upstairs to the Audio/Visual Room, Joe could sense the sidelong glances, the guarded looks, the whispered comments. A few of his old colleagues came up sheepishly to shake his hand, Joe barely responding, the two-year chasm of time and experience too wide to cross, even to contemplate.

260

There were two detectives already at work in the Audio/Visual Room. They glanced up when Joe and McInnis entered, then hastily left the office on McInnis's thumbed command. He then led Joe across the cluttered room to a desk by the window where a piece of high-tech electronic gadgetry held pride of place alongside a comparatively cheap-looking tape-recorder. Outside, the Salisbury Crags rose sheer towards the dark blue sky.

Joe said, 'You remember the Acid Killer's first victim?'

McInnis frowned for a moment, then nodded. 'They found him up there, at the foot of the Crags.'

'Look it up in the files,' Joe said. 'Now you know who you're looking for, I think you'll find all the evidence you need.'

'I think you're probably right.' McInnis nodded at the machine on the table. 'Know what that is, Joe? It's what they call an F1 Analog/Digital Converter.'

'Which explains everything.'

The detective tried to look hurt. 'Apparently a lot of recording studios use them to store their final mixes. What they do is pass the mix through one of these machines, thus converting the analogous sound into a digital – that is, binary – code which can then be simply recorded on to any magnetic tape. Which is why, when we first played the Betamax tapes back on video, all we got was a screenful of ones and zeros.'

'Wylie gave me a guided tour through all his equipment,' Joe said, 'but I never saw a machine like that.'

'Man who runs the electrical repair shop downstairs from Wylie? He had it in for repair. It was only when we got round to questioning him that we put two and two together.'

'And now you've converted it all back to its original state?'

McInnis nodded. 'But I must warn you again, Joe, you're not going to like it.'

'There's nothing Billy or Rankine could either do or say would surprise me any more.'

McInnis took a cassette from his pocket, passed it across the table. 'This copy's for you, Joe. I know it's against all regulations but what the hell, like you said, we owe you something.'

'What is it, a recording of Vass's torture? His murder?'

'Joe, listen—'

'Or worse? Rankine singing in his bath?'

'Joe, would you listen a moment?' McInnis having to raise his voice to cut Joe off. 'This is the tape Wylie died for, why his place was ripped apart. Rankine didn't just stop at having Wylie bug all his business associates and RanCor partners. I mean, he must've been really paranoid, Joe, to do something like this.'

'Like what?' The cold knot suddenly tight in his stomach.

'Like bugging his daughter's flat.' The detective avoiding Joe's stare as he added, 'The flat you shared – and in which she died.'

Joe felt the world tilt away. Time passed. Or maybe it didn't. When he eventually spoke, his voice seemed to come from a long way off. 'I want to hear it,' he said. 'Now.'

'Joe, please, don't. You don't want to listen to this, not now. I strongly advise against it.'

Joe pushed the cassette back across the table. 'Now.'

McInnis inserted the tape into the recorder, then rose to leave. 'I'm sorry, Joe,' he said, sadness softening his voice. 'I'll be next door if you want me.' The door closed gently behind him.

Joe stares down at the table with his head in his hands. He is aware of nothing but the sound of Karen's voice.

She is singing. One of the songs she sings with the band. She sings as she irons. He can hear the hiss of steam and the creak of the ironing-board as she presses their clothes for the honeymoon. Singing because she is happy. Because the next day she'll a'married be, then off and winging her way towards the Mediterranean sun.

Suddenly the doorbell rings. She stops singing.

'Who the hell can that be?' she murmurs to herself.

Fading footsteps. Rattle of chain on the front door. Barely audible, *'Dad! What on earth are you doing here?'*

Mumbled reply, approaching footsteps.

'You just missed him,' Karen says. *'He's been called out – a stabbing in Muirhouse or something. You want coffee?'*

Rankine snorts. *'You're still determined to go through with this, then – this farce?'*

'It's not a farce, Dad, it's a wedding. And if that's the only reason you came, to try and put me off again, forget it.'

Over the sound of a running tap, Rankine says:

'Do you really hate me so much?'

'Hate's got nothing to do with it. This is about love, Dad, can't you understand? I love Joe and I'm going to marry him, and there's nothing you can do or say that will ever change my mind.'

'You forget that I love you, too, Karen. You're all I have left.'

'You have your business,' Karen retorts, anger bristling on her

voice. '*And that creepy little man who follows you round flashing the world his mean, dirty looks.*'

'*See what he's done? He's turned you against me – Karen, my own daughter. We used to be so close, a real family, until Costello came along. Can't you see that? He's using you, has been from the word go. Now he gets to me the only way he can, through you.*'

'*Christ, Dad, can't you forget your damned obsession just for a day?*' The sound of percolating coffee in the background, cups being placed on saucers.

'*Forget it for a day and regret it the rest of my life? I'm sorry, Karen, but I'm not the only one obsessed. I wish you could see it. Costello's been after me for years, on account of his father. Have you never heard of "vendetta"? These Italians have memories longer than their ancestral trees.*'

Karen sighs. '*Dad, I'm not going to go through all this again. Especially on the eve of what is supposed to be the happiest day of my life.*'

'*I can't let you go through with it. I want you to call it off.*'

'*Call it off?*' Karen sounds incredulous. '*Call it off?*'

'*Tell him you've had a change of heart, Karen. I'll make it up to you, darling, anything you want.*' There is an understone of desperation in Rankine's voice. '*Name it and it's yours. You want a new car? A bigger flat? The villa in Spain?*'

'*Want, want, want, everything in your life is want, Dad. You don't know the meaning of need. You think money is the answer to all your problems, the key to everyone's hearts. You tried to buy my love as a child, now you're trying to buy it again. Only this time the price is one you could never afford, not even with all the money in the world.*'

'*I can't let you go through with it.*'

'*You can't let me go through with it? How the hell're you going to stop me?*'

'*I'll cut you out of my will.*'

'*You're threatening me? Your own daughter?*'

'*I mean it, Karen.*'

'*And so do I. You do* anything *to spoil the wedding tomorrow and I swear to God I'll tell Joe about the night Cosmo Vass died.*'

For ten seconds, there is silence. The tension in the room almost crackles. Rankine speaks eventually, a rasping edge to his voice:

'*And what would you tell him, Karen?*'

'*That you weren't where you claimed to be that night. That you made me tell the police you were home with me, when in fact you were out.'*

'I told you where I was, with a . . . friend of mine.'

'Kelly, you said her name was.'

'That's right – Kelly.'

'Only you never went there that night. I phoned up and she said she hadn't seen you for at least a couple of weeks. You lied to me.'

'You phoned her up?'

'A fax came through from your office and I thought it might've been urgent. Her number was in your book.'

Rankine forces a laugh. *'And you seriously think I had a hand in Vass's death? Come on, Karen, look at me. I'm your father, not some psychopathic nutcase.'*

'I heard you, Dad, I heard you when you came back that night with your creepy little bodyguard. You came up to my room to check I was asleep, then went downstairs to let the creep in through the back door. You left the library door open.'

'You were spying on me?'

'You'd lied to me.'

'You heard everything?'

'Enough.'

'So why haven't you told Costello?'

'How could I?' Her anguish is clearly audible. *'Tell the man I love that my father's involved in murder? Have him drop me like a hot brick?'*

'Karen, I'm sorry.'

'Get away! Don't touch me! You're not my father any more.'

'Karen, you must realise now that you can't marry him. If he were to find out . . .'

'I'd let him throw you to the dogs.'

'I can't take that risk, Karen.'

'No? Then how're you going to stop me? Kill me? The same way you drove my mother to her grave?'

The sound of the slap is like a pistol shot. The ironing-board crashes to the floor. A coffee-cup smashes. A dull thud as the iron – or something else – bounces off solid wood. For a moment, silence. Then:

'Karen! Karen! Don't do this to me! Oh my God. Karen, say something, speak to me. Oh God, oh God, oh God. Karen, no, you can't be, speak to me, speak to me, SPEAK TO ME!'

For the next five minutes, the sound of Rankine sobbing and

moaning, then mumbling to himself as he moves around the room. Eventually he picks up the phone and dials.

'*Yeah?*'

'*Billy! Thank God! You've got to get over here. Something dreadful's happened.*'

'*You run out of paperclips again?*'

'*Billy, you ever want to breathe through your face again, get over here now!*'

'*Sure, boss, whatever you say. Where's here?*'

'*My daughter's flat.*'

'*What the hell you doing there? I thought you weren't talking.*'

'*Just move your fucking arse, Billy!*'

The phone slams down.

Rankine moves about the room. Every now and then a sob breaks from his lips. He snivels and sniffs and mutters to himself until, some time later, the doorbell rings.

'*So what's the big emergency, boss?*' The front door slams. '*Someone stole the bride or—*' Billy breaks off as his footsteps enter the sitting-room. '*Holy shit!*'

'*What am I going to do, Billy?*'

'*Is she . . . dead?*'

'*It was an accident. I didn't mean to . . .*'

'*You hit her?*'

'*It was just a slap, Billy. She . . . she . . .*'

'*Christ, look at the blood. She must've hit her head when she fell. There's more there, on the corner of that chest.*'

'*What am I going to do, Billy?*'

'*Call the polis?*'

'*I call them in an we both go down.*'

'*Good point. Fuck, Costello's going to go crazy when he finds out. Where is he, do you know?*'

'*He left for work just before I arrived. Out at Muirhouse, Karen said.*'

'*Okay. Try it like this. Maybe he and Karen had an argument. He slapped her, she fell down and hit her head, suddenly he's got a body on his hands. What does he do? He messes up the room, knocks over some furniture, makes it look like someone broke in and murdered his fiancée. Then he goes off to work and when he returns, he can play the grieving spouse. How's that sound?*'

'*Why did they argue?*' Rankine asks.

'*She found the money, of course.*'

'*The money! Christ, I'd forgotten about the money. Where did Wylie stash it?*'

'*Under the floorboards in the hall, he said.*' Billy clapped and rubbed his hands together. '*Better and better. Right. This is what we do. First, you get as far from here as you can, find yourself a good strong alibi while Billy cleans up your mess. Did anyone see you arrive?*'

'*Nuh. Not that I know of.*'

'*Good. Then make sure no one sees you leave.*'

'*What will you do about the money?*'

'*Rip up a few of the boards, let the polis find it. What's the name of that Southside cop who does you all those favours? Kylie, was it? Kylie Minogue?*'

'*Kerley. Sergeant Kerley.*'

'*Okay. He gets an anonymous call. Someone tips him off, says something about a disturbance at this address. The sound of shots.*'

'*You've got your gun?*'

'*You said it was urgent, Jackie-boy.*'

'*Don't call me that! Don't ever call me that!*'

'*You just killed your daughter and you're worried about what I call you? Shit!*'

Rankine makes strangled sounds, as though struggling for air. Billy says:

'*Okay, okay, don't get mad. Just leave this all to Billy and we'll talk again later.*'

'*I'm sorry. I just . . . I mean . . .*'

'*Yeah, yeah, on yer bike. Come on, now . . .*'

Their footsteps fade, the front door opens and slams. Billy returns. He is whistling. The Who, 'Won't Get Fooled Again.'

Suddenly the sound of crashing furniture.

Then silence, over which Billy talks to himself.

'*Decisions, decisions, hum-de-hum. Through the mouth? Nah, too much like a suicide. The forehead then, right between the eyes? Nah, not gruesome enough. Gotta make the bastards puke. The eyes, then? Yeah, that's the one! Pop a pellet through both her gorgeous eyes and make it look like a mafia hit. Okay, decision made, now what else? Mmm. Nice looking girl.*' The rustle of clothing, a zipper being drawn. '*Mmm. Very nice. Well, what do you know . . . same colour as her hair. And still warm. I wonder . . .*'

The telephone interrupts.

'*Shit!*'

Billy lets it ring. It stops after twelve.

'*Fuck, I better move.*'

Two loud reports are followed by total silence.

Joe sits there, rocking over the table, tufts of hair tight in clenched-white fists as he bangs his forehead off the tear-stained tabletop, again and again and again. All he can hear are the echoes of the shots reverberating around the walls of his skull.

Detective Sergeant Bob McInnis watched from his office window as his former partner left the station, walking slowly down the Pleasance. He came to a decision, turned to Bruce and nodded.

'Okay,' he said, 'follow him.'

There are wintry Edinburgh days so sharp that a single breath can slice your lungs. Afternoons when the air is so crisp the silhouette of the city seems razor-cut into the powder-blue sky. Evenings when corrugated clouds hang brittle on the horizon, as though sculptured in ice and stained with the blood of a fast-dying sun. Today was such a day; this evening, such an evening.

Joe came out of the Southside Divisional Headquarters and stood for a moment drinking in the air. It was cool, but not cool enough. He began to walk.

There is also an anger so hot, so intense, it burns like ice. A volcanic anger that knows only violent release. That freezes emotions, yet boils the blood. Compared to the blindness of such an anger, love is nothing but a little shortsighted.

He entered the pub, went straight to the phone.

Grace answered on the second ring.

Joe said, 'Has he phoned yet?'

'You're out? Where are you?'

'The Auld Hoose. Has he phoned yet?'

'Ten minutes ago. He wants to meet tonight. Out of town.'

'Where?'

'The Forth Rail Bridge. Midnight.'

Joe thought for a moment and then asked if Andrea was there.

'Why?' Grace asked.

'I want Jay's gun.'

CHAPTER 35

Joe walked slowly along the northbound platform, leaving the small, deserted station of Dalmeny lightless behind him. The rain had passed, the night was quiet, the moonless sky black with sheeted cloud. A chill north-easterly wind flapped the tails of his Drizabone stockman's coat, causing the barrel of the sawn-off to bang gently against his leg. The cord from which it hung chafed the side of his neck. He reached the end of the platform, dropped to the track, continued, more cautiously now, out along the South Approach Viaduct towards the Queensferry Cantilever.

Joe had never known his grandfather, Uberto – who had died that fateful night on the *Arandora Star*, crushed beneath the stern-gun as it toppled from the aft-deck to the icy waters below – though in a strange sense he felt as if he had. Ancestry in his genes, perhaps. It was his own father, Aldo, who had brought the man alive in the young Joe's mind. Aldo had worshipped his father, and always took great pride in the fact that a Costello had helped construct what was referred to at the time as the first industrial and engineering wonder of the modern world. He took so much pride, in fact, that he knew the history of the bridge by heart. Winter evenings, he and Joe would sit by the glowing hearth and Joe would listen to the story of its construction, enthralled by the sheer magnitude of the engineers' vision. Now, as he approached the dark looming steelwork along the narrow catwalk, the glossy black waters 150 feet below, he tried to recall some of the details of his father's bedtime stories.

269

Better that, he thought, than fill his mind again with the echoes of gunshots that seemed never to end. He pushed on through the snapping wind.

The first attack of the Second World War on mainland Great Britain, he recalled, occurred on 16 October 1939 when German bombers tilted at the naval installations along the Forth, their main target the Royal Naval dockyard at Rosyth. One lone bomber, however, became isolated from the rest of its squadron and, running for its life, loosed its load over the Forth Bridge.

And missed. The bombs did, though, manage to cause a small amount of damage to a passing ship, but failed to achieve any loss of life. Which, Aldo always reminded Joe, was more than could be said for the seven years between 1883 and 1890, when fifty-seven workers died during the bridge's construction.

The sound of metal clanking on metal came to him suddenly through the gusting wind. He pressed himself quickly into the deepest shadow of the superstructure, his hand tightening on the stock of the sawn-off as he tried to filter out the soughing moans of the wind. The noise continued, a hollow rhythmic beat, coming from somewhere up ahead . . . overhead.

A loose cable or hawser, Joe decided, thrashing the steelwork in time to the squalling wind. He released his pent-up breath, relaxed his grip on the sawn-off.

Anyway, he thought, Billy would be somewhere down on the track, not hidden high in the crutch of the cantilever tower. When the showdown came he would want to be as close to Costello as possible, so he could look in Joe's eyes and gloat. Such is the nature of revenge: a meal best served cold, and intimately savoured. There would be no snipers aloft among the whistling cables, no nightsights trained on the glow of his racing heart. No. It would be just Billy and Joe, his father and Dodds. If his father was still alive.

He pressed forward, cautiously now, edging along the shadowed parapet. Ahead of him, the two sets of tracks narrowed into darkness.

Aldo's favourite story was that of two men who died during the laying of the bridge's foundations, whose bones now lay trapped for ever in the airless *caisson* beneath the murky waters of the firth below. Uberto, who had been brought over as cheap labour from Italy by the French firm contracted to work on the foundations, had been employed on the same gang as the two unfortunates. The two men in question, it was later revealed, had been working at a lower level of the *caisson* – a large watertight chamber used for laying foundations underwater – their presence forgotten by the men above – who had already almost completely closed off the lower section – until too late.

Rescue was ruled an impossibility. The contractors were called and there were hurried negotiations with the two men's relatives. Eventually an agreement was reached whereby compensation would be paid to the relatives and a last supper of poisoned food lowered to the two trapped men.

Nice work if you could get it, Joe thought, now approaching the Inch Garvie Cantilever, the mid-section of the bridge. In the quiet of the midnight chill, he had often wondered if the two doomed men had been aware of their fate, whether they had knowingly consumed their poisoned fare. Right now, however, he was wondering if a man could survive a 150-ft fall to the water below, and how long he might live in the swift, icy water; whether he could last long enough to make Inch Garvie Island or either of the distant shores.

Probably not, was his conclusion.

He could now make out dim lights on the northern shore, flickering through the swirling mist: there the dockyard, there North Queensferry, there the paper-mill and there, suddenly, directly ahead, pinning Joe like a fly to a wall, the beam of a powerful torch. Behind it, a shadowy figure moved.

And spoke: 'Stop. Not another step,' The voice Billy's.

Joe stopped, right hand deep in his coat, holding the squat but comforting bulk of the sawn-off hard against his hip.

He shielded his eyes and said, 'So what happens now?'

'We wait.' Billy sniffed the air like a bloodhound. 'To see if you've brought any uninvited guests along.'

'I came alone.'

Billy McCulloch played the torch-beam over Joe, across the tracks and into the darkness behind. 'That's what they say in the films, Joe, when they have half the fucking polis in the world waiting around the corner.' He peered into the murk a moment longer, then, apparently satisfied, positioned the torch on the parapet so it lit up the thirty-yard space between them. 'Did you get my message?'

'What message?'

'Wylie.'

'Aye,' Joe said. 'Loud and clear.'

'You think I hammered the point home?'

'You're sick, McCulloch, sick as your sense of humour. Where's my father?'

'He's back along the line with Dodds. Waiting to see if he lives or dies. See the torch? All I need to do is flash it a couple of times and your old man takes his last big swallow.'

'And Rankine?'

Billy turned his head a fraction and spoke from the corner of his mouth. 'You still there, Jackie-boy?'

'Get on with it, Billy!' Rankine's growl coming out of the shadow, fifty yards back on the other side of the tracks. 'Stop wasting time!'

'Does that answer your question, Costello?'

Joe said, 'So how d'you want to play this?'

Billy grinned, white teeth flashing in the torchlight, as he whipped the gun from his pocket and aimed it at Joe.

Joe, caught unaware, stood as motionless as time, his thoughts colliding like telescoped cars in a motorway pile-up as the barrel of the gun held him hypnotised, muscles locked.

'Do it, Billy!' Rankine yelled. 'Do it now!'

A revolver, Joe noticed, what looked like a .38. The same kind of gun used to shoot out Karen's eyes.

Billy's grin now a clench of teeth as he suddenly shifted aim and fired over Joe's left shoulder, the sound of the shot a flat crack muffled by the mist. Joe moved instinctively, diving to his side in a roll that brought him up hard against the parapet, the sawn-off under his coat slamming painfully into his ribs. He hoped the safety was still on.

Billy laughed and fired off another shot down the tracks, the clang as it ricocheted off the steel framework louder than the first. Then silence crowded in as Billy covered him again.

'Feeling tired, Costello? All this excitement getting to you?'

Joe picked himself up, dusted himself down.

'What the hell're you doing, Billy?' Rankine shouted, 'Hurry up and get it over with.'

'Checking he ain't brought any of his friends along.' McCulloch's breath rasped like a saw; he seemed about as calm as a man with his finger in a socket.

Joe took a half-step forward; he was now side-on to Billy, his right hand in the folds of his coat, gripping the stock of the sawn-off. He eased his finger into the trigger-guard, braced his thumb against the safety. Then slipped his left hand into his pocket.

'Hold it there, Costello! Let's see what you've got in your pocket. Slowly now.'

Joe remained motionless.

'Either that or your old man dives.' Billy obviously enjoying himself now.

Rankine's voice once more emerged from the mist. 'What are you waiting for? Kill him now and stop playing games.'

'Take it out slowly, Joe, place it down on the sleeper.'

Joe removed his hand, clutching the small pocket dictaphone. He laid it on the sleeper.

'Now back off.'

Joe backed off.

Billy edged forward, gun-arm extended, eyes fixed unwaveringly on Joe as he squatted to pick up the dictaphone.

'Music while you work, Joe?'

'You ought to give it a listen. Relive a few old memories.'

McCulloch frowned. 'I hope it ain't what I think it is,' he said.

'Play it and see. Press the red button on the top.'

In the split second that Billy took his eyes off Joe to find and press the button, Joe swung up the barrel of the shotgun and centred it squarely on McCulloch.

The tape began to play.

The scrawny old nutcase was leaning over the parapet, mumbling to himself as he watched the sliding water black below. The old man so frail, Dodds had to grip him tight in case another squall came and whipped the man away.

As he waited for Billy's signal, Dodds squinted into the darkness. He saw no fleeting shadows, no flashing torch. Behind him on the North Approach Viaduct the thin gauze of the Fife shore mist was already beginning to disperse in the squalling wind that had seemingly come from nowhere. Dodds returned to his thoughts.

His plan.

It was simple. When Billy flashed his signal down the line, Dodds would clip the old man's head and leave him lying out of sight by the side of the tracks. Then he'd make his way up the bridge towards Billy and the boss. Billy would say, Hey, moron, where's the old goat? And Dodds would tell him, Over the side, Billy-boy, isn't that what you wanted? And Billy would come up close the way he

liked to do and peer in Dodds's face as he said something witty,
cutting Dodds down with his piercing sarcasm, the way he'd done
it already a hundred times too many. And Dodds would smile his
vacant smile and close his fist around Billy's gun-hand and twist
until he heard the wrist go snap and the gun fall to the tracks. Then
he'd grab the little fuck by the throat and lift him off the ground
and watch the pleading eyes go all dim and distant. Maybe he'd say
something himself, just to show the little shit how wrong a man can
be. Then he'd look across at the boss and the boss would say, Do it,
Dodds, and Dodds would hang McCulloch over the parapet by his
feet and hold him there for as long as he could before he released
his grip and listened to Billy go aaaaaaaaaaaah all the way down.
Then maybe rush to the other side of the bridge and count the
seconds before Billy emerged.

Aye. That's how he'd do it. And maybe leave a little room for
improvisation, too – as Billy had always advised.

Suddenly, the sound of shots came to him through the murk. Two
– then silence again but for the howl of gusting wind. Two shots.
What did two shots mean? It was all over? That Billy would soon
be signalling down the line?

Costello squirmed in Dodds's grasp, brought alive by the sound
of the shots. 'Abandon ship! Abandon ship!' he yelled, his voice
as shrill as grating metal in the stillness of the night. 'Every man
for himself!'

Then, with a strength that took Dodds by surprise, the old man
broke free and lurched staggering back down the tracks towards
the centre of the bridge. Dodds stood there for a second with his
mouth ajar, then lumbered after the old crazy.

Somewhere in the distance, beyond the northern shore, a horn
sounded: the two-tone horn of a southbound train. But Dodds
didn't hear it; he was too busy running punchlines through his
mind.

Below him the tracks began to hum.

They stood facing each other with cocked unwavering guns as the
tinny voices came from the dictaphone in Billy's hand.

'Karen, I'm sorry.'

'Get away! Don't touch me! You're not my father any more.'

*'Karen, you must realise now that you can't marry him. If he were
to find out . . .'*

'I'd let him throw you to the dogs.'

'I can't take that risk, Karen.'

'No? Then how're you going to stop me? Kill me? The same way you drove my mother to her grave?'

The sound of the slap still like a pistol shot.

Joe yelled, 'Recognise the voice, Rankine? That's your daughter talking. Karen. Remember her?'

The wind rose suddenly to whip the recorded words away; maybe Rankine heard them, maybe he didn't. Or maybe, like Joe, they were already cut like scars in his mind.

'I've got the tape, Jackie-boy, I've got the tape!'

'A copy,' Joe said, 'just a copy. The police have the original. It's all over for you now.'

'Talk,' Billy screamed, 'you're nothing but talk!'

Suddenly Rankine broke from the shadows, his gait a drunken lurch as he held the parapet for support. Not the upright bear of a man Joe had last seen two years ago, but a man now shrivelled and bent, with a drawn and jaundiced face beneath an unkempt beard now twisted by hate. 'Kill him, Billy! Do it now!'

Then he saw the shotgun in Joe's hands, and stopped.

Both of them now on the far side of the tracks, but McCulloch ignoring Rankine, standing there with his gun-hand shaking, head cocked, as though deep in thought and trying to come to terms with the changed situation.

Looking for a way out.

Joe said, 'It's over, McCulloch, end of game.'

'Not till the final whistle, it ain't.'

Out of the darkness and across the night, a whistle shrilled, once, twice, from close to the northern shore.

'End of game, McCulloch.'

Looking past Billy, Joe saw dim lights moving towards them. Felt the first vibrations through the soles of his shoes. Neither Rankine nor Billy seemed aware of the train's approach: Rankine yelling at McCulloch to end it quick, the wee Gorgie wideboy dropping to a semi-crouch, both hands now on the .38 as he swung it jerkily from Joe to Rankine and back to Joe, knuckles blanching around the trigger-guard as he tried to reach a decision behind wild, fear-fucked eyes. Suddenly, Aldo Costello broke from the darkness.

'Abandon ship!' he shrieked, staggering to a halt. 'Every man for himself!' Then he noticed the guns, the figures of Rankine, McCulloch and Joe locked in deadly stalemate, and froze. 'Joe . . .'

'Stay out of it, Dad!' Sawn-off steady in Joe's sweating hands, taking the pressure now as he concentrated solely on McCulloch, blanking out both Rankine and his father, no threat there, but where the hell was Dodds?

Billy yelled, 'Over here, old man, or your precious son dies!'

Before Joe could shout or his father move, Dodds lumbered, panting, up the track.

'Train . . . coming . . .' he wheezed, doubled over with his hands on his knees, gulping at the air like a drowning man, face turned to Rankine as though waiting for some kind of signal.

From the corner of his eye, Joe caught Rankine's almost imperceptible nod.

Typical, Billy thought, fucking typical. Here they were, stuck in the middle of a showdown, only seconds away from a bloodbath, and British fucking Rail, late as usual, was gonna drive a bloody freight-train right through the proceedings. Bad enough that Dodds had let the old fuckwit go, bad enough that Joe Costello had brought out a sawn-off from the likes of nowhere and now had both barrels square on Billy's chest making his skin crawl and prickle in sweat. Bad enough the cops had the tape and for all he knew were crawling along the tracks this very moment coming to blow him away, and British Rail couldn't even run a train on time . . . But what was worse than all that, what pierced him to his core and brought his blood to the boil was Jackie-boy Rankine making eyes at the moron, some kind of unspoken dialogue passing between them. Billy was beginning to feel like he wasn't on the bridge at all, had somehow slipped through a Time Tunnel, back a couple a thousand years, and now here he was, wearing a sheet and fucking sandals, stood in a Forum with a bouquet of leaves in his hair, and his name was suddenly Julius Caesar and all the baldie-heided bumtonguers in their fancy robes and kytes way out to here were crowding in, with smiles on their faces and chibs in their hands, and there was his best mate Brutus saying . . .

'Hey, Billy . . .'

Dodds stepped forward, picking his way across the tracks, stopping a few paces to Billy's left, out of the line of fire.

Billy smiled. Then snapped his gun-arm round and centred the sight on old Fuckwit Costello's scrawny chest before anyone could even make a move. No one tried. Joe Costello, now to his right and a blur on the edge of his vision, presented no danger, so long as his father remained alive. So forget him. Concentrate on the backstabbers. On the timing. On the lights coming out of the dark behind the old man, the train on the Northern Approach now, the sound of its diesel coming to him through lulls in the gusting wind. Billy smiled again, back in control. 'Hey, moron . . .' he said.

Dodds had this look in his eye, kind of smug, kind of crafty, kind of eager. He took a step closer, eyebrows raised, arms out by his sides in a kind of shrug, as though to say, 'what can I say?' So Billy moved the barrel a fraction and shot him once in each knee, retraining the gun on the old Costello before his son could even blink. Then he watched the moron buckle to the track, surprise opening up his features the way a good sharp axe would do. Not so fucking smug or crafty now, not so eager to please his master any more. Some people live and learn, Billy thought. Others just live and die.

The southbound track began to hum.

Dodds was moaning, staring at his bloodied legs, the shards of bone sticking out through his trousers. Rankine leant weakly against the parapet, his breath rasping, his face ashen and eyes wide. Joe still held the sawn-off on Billy, and Billy still covered Aldo with the .38. The train whistle sounded again, louder now, closer.

Joe waited. There was little else he could do.

Dodds tried to gain his feet. Like an elephant smashed on rotting apples. As though he'd forgotten about his shattered kneecaps. He held his hand up to Billy, eyes as round and empty as a beggar's bowl. Billy smiled down at him and, shaking his head, said, 'Et tu, Moron.'

Dodds cocked his head and frowned. The question died on his lips. The bullet smashed through his nose and blew his brains out the back of his head. He slumped to the track and lay still. Joe tensed, his finger squeezing on the trigger, but too late. Billy again had his father covered. Was moving now, stepping sideways, away from Joe, towards the far parapet and Rankine, gun-hand steady on Aldo, who was trembling visibly, staring open-mouthed from Dodds to Joe, Joe to Dodds. Rankine backed away as Billy approached. Slipped and fell. Billy grabbed his collar and hauled him to his feet.

Rankine cried, 'No, Billy, please!' as McCulloch put him in a neck-lock and, using him as a shield, turned his gun on Joe.

Joe saw the barrel move, his actions instinctive, dived to the catwalk in a parachutist's roll as a kaleidoscope of impressions assaulted his senses: the sound of a bullet ricocheting off one of the stanchions, Rankine's half-choked screams shredding the night, the thrumming tracks and roar of the diesel as it hurtled towards them, and a second loud clang as Billy fired again and missed. Joe came out of the roll and on to his feet in one fluid motion, the sawn-off already swinging round on the two men struggling between the tracks. He saw his father on his knees, crawling to the far side of the bridge and, from the corner of his eye, the train careering towards them at breakneck speed, fifty yards off, forty, thirty . . .

Joe steadied the stock and fired. The shot went wide. Billy laughed, a wolf baying at the moon, then placed his foot in the small of Rankine's back and pushed. The old man flew across the tracks and stumbled into the path of the oncoming train. Billy emptied his gun at Joe. One of the bullets caught Rankine in the spine. He collapsed across the rail, the sound of the train deafening, almost upon them, as Joe braced himself and fired again. He had a fleeting impression of Billy staggering, dropping to one knee, moments before the train hit. Rankine exploded in a spray of flying blood.

Joe stood there, drenched, covered in matter as the train thundered by, only a foot or eighty from his face. With shaking hands, he ejected the two spent cartridges and reloaded. Then wiped the blood from his eyes and waited for the end of the game.

His father sat propped against the parapet, blood seeping from a gash over his swelling right eye. The train had come to a halt half a mile down the track. A dozen torches swayed in their direction. Behind them, men in uniform trotted along the tracks.

Joe knelt by his father.

'Billy?' he asked.

The old man turned to stare down at the sliding dark water below. After a moment he turned back to Joe and smiled his toothy smile. 'Swimming.'

CHAPTER 36

Flames leapt from the ground-floor windows as panes cracked and shattered. Smoke billowed from the roof into the midnight sky. Sirens wailed, still a long way off. Andrea sat in the Porsche, talking to Jay on the phone as Joe, his father and Grace stood nearby, watching the house burn.

'Dead,' Andrea said, 'and Billy McCulloch, too.'

'The details, woman, give me the details!'

'Billy shot Jack and Jack fell under a train,' Andrea said, not even trying to conceal the sneer from her voice. 'You want me to describe how they shovelled him up into little plastic bags?'

'And Billy?'

'Joe says he wounded him, that he must have gone over the edge. Police found bloodstains on the parapet and recovered his gun.'

'What about *my* fucking gun?'

'Joe knows roughly where it is.'

'Aye? And where's that?'

'At the bottom of the Forth.'

'A thousand quids' worth of gun and you let him cut down the barrels, then throw it away? You and me, we're going to have to have a damn good talk when I get back. You got that?'

'Yes, Jay, I got that.' With a sigh.

'So what about the polis? They going to leave me alone now?'

'The danger's over, Jay. You can crawl out of your hole now.'

'Speak of the devil, she's just come in.'

279

Andrea smiled into the mouthpiece. 'I hope she's worth it, darling, because I'm citing her as co-respondent.'

'You're filing for divorce?'

'Darling, I'm going to take you to the cleaners.'

'Yeah, sure. Just like all the other times.'

Andrea was interrupted by the crash of falling masonry.

Jay said, 'What the hell's going on there?' Sounding worried, his voice rising. 'What's that noise?'

'Just a fire, darling, nothing serious.'

'Fire? What fire, where?'

'The house, Jay. It's almost reached the first floor.'

'You what?' Jay screamed. 'Call the fucking Fire Brigade!'

'What, on Hogmanay? Have a heart, darling, it's only a house.'

'ANDREA!'

'Happy new year, darling.'

She climbed from the car to join Joe, Grace and Aldo, standing arm in arm as they watched the blaze take hold. The heat was hot on her face.

Grace slipped her arm around Andrea. 'You're a quick learner,' she said.

'Jay always liked to come home to a real fire.'

Aldo looked up into her eyes and smiled his beautiful crazy smile. 'A real fire!' he exclaimed, his eyes suddenly alight with a dawning revelation. 'Now *that*'s what I like. That's what me and the boys *really* like.' He turned to Joe. 'Eh, son?'

Joe stared deep into the leaping flames, watching the glittering sparks shoot towards the sky, like the spirits of his memories, freed at last from the frozen depths of the midnight chill. As free from him now as he was from them. He turned to his father.

'You know what I'd like right now?'

Aldo shrugged and shook his head.

'A biscuit,' Joe said. 'That's what I'd really like.'